"This provocative anthology is as entertaining and original as it is seductive." —*Heart & Soul*

"Whether subtle, romantic, or graphic, *Brown Sugar* represents some of contemporary African American literature's best voices." —*Library Journal*

"*Brown Sugar* is a celebration of sex and sensuality. The stories demonstrate an incredible diversity of settings, characters, and sensibilities. [*Brown Sugar*] liberates black sensuality from typical American standards of love and beauty." —*Booklist*

"[The] *Brown Sugar* series spices book sales among African Americans." —*St. Louis Post-Dispatch*

"*Brown Sugar* . . . has . . . depth . . . feeling, emotion, humor, and heart. It showcases the talents of some really good writers many may already know, and others people should definitely get to know." —*Savoy*

EROTIC
TRAVEL
TALES

Wanderlust

Edited by Carol Taylor

A PLUME BOOK

PLUME
Published by Penguin Group
Penguin Group (USA) Inc., 375 Hudson Street, New York, New York 10014, USA
Penguin Group (Canada), 90 Eglinton Avenue East, Suite 700, Toronto, Ontario,
Canada M4P 2Y3 (a division of Pearson Penguin Canada Inc.)
Penguin Books Ltd., 80 Strand, London WC2R ORL, England
Penguin Ireland, 25 St. Stephen's Green,
Dublin 2, Ireland (a division of Penguin Books Ltd.)
Penguin Group (Australia), 250 Camberwell Road, Camberwell, Victoria 3124,
Australia (a division of Pearson Australia Group Pty. Ltd.)
Penguin Books India Pvt. Ltd., 11 Community Centre, Panchsheel Park,
New Delhi – 110 017, India
Penguin Group (NZ), cnr Airborne and Rosedale Roads, Albany,
Auckland 1310, New Zealand (a division of Pearson New Zealand Ltd.)
Penguin Books (South Africa) (Pty.) Ltd., 24 Sturdee Avenue,
Rosebank, Johannesburg 2196, South Africa

Penguin Books Ltd., Registered Offices: 80 Strand, London WC2R ORL, England

First published by Plume, a member of Penguin Group (USA) Inc.

Copyright © Carol Taylor, 2006
All rights reserved
ISBN 0-7394-6239-3

Printed in the United States of America
Set in Goudy

Wanderlust is dedicated to lovers,
and lovers of fiction and travel

CONTENTS

ACKNOWLEDGMENTS

As always, many thanks to my agent, Tanya McKinnon, for her smarts, savvy, and good-humored guidance, and to my editor, Brett Kelly. Thanks to my family for making me who I am; without you I am nothing. Much gratitude to all the cool writers who hooked me up with other cool writers, and who've so fearlessly created the original stories in *Wanderlust*; you are on the cutting edge. My deepest thanks to the readers for supporting short-story anthologies, where we find some of today's best fiction.

"We don't take a trip, a trip takes us."

—JOHN STEINBECK

INTRODUCTION

*B*rown Sugar: A Collection of Erotic Black Fiction became an instant classic when it broke new ground with a steamy and stellar collection of erotic black fiction that garnered critical acclaim and commercial success after hitting the number two spot on the *Los Angeles Times* Bestseller List. The *Brown Sugar* series has brought together some of the most acclaimed voices in contemporary black fiction: bestselling commercial authors, critically acclaimed literary writers, and award-winning performance poets. Their stories go beyond sex to illustrate issues of race, identity, beauty, and relationships.

Black men and women have found many things to relate to in the stories because they truly represented what makes us tick sexually and emotionally. *Brown Sugar* became a bestseller because the stories were not just about sex; they were sexy stories about black life, in all its myriad forms. That's the beauty of being black, our diversity. And though we don't know it, our diversity is also our greatest strength. You may have been born in the North, or South, or uptown, or down. You may come from the Caribbean or England, or the Caribbean via England. You may hail from the East Coast or the West, or from somewhere in the middle of

America. Though you are black, you may also be French, Asian, Italian, Jewish, or a mix of all of them.

We Don't Take a Trip, a Trip Takes Us

As black Americans, it's easy to forget that we are world travelers. We didn't start in America. We started far from it. Our ancestors come from all over Europe, Egypt, the Middle East, Asia, South America, the Caribbean, and Africa. We are children of the world, and the world can teach us about each other and ourselves. America is not the world, and we are not only American. There are as many different types of black people as there are countries in Africa where we originated.

If you've never left the country, or barely left the neighborhood where you were born and grew up, I urge you, *get out of town*. Hell, get out of the country. Travel allows you to meet other peoples and to put yourself and your world in perspective. You'll come back with a better understanding of who you are and your place in the world. Travel gives you unimpeded access to other cultures, food, books, and viewpoints. You can hear firsthand how the rest of the world feels about your country. And you can experience how other cultures, cities, and societies function. When you explore other continents, cultures, and peoples, you'll meet French, Italian, German, Dutch, Spanish, Scandinavian, Asian and British blacks. You'll see how they live, and you'll be able to reference yourself against them.

I've been traveling since very young, first from the island of my birth, then across America, and later to Europe. At this point it's probably easier to say where I haven't been than where I have. Before I leave, half my suitcase is taken up by books, notebooks, and maps. When I get back home, I'll have even more. I send postcards to myself from every place I've been. As soon as I am on the ground, I buy a batch of cards and write a note about what's happened up to that point. When I get home and recover from jet lag and bad airplane food, I'll reach into my stash of postcards and relive my entire trip.

This is what has allowed me to remember, in almost exact detail, the countries and cities I've explored, the foods I've eaten, and the people I've met. Beyond anything else, one of the most important reasons to travel is to meet people and explore other cultures. You might surprise yourself and meet one of the loves of your life, like I did in Amsterdam. Let me share that story with you.

Dutch Treat

I woke the next morning, sore and satisfied, my muscles aching from the night of lovemaking, alone in the big rumpled bed, thinking about the man I'd met just the day before. I was still stunned with desire. I didn't know what had come over me, but I didn't regret one delicious moment of it even though I had been seeing someone else for a year now; "almost engaged," Tyler had even joked.

Tyler Landry was everything I'd thought I wanted. A doctor, he was successful and good-looking. I'd been told by too many girlfriends that I should thank my lucky stars for him because at my age (which was the north side of thirty-five), he was a good catch.

A Creole, he was light-skinned, wavy-haired, his eyes a compelling mix of greens and browns. I knew he'd be a good mix for my chocolate complexion. If we had kids, they'd be more milk chocolate and less bittersweet. This pleased my parents to no end—having come from the generation where you married to lighten your progeny (even though they hadn't). They'd always steered their kids away from relationships with darker sweethearts. Tyler had even started dropping hints about getting married.

But in bed, he left me wanting.

I applied for the writer-in-residence position in the Netherlands to buy time to think about what I *wanted*, as opposed to what everyone else thought I *needed*: a secure relationship with a nice man whom everyone liked and approved of, even my father. *Hell*, I liked him, too, even loved him at times, but there wasn't that heart-pounding want, that *need*, that rush of desire when he touched me. That was what I wanted from the person I was going to spend the rest of my life with.

This was not something I could share with Tyler, a sweet, good-natured man always falling over himself trying to please me.

■ ■ ■

I met Malik my last day in Amsterdam. It was a good thing he spoke English, because I knew only one word in Wolof and my French was laughable. But English I could manage.

I was staying about fifteen minutes southwest by train, in Leiden—a charming city situated on large canals whose twenty thousand students gave it a cheerful intellectual aura. I was writer-in-residence at the university, but I was in Amsterdam for the weekend as a guest of my Dutch publisher promoting my book—which had become a bestseller in the Netherlands—at the annual book fair.

I'm here, getting paid to live in Holland. My book is doing well, and I've got nothing to do for the next several months but read and write, and talk about reading and writing. I was already the happiest girl in the world. Then Malik walked up to me.

I felt him before I saw him.

I was standing at the bar in the hotel restaurant waiting to be seated. I'd seen him at the book fair over the last two days. We're hard to miss here, as there are so few of us. He was black, but I didn't think he was American. He was so elegant in his three-piece suit; I'd first thought British. But when I heard him speaking French, I figured West African.

He stood there looking at me, his eyes moving boldly over my five-foot-ten frame. My hair's unruly kinks momentarily tamed for the fair. His eyes traveled down to the swell of my breasts beneath my white silk shirt; one button, opened now at the end of the day, exposed a glimpse of creamy lace.

His eyes continued down the length of my chocolate brown light wool suit, the one-button jacket tightly cinched at the waist, accentuating my curves. Then to the brown woolen pants, cuffed above the high-heeled brown crocodile pumps. His eyes came to rest on my lips, which were full and plump and stained with the mocha lipstick I'd just applied in the ladies' room. His eyes then met mine.

I almost blushed, which is something, for me. But I met his gaze evenly. He was dark, almost blue-black, the color of polished ebony. His cheekbones were defined and sloping, his almond-shaped eyes surrounded by full lashes. His lips were as plump as my own, but I could see a few fine lines around them. On his chin was a deep vertical cleft I wanted to place my tongue inside.

He was completely bald; his head looked freshly shaved. About six foot two, he was stocky and stylish, in a midnight blue suit with a fine gray pinstripe, a sky blue silk shirt beneath. His tie was silk and the same blue as his shirt. At his wrist was a gold watch. As I looked back at him, he stood there watching me. When my eyes returned to his face, he smiled, his lips parting to reveal straight white teeth.

He looked at the conference label on my lapel. "Carol Taylor, Author," he said, his voice a rich baritone, with a slight lilt.

"You have a beautiful name, *Carol*." He rolled out the second half of my name, like the French. "Do you know it means to bring forth joyous song?"

"I do, actually. Like Christmas carol," I answered.

"What are you doing at the book fair?" he asked, as though we'd been friends for years.

"You ask a lot of questions," I said, smiling. "And you are . . . ?"

He offered his hand.

"My name is Malik Touré. I'm here promoting a series of audio-books on language. And I see you are an author."

"I'm here as a guest of my publisher promoting my book. I'm a writer and editorial consultant. I live in New York. I'm also a writer-in-residence at Leiden, but I'm here in Amsterdam through the weekend."

"How old are you, *Carol?*"

"I'm thirty-five."

"Are you married?"

I thought about Tyler for a split second, then answered, "No."
"Good," he said.

■ ■ ■

When the host arrived to show me to my table, Malik took my arm and escorted me to the banquette. After I'd sat down, he indicated the seat across from me. When I nodded, he slipped out of his jacket and sat down.

I could tell he was African as soon as he looked at me. He was so self-assured, meeting my eyes, his head high and shoulders back. Like he was royalty, like he owned the joint and everyone was there to cater to him. I'd heard him speaking French, so I guessed West Africa, the Ivory Coast or Benin, maybe, or perhaps Senegal.

"Are you West African?" I asked.

He looked surprised but just for a second.

"Very good, yes, I'm Senegalese, Wolof, from the coast of Senegal. I live now in Paris, but I grew up in Dakar, the capital."

"*Asalamalekum,*" I welcomed him.

Most Wolof are Muslim, converts of Islam.

"*Asalamalekum,*" he returned. "You are full of surprises. And you are from where?" he asked me.

"I'm Jamaican, but I grew up in America."

"Ahh," he said, "you're British. That explains it."

"No," I corrected him. "I'm *Jamaican.*"

"But Jamaica is a British colony."

"Not since 1962. But that wouldn't make me British. Senegal was a French colony. Does that make you French?" I asked.

He smiled and held up his hands.

"It was meant as a compliment. Your speech, it's not that of an American black. And now I understand why." He arched a brow. "Don't tell me you've never heard that?"

He had a point. I'd perplexed far too many ignorant white people who after a moment or two of polite cocktail conversation would cock their head and give me a piercing look. "Where *are* you from?" they'd ask, brows knit.

"I'm Jamaican," I'd answer, and they'd nod like this answered something. "Ahh, I didn't think you were American, you speak so *well*."

You're so well-spoken, I'd correct them in my head.

They'd give it as a compliment, not knowing it was an insult—that because I was black I should not be well-spoken.

"You should get out more," I'd usually say. Then I'd smile and walk away. It was tiresome that in this age some white people still didn't know enough black people who could hold a conversation, in a couple different languages even.

I smiled at Malik. "I couldn't quite place you either, but now I know why. It's because you're African. Are you a writer?" I asked.

"No. I own a language software and licensing firm based in Paris. But I have an apartment in New York. I've been here since Thursday night. I'm forty-two years old. Unmarried. No children."

■ ■ ■

We sat an hour later, in a room by now thick with bluish gray smoke curling in tendrils around our heads, drinking chilled thimble-sized glasses of Genever—Dutch gin made from juniper berries—with Heineken chasers.

Malik pulled a cigarette out of the pack in his breast pocket along with a silver Zippo lighter. He tamped one cigarette out into the palm of his hand, then placed it gently to his lips. Sparking the lighter, he inhaled and then exhaled up toward the ceiling. It would take him all of ten seconds, but he did it with such care that it seemed choreographed to perfection. When I gave him a questioning look, he indicated the cigarette.

"Do you disapprove?"

"I think it's a stupid thing to do, for someone who seems so smart."

He sat back and crossed his legs. Taking another drag, he blew it again toward the ceiling and looked at me.

"You Americans like to pass judgment. I believe I should be responsible for me. Yes? This is why I prefer Europe. Here we are trusted to be responsible for ourselves. You black Americans are so provincial; you think in Africa we are this one big tribe that is all the same. Can you name me three African countries?" he challenged.

Oh no, he did not, I thought.

"Hey, don't get all African on me. If you've lived in the states, you know all blacks are not provincial, in the same way that not all Africans are arrogant. Maybe *you* should get out more."

When he didn't respond, I went on, "Now let's see." I started ticking them off my fingers, "Kenya, Mozambique, Benin, Ghana, Nigeria, Zimbabwe."

"Okay, okay," he said. "I give up."

"And if I'm not mistaken, weren't the Wolof known for capturing and selling Africans to the Europeans during the slave trade? I don't think you should feel too good about your people's contribution to black American history."

He sighed. "I don't, and I've been trying to make up for it ever since." He leaned forward in his seat. "America wants to pretend it's come far, but it's still the Antebellum, isn't it? How do you stand it? Every time I go to America I can't wait to leave. I feel like a second-class citizen. And not because I'm *African*, because I'm *black*."

Waving over the waiter, he stubbed out the cigarette in the ashtray, then placed it and the Zippo onto the waiter's tray, and told him to take it away.

He then leaned forward and took my hand in his.

"And I would like to get to know you better. What do you think about that?"

Definitely African, I thought. I wondered how I'd missed it.

I found it funny I had come to Amsterdam and met an African who lived in New York.

■ ■ ■

This was my second trip to the Netherlands. The first time was about a year before, when I'd done a quick tour of Europe. Although I'd stayed in Paris, Rome, Tuscany, Munich, and Antwerp, it was Amsterdam that I swore I'd return to one day to live.

The Dutch do things differently. Amsterdam is proof. With its scenic, romantic canals and a peaceful city center, it's an offbeat metropolis with world-class museums, cutting-edge art, music, and fashion, and beautiful and cosmopolitan people. Amsterdam is steeped in its Dutch *gezellig* spirit. Loosely translated, *gezellig* describes kicking back, mellowing out, and not getting hung up on someone else's preferences. It seemed a lot like me.

The Dutch seem to enjoy life the most and feel the least guilty about its pleasures. Compare the Dutch to other nationalities: Germans, living up to their stereotypes, take the least pleasure in life, yet feel the guiltiest about it. The English are somewhere in the middle, with equal amounts of pleasure and guilt. America has the most amount of pleasure but also a fair amount of guilt about it.

Yes, Amsterdam is a city with *legal* sex and drugs, but it also has so many other goods things going for it (for example, success with race relations, urban sprawl, and poverty). The availability of sex and drugs is actually the end product of careful planning.

■ ■ ■

Malik and I spent most of the afternoon together. Following the canals north, we explored the elegant nineteenth-century streets of Oud Zuid, walking in the gorgeous Vondelpark, which is an oasis of green in the middle of the city. We ended the day with dinner at Malik's favorite West African restaurant in fashionable Jordaan, an area with trendy bars and restaurants and a steady stream of young, beautiful, and cashed-out locals. As we walked we talked about the differences between Africans and black Americans. How Africans didn't see blacks as African but as American. He told me how it would amuse him and his friends to see the crowds of black Americans getting off the plane in Africa in their kente cloth outfits and head wraps, not knowing what the design on the fabric meant or how to wrap their heads correctly.

Over dinner Malik explained that the origins of kente cloth dated back to twelfth-century Africa, in the country of Ghana. Behind each design was deep symbolic meaning. Kente cloth came to represent the history, philosophy, ethics, and moral values in African culture.

To be honest, I hadn't known any of this, but then again I didn't wear kente cloth. Now I could. It was enlightening to hear how Africans saw black Americans and to understand that even though blacks felt a kinship to Mama Africa, Africans didn't necessarily see black Americans as their long-lost brothers and sisters. And how could they? We are, after all, Americans.

Without asking, Malik ordered for me in Wolof, his favorite dish, *ceebu jen*. When the waiter had walked away, he'd said, "I hope you don't mind, I think you'll like it. It's a fish and rice dish. You're Jamaican. You like fish and rice, yes? And it's spicy, like you."

It was spicy like me, and I liked it.

■ ■ ■

Now, back in Amsterdam, Sunday night. In the morning he'd be leaving for Paris and I'd be heading out to Leiden. We sat in the hotel bar, neither one of us wanting to end the evening.

When the waiter left, he said, "I want you to do something for me."

"Oh?"

"Yes, I've given you something you wanted, now I want something from you."

"What might that be?"

He leaned across the table and took hold of my hand. "I want to make love to you."

You couldn't fault the man for trying.

I sat back in my chair and looked at him. "Since you're being so straightforward, I'll be as well. Why should I let you?"

"Because I've given up smoking for you." He laughed.

"Not for me," I corrected. "For you. If you want to kill yourself, go ahead. What does that have to do with me?" I joked.

"No, it's for you. We are going to continue seeing each other, so I'm quitting for you," he said, taking a sip of his drink.

When I just sat there looking at him, he continued, "And because I want to and because you want me to. You seem so proper and, though you'll deny it, *British*. But underneath is a fiery Jamaican."

I couldn't argue with him.

■ ■ ■

This is how we ended up in his hotel room.

Leaving me standing at the door, Malik walked into the room. Silhouetted by the soft light coming in from the windows, he took off his suit jacket, throwing it across the leather couch, loosened his tie, and slid it from his neck. His deep ebony skin seemed to glow in the half-light. Like my dad would say, he was "blackity black *black*." My parents would freak.

He took off his watch, walked to the balcony, and closed the drapes. The room was plunged into darkness. What was I doing, I asked myself, locked in a strange man's room? Sure, we'd hung out and had a good time. And we had chemistry, but I didn't really know much about him beyond his name and his nationality. Actually, I'd Googled him before we'd gone out and discovered he was CEO of Touré Technologies, main offices in Paris, France. Forty-two. Unmarried. A girl can't be too careful.

A moment later the room was bathed in a soft warm light and Malik was standing at the edge of the bed, his shirtsleeves rolled up to reveal strong forearms and muscular biceps.

"I've been watching you since you arrived, *Carol*. I find you very attractive, poised, and elegant. Have you ever made love to an African? I'm sure Africans have wanted to make love to you. I want to make love to you. Do you want to make love to me?"

I searched my brain for a rational answer. What *was* I doing here? I thought again. What about Tyler? Had I lost my mind? Malik stood watching me. He arched an eyebrow. "Yes?"

A million thoughts rushed through my head as Malik stood there watching me. "Yes."

"Come here," he said. Before I knew I'd even moved, I was standing in front of him.

"Unbutton your jacket. I want to look at you."

I undid the button at my waist.

"Take it off."

I did as I was instructed. Sliding the jacket off my shoulder, letting it fall to the floor.

"Good."

Malik stood looking at me, his eyes leaving no part of me untouched. "Don't move," he whispered. He walked around me, picking up my jacket and tossing it to join his on the couch, his movements confident and deliberate. Then he stood behind me, his breath warm on my neck.

"Unbutton your shirt."

Again I did as instructed, pulling my shirt free of my waistband. The creamy lace of my bra was all that covered me.

He undid the clasps of my bra, separated the cups, and pushed the straps off my shoulders, my shirt sliding to the floor along with it. I stood topless in front of him, the air cooling the light perspiration on my chest. His hands went to my waist, unbuckling my leather belt and opening the button of my waistband to reveal the matching cream lace thong I wore. Pushing my pants down my hips, Malik told me to step out of them. I did.

He unbuttoned his shirt and threw it onto the couch. He had a nicely muscled chest that was as completely hairless as he was bald. He took my hand by the wrist and pulled me toward him.

■ ■ ■

When I woke the next morning, sore and satisfied, my muscles aching from the night of lovemaking, I was alone in the big rumpled bed. The pillow beside mine smelling of musk and sandalwood reminded me of Malik and the night before. He'd risen early to catch his plane back to Paris, leaving me with breakfast, his business card, and a credit card number to purchase a flight to Paris the following week. As I lay in bed I started packing my things in my mind, wondering what my father would think of Malik and rehearsing what I would say to Tyler.

No Truth but in Transit

If "there is no truth but in transit," then it's no coincidence that we are our most uninhibited when we travel. It is out of town when we are most willing to be wanton. Travel and sex, my two favorite pastimes, just seem to happen more often together. In different places, I guess we can be different people, out of place and out of context.

The stories in *Wanderlust* explore the desires we all have to be someone else outside the confines of "home"—whether we've acted on them or not—and will strike a chord with anyone who has ever been drawn to a foreign country and into a relationship with someone they met there. Less a guidebook than an erotic travelogue, these edgy, atmospheric, and erotically charged stories take place around the world, and although they are set in different countries, the characters are people you will recognize. Contemporary, enlightening, and sexy, they take you from Parisian streets to Jamaican beaches, from the Barbadian mountainside to Costa Rican towns, from the African countryside to Italian beaches for moonlit nights and sun-kissed skin.

Sex is everywhere in these stories, and not just in the act. It's in the words and the gestures. It's in the setting and the mood. Though many of these characters don't speak the same language, it hasn't stopped them from understanding each other's needs or desires. To be honest, the best sex I've ever had often has been without a word being spoken. If you're on the same page, who needs words? They often just get in the way.

Let's Trip

Nine of the writers included in *Wanderlust* I invited because I like what they're doing. Four writers were selected from stories submitted in response to an open call on my Web site to writers—published or not—who wanted to be in the anthology. These writers—SékouWrites, Melvin E. Lewis, Carol Amorosa, and Deep Bronze—impressed me with their stories, their writing, and their passion for both. There's no doubt you'll be hearing a lot more from them.

Each story is a gem. Let Glenville Lovell's rich and seductive prose transport you to his Barbados, here a country of great beauty and dark secrets in "Sexing the Mountain." Nina Foxx's haunting and sexy "The Rule of One Thousand" is about a woman getting over a breakup with the aid of an unlikely lover, and tests our beliefs as much as our boundaries. Sékou Writes's "Pink Tiara Rainbows" is as much a metaphysical trip as a physical one where we go from the banks of the Nile and across America as several lives are touched and changed by an unlikely object. Then let Miles Marshall Lewis escort you through the Paris arrondissements and the *calles* of Spain as an American contemplates the two *irrésistible* women in his life: one who loves him and the one whom he loves, but who doesn't love him back. Isn't that always the case?

From there it's a quick trip to Italy with Sandra Kitt for a midnight rendezvous on the moonlit beach of Taormina. A young woman's vacation is starting to come undone until "The Fixer" steps out of the ocean and into her arms. It's a night neither she nor you will soon forget. Brandon Massey's "La Segua" is a supernatural tale of danger and desire when a man in the grips of a midlife crisis runs from his wife and life to Costa Rica and loses himself in the arms of another woman. When his betrayal comes back to haunt him, his only chance is the love of his wife. Hopefully, it won't be too late. When you're done, leave the lush countryside of Costa Rica for the sugarcane counties of Puerto Rico, the rich and verdant rain forests teeming with flora and fauna, and the cobblestone streets of San Juan in Melvin E. Lewis's "La Linea Negra," where an American and a Latina, as different as night and day, navigate the intricacies of race, color, and country to fall in love. Next, trip with Tracy Price-Thompson in *Hawaii Five-Oh!* Her sexually adventurous heroine finds more than she expects but exactly what she needs in the gorgeous islands of Hawaii. You'll be packing your bags before you finish the story. Then, head on to Mama Africa with Sandra Jackson-Opoku's wry and funny "Fort Jesus." On location for a music video set in Mombassa, the director's life starts to mirror the scene he is trying to shoot as he falls for an African woman destined for another man. Years later, he sits recounting his tragic tale and is taken back to the shores of Africa and the woman he can't forget. Jamaica's next, the island of my birth, where Angela, the namesake and narrator of Carol Amorosa's sexy and insightful story, tries to stop herself from falling as hard for the Jamaican men as she has for the Jamaican country, even as she tries to sort out her life as a vibrant and sexual woman no longer in the flush of youth.

Venture north of the border with Nalo Hopkinson to Vancouver, where her deliciously hot and horny story "Blackberries" illustrates how friendship and desire are intertwined and often inescapable as three old friends explore more than the dunes, amid the tall grass of Wreck Beach. Back in the States you'll feel like you're still in Europe as Jervey Tervalon's "The Grim Gumbo of Love" takes you inside his dark and gritty New Orleans, with its overwhelmingly heady mix of sex and black magic. Travel to the other side of the country for an encounter in an unlikely place in Deep Bronze's raunchy and arousing "Just Another Day," where two straphangers surprise themselves and each other during a ride on the el. Though I don't recommend you try this at home, it shows that love can be found in even the most unlikely of places. Then let Preston L. Allen show you the "Southernmost Triangle" in the Florida Keys. You'll find a most unusually entangled relationship amid a sexually adventurous threesome whose desire is fueled by equal parts love, lust, and regret.

You won't close this book unaffected—compelling stories all. You'll find them more familiar than not, even as they introduce you to places you've never been and experiences you might never have dreamed of.

Wanderlust

SEXING THE MOUNTAIN

Glenville Lovell

"The most beautiful place I know."

Iris spoke these words with the proprietary pleasure of a long-held secret. A secret being revealed for the first time, but which, now released to her lover, would seep into the ground to flow to the sea for no others to hear but the fish and their hunters.

Moses was her lover.

That thought filled her with more joy than she could've ever imagined. At the same time it filled her with anxiety. Could he also be her brother? Every chance now she searched him for her father's imprint, for signs of herself since everyone said she was the spitting image of her father: in the shape of his feet, the length of his fingers, the scale of his cheeks, the light in his smile.

But he bore no obvious resemblance, no footprint leading back to her family tree. Except for the motionless clarity of his deep, brooding eyes, he was everything of his grandmother: the slope of his forehead, his ample lips, the tilt of his nose, down to the impeccable curl of his fleshy ears. But what about *his* voice, brimming with authority and wit. Wasn't there something of her father there?

It would've been so much simpler to dismiss it all as paranoia hatched from a story overheard when she was a little girl. But in a country of dark secrets, every bout of paranoia had to be remedied, so she'd asked her friend Darian, a lawyer, to sift through his birth records at the Barbados Registry. What was revealed only added to her confusion. Moses was five years her junior, and his father had not been identified on the birth certificate.

She'd never brought anyone to this place since she discovered it one bright night twelve years ago. Driving back from a moonlight picnic near Bathsheba, she'd taken a wrong turn, landing in a ditch. Save for the fireflies, everything was asleep at that hour as she got out to walk for help. Hugging the eastern coastline all the way from Saint Andrew to Saint John, Iris could hear the Atlantic Ocean pummeling the rocks not far off.

Scooting down a steep dirt track hedged in by canes on one side and the manic raw smell of the sea increasing on the other, she decided to forego the search for help—it was already four in the morning and daybreak was near anyway—deciding instead to let her ears lead her to the sea where she would sit until sunrise.

A tiny path off to her right drew her through a banana grove. Shadows abounded in the field of stunted plants. Backs glistening, tiny crabs scampered across the full moon, which lay splattered on the ground in front of her.

Winding tighter with each yard, the narrow path edged uphill, one side falling off into a steep gully. Iris held on to branches for balance as she wound her way up. After climbing another fifty yards she suddenly broke free onto a hilltop oasis of light at the edge of the sea. The grassy plateau spanned an area of forty square yards. A huge stone mass rose out of the ground ten yards away. A giant without a head. Smaller stone-children huddled around. Beyond the family of stones a solitary hut stood out against the sky, its bleak posture contradicting the impatient white-headed sea god thundering against the rocks. Overwhelmed by the austere beauty around her, Iris walked closer to the edge. The water shimmered and slashed at the stony cliff face, spitting needle-sharp streams of water toward her and leaving what looked like rainbows in the air.

It became her secret haven; she returned every chance she got. Always alone. Anytime Iris began to doubt herself, or felt overwhelmed by the enormity of her work, she returned at the full moon, to sip from this magic cup of thundering sea, to be reminded that only Nature could afford the extravagance of self-pity.

Here, on this plateau on the eastern edge of Barbados, she was a woman without fear, without contradictions, omnipotent, belonging to no place but this oasis where in the blue brightness of the moonlight her mind and spirit roamed free as she witnessed rainbows unfold in sea spray. That was why she'd never brought anyone here. Who'd believe her?

Moses might believe.

Here was a man who might dream of iridescent rainbows kissing the sea at night. Here was a man she might also have to kiss good-bye.

■ ■ ■

Iris had met Moses two months ago in New York at a reception for visiting Barbadian artists whose work was on exhibit at the Barbados Consulate. She'd left the island of Barbados at the age of twelve with her parents, both university lecturers, when her father accepted a professorship in literature at Morgan State University.

Her parents divorced two years later and her mother returned home. She stayed behind with her father, graduating from Columbia University College of Physicians and Surgeons at the age of twenty-three.

She interned at New York-Presbyterian, remaining there for three years after becoming certified. For the past seven years she'd been on staff in the department of gastroenterology at NYU Medical Center, a job she loved.

Moses's work had been the most distinctive on display that evening at the consulate, in particular his oversize heads of old men and women in burnished mahogany. It wasn't just the gracefulness of execution but the dignity evident in each face, as if the artist had inhabited the souls of his subjects.

Iris sought him out at the reception to express her appreciation. How powerfully she was drawn to him surprised her; his warm inviting voice proved so beguiling she shocked herself by asking him to dinner. He declined, saying that he was leaving the next day.

Her disappointment was palpable; in fact, it frightened her. Before they parted company he invited her to visit his studio whenever she was in Barbados.

Unable to get him out of her mind, Iris decided to take two weeks off and head to Barbados, telling herself she was going to see her mother and family. It was an impulsive act, something she was not known for, having calculated and planned just about every step of her life up to that point. But in the short time with him, Iris experienced an emotion she could only describe as a waterfall in her soul, as if someone had opened a curtain revealing her own private beach in paradise. She could've listened to the lilting rhythm of his voice all night, and there was a purity about his passion that was almost hypnotic.

She'd never been frivolous or capricious when it came to men. Though she'd only had one long-term relationship, which ended because she had to choose between him and her work, she'd been blessed with good looks and never lacked for suitors.

Lately, she'd felt herself being pursued by an unlikely suitor: loneliness. It didn't help that at the age of thirty-five she also found herself experiencing a burgeoning sexual appetite.

Moses lived a modest life with his blind grandmother in the Chalky Mount area, the only hilly part on an otherwise flat island. Their small wooden house, settled in the yawn of a wide-branched plum tree, was where she spent her second night on the island. That night after they'd made love for the first time, he told her that his name was chosen because he was born on a grassy knoll near a pond not far away. Moses also revealed that he didn't know his father but knew he'd been a university lecturer for whom his mother worked before she left the island for England.

It brought to mind a rumor Iris had heard growing up. Someone in her family had let slip that her father had impregnated a housekeeper and had paid her a sum of money to keep quiet. Perhaps it was just a coincidence. But Barbados was a very small place, so small in fact that there was little room for coincidences. In a country of only 166 square miles, every coincidence had the likelihood of being part of a truth.

That night Iris questioned her mother, who was reluctant to revisit the scandal. Finally, she admitted that the young woman in question had lived in the Chalky Mount area, and though her father denied making the girl pregnant, she never believed him.

There was nothing more her mother could tell her. She didn't remember the young woman's name, though at Iris's insistence she promised to look through her records for anything that might refresh her memory. At this point her curiosity had reached its peak, and doubt had settled like a cloud. This morning her mother told her that she'd unearthed some papers bearing the young woman's name. Miriam.

Her heart sunk. Miriam. The same as Moses's mother. There was only one way to know for sure now. She would have to get in touch with her father.

■ ■ ■

Moses came up behind her, collecting her in his arms, nestling his head on her neck.

"What do you think about this place?" she asked him.

He released her and walked off a couple yards, face serious, hands akimbo, feet astraddle two stones. He seemed to be waiting for something to happen. The sea splashed over the edge of the cliff, dousing the grass, sprinkling them with fine mist.

"I see a rainbow."

Her heart skipped. Surely, he couldn't have read her mind.

"You can't see rainbows at night." Her laugh was timorous as she waited for him to answer her. But he said nothing more.

This place turned Iris into a child. An effect she could not explain to anyone, something that could only be understood through divine perception. As he walked closer to the edge of the cliff, so close she thought he might jump, she wondered if somehow he'd sensed that.

She lay on the grass facing the moon, with eyes closed, ears opened. The sound of the sea becoming air filled her with a dull fire, making her nerves raw with excitement, making her twitch and pulse to a magical drumbeat as she waited for Moses to make love to her.

She knew she shouldn't entertain any thoughts of him touching her again until she had sated her curiosity about his father, but here, on this hill, it was impossible to contain her desire for him.

She heard her name and jumped up.

Iris! Iris!

She started toward him, but realizing he wasn't calling her, she stopped. He was staring into the distance, calling her name over the sea. Calling and waiting. And calling and waiting. It was a magical sound. After a few minutes of this he came to her.

"What were you doing?" she asked.

An impish smile crept into his eyes. "I just give your name to the sea. Tomorrow I go see if the wind bring it back to me."

"And what would that mean?"

"That you will be mine forever."

The smile spread over his face as he slid to the ground at her feet. He stretched himself out, a fabulous avian creature with long black wings. She studied him—the expanded cheekbones, the tapered nose, the patch of premature gray—and knew she could love this man with her soul, with an abandon she knew she kept in reserve.

"Moses, there's something I have to tell you."

"Later."

"No, we have to talk about it now."

"It can wait. This is not a time for talking. This is not a place for talking."

He reached under her shirt and squeezed her nipples hard. The combined pleasure and pain tied her tongue. With a soft moan she wormed onto him, draping herself over him like a flag. He slipped his hand under her skirt knowing he would find her naked there. She wanted to pull away, to stop him, but she also wanted more than anything for him to touch her there, in that sweet place. His soft kisses on her neck were sweeter than moonlight. She couldn't move. She sensed, too, that her pussy was obscenely swollen, for she was filled with a vertiginous lust. A lust that no other man had ever inspired in her. She'd lost the will to stop him now. She unbuckled his pants and touched him. Flaccid with a warm thick softness like a newborn puppy. She put him in her mouth. He rose quickly and abundantly. His breathing changed, quickening. She pulled his pants completely off. He rubbed his ankle against her ass. Dark skin glistening on light skin. Moonlight shining on naked sea.

Snaking the skirt up her thighs, beyond the boundary of her ass, his fingers encircled her clit and she cried out, her voice echoing deep and long. Riding his hand, she collapsed on top of him. Her passion became like the sea. Dark and relentless. Letting his hardness rub against her stomach, she massaged one of his testicles gently against her clit. She loved the odd feeling it produced there, the tightening it caused in the muscles around her pelvis. Shedding her skirt, she shifted to guide him inside her, but he stopped her. Sitting up, he forced her down onto her back. She drew her legs up to her chest, expecting him to enter her, but he pushed them down, entreating her to lie still. Crouched on his haunches, with a look of exquisite wonder on his face, he began to caress her, sliding his hands over her entire body like a sculptor shaping clay. Her skin tingled where his calluses scraped her. His large hands gobbled up her body with each stroke. But the reverence of his touch drove her crazy. Now he was reciting something like a mantra, to himself or to her, she couldn't tell. *You are worthy. You are worthy. You are worthy.* She felt her body melt into the grass, her spirit yielding to the altar of air as he continued to caress her, replacing his hands with his mouth.

Every inch of her being was aroused. She no longer knew exactly where his mouth was. Whether it was touching her neck, gnawing her belly, enveloping her pussy. She had been set afire on the grass pyre. Her entire body had become one nerve, her every sense intensified. She could smell the sweet sourness of the grass; she could feel the heat seeping from the ground underneath her, the sharpness of a single blade of grass tickling the crack of her ass; she could hear the wind trapped between their bodies. She imagined that her clit had fattened beyond recognition under assault from his tongue. And when she closed her eyes, the first wave came. The first fall over the cliff. The first tingly touch of the rainbow. She endured it, and when she thought it would end, another wave came, longer, more intense. And when that was about to pass, another one came, a shinier wave, brighter and wider, from so deep inside her she just knew her body would explode. Night surged around them. Stars scarred the glistening sky as she disappeared inside that wave until it passed.

Afterward they lay wrapped around each other like a hungry love-vine ensnaring itself. Her head full of the music of love. His head swelling with the echo of the high-pitched voice of Jackie Opel, which always came to him after sex.

He cracked the silence. "I have music in my head."

There was a pause.

Then a giggle, from Iris. "I was about to say the same thing."

"What kind of music you hearing?"

"Jackie Opel, for some reason. 'Eternal Love.'"

He sat up smiling. "You serious?"

"I didn't think I liked him. Then I heard this song that morning I left your house, and I haven't been able to get it out of my head."

He lay down again. "Listening to Jackie does give me such a special feeling. Like listening to the land sing. I don't know any other way to describe it. He had the spirit of this whole country in his voice."

"I think you do, too, in your hands."

"Me?"

"Yes, you're a great artist."

"I ain't no Jackie Opel."

"Your ability to bring out the beauty and dignity in the faces of people who've obviously lived hard lives, to illuminate the darkness in their past, is a special gift."

"I'm just a man trying to find the purpose to his life, that's all."

"I love your work," Iris said. "And I love you. And I'm not sure if I can give you up."

"Why would you have to give me up?"

At that moment she couldn't bring herself to tell him why.

"I'll tell you tomorrow."

She snuggled into him. He welcomed her warm body. They closed their eyes. The fat moon hovering above lulled them to sleep.

The morning glow spreading over Saint John found two love-drunks asleep atop the hillside. Sheep emerged from the dream Moses was having, and when he woke, he saw them filing from the hut behind him. A small frail man, already dispirited, lurched after them, hollering angry orders to no avail. The sheep pranced around, joyous in their freedom, more attuned to the natural beauty around them than their ill-tempered master. Moses looked at Iris, still asleep, and felt lucky. Could this woman possibly love him?

Iris woke a few minutes later to Moses stretching his wings and felt special under them. Beyond the cliff, gulls and egrets seemed to pause midflight, showing off what real birds could do as they balanced between heaven and earth. Over the cliff last night's foaming rage had been replaced by a timid squall gently kissing green coral stone.

As the old man and his sheep disappeared from view, Iris and Moses made their way down the ridge to the car parked under a breadfruit tree. Dew covered its black metal skin. In the valley the air was damp.

"What did the wind say to you this morning?" she asked as they settled into the car. "Did it bring my name back?"

"That's between me and the wind." He smiled mysteriously and leaned back into the seat.

They drove west into the heart of the country. Moses, aware that they weren't heading toward his home in Saint Andrew, asked where they were going.

"To my home," she replied. "I have something to show you."

The road was quiet for a Monday morning. They met few cars on the way. The human traffic along the side of the road was heavy, however, mostly women in drab laborers' rags, heads covered with bright colored cloths or subdued under Panama hats, hoes draped across their shoulders on their way to clean ditches at some plantation. The soft roar of wind through serpentine grass bid these spirited workers welcome, but the incipient sun in the east, preparing for a fiery solo center sky, augured a tough day ahead. Moses could hear them singing and trailed their cheerful steps as far as he could without straining his neck. In the evening they would return, heads down, too weary to sing.

Half an hour later they turned into the driveway of a house on Pine Road, one of the most upscale neighborhoods on the island, a place where not so long ago only white people lived. Moses eyed the sumptuous gardens and the pristine surroundings as he got out of the car. A bull of a man with the biceps of a bodybuilder was clipping a hedge.

"Morning, Miss Sinclair," the man greeted Iris.

"Morning, Caswell. Caswell, this is Moses."

Caswell looked Moses up and down, settling his eyes on Moses's feet, noticed how ill-fitting his sandals were, then began to snigger as Moses extended his hand. Moses withdrew his hand, staring angrily at the man.

"What you laughing at, man?" he demanded.

Caswell glanced in Iris's direction. She was standing on the first rung of the steps, and a scowl advanced over her face. Caswell broke off his snickering and returned to his work.

"Come on, Moses," Iris said.

■ ■ ■

Iris's bedroom was in the western part of the house and, like all the other rooms, looked out onto the ubiquitous garden. Fine mahogany furniture, including an ornate four-poster bed with carved frames and a caned rocking chair, endowed the room with an old-world atmosphere. A red vase filled with fresh flowers sat on a high-legged mahogany console.

She walked over to the dresser and picked up a photograph in a shiny black frame, handing it to him.

He stared at the black-and-white picture of a stocky man in a suit leaning against a car.

"That is my father." She paused, not sure how to continue. "There was a rumor that my father had a child by a woman living in Chalky Mount. Her name was Miriam. I don't know if it's true. I never met this sibling. But there's something about your voice and the way you laugh that . . ."

Moses started to laugh. "You think I might be your brother?"

"It is possible."

"That is so ridiculous."

"Trust me, Moses. I don't want to believe it. But I've trained myself to be rational about things . . . To examine and question."

"I don't care what you've been trained to do. This is the craziest thing I ever heard. How can I be your brother? I don't look nothing like you or that man in that picture. Besides, my father's dead. I already tell you so."

"But you don't know who he was."

"Who cares? He's dead, so forget about it. If your father fucked a woman in Chalky Mount named Miriam, it wasn't my mother."

"You know, the one thing about growing up here that I've never really been able to shake was the feeling that there were secrets all around me. In the air. The way blackbirds stared at me. The way people walked with their heads down. I could never seem to shake it. When I went to sleep at night I often had this feeling that the trees were whispering things to me that I couldn't understand. Did you ever feel like that?"

"Yes, but I got used to it fast. This is a country of secrets. Thanks to the British."

They stared at each other from across the room.

"Where's your father, anyway?" he asked.

"In Egypt. He retired from the university two years ago."

"What's he doing there?"

"Researching the Abydos mystery plays. He's always had a fascination with Egypt and its ancient rituals. The Pharaohs, the mystery religions, the deities, and stuff like that. Actually, he told me something he discovered sometime ago about the origin of one of the Moses stories in the Bible. He claims that the bridegroom of blood story is an adaptation of the Egyptian myth of Isis and Osiris."

"The *what* story?"

She laughed. "You don't read the Bible, do you?"

"No, and especially not about Moses." He stared earnestly into her face. "There's something I want to know from you."

"Yes . . ."

"You came down here just to be with me, didn't you?"

She laughed. "Is that what you think?"

"Yes." He sat on the bed.

"What if I said I did?" She followed him instinctively.

"What do you want from me?"

"I don't know. I'm afraid to ask for anything. Just in case . . ."

"Just in case what . . . I'm your brother? Get that out of your head." His voice was emphatic like a strummed guitar.

"Can I have your love?"

"You have everything anybody could want. You come from a well-off family. You got money. You live in New York. Why do you want my love? You hardly know me. Are you willing to give up all that for my love?"

"Is that what you want to hear?"

With a raffish smile he netted her in his arms. "Yes, I want to hear that you would give up everything for me. I want to hear you say you could love me more than anything. Can you say that?"

"I could, but I won't."

His fingers began to dance a tango on her behind.

"No, Moses, we can't do this anymore. Not until we're sure," she begged, but already she knew she'd been rendered powerless by his touch.

He pushed her firmly down onto the bed and wedged his legs between hers, forcing them apart, sliding his hands over her ass, dipping his fingers in the crack, searching for her pussy. He found it slick with her juices.

"Moses . . ." Her voice was a mere whimper now.

He didn't reply. Working another finger into her pussy and one in her ass, he enticed soft moans from her throat. He slithered his wiry body down onto hers, at the same time pushing her skirt up above her waist. Meeting little resistance now, he spread her legs wider, holding her ass in his hands, kneading the cheeks gently, inserting his tongue, licking her from crack to clit.

"What if I'm your brother?"

"I don't care," she whispered.

"Beg for the dick," he ordered.

"Please, baby. Please, fuck me."

"How do you want it?"

"Like this, baby."

"From behind?"

"Yes, from behind."

She'd never felt such quivering desire, never experienced this depth of depraved pleasure and abandon. Head down and ass up, she welcomed and celebrated the slow, aggregated sensations of his dick sliding into her.

Her emotions were coming from a place she couldn't identify deep within her core, radiating outward, brushing every nerve within her, expanding up through her stomach, chest, and neck.

Slowly he began to work in and out of her, drawing wet sounds from deep within her. He quickened his pace and she increased the volume of her cries, her body beginning to shake uncontrollably.

She surrendered herself completely to the mystical drumbeat of his rhythm, heavy as the bough of a tamarind tree, capturing her spirit with the fury of its pounding, taking her breath away with the intensity of his tempo. Even her bones seemed to shake as if wanting to break free. Her heart had been attuned to his rhythm from the moment they met, and she was now unable to say no to his spirit.

Who was this man? And what was he doing to her? How did he make her feel this way after only a few short days?

His tongue lapped away the sweat from her neck, his large calloused hands exploring the roundness of her hip with sureness, as if he'd roamed the sharp terrain all his life. He seemed to be pulling her across time, across burning fields of dead languages. She tried to speak but her tongue was tied.

"I'm getting ready to come, baby," he cried.

She wanted to tell him he was welcome to grow his seed inside her, even if he was her brother, but he had already scorched language from her mind.

She caught his flame and it ignited her. Her own cries were elusive, fluttering away like a spider's web in a breeze.

They collapsed on the bed in each other's arms. She could not get enough of him and cried out when he withdrew. He kissed her; she cuddled up to him, their bodies still warm and wet.

JUST ANOTHER DAY

Deep Bronze

I do it for the excitement, the attention. Yeah, and I knew one day that I might get caught. Some nights there's a cop on; and damn near every night those *transit preachers* are on the el witnessing and asking for donations in exchange for stale peanuts and M&Ms. After a while, they really start to bug you with their "hell and damnation" lectures, testimonials, and sermonizing.

> *. . . givin' honor to God I greet you this evening, brothas and sistahs. I want you to bear witness this evening that He done brought me from a mighty long way. . . . I was out here strung out on heroin, cigarettes, alcohol and . . . prostituting and pimping myself just six months ago, but oh happy day . . . I got these fund-raisers . . . brothas and sistahs, can you spare some change? . . .*

I'm trying to figure out how I'm gonna pass the bar, and these fools always wanna get on the train with that shit. And that night I was not in the mood for it. All I wanted was to sit in my seat and do my thing.

I always sat in the first seat by the door, in the last car, because I *wanted* to be seen. I guess you could call me some kind of freak, but I like the excitement. I've always liked being watched. But you know what they say: Be careful what you wish for, because you just might get it.

Every Wednesday I take the same route home. I get on the 7:15 Red Line and head to the South Side. Most times I see the same faces. Generally, I'm the only one in that last car for the first couple of stops. But by the time we get to Loyola, there are usually a couple college girls who I can fuck with back there. Most of the time they just giggle, but sometimes there's a snooty one who gets offended and moves. But that night was different.

■ ■ ■

I was tired that night and ready to get home. I nearly missed the train and had to jump on the last car. I never liked riding in the last car because it seems disconnected from the rest of the train. So despite my usual preference, I stayed in that last car and settled in for the long ride. Although the crazies were always out at night, I enjoyed riding the el. The train was long and fast, yet gentle; smooth yet full of friction—it reminded me of beautiful sex and a good dick. I was tense that night, and anything that made me *think* of a strong, hard dick was just what I needed.

My new job up north was cool, but it wore me out. Regular clients took a lot of energy, but most of them were cool guys; they just needed someone to talk to them, listen to them, and make them feel like the great Adonis. I was good at my job, but it was taxing.

And then there was my lackluster personal life. Sometimes my job interfered with my relationships. The men I dated were always turned on by my job, but eventually they'd say I was playing head games or trying to control them. The last one just straight up called me a ho one night, so I let his ass go. I really liked him, but if he calls you a ho, he'll eventually treat you like a ho. But I missed Rod. I missed his hand on the small of my back, his tongue tickling my earlobe, and the way my pussy got wet just thinking about him. We met on the train, ironically. He was large but not awkward or imposing, tall, at least six foot two, and dark.

I was mesmerized when he sat down and opened his newspaper. I've always loved guys who were well-read and up on current events. And just like he got on the train, that's how he entered my tunnel every night for the past year—strong and confident. Yes, I missed Rod, and that was a big reason for the tension I had. It was in my neck and shoulders, like a hundred kisses; in my hips and legs, like a thousand caresses; and in my waist and vagina, like a million gyrating orgasms kneading into my center. So I needed this quiet time to just mellow. And for whatever the train offered at night—crazies, evangelists, and perverts—it most often offered solace, an unsuspecting portal into the erotic valleys of my memory.

And then I saw him. Actually, he looked crazy. Not like the folks who talk to their elbows and imaginary friends, but in a perverted kind of way. He got on after I'd sat down. He reminded me of Rod, but he wasn't as dark. He was a little lighter and looked like a GQ model or something. He was well dressed and smelled exotic, like *tchourai*, that Senegalese incense you always smell in those African restaurants and dress shops. Now that turned me on. Some of the best lovin' I ever had came from a man I once knew from Senegal. I never really thought of him anymore, only when I smelled *tchourai*. And the last thing I needed that night were more reminders of the sex I *wasn't* getting. I decided to cast my desperate eyes away from him before he smelled *me*—my loneliness and my growing desire. I closed my eyes.

■ ■ ■

I saw her when I first got on; that's why I sat close to her. I guess I wanted her to be a part of my fantasy. She was a nice-lookin' woman. You ever heard "Brick House" by the Commodores? Well, that's what she was—stacked. Five foot three and maybe 145 pounds. She had deep, dark, almond-shaped eyes, and big pretty lips. Those lips were made for a Cover Girl commercial—thick, round, and sensual. They weren't big like Adele Givens's, but more like the old girl on *Martin*. The kind that could give good head. And she had on this lipstick that made them shimmer. I could easily imagine her doing to me what I had to do to myself.

And titties—I'm a titty man so I can tell you 'bout some titties. She was a 40DD, and in my book that's perfect—a *brick house*. So yeah, I sat near her because I wanted to watch her. I wanted to watch her sleep . . . see her breasts bounce as the train jerked along . . . fantasize about her going down on me when we went deep down, under the city, into the subway. She was beautiful and I *needed* to feel close to her, if only in my fantasy.

■ ■ ■

"Long day?"

I opened my eyes reluctantly. I didn't want to be rude. I knew he was talking to me.

"No, not really. I'm just tired, a little tense, and ready to get in for the night."

"Yeah, it's been a long week for me, too."

I closed my eyes again. I hoped he wasn't gonna be a talker. It was a long ride and I just wanted to chill. I wanted the swaying of the train to take me to my special place that night. All I wanted was to dream about my last sexual encounter with Rod . . . the rhythm, the stroking, and the moaning. Hell, I wanted to think about his long, perfect dick inside my pussy, going deeper into my tunnel. What I *didn't* want was GQ interfering with the only plea-sure I had left. So I snuggled back into my seat like it was the strong, protective arms of my lover, pulled my wrap around my shoulders, and drifted back into dreamland ecstasy.

■ ■ ■

Working at the law firm of Baptiste, DuBois, Ndiaye, & Adeyinka was difficult. The other paralegals were women, so I al-ways seemed out of place. It was hard working as a glorified secre-tary to the partners and even more difficult trying to win their respect. It was tough going to law school and then working in that kind of environment. I was always stressed out.

A couple of months ago the pressure got to be too much. I didn't have a woman, and, frankly, that may have added to my stress. But hell, I needed to have a good time. At first I tried going to strip clubs with my boys. But that didn't work. It was cool at first, all those females coming over to our table, shaking their asses and titties, sitting on my lap grinding and everything. But I wasn't in control. It was always just a tease. Then I tried to watch videos, and that was straight up boring. Hell, one time I saw this chick I used to go to school with. We all knew she was in some porno flicks, but none of us had ever *seen* her. When I saw her on-screen, it was pretty fucked up. After that, I didn't really wanna watch that shit too much. So between doing this, and phone sex, that was the only way I could feel in control and release some stress. I ain't never raped a woman or nothing like that, but I like to be in control. I like to dominate the situation. I guess that's why I always dated little, petite women, so that I could tower over them. Hell, that's probably why I want to be a lawyer, too—for the power. We all have fetishes and fantasies, and mine was doing it on the train. So that night she seemed like the perfect woman to be in my fantasy. And the truth is, I'm a sucker for pretty women with big titties.

"So you work up north?"

"Yeah, I do."

I could tell she was trying to take a nap or something, but I wanted her to talk to me. I wanted to hear her voice in my head. When I saw her lips move I wanted to imagine them wrapped around my dick, moving up and down my head with juicy strokes. So I *needed* her to talk to me.

■ ■ ■

"What kind of work you do?"

I could tell he wasn't going to just let me be in peace. GQ wanted to make small talk, and I wanted to have an orgasm. I was leaving Evanston later than normal, and usually at this time it's seductively quiet, but as fate would have it, I sat in the last car only to be harassed by a man who, on another night, would have been a nice riding companion.

"Customer service."

"Oh. I'm a paralegal, but I'm in law school."

I was unimpressed. On a good night I might have chatted with him, but tonight I was just too full of tension and just not feeling the whole small-talk thing. I was missing my man and the mystical, magical way he used to make me feel. So if I couldn't have Rod, the least I could have were my memories. Those memories of his tongue lashing my insides, making me promise not to be a naughty girl anymore, but knowing that I would be bad, just to feel him inside me over and over again. If nothing else, I could have my memories . . . those fleeting memories of his sliding down into my tunnel, searching for its depths, and releasing oceans from the orgasmic fluid of my center. I just wanted to *be*, and this man wanted to talk and insert himself in places where I did not want to welcome him.

I tried to find refuge in my seat and warmth inside of my wrap. I buried my head into the corner, like I used to lay my head against Rod's strong bare chest. I closed my eyes, determined and desperate to have my fantasy.

■ ■ ■

I knew she didn't want to be bothered, but I needed her. I didn't know her, but I needed her comfort, her warmth, and the fantasy of her. But she was determined to sleep, determined to ignore the passion that was welling up inside of me and making my manhood grow right in front of her. I *needed* her to see what she was doing to me. But she wanted to resist me.

I put my hand inside my pants. My dick was already wet, crying for attention. The blood vessels started to constrict and I grew. It was hard now, and like a wild animal, it leaped out of my underwear and onto my lap. It was big, strong, and black. And I stroked it.

I remembered when Sheila used to stroke it the same way. Rubbing . . . pulling . . . kneading it until I moaned. Then she would bring me inside of her. In her mouth I would find Eden. She would pleasure me with long, deep strokes, making my dick grow and swell like the tides of the Atlantic Ocean. In her mouth I would melt like a pat of butter inside a warm bowl. And she would look up at me, teasing me with those pretty brown eyes. Seducing me with her half smile, she would suck my dick until I came. For her, I would come again and again, and she'd lick every bit as she circled my head with her tongue. Then she would roll over on her back and pull me to her. I would make my way into her garden and find heaven. Lush and fertile, her scent and juices flowed from her core. She was good, always so sweet. When I would taste her, it was like vanilla and apricot, dripping with honey swirls. I would fill my mouth with her juice and drink.

■ ■ ■

I was glad when he finally stopped talking. The train had lulled me back to Rod. He was touching me. I felt his hands gently pulling my nipples. He loved my big titties. He used to sit next to me and just play with them. His hands were big, but he was gentle with me. He was always gentle. When he put them in his mouth, he made liquid loops around them until they grew. I felt him there with me. My back arched and I drifted into ecstasy.

■ ■ ■

I didn't know what to do to make her look at me. I wanted her. I wanted to hear her voice again. But I had nothing to say. I liked the silence but needed the seduction of her voice to envelop me. If I spoke, she would *see* me, and it would give me the rush I needed.

■ ■ ■

"So . . . you live on the South Side?"
Damn. Just as my pussy started to throb, he spoke to me. I wanted to act like I was sleep, but it was hard for me to just ignore people. And besides, I figured that he probably saw my hand moving inside my wrap and knew that I was awake.
"Yeah, on the Southea . . ."
I stopped in midsentence. I couldn't believe it—GQ was jacking off. His dick was in his hand and he was strokin' it. I was

shocked. And he had to know that if he spoke to me, I would see him. *He wanted me to see him.*

■ ■ ■

She was shocked, but she didn't move. It was a brief moment, but it felt like hours. I didn't even stop when she looked, just kept strokin' my manhood. My dick was rock hard and I had gotten more excited.

■ ■ ■

I didn't look away. I couldn't. His dick was big and inviting. It had been so long since Rod and I made love. His dick was in his hand, and as he stroked it I felt quivers up my spine. I didn't know what to do. I wanted to get up, but I couldn't move. I was chained to the seat, and my eyes were fixed on him and the beautiful thing he held in his hand. I wanted to watch him, like I had done with Rod so many times before. Rod knew it was my fetish, the thing that truly turned me on. Whenever I was holding out, he wouldn't beg; he would just get undressed and watch TV. And while he sat there, he would start to masturbate. He knew it was my weakness. And once I saw him strokin' that thing, I would get wild. I'd be all over him, sucking his dick deep into my mouth. He would thrust harder, deeper into my mouth, and I would take him. I would swallow him up trying to get to the joy of his center. I loved to give him head; it was never a chore for me. I missed pleasing him. And now here I was, horny and hot, sitting in front of a stranger who was stroking his dick like he knew my secret.

■ ■ ■

"Yeah, I live over East. You?"
"Over on Cottage by Chicago State."
She picked up her sentence like nothing happened. But she was still looking at me. Usually, women get scared or offended and move away. She was different. I could tell she was still rubbing her nipple. I looked at her, and her eyes locked on me. She wasn't offended; she was getting off on it.

■ ■ ■

I don't know why he sat there rubbing himself in front of me, but I didn't care. My life had become so boring, I welcomed the excitement. Even at work, I was getting all the same calls so I didn't have anyone new to be with, to experiment with. This was perverse, but I wanted to do it with him.

His dick was a huge mass of beautiful muscle. Circumcised. And as he stroked it, I could see that it was wet. He must have been doing it for a while before I opened my eyes. We were the only two in the last section of the car. There were others in front of us, but we didn't care. He stroked his dick and my pussy contracted. This strange man on the el wanted me to be a part of his fantasy. He wanted me to watch him. So I did.

■ ■ ■

I looked deep into her eyes as I stroked my dick. She stared back at me boldly, blazing her face into the recesses of my mind. She was comfortable and I enjoyed her watching. The other people on the el weren't paying any attention to us.

I grabbed my balls in my hand and shook them. And then, returning my hand to my dick, I beat it on my left thigh. She moaned. Her back arched, and it felt good doing this to her. It felt good making her come into my fantasy, making her participate in my pleasure.

"How far south you going?"

"Eighty-seventh."

■ ■ ■

Every day I give men, and sometimes women, their fantasies. I give them what their lovers can't or won't. My job is to please them and tease them. So that night, if I was giving him *his* fantasy, I wanted to get mine, too.

I knew his type. He was a control freak, liked to dominate. Flashers, exhibitionists, and voyeurs like to control their environments. A lot of the men I worked for were like that, too. They couldn't control their sexual experiences at home, but they could with me. They call and tell *me* what *I'm* wearing just for them, what they want to do to me, what they want me to do to them. It's always about control. He was no different. But I was willing and happy to oblige him. He was exactly what I needed right now. I didn't know what he wanted from me, but I was glad that for once someone could be *my* fantasy.

■ ■ ■

"What's your name?"

"Syn."

"Syn? What kind of name is that?"

"It's just my name. What's yours?"

We didn't stop. She licked those big, beautiful lips and slid her hand between her legs. She began to rub the inside of her thigh. She made strong, deep strokes, and I became even more aroused.

"Andre . . . Dre for short."

I imagined her thighs on my shoulders, my tongue buried deep inside her. I could feel my tongue thrusting between her legs, making her moist with excitement.

"Do you like this, Dre?"

"Yes."

■ ■ ■

His voice was faint. I'd made him quiver. He wanted me as much as I wanted him. I played with him and he liked that. He started the game, but I was gonna finish it. He wanted to use me for his pleasure, but in the end he would be mine.

I slid my hand underneath my skirt. It was Wednesday, *no panty day*. So he saw all of me. My finger glided deep into my pussy. Inside I felt the warm heat of myself. I licked my lips. The passion inside me was growing, and I thought I would come at any moment. Pushing deeper, I tickled the walls of my vagina and imagined his tongue stroking me there.

■ ■ ■

"Don't stop," I begged.

She was blowing my mind. I never thought she would participate. I wanted to be in control, but she was controlling me. I came on my slacks, but I was still hard and growing again. I wanted her. She was mysterious and free. She was like no one I had ever met, and the experience was like nothing I had ever imagined.

■ ■ ■

He was begging. He asked softly, but there was pleading in his voice. I had him and he had me. I couldn't stop. I wanted this. I wanted him to make me feel special, sexy. I wanted to feel like the woman I was with Rod. I wanted to be free and uninhibited, and he offered me that. He excited me and I was open to it.

■ ■ ■

I couldn't believe I'd said it. I wanted to fuck her, but it wasn't about that, really. We were sharing something together, if only for that one night. I swear I would have eaten her pussy if she'd asked.

More people were getting on the train, but we didn't stop. We couldn't stop. We were outside ourselves, captured in this moment. We were captives in our own sexual fantasies, and nothing but the excitement of an orgasm could liberate us.

■ ■ ■

"I won't."

GQ had come on his slacks, but he was ready again. Growing bigger and bigger, his dick seemed to call me. I wanted to fuck him. I wanted to sit on his lap and ride. I wanted him deep inside me like the train in the tunnel.

I knew we would get to my stop soon, but I wanted to blaze a memory in his mind that his dick would never forget. As much as he wanted to shock me, I shocked him. I opened myself up to him. I let him come inside my mind, and it felt good. Most people won't let themselves be free like that, but we did that night.

■ ■ ■

I stopped wanting to be in control and began to really remember what it was like to make love to a *free* woman. When Sheila left, I didn't think I would have that again, but Syn showed me that at any moment, in any place, at any time you never know how your night will unfold. We were at Sixty-ninth and it would only be a few more minutes before she got off. I didn't want this night to end. I wanted to ask for her number, or give her my card, but it seemed awkward. I didn't think we could move beyond this night and explore a relationship, but I wanted to get to know her.

■ ■ ■

I rubbed the back of my neck. My breathing was heavy and I was ready. I was about to have an orgasm on the el, and I didn't care. I was about to come with him on the el. I don't know if I could have been so free with Rod in that situation, but this felt good. I licked my lips, moaned from deep within the inferno that was my pussy, and then . . . it happened.

"I . . . 'm coming. I'm com . . . ing."

I wanted to rush over there and swallow that joy coming from inside of him, but I didn't. I sat there, and with all the pent-up energy I had, I fucked myself. I thrust my finger deeper and deeper into my pussy until it erupted like a volcano releasing hot liquid down my thigh. I wiped it up with my finger and placed it deep into my mouth.

■ ■ ■

She made me come. She didn't touch me and she made me come. I was shocked. I didn't know what to say or do after that. When I call the phone sex place, I always talk to this one chick, Stacey. She excites me and I get off on her, but this was different. This woman didn't talk dirty to me and she didn't touch me; she just *felt* me. I guess we felt each other.

Syn was finally getting off and my fantasy was over. She fulfilled it and I was fucked up. She was the kind of woman every man dreams of. Syn was fine and she seemed like an intelligent woman, but most of all she was a true freak. She's not the kind that you'd ever see in a porn movie, but the kind who rocks your world and makes your dick hard just thinking about her. She was *my fantasy* and would probably be some other man's woman.

I wanted to say thank you or something, but that was stupid, and the words were stuck somewhere between my balls and my dick, leaving me speechless. I had cleaned up and put my dick back inside my pants, but she was all over me. I closed my eyes and I could still see her pussy peeking out from underneath her skirt. She was in my mind and would probably be there for a long time to come. I imagined that my dick would rise every time I thought of her.

■ ■ ■

Eighty-seventh was the next stop and I had to get up. I was starting to feel awkward. I wanted to give him my number, but that seemed trite. I don't know if I thought that he and I could really move beyond this experience and talk, but I was willing to try. But first, I had to ask . . .

"Do you do this often?"

"I like to masturbate on the train. I've always fantasized about having a voyeuristic experience, but I never had—until now. Why did you do this with me?"

"Sometimes when I get on the train I think of my ex and how we used to make love. When I get home, I masturbate and then get really sad over not being with him anymore. So tonight I figured that I would masturbate on the train with you, and then when I get home it might be the first night I don't think about him."

■ ■ ■

She was beautiful and seemed sincere. She stood up and she was definitely a brick house. I wanted to see her again. Yeah, I wanted to make love to her. But more than that, I wanted to get to know her, so confident, beautiful, and free to just be in the moment. I liked her energy and wanted to relive that night for years to come. It may not have been realistic, but I was going to ask her out.

■ ■ ■

That night, the whole experience, seemed more surreal than anything I could ever read about. It was the most daring thing I had ever done. He made it easy for me to do. Normally, I never would have done something like that, but that night was so differ-ent. I felt free and I *needed* to be. It's been so long since I felt that sexy, felt like there was someone I could turn on. It felt good, and deep down I hoped to feel that way again.

■ ■ ■

"Syn, I know this may be kinda awkward, but I would like to see you again."

I didn't know what she was going to say, but I decided to go for it. If she turned me down, I would still have my memory of that night. So I stepped out on a limb. Hell, that girl had my ass fucked up because not once did I think about how I would feel if she turned me down. In a word . . . sprung. But hell, I've been sprung on worse.

■ ■ ■

I didn't know what to say. See, in a way, I've been down this road before. In one way or another, I turn guys on. But eventually, the job gets in the way and they grow tired of their woman having phone sex with other men. My life is such a contradiction when it comes to my lovers. Yeah, he started that thing on the el that night, but six or nine months down the road, *whore* will be on the tip of his tongue when he feels like he's *competing* against my job and all the men I talk to. Maybe he would be like all the rest . . . maybe he would be different. I wanted to find out, but I didn't know what to do.

I didn't say a word. I got off the el and rode up the escalator. I felt satisfied. Not just satisfied cause I did a freak move on his ass, but be-cause he touched me somewhere very deep down inside. As I walked up the street, I knew that when I went home I would take out my vi-brator and think of him all over again. He made my pussy wet and never touched it. I imagined him eating me and thrusting his dick deep inside me. I pulled the wrap tighter around my shoulders and smiled. It was a smile that reached up to my lips and sparkled in my eyes. A man that could make me smile like that *deserved* a date. I walked along Chatham Village enjoying the fall breeze. I was happy and for once not tense. And I knew that would be the first night that I didn't lie in bed fantasizing about Rod. The unexpected bonus was that Dre would fill the next chapter of my novel.

Someone working as a phone sex operator always has a lot to write about. The wind was stirring around me, and it was a beautiful night. I was satisfied because on that night I reclaimed my femininity in the most awesome and adventurous way. Yes, I was still beautiful and desirable. Maybe I am a freak, but that doesn't take away from the person I am, or *make me* the woman that I am. Without Rod, life would still throw me surprises and offer excitement. After all, that night on the train was just another day, only this time I was the one being pleased.

■ ■ ■

When she didn't speak, I didn't know what to think. I thought that maybe I had turned her off. But then she smiled and handed me her card. I put it in my pocket and decided to take it out when I got home. Our fantasy had come to an end, but I wanted it to last a little longer.

I said good night, but she didn't answer; she just turned around and got off the el. I watched her walk to the escalator and wondered what just happened. Never in my wildest dreams could I have imagined an evening so perfect.

I was at Ninety-fifth and it was time to face the world again. I walked up the stairs and out to the street. It wasn't too cold, so I walked the twelve blocks home. Walking gave me a chance to think about Syn. It was a sexy name, and I wondered whether it was her real one. I pulled out her card. Some women are just amazing. Some women exude a certain kind of confidence, and Syn was one of them. I'd never met anyone like her, and I knew that I probably never would. I was scared to call her, but after I read her card, I *knew* that I would call her the next day. Her card was enough to make me take my chances.

Synful Secrets . . . for every man who wants a little Syn in his life . . .

Call Synthia . . . 555-SYN-FULL

IRRÉSISTIBLE

Miles Marshall Lewis

It was late February and I needed some fresh air. I walked the streets of Paris alone with my eyes swollen with tears. I found it so bitterly ironic to be heartbroken in the romantic City of Lights. I'd come an awfully long way for this shit to be happening; I'd sold myself a dream.

I was out there to sulk. I took a seat on a street-side bench, its chipped green paint revealing the plywood underneath, and lit a cigarette. The neon lights of French signs refracted through my tears. I took a drag and the lump in my throat seemed to grow that much heavier. Then I thought of Solange, asleep upstairs. And my tears started to fall.

I didn't understand how I could have loved her so much without her ever loving me. Clearly, she wanted to call the shots, but I had allowed her that. When I was planning to visit, her letters implied, *Play my way or not at all*, not *I don't want to play*. We did kiss, on two separate occasions, since my arrival at Charles de Gaulle airport two days ago. I held her at night, staying in her studio for the week, but it just made matters worse. When she fell asleep and her breathing slowed, I fought the urge to lift her nightgown inch by inch and explore her body. My heart raced watching her breasts slowly rise and fall under the sheets. God, the pleasure I could have given her; she just didn't understand.

I let my tears fall. The busy thoroughfare of avenue d'Italie was empty at three in the morning. I felt the puffiness of my eyes, tears drying on cheeks only to be replaced by new ones following their tracks. I aimed for one last cry to finally rid my system of Solange. If only she would say in so many words that she didn't have feelings for me, that I was not attractive to her, something. Why kiss me twice if she wasn't interested in me? Why build false hope with letters and calls? Who would purposely do such a thing?

I lit a fresh cigarette with the old and flicked it away. A homeless man approached from the far end of the street, and I rose to walk. This was somewhat dangerous, being out late in Paris with next to no knowledge of the native tongue. I'd left my passport in Solange's flat, grabbing as little as possible to avoid waking her. It would be unfortunate to get into a confrontation of some sort without identification.

Wiping my face, I remembered my first night in town. Solange and I went straight to the Eiffel Tower. I felt like a king, strolling Trocadéro with the girl of my dreams. The history of Paris, the smells, the architecture—all were overwhelming. We decided to walk to the third level and made it only to the second due to exhaustion, but I couldn't imagine the view being more beautiful. If I knew more French, I'd become an expatriate, I thought. I'd find a nightclub to spin at, convince Solange to stay after she graduated, and make babies. She knew the language; she could still follow her dreams to sing and record CDs in French. I remember the thrill of holding her by the waist as a Parisian snapped our picture.

We walked the night streets, hand in hand, crossing the river with cars whizzing on the overpass. Strolling alongside the Seine, its cobblestone walkway imbedded with Heineken bottle caps, rays from a crescent moon shimmered off the waves, illuminating the olive green hue of the river. In the taxicab to her flat, my arm rested around her shoulder until she nuzzled up to me for warmth, fending off the late-winter chill. In bed together for the first time I felt the strongest sensation in my stomach, akin to what I had felt as a child in the Bronx, being pushed high and hard by my mother on the metal swings of Claremont Park, or the butterflies I felt in the second grade when I lent that pencil to Eileen.

"Can I have a good-night kiss?"

"You can come get one."

And so I knew the wetness of her mouth, my hand grasping the back of her head, fingers feeling their way through her braids. This was what I'd awaited, dreamed of, ever since planning my trip late last year. Later in bed, she denied my request for another kiss. Still, I felt vindicated, knowing my feelings were somewhat reciprocated. Sleep came easy, my dreams animated.

Yesterday we awakened midafternoon to travel northeast to the twentieth arrondissement, to walk the winding paths of the Père Lachaise cemetery. I wanted to see the graves of the great authors I'd read in French class at Morehouse. She'd not been since her arrival in the fall, and I told her about the works of Marcel Proust and Honoré de Balzac. Crude graffiti directed us to Jim Morrison's final resting place, and we debated his importance (or lack thereof) as we returned to the thirteenth arrondissement. We drank Bordeaux as I oiled her feet, sensuously massaging them to my inner boiling point. Reaching the threshold of my self-control, I slid myself between her legs and, without asking permission, began to kiss her again. Grinding, wrapping her legs around my waist, her moans of approval strengthened my resolve. But we stopped all too suddenly. A low-tolerance lightweight, Solange blamed her behavior on the wine and went to the bathroom to compose herself.

We then left her flat for La Maroquinerie in the twentieth arrondissement and danced the alcohol out of our systems till it closed at one thirty. Paying ten euros each for our two hours, I paid special attention to the DJ even as we guzzled Evian at the bar, talking. "Sunset People" by Donna Summer got the crowd live; Solange knew some of the people from her classes at École Normale de Musique. Sizing up DJ Taishi's disjointed style against my own deejaying skills, there seemed little rhyme or reason to his selections. A drunken couple began making out in the corner during "Everybody Wants to Rule the World." "Walk on the Wild Side" sent everyone remaining out into the night. In the taxi home, Solange made it clear that nothing else would happen between us during my stay.

I want a woman to want me as much as I want her. I've never been the type to force myself on a girl. But Solange gave indications that my advances were permissible, desired even. I thought things were going so well, but I could abstain from pushing up on her if she wasn't clear about what she wanted.

Exhausting my memory of our romantic tryst, I returned to 18 rue du Moulinet, entered the code to gain entrance to her building, and slowly pushed open the apartment door I'd left slightly cracked a half hour earlier. Seeing Solange sound asleep, I sighed deeply and began to undress.

Still sleeping, Solange—whom I was afraid I might love—sidled up against me. I fit myself against the angles of her back, and my arm crept slowly around her waist.

■ ■ ■

I awoke at noon to the sound of running water as Solange showered in the corner stall, the outline of her body moving behind the thin curtain. I debated masturbation as she caressed herself with soap. She bent over to wash her feet and I rose to play some Miles Davis. The late jazz legend once said that by playing the blues in a certain key he could forget his wife if she deserted him. Trying to tune into that sentiment, I scanned frantically for *Bitches Brew* in my laptop's library.

"Hey, sleepyhead," Solange said, peeking out from behind the curtain. "I was so drunk last night. Hand me a towel? It's cold!"

Her heater was pretty low maintenance and she often refused to turn it on, to lower her expenses. During the daylight hours, with warm sun rays peering through the windows, running the heat was out of the question.

Within the hour, we were miles away at Notre Dame. The sky was darkest gray in late afternoon, hazy rain misting the air. Not quite wet enough for an umbrella, the moisture collected on our faces with every step. Walking inside, I was in awe. If God dwelled inside a church, She dwelled in Notre Dame. Silence pervaded the cathedral. I watched as Solange walked over to a row of candles, then one by one began to light wicks that had burned out. I could not help but imagine walking through the Jardin des Tuileries hand in hand, discussing baby names.

We walked from the Tolbiac metro station back to her flat in silence. Absorbed in thought, I contemplated my old soul. I had always favored ballads and tales of unrequited love to more uplifting fare. Perhaps I somehow preferred being slightly depressed and unsatisfied to a state of comfort. After all, there was another relationship I could have been perfectly content with, but something about the challenge of wooing Solange attracted me.

In the kitchen, she began preparing vegetables for a salad. I resumed the jazz and started yet another decision about our relationship. I would go for broke. Perhaps complete honesty would ease my mind and make it easier to let go. She didn't know all the details of what led us to this impasse, and maybe her knowing would take us to another level. If I was wrong, at least I would've played my final hand. I could rest easy knowing I'd done everything within my power to convey my feelings toward her. And if I was right, well, we could build on a more solid, honest foundation.

"Solange?"

"*Oui?* Could you turn that down a little?" She turned to me, an apologetic smirk on her moon-shaped face. Two braids careened down the side of her light-skinned profile, her rear shaking as she diced cucumbers for a salad. With the Chinatown of Paris around the corner, we planned to finish some leftover Vietnamese food. I muted Miles's trumpet and searched for the right words.

"You know when we met, like, three years ago?"

"*Ouais* . . ." Her tone told me she expected yet another come-on. Still, her attitude, that spunk, was what made it so difficult for me to leave her be.

"Solange, I got a problem I wanna talk to you about. I kinda need your help—"

"You didn't have to turn it off, just so I can hear you. You and that music . . ." The puffy rouge lips she formed her words with made things harder.

"Aiight, well, there's this girl I met, like, three years ago."

Solange beamed a knowing smile.

Receiving a letter from Charlene lifted my spirits, which was no easy feat. I felt thoroughly exhausted. I'd carried several thick textbooks in a knapsack on an overcrowded, stifling hot bus creeping slowly up Buford Highway. In a mailbox stuffed with bill notices, I was elated to find an envelope postmarked from Madrid. Sitting on a beanbag in my living room, preparing boiling water on the stove, I squinted at the small schoolgirlish handwriting.

Querida Kit,

I don't even know where to start. Well, let me start by saying that I miss you sooo much! This 2-wk. traveling seminar seems like forever. I can't believe I have 16 more wks. here in Spain. Oh, you must let me know what you want me to bring you as u r SO HARD TO PLEASE! How is school? Who have you seen and been with?

Don't forget to start saving your money and investigating flights to Spain so you can come see your "Bougie" for Thanksgiving! Kit, no matter what, I'm (almost) always thinking of you, and you don't have to worry about a thing. Brooklyn says hi and we are always thinking of our boyfriends. We're all oh so horny (smile)! We leave Madrid for Grenada on Friday. I can't believe I haven't started school yet!

I will call you as soon as I get to Grenada (you probably won't even have this letter by then). I love you so dearly. Please take good care of yourself and, of course, my heart.

Lonely & lovingly, Charlene T. Wright

The doorbell rang, reminding me of Max and his visit from the Bronx to Atlanta.

"Peace, God!"

"Peace." We laughed and slapped hands, then I searched for tea bags and honey in my cabinet. Max had changed slightly since we'd last seen one another. His hair was almost completely sheared off and faded bald at the sides like my own. His muscularity and size had diminished, the result of a more conscientious diet. Max was now almost as slim as I.

"I got a letter from Charlene today, dude. You know she's studying in Spain?"

"Yeah, I remember you telling me she was gonna make that move. That's fly, man. She speaks Spanish?"

"Does she. She's nice with the verbs; fuck what you heard. I cheat through most of my French exams, but she can flow with the *español*. I'm going out there for Thanksgiving."

My confession produced a simper on Max's face that I was all too familiar with, having known him since childhood. Max and I were a lot alike, but there were points where our personalities diverged. This was one of them. Over the years, I'd detected a distinct pessimistic streak in my homeboy's outlook. The elongated conversations we used to have as college roommates (before Max dropped out) were usually so prolonged because of Max's questioning nature and my having to support every last detail of my position to his satisfaction. Knowing Max, I anticipated his doubtfulness in considering my visiting Charlene. I didn't own a passport, had never been to Europe, and neither of us knew anyone who had. Max took that into account, no doubt, which added to the consideration of the great expense of traveling to Spain.

"That's a cool idea," he said. "Do you have dough for that, though?"

"It might not cost all that much. I already got my ticket."

"Yeah, right. For real?"

"Yeah. I got a hookup with a fat student discount. I bought it with money I'm supposed to use for tuition, so I hope my financial aid covers me. If not, I owe the school four hundred dollars. I'm thinking about spending money to take over there now, though. I just started selling mix tapes at Little Five Points. I made bank last Friday. Charlene doesn't know I got my ticket yet."

"That's hot. Can you stay with her?"

"She's staying with a Spanish family. I'm writing her back to ask about hotels and shit. I wish I could stay with her. That's probably two hundred dollars right there. You want some tea?"

"Let me see the box." Max had recently become hyperconscious about what he put into his system since joining the Nation of Islam months ago. The religious doctrines of the Nation of Islam forbid the ingestion of pork or any of its remote by-products. Max had committed these polysyllabic by-products to memory, avidly scanning the ingredients of my chamomile tea.

"Yeah, I'll take a cup, thanks."

Apparently, Celestial Seasonings passed his inspection.

"You want honey?" I asked, pouring the boiling water into coffee mugs.

"Let me see the honey," he replied.

"I need to talk about Charlene."

There was a heartbeat pause. "She cheated over there?"

"Nah!" I laughed, and he joined in. "Nothing like that. I'm just trying to figure out where to go from here. I'm starting to feel like . . . almost like I'm settling. You were there when I first met Charlene. I didn't even like her; I though she was aiight. Now it's going on two years!"

"She macked you, God. Charlene's a mack."

I laughed. "I guess so."

"Your feelings can change. They can get stronger. You're the only one who can really know if your feelings got stronger or if you just said, 'She's feeling me, so I'm gonna chill.' "

"Yeah, well, I'm not sure. I do have a love for Charlene. I'm just not sure if I'm *in* love with her. I care for her a whole lot. That might be the most in love I'm ever gonna get. Who really knows? She talks about being so in love with me all the time, but maybe her actual feelings for me aren't any stronger than mine for her. But then I've always felt stronger about Solange."

"You think you might be in love with Solange?" Max said, his voice tinged with that familiar disbelieving tone.

"I don't know, dude. I mean, I know she was never really even my girl. And we never had sex—"

"Well, maybe that's it," he interrupted. "Maybe you just want Solange because she never put out, because you never had her open like Charlene. Don't leave her for Solange. She's shady. I said that since the beginning. Man, I got the inside track, Caldonia's been telling me the scoop."

Caldonia was a girl we knew from around the Edenwald projects, a mutual friend of Max and Solange's.

"They don't even roll no more," he continued. "Solange don't be callin' nobody since she started school at Sarah Lawrence, like she's all that. Even worse since she took off to study in Paris. Wait till you get home. I got these flicks of Solange with Petronila from back in the day. She looks busted."

"Word?" We laughed. At this point, I was interested in finding a crack in her flawless veneer.

"I thought to myself from jump, This sister is from around here; how come we never noticed her before? She used to look all frumpy, braces and stuff. She had a wack perm. Back in the day her moms wouldn't let her wear makeup. Petronila gave me the full 411. Solange even likes you, but I'm sayin', leave that alone. I know her style. She's gonna make a brother do cartwheels for the pussy because she used to get dissed. Mad cats probably just hit it and broke out, so now she's on some revenge shit."

"Okay, I thought of that, and that could be true. But I was always more hyped about her than about Charlene."

"Kit . . ." He took a sip of the steaming tea. "You might have to chill on that. It looks like she's not trying to go there. You're tripping on this triangle thing when, really, Solange isn't an option for you, and she might never be. Charlene is a good woman, God—she's solid earth. I don't see any reason for you to mess that up. A lot of brothers would trip to have Charlene in their corner like that. Don't get me wrong, don't settle. If you're not happy, then breeze. But you need to think about if you're really unhappy, and how unhappy you could be. You know what I'm saying? How unhappy some brothers already are."

Kit,

Don't you know that I hear you in the music I listen to, see "you & I" when I sometimes see Spanish lovers, I feel you . . . even throughout my extreme moments of loneliness, and, most of all, I meet you in my dreams . . . the only REAL place that I can truly communicate with you in whichever way my unconscious mind and broken heart desire.

I mean . . . shit, I knew I would miss you greatly, but DAMN, KIT, I REALLY MISS YOU! So much that I can't even fathom being with someone else. Sooo many Spanish men, not guys (well, some of them), but men have come on to me. I can only think of you, and then I become repulsed!

Did you know that one of my ultimate goals in life is to continue to shower my love upon you, to share my sacred fountains and springs with you, to mix my showers with yours . . . with your aphrodisiacs, to give birth to something that could have eternal beauty? (Long question, huh?)

I must admit that I was ecstatic to get your letter yesterday. I'm so glad you're coming to Spain to see me, to share this experience with me. Occasionally, your extreme desire and will to do things (anything . . . like buy a rare 12-inch of some sort) can annoy me; however, it has also become a very admirable quality at times like this: You're coming through to see me here! (Of course, this is not the first time you've come through for me. Don't get me wrong.) It makes me realize that I am sometimes too complacent about doing certain things, and that sometimes ALL is possible and within your power or control if you want it to be! (I love the way we complement each other.) I'm so proud to be your woman! Every girl on my program w/ a steady boyfriend is GREEN w/ envy because you're coming, and I love it, and I love you for it!

You can stay with some friends of mine who have apartments here if you want. The only problem is that I know I will be staying with you every night, and we may want our privacy. Well, in any case, I'm still looking into hostels and pensiones for us during that glorious week (cheap ones, of course).

Well, *mi amor*, I must retire. It is 2 A.M. here and I must get
my beauty rest. I'm so glad you say I was a best friend of yours
at school because you're my best friend. I love you, Kit. Don't
ever forget that. I hope that statement never loses its meaning
or becomes a memory. I have a picture of you that I keep on my
nightstand. I have shed some tears, but all in the name of love.

Stay handsome, intelligent, and the awesome BLACK
MAN that you are spiritually, physically, and psychologically. I
eagerly await your arrival in November. Until then, God bless
you & keep you. Don't party too much, and give regards to my
future in-laws. I have not cheated and have no intentions of
doing so, and I expect the same of you. *Pax, amor, y felici-
dades* . . . (translate it!)

Much love, Charlene T. Wright

I collected the letters I'd been reading throughout the course of
my intercontinental flight over the Atlantic and placed them
back into their envelopes. Looking out the window to my left, a
Spanish landscape of mountains was draped with clouds and mist.
Hours earlier, during a stopover in New York, Mom and my grandparents met me at JFK airport to see me off and line my pockets
with extra cash. It would come in handy; the dollar and the exchange rate were weak in Europe.

Packing away Charlene's letters into my carry-on, I thought of
the subliminal messages I'd unsuccessfully tried to plant in my own
letters to her. I remember phrasing certain comments just so,
about relationships of convenience and being unworthy of her un-
conditional love. She spoke of my family as future in-laws, and I'd
never seen her as my wife. I tried to find ways to slowly let her
down within the confines of the labyrinth of emotional lies I'd
constructed over time. I cared for Charlene, but in the two years
of our relationship, I'd failed to cultivate the same strong feelings
she felt for me, and I doubted I ever would.

I'd first met Charlene over the telephone, through a mutual
homegirl who'd dropped out of Clark University. She'd seen my

picture and thought I was cute; I had no idea how she looked, but she piqued my interest—all talkative Valley-girl English and wide-eyed rap reverence. Charlene was a West End girl with a ghetto pass, taking her Calhoun private school education straight up into DJ Funkmaster Flex night at the Tunnel every Sunday. Weeks after we first spoke, she visited Spelman to decide if she'd be attending in the fall, and we fucked immediately. Our relationship just sort of happened. I went with the flow, falling into "us" without fully deciding if we were right for each other. Charlene was a hip-hop bourgeois sorority girl, and our college sweetheart status in the Morehouse-Spelman community was a definite ego booster. But it often left me feeling untrue to myself. I felt the imbalance in our feelings on a regular basis, especially considering how much I cared for Solange.

After the airplane touched down in Madrid, I collected my luggage and cleared my passport and belongings through customs. Then I stood alone in the Aeropuerto de Barajas, arms weighted down at my sides with a mass of suitcases, absorbing my surroundings. Smoke from various cigars and cigarettes wafted through the air, the product of older Spanish men in unassuming suits. My rudimentary Spanish was not enough to interpret the language enveloping me. I felt a frisson of fear. Charlene would be my only comfort zone in a foreign land thousands of miles away from a world I'd never ventured outside of until now. I searched the area for her face and began walking.

Following the general direction of others from my flight, staring dumbfounded at imperceptible Spanish signs, I happened upon a set of large sliding doors. On the other side stood native citizens awaiting those from our flight. I spotted Charlene and my heart was immediately put at ease.

I paused with my luggage to strap on a pair of black wraparound shades and walked through the doors. I watched Charlene's eyes dart around in expectation and crept up beside her. She wore a salmon pink and apple green Alpha Kappa Alpha sorority jacket with a mohair scarf tied round her neck, tight Baby Phat jeans hugging her Coke-bottle figure. Sidling alongside her newly curvaceous frame (Spanish food is evidently delicious), I could see the black of a G-string triangle peeking below the flaming sun tattoo at her waistline. Her bangs were freshly cut, her perm freshly pressed; I could smell the pink lotion amid the citrus scent of her CK One and the Juicy Fruit she stood smacking away on. Throughout her time in Spain, Charlene remained a high-maintenance cutie.

"Kit!"

"Hey there, Bougie . . ." We embraced, her hold on me firm with emotion and yearning. We boarded a train leaving the airport for Sol, the center of Madrid where Charlene found an affordable hostel for us.

"I can't believe I'm here," I said in a hushed tone, so as not to draw attention to my English.

"Me either, honey. I'm so excited! I couldn't sleep last night because I was so happy you were actually coming in the morning, then I got afraid I would oversleep because it got so late. Do you have jet lag? Are you tired? How was the flight? Before I forget, you have to change money at El Corté Ingles to pay for the hostel. They have good exchange rates for pensiones; it's like the Macy's of Madrid. So what about the flight?"

"It was cool. I'm not really tired; I read your letters all the way over."

"You did? Ohmigod, that's so sweet. You really have them all? You know, when we get you settled, we should maybe take a little nap before getting into anything." Charlene gave me a knowing look and we both began laughing at her sexual innuendo, and at the fact that no one around us on the metro could possibly understand our cryptic English.

From the window, squat centuries-old buildings flashed by in the two-minute intervals of metro stops. America is just a baby, I thought, mentally comparing these wired-for-electricity castles to the skyscrapers I was used to as a native New Yorker. There, baseball caps are omnipresent on the 5 train. Here, Spanish men sported fedoras like something out of news footage from the 1950s. Bright signs in primary colors of yellow, red, and black reading ESPAÑA welcomed me at every turn.

At the Hostal Riosol, we encountered a minor problem with the aged, bespectacled check-in lady. I'd have to pay a slightly higher rate in order for Charlene to stay with me throughout the week, even with the discount from my International Student ID. Charlene agreed to reimburse me for the excess charge, as we rode a phone-booth-sized elevator to the second level. My room wasn't much bigger than the elevator; the full-size bed, night table, sink, shower, and closet left minimal space to lay my suitcases. Our toilet was in the hall.

Charlene walked toward the wall-length windows that led to a small veranda to open the curtains, but I pulled her back to me as she feigned shock and annoyance. I gathered the sides of her blouse in my fists and yanked her snaps open. We kissed. I held her close, her black satin bra against my thick flannel shirt. Our kisses were soft; no words were needed. I unzipped the front of her jeans, my hands along the round contours of her waist. I felt a tingle of anticipation unlike anything I'd experienced with Charlene since the beginning of our relationship. Soon we were naked to the morning chill in the room and scampered underneath the comforter and sheets.

Following her lead, I saw Charlene's body as a stranger's, with a vague familiarity. Her once petite form had blossomed with a few pounds and exercise into a sublimely curvy figure. My scale weighing Charlene against Solange was obliterated. Since meeting Solange the month after Charlene two years back, I'd constantly sized them up against each other. But in this moment, Charlene was all I needed, clutching her soft, smallish breasts as I stared in her eyes, absorbed in amorous thoughts. I came quickly; no sex for three months seemed like forever and a day.

It was the second time that moved the earth. (Isn't it always?) Charlene programmed her iPod to the brisk Brazilian percussion of the *Orfeo Negro* soundtrack, and lay with her stomach to the mattress. My sweaty chest touching her back, I was soon stiff again against the puffy pillows of her thick cheeks. Wrapped in my arms, she spoke casually, conversationally, about the legal troubles of Lil' Kim—my right hand in hers as our middle fingers competed for her swollen, slick clit; my left massaging the flesh of her booty, a thumb swathed in Vaseline Lip Therapy slowly entering and exiting her ass.

"And so Kim. She. Mmm. She didn't want to drop dime on her boys from Junior Mafia, but—oh, Kit, slower, easy—but. Like that. Mmmmm." Laid-back, non sequitur banter always turned us on during foreplay, while we acted for as long as possible as if what was happening wasn't.

Back at school, Charlene allowed me to hump the deep cleavage of her apple-shaped ass as a consolation for her being too exhausted for sex sometimes, her booty eventually damp with come and lubrication after drunken, late-night beer bashes. It was months before we experimented with fingers in forbidden places. And we didn't totally take it there until August, days before she left for Spain, but our international phone sex covered all imaginable variations of our little experiment, and what lay in store for my visit. My head entered, slowly. I gripped myself in my hand as if what I held wasn't me, like I was gradually easing a dildo into Charlene from behind.

"But. She. Told the judge . . ."

"Mm-hmm?" I murmured, my breath hot on her ear.

"Kim told. The judge . . ." Charlene giggled seductively, still working her soaked finger and mine overtime at stroking her button. We were talking about Lil' Kim—this wasn't happening (surely not to bougie Charlene, the refined, pinky-in-the-air, Spelman honor student), but it *was* happening. I inched in deeper, deeper still until I released my hold and let my hips take over the motion.

"So. If. She. Goes. To. Jail . . . Kit, fuck!"

And I honestly couldn't tell the difference; this felt just like Charlene's wonderful pussy. I let her control the movement, her bottom rising to bump against me, then falling back to the sheets. She called my name, she called out to Christ, she cursed again and again. I couldn't believe I wasn't hurting her—glad, naturally, but this was so new to us both. Our last time months ago, she said she couldn't understand where exactly her orgasm was springing from.

But here it came again: She screamed out loudly to God one last time, her plump ass splayed against my sweaty thighs, shuddering softly. Barely containing myself, I pulled out seconds later to pump all over her backside tattoo of the sun. Taboo desires ran through my mind as my warm rush spread across her butt—*she likes it like this? I've been waiting for this for sooo long, and I can't believe she's such an undercover freak!* I live too much in my mind.

A minute passed holding one another before I mentioned, still breathing hard, "Yeah, I mean, if Kim gets time, then where does that leave Lil' Cease?"

■ ■ ■

"So when are you two getting engaged?" Brooklyn asked. The night after my arrival, Charlene brought me to Archy's to hear Spanish DJs and experience their nightlife. Paying our pensiones, we heard a DJ mix "Sex Shooter" into a "Sugar Walls" remix beyond the huge doors. Archy's was a high-end club, filled with the movers and shakers of the Spanish scene. In her brief time in Madrid, Charlene and her friends encountered Pedro Almodóvar, Bebel Gilberto, and Antonio Banderas in Archy's VIP section on various nights. Brooklyn had been fucking one of the bartenders all semester (a Gael García Bernal look-alike), which is how we bypassed their velvet-rope selection. We sat on a sofa with Brooklyn, drinking and talking.

"Child, we ain't doing shit until Kit can keep his eyes off other women," Charlene chided. The girls laughed, eager for my defense.

"I swear I wasn't looking at her," I remarked, smiling. The hostess at the door of Archy's was a tall Spanish bottle blonde wearing black leather pants with a thin, transparent black top. Her breasts were in full view.

"Yeah, right," Brooklyn said, exhaling cigarette smoke. "We saw you when we walked in. Charlene tapped me!"

"You just have to instigate, huh? Yeah, well, of course I looked at her. You can see her fuckin' tits! But I wasn't staring at her. Every guy here has looked at her. That's why she wore the shirt in the first place."

"That's bullshit, Kit! That's sexist!" Charlene said, the synthesizers of André Cymone's "The Dance Electric" threatening to drown out her voice. "Maybe she just wore that for herself because it made her feel good. When I go out wearing something sexy, I'm not dressing for other people, I'm dressing for myself." She downed her third gin and tonic, slamming the glass down on the table.

"First of all, you don't be going places naked like that." She smiled. "Her shit is completely see-through, her nipples all hard."

"How do you know, though?" Brooklyn protested with intoxicated excitement. "You were looking at her shit. How do you know her nipples are hard?" We all laughed.

"You can't understand a woman's frame of mind," Charlene said. "You don't know what it's like to get pretty. When me and Brooklyn want to feel good, we can do stuff guys know nothing about—like wearing silk underwear, or giving ourselves a facial so we know we look our best. A special shade of lipstick or a new hairdo can make a girl feel better about herself. Guys don't have an equivalent to that, so you can't really understand what I'm talking about. Y'all are so egotistical anyway that of course you think it's all for you, but don't sweat yourself!"

The girls whooped and hollered, slapping each other's hands in solidarity. The DJ mixed in "Irresistible Bitch" by Prince, the author of everything we'd heard since entering Archy's. Spaniards rushed the dance floor.

"Aiight, whatever, you got it. Charlene, let me get a cigarette?"

"A cigarette? Mr. Jackson is not asking me for a cigarette!" I didn't smoke cigarettes, often chastising Charlene for smoking and breaking her cigarettes in half. I smoked weed, but cigarettes were a greater cancer-causing danger.

"Y'all are smoking. Everyone in this country smokes."

"Here," Charlene said, lighting a match against a matchbox. "These are Nobels. The buzz is kinda strong—"

"I'll be okay, thanks." We shared a caring glance.

"Lord, your guys' relationship . . ." Brooklyn said.

"What?" Charlene said, blushing. "Stop it, Lyn."

"You stop it, girl. You know what I'm talking about. It's like y'all are best friends. There are things I could never tell J. J. at home, but Kit—child, let me tell you—Charlene tells you everything, honey. I swear, y'all are my favorite couple. I can feel the love between you."

"Why you puttin' us on the spot?" Charlene said, laughing.

"The way Kit looks at you sometimes, I hope I find a love like that. You talk like a brother and sister almost, but I know y'all be swinging from chandeliers, too."

■ ■ ■

Cigarettes in hand, Charlene and I walked from El Museo Nacional Centro de Arte Reina Sofía to a restaurant specializing in appetizers and desserts. At the museum, Charlene led us directly to Joan Miró's *Inverted Personages*. Earlier in the week, we'd bought identical T-shirts with the painting emblazoned on the front. Wandering around Madrid, I took notice of the Spanish. Women were beautiful: wavy locks tumbling over lithe shoulders or restrained in stylish buns, colorful skirts revealing stunning legs sheathed in chic stockings, flirtatious glances. Men seemed especially fit, slim, and styled in a range of conservative suits or American sportswear: Adidas sweatpants, fleece-lined denim Levi's jackets. Americans suddenly seemed grossly overweight.

"I love Miró so much," Charlene said, comparing the historic Prado museum to the more modern Museo Nacional Centro de Arte Reina Sofía. "The Prado is so historical and my art class is just so interesting. For instance, an impressionist painter can look at something, any object, and see it differently every time they see it. It's a capture-the-moment technique. If I was a painter and I had to paint you using this technique, I might paint *Kit in the Morning*, *Kit in the Afternoon*, and *Kit in the Evening*. I would have to paint so many paintings of you because I have so many impressions of you."

"Okay. That's fly," I said, distracted. I was too lost in the moment to be interested in impressionism. The melodiousness of Charlene's white-girl cadence was more captivating to me than what she was saying. Walking the streets of Madrid with a girl who loved me, smoking cigarettes, and discussing impressionism at twenty, I was gassed. Noticing the tags of Spanish graf writers along the way, I made a mental note that the graffiti was as significant to me as the impressionist art she'd seen at the Prado.

During the remaining days of my stay, Charlene and I ate a simulated Thanksgiving dinner with the family she lived with, the Guitards. The frail older couple lived near the Tirso de Molina metro stop, and cooked a three-course meal of salad, *tortilla de patata*, and rice pudding. Charlene and I frequented a bar, drinking cheap pitchers of sangria, popping pensiones into the jukebox, and continued to make love nightly. At the airport, Charlene cried in my arms. I consoled her and boarded my airplane. As the plane lifted off, my mind was consumed in deep thought.

Many of the homeboys I grew up with in Edenwald remain there, the same forty ounces in their hands. Some were killed; others were locked up for killing or dealing. College might've saved me. I felt changed having left the Bronx, New York City, the United States altogether. My world perspective would never be able to shrink back to the four corners of the blocks I grew up on. *Gracias*, Madrid.

Above the clouds over the Atlantic, I contemplated Solange and Charlene. I had no idea how to resolve the emotional conflict of my feelings. Despite the platonic nature of our relationship, I continued to see Solange as my ideal love interest. And though I'd just traveled thousands of miles to visit Charlene, whose deep love led her to bawl on my shoulder an hour ago, I still felt our partnership would end eventually. Maybe the time had arrived to proposition Solange again. It had been years since she brushed me off; enough time had passed for her to feel differently.

I nodded away in my window seat until a stewardess sashayed down the aisle with drinks and salted peanuts.

■ ■ ■

I'd finally filled Solange in completely on all the details surrounding what had happened after our brief courtship, and her initial rejection, when my relationship with Charlene kicked off full strength. The story of Charlene and me took us through salad, Nutella on toast, and leftover *pho* noodles, then finally the better half of a bottle of Pinot Noir. Totally unloading myself was extremely cathartic, a load off my mind and heart. I could withstand her rejection now; I knew there was nothing more I could do. After nearly three years, either I would at long last receive some emotional response from Solange or again be rejected. But at least I'd tried. Like Charlene four months ago, I'd accepted Solange's invitation to visit her studying abroad, in order to see how she really felt about me. Bougie had no idea.

"So I need to know, Solange: How do you feel about me? What do you think I should do about her? Any resemblance to anyone you might know is just coincidence, of course."

She laughed. "I don't know, Kit. Early on, I just started to feel like I couldn't live up to what you built me up to be. Maybe you saw something in me that even I hadn't seen yet, but I felt like I was on a pedestal. It was pressure. I thought maybe you just liked this image you had of me, but all I could ever do is be myself. Don't leave this poor girl for me, Kit. I'm not worth it, believe me. Just turn around and don't look back," she said, affecting the melodrama of a typical 1940s screen siren. "I'm no good for you! Seriously, you're not even really my type. I like guys like my dad, hoodlums and athletic types. It wouldn't work. It sounds like you're just tired of her anyway. If you leave her, don't do it because of me. I just never thought of us the way that you do."

"I figured maybe I was making progress with you. Like chiseling away at a rock," I said, joking.

"Gee, thanks a lot. Well, you can't make somebody love you," she said matter-of-factly.

"True. It's all good. It was the pussyfooting around and being in the dark that was really fuckin' with me."

" 'Being in the dark'? God, guys just hear what they want to hear. I never said anything to you that was at all ambiguous."

"Well . . . I still don't know what to do about Charlene. I feel like I know how she's gonna respond in our conversations, how she feels about everything, at what point she's gonna have an orgasm. I'm getting bored."

"You're gonna get married. It's so obvious. You're complaining, whimpering, and whining. Y'all are gonna end up married. I think you should just stick it out. Unless you're *that* miserable."

■ ■ ■

I soaped and rinsed the dishes. Solange turned her heater on, for a change, and dressed for bed. The relief I felt simply knowing the truth was immense. Having a clearer understanding of where we stood lifted a burden on my heart that I'd been carrying for far too long. I changed into my sweats until the room warmed up. Solange and I finished off the wine.

I switched off the lights, save for the bloodred nightlight, and selected some music from my laptop, feeling buzzed. I grabbed Solange's massage oil from the bathroom and walked toward the futon. The airy singing of Vanessa Paradis floated lightly through the air over funky tambourines and fatback drums. After a sip of wine, Solange stripped off her fitted Supergirl T-shirt under the dim burgundy light and unhooked her sheer bra. I'd never seen her breasts. Everything was larger than I imagined. The circles surrounding her nipples took up more than the size of a half dollar, an apricot color blending in with the rest of her chest. Charlene was much more booty-blessed than top-heavy, and Solange's full chest thrust out boldly in view made my dick heavy. I got excited, caught up in visualizing what could happen. But my feelings were different somehow. The pretending between us was gone. Solange no longer intimidated me; it was the first time I realized she had. Standing shirtless under the crimson glow, she was exposed to me for the first time.

She lay on her fabulous tits as I sat beside her on the mattress. The oil in my hands slipped through my fingers like something intangible, impossible to grasp. I rubbed my palms together before applying them to the smooth angles of her bare back. She moaned with approval as my fingers wound circles down her neck, pressing her tense shoulders. Working my hands up and down the sides of her back, I brushed past the heft of her breasts in an unasked question. She lifted up and I caressed them with my hands, lightly pinching the tips to rigid attention. My hands skimmed farther down to the swell of her behind. Solange murmured a faint "mm-hmm" as I slid her panties off along with her sweatpants.

She twisted over, naked and open to me for the first time. I playfully poured the remaining drops of wine over her breasts and sucked them delicately, licking warm lines through the spilled Pinot. Nibbling the crinkled flesh of her nipples made her moan louder, her hips beginning a fidgety squirm. I quickly stripped and lay beside her. The past three years and these last three days in Paris had led us to this moment.

Solange turned to face me, her hand reaching between my thighs, her mouth moist against my stomach, chest, and neck. We kissed wet and deeply, my slippery hands massaging her backside. With a smile, she stretched for the container of Nutella on her nightstand. Unscrewing the lid and dipping her fingers into the hazelnut and cocoa spread, she brought her hand back between my thighs. My hardness sticky with chocolate, Solange kissed my navel and then licked slow, teasing traces along the underside of my erection. It could've exploded right then, twitching practically on its own as she grasped the length tightly and swallowed deeply again and again. As the Nutella gradually disappeared, Solange stroked me into her mouth, dancing her tongue over my crown, sucking delightedly. My hand fondled her neck as hers fondled me. Just before I lost control, she rose and we exchanged sweet delicious kisses.

I held her tightly at the hips and lifted her onto my lap. Gazing at me, she reached near the Nutella, smiled again, and handed me a lubricated Durex. I slipped it on quickly and slid into her. Entering deeper with every movement as we held each other, Solange whispered French in my ear in response to my moaning.

"C'est bon . . . J'adore . . . Baises-moi . . ."

I laid her back down and mounted her, her legs curled to the ceiling. Our motion resumed instinctually, primitively, and I knew there would be no respite until I made Solange surrender to me, our bucking and rolling building up to that release. I watched her beneath me, her chest heaving in circles with every contact, eyes rolling beneath her closed lids, face fixed in anticipation of an arriving promise. Her braids tangled beneath her head, lashes glistening with the wetness of tears, her body moist with sweat. Our sounds of love mixed with her hushed sobs and whispered words of pleasure brought my own climax rushing forward. Solange cried out and came. I could feel the pulsing between her legs as she peaked, over and over. Pushing into her, enjoying the final sights and sounds of this fantasy come true, I hoisted her ankles over my shoulders, held her breasts firm, and came deeply.

Then we lay in silence, the pounding of our hearts slowing. I was the first to move, tossing the condom into the wastebasket and walking over to my laptop, ever the DJ. I returned to the bed with a bottle of Contrex mineral water, André 3000 crooning "Prototype" at my back. In bed we faced one another in the rays of the scarlet nightlight.

"Thank you," Solange said softly.

I stammered before offering, "Thank *you*. If I say anything right now, it's just gonna sound corny. . . ."

"Yeah, I know. I . . . don't know what happened," she agreed, smiling.

"So do you regret it?" I had to ask, at the risk of ruining the mood.

"No. I think it's funny that we waited so long, but I'm glad we did. I never meant to be a bitch, Kit. But no girl wants to be used. It was hard to tell if you wanted me for me or if you just wanted to check me off your list. It's happened to me before. Guys can be assholes. I thought the sex would be better if we both waited it out. But I think you should stay with your girlfriend. I'm really trying my best to give Beyoncé and Alicia Keys a run for their money; I don't have time for a boyfriend right now."

"I just wish you'd said that from jump," I replied. "But I guess I understand. I'm totally blissed out right now, I'll have to think about it tomorrow." We laughed. "Good night, Solange." I leaned over, kissing her full lips.

"*Bonne nuit*, Kit." We curled up together and I held her until the morning.

■ ■ ■

The remaining four days of my visit were peaceful and relaxed. Solange and I ventured to Montmartre to feast at Haynes Grill, Europe's first soul-food restaurant. For a historic bistro so central to the life of black American expatriates back in the day, Haynes Grill disappointed. It was in need of renovation, the cornbread was dry, the ambiance was barely saved by a jazz trio, and the food just okay. Sean Combs would clean up with a Justin's in Paris, I thought as we walked to the Jardin du Luxembourg. The box-shaped plane trees gave so much character to the park; the maples in Central Park were no comparison. Solange ordered her crêpe with Nutella, causing us to laugh at our private joke.

I contemplated what Solange said the next day, as she attended her music theory class. When she began her cat-and-mouse game years back when we met, I did honestly lose sight of whether I was genuinely falling in love or becoming obsessed with the chase. With her aspiring music career, Solange appealed to my creative side while Charlene, I suppose, appealed to my buppie pretensions. Each girl gave me passage to a different world, nurtured a different side of who I was becoming. I was better off with Charlene for the time being. "If you can't be with the one you love, love the one you're with," true. But I was already beginning to see my "love" for Solange as an infatuation that had already extended for far too long.

In my final moments in Paris at Charles de Gaulle, Solange and I stood at the gate holding hands silently. When my final call was announced, we both smiled. She kissed me twice on the cheeks before I boarded the plane.

I turned back to look at her a final time—recalling Charlene's tears when I left Spain months ago—but Solange had turned to walk away. I turned again and stepped onto the plane.

THE RULE OF
ONE THOUSAND

Nina Foxx

My apartment was half-empty. I stood in the shell of what had been my life for the past year and a half and looked around. Ahmad, my now ex-boyfriend, had been thorough. He'd taken everything that was his and some things that weren't—moving out of my apartment while I was away on a business trip. There was a note sticking to the front of my fireplace, strategically placed at my eye level. I snatched it; the rustling of the paper in the quiet apartment made me jump.

> Leslie,
>
> I was already more committed to you than most people are to anything in their lives. Too bad you needed a piece of paper to let you know that. You know how to reach me.
>
> Ahmad

He'd written on fancy paper, the kind you find in specialty stores. Knowing Ahmad, he might have even made it himself. He was the type to carefully plan out every detail of his exit. I dropped it without even folding it and watched as it fluttered to the floor.

I felt as empty as the room I stood in. Ahmad had managed to get the upper hand by leaving first. He'd left me wounded. All I wanted was to hide my head in the ground and lick my wounds. I couldn't even remember what we'd fought about this time. And since we had been giving each other paper cuts for months, it was only appropriate that he made his exit the way he had.

My footsteps echoed as I walked through the rooms surveying what was left behind. It wasn't much. Most of what had made the place comfortable had been his. Ahmad was the one into comfort and things like that. I was the driven one in our relationship, the one who made plans and then made plans to achieve those plans. I never had time to really furnish my apartment before he moved in. I didn't even know how to grieve his leaving. I told myself that it was okay that he was gone, that he'd been just holding me back anyway. I didn't believe it.

I swallowed heavily. His scent was fading and even I couldn't deny that the place felt empty without him. It was my fault. I'd given him an ultimatum, things he had to do to stay, and he'd made a choice. I couldn't fault him for that, even if it wasn't the choice I wanted.

Ahmad had let me know where he stood on the subject of marriage from the very beginning. He didn't want modern institutions—institutions that had perhaps outlived their usefulness—to define his life.

"No man can put on paper what I feel," he'd said. "The concept of marriage was designed to keep women in a position of servitude to men. I don't want a servant, I want a partner. A soul mate."

I'd thought he was charming, talking out of the side of his mouth. He couldn't have really believed what he said. I remember thinking that if he loved me like he said, he would give me what I wanted. And I wanted to be legally married. To have it on paper that he would be as committed to me as I would be to him. I was wrong.

He was the artist, the one comfortable in places I was not. Ahmad freelanced for a living, never sure where his next paycheck was coming from, but he was happy. It didn't bother him to pay all his bills at the last minute, and he never thought to plan for the future when a big windfall did come in. Ahmad always wanted to celebrate the here and now. I was the one who needed the guarantees and certainty, some kind of confirmation that I was doing what I was supposed to be doing. I worked as a technical writer instead of doing the writing I knew I was capable of. I was compelled to try and move faster than my thirty-two-year-old biological clock was ticking. I'd wanted the regular paycheck and the predictable life. Well, I had that certainty now. I was certain that I lived alone, again.

I slept fitfully. Memories of us together kept running through my mind. Recent ones were of shouting and senseless arguments. Then I dreamed of the future we were not to have. Trying to surface were memories of Ahmad running his strong, thick fingers through my fuzzy hair and rubbing my back with all-natural soap that made suds the same color as his deep caramel skin. Those were the things I liked. Unfortunately, those were also the things that didn't last past the three-month excitement of our initial infatuation. I didn't understand. I thought I had done everything right this time. We should have worked.

At 7 A.M., I slipped out of bed and into my jeans. The almost-naked apartment was like a prison. I knew he was gone, but I kept expecting him to walk through the door at any moment. I let the door slam behind me as I ventured outside to find something more productive to do than listening to the clock tick or tossing and turning in a half-occupied bed.

Second Avenue, like most other parts of New York, was already bustling, even though it was a weekend. I stopped for coffee and sipped it too fast, then walked for a while, staring down at the sidewalk as it streamed endlessly under my feet. I searched for something that could make it better, but I had no idea what.

Then I saw a poster in the window of a travel agency. Ahmad always urged me to be more spontaneous. Maybe he was right. I needed adventure, exotic surroundings, and remote locations. I needed a change to help me put things back together in my head.

■ ■ ■

The ship was beautiful. I was intrigued by her from the very beginning. The *Sea Breeze II* had been the first Big Red Boat. It had been designed to be a traveling amusement park, ferrying children and their parents on endless Disney voyages. The ship had been bought and sold time and time again. She was now a small ship by today's standards. That is what the travel agent had told me. The fact that the ship had more history on the ocean than I ever had with anyone was fascinating to me.

Much less glitzy than some of the newer cruise ships in the industry, the *Sea Breeze* now only did adventure sailings to smaller ports that were off the beaten track and away from the crowds. Her patrons were older, more moneyed types, people in search of a vacation away from the overcrowded theme park–like ports. It sailed a different itinerary every week, so many of the passengers had been on board for a month or more.

I marveled at the workmanship as I made my way to my cabin. You didn't see woodwork like this on cruise ships anymore. Too expensive and the craftsmanship would be lost on the crowds. I looked closer; it was so beautiful it looked like it belonged in a museum behind glass, to be admired and not touched. I ran my hand down the wall, savoring the feel of the wood under my fingers. I was sure the ship could whisper stories of past voyages and passengers if I listened hard enough. I planned to discover some adventure of my own during the seven days I would be aboard; it was time for me to be more adventurous.

My cabin was in the bottom of the ship, oddly shaped with a small porthole to see outside, but I didn't care. I didn't plan to spend much time in the cabin anyway. The ship would sail in a few minutes and it would be dark soon. I was anxious to discover the secrets of the *Sea Breeze* and its virtually unknown Central American ports. Hopefully, I would be doing some self-exploration at the same time, discovering things about myself that I had yet to understand. I wanted to stay busy to leave myself no time to miss Ahmad.

I got settled in my cabin and then went on deck to watch the sunset. The Miami sky was virtually cloudless, and as it faded from blue to red, I felt my stress melt away, too. A handsome waiter walked up and slid a drink onto the small table near my chair. I shook my head.

"I didn't order yet," I said.

"You didn't have to." His voice was heavy with a lilt I recognized as Trinidadian. "We know what you want here."

I read his name tag. It was starting already. "Oh, *really?* . . . Delroy?" I wondered if they were taught this when they first signed on to be a part of the ship's crew; charm the ladies, make them happy.

"Yes, the ship knows. Did they tell you she was haunted?"

I laughed. "No, they didn't. But that makes two of us." I smiled. My quip was lost on him. He had no idea how my recent breakup was haunting my mind. "I suppose she tells you what each passenger wants, then?"

He nodded.

"Uh-huh. Well, then she must have told you that I don't believe in ghosts and am not the type to fall for gimmicks. Thanks for the drink, but I'm here already. I already bought a ticket." I looked away, dismissing him. He could take his flattery over to someone it would work on.

He shrugged, then walked away, leaving me to my thoughts. The steel band started up, making the wooden deck rumble. I sipped my drink, smiling, and watched the coastline of the United States slip by. The sway of the boat as we made our way south was calming. It had only been a few minutes and I already felt swept away.

We had a day at sea before we would reach our first stop in Honduras.

■ ■ ■

The dancehall was empty. The DJ was playing as if he had a room full of people as the eighties disco lights swirled in the dark room. The disco was in the bow of the ship, at the very bottom and also oddly shaped—probably an afterthought. It was easy to feel the ship sway here, and I found myself losing my equilibrium. I spotted a booth at the back of the room, walked over, and slid into it.

As I stared at the drink menu in front of me, I became aware of another presence. I looked up just as someone slid into the booth across from me.

"I'm sitting here," I said.

"And I am too."

I sat speechless. He was a big man. Muscular, his skin a beautiful cocoa brown. But that was not what took my words away. It was his eyes. They were light brown, similar to Ahmad's, but much deeper and more mysterious. I could feel the secrets inside calling me, drawing me in.

He smiled. "Unless, of course, you mind. You are here alone, right?"

Before I could answer, Delroy approached. He didn't speak, just placed a drink in front of me. His face held a knowing smile as he left. I cleared my throat.

"I am."

"Good." He spoke with an accent that I couldn't place.

"Where are you from?" I asked, sipping my drink. The waiter had been right on. It was a very good drink.

"From Brazil. But I have lived a lot of places. My name is Oba. Pleased to meet you."

The warmth of the drink quickly took over me, and I relaxed. "Leslie."

An awkward silence was between us for a few minutes. I looked at my drink, stealing a few glances at him through my lowered eyelashes. He looked as delicious as my drink.

He tapped me on the back of my hand. "Let's go on deck so we can talk. It will be quiet there."

I wanted to go, but I knew that I should be careful or I would find myself right back where I started. He was a stranger, yet he somehow felt familiar. "I can't. I mean I shouldn't."

He gave me that sexy smile again, showing me a deep dimple. My insides melted and my apprehensions floated away. It felt good to be moved that way after spending weeks feeling tense. Oba oozed a sensuality that I had only previously read about.

"Don't be ridiculous. Of course you can. We are at sea. The Rule of One Thousand is in effect here." He took my hand.

"And that is?"

"When you are more than one thousand miles away from home, you can do as you please. There is no one here to tell you otherwise."

"That's corny," I said, smiling. I held on to him for balance as we went on deck.

"Maybe. But you're coming with me, aren't you?"

I let him guide me up to the deck. We walked to the nearly deserted rear of the ship and settled by the empty hot tub. I perched on the edge and Oba pulled up a chair, sitting so close that his lanky legs made a V around me, but not so close that he was touching me.

The full moon illuminated the deck. The ship was moving fast enough that the cool wind tousled my hair. The hum of the ship's motors was hypnotizing as it moved through the deep, black water. I didn't want to be sucked in by the romantic setting. If I had been the type to get swept up in the romance, I would have still been as cautious as I was. Even romantics learn from their past experiences, and Ahmad had taught me a lot about going slow.

Oba cleared his throat and leaned in. "So, what are you running from?"

I crossed my legs underneath my full peasant skirt and smiled. "What do you mean?"

"Most people don't take vacations by themselves. Are you trying to get away from something?"

I was startled. Perhaps the glint I had seen in Oba's eyes was his perceptiveness. He had gone straight to the point. It was eerie. Even though the night was warm, I felt a chill run up my spine.

"I'm not running—" I lifted my chin defensively.

He smiled knowingly. He didn't believe me. I wasn't sure I did.

"If you say so." He leaned in closer as if he had a secret to tell.

I shivered again and inhaled his smell. He smelled of woods and a gentle musk. Oba ran his tongue across his thick, smooth lips. I swallowed.

"I took my first voyage because I had my heart broken. I thought she was the love of my life."

I caught my breath. It was as if Oba was telling my story. "Was she?"

He shook his head slowly, never breaking eye contact. "No, she wasn't. I discovered that I loved the sea more."

I laughed at that. "I don't get it."

"What's to get? If she had accepted my proposal, I would have never known that I enjoyed the freedom to travel the world, something I could not have had with a wife and family, not at that time. Most people never discover what they truly love until it is too late."

We paused as another couple strolled past us on the deck, hand in hand. I looked down to the edge of the hot tub where I had placed my drink. I took a sip.

"Maybe this is an opportunity," I said.

A half smile crossed Oba's face, and I could tell he was waiting for me to continue, but he didn't interrupt.

"I was only looking at the bad side, feeling sorry for myself."

"Were you?"

"I was trying to make him do what I wanted, what I thought was the best thing. He always said he didn't want to get married."

"Not everyone does."

I nodded. "I used to find that hard to believe. After he said no, I couldn't hear what he had to say."

We didn't talk anymore. We watched the orange moon together as I contemplated what he'd said. I felt close to him, knowing that his experience was somehow similar to mine. He just seemed to be so much wiser from it.

As we sat there I realized that Oba was familiar, as if he had come on the cruise just to meet me. Up to then I had been too practical to believe in karma, but it was like he had been sent to me. He had an aura about him that glowed brighter than the other passengers. My adventure ship was becoming a love boat. I was falling.

■ ■ ■

The next day, I looked for him at breakfast and then at lunch. My eyes darted around the room hopefully, but Oba was nowhere to be found. By dinnertime, I was sulking openly. I sat by the empty pool afterward, staring out over the horizon. The wooden deck, although worn, had been meticulously cleaned. People around me sat in groups of twos and threes, most dressed in tropical clothing, bright colors that should have cheered me up. The ship's engine sounded like a hum in this section of the ship, and their hushed tones blended together with the sound.

"Why so glum?" Oba's lilt was as musical as it had been the night before. He'd walked up behind me, the sounds of his footsteps covered by the never-ending hum of the ship.

I straightened my face. "I'm not glum, just pensive." I didn't want to smile. He didn't need to know that I had been wishing for him.

"I see," he said. "Did you have a good day? Days at sea are good for thinking." Oba stood behind me, putting his hands on my shoulders. My hair moved lightly in the breeze, and he brushed a lock of hair away from my face, letting his finger trail sensuously down my neck.

My heartbeat throbbed in my ears. "I thought I would see you somewhere today. Did you sleep all day?"

He smiled but didn't answer. Instead, he pulled a chair over and sat very close to me. He had the same effect he'd had on me the night before. Every pore in my body became aware of him. My mood instantly lifted. Oba put his mouth very close to my ear. His breath caressed my ear as he spoke.

"Thirsty?" he asked. His husky voice was barely above a whisper. The air suddenly felt heavy. I swallowed, nodding.

Delroy suddenly appeared and placed a drink on the small white plastic table near our chairs. After a few deep sips, I was more comfortable and felt courage begin to course through my body. I leaned into Oba. My boldness surprised me. I did not recognize this new me, no longer afraid to take a chance or act on impulse.

"We'll be in Honduras tomorrow. Ever been there?" he asked me.

I shook my head. Other than business travel, I hadn't been anywhere.

He captured my eyes with his. "You should get some rest, then. It will make you tired. Honduras can be very intense." His voice sent a ripple of awareness through me.

"You're right. Of course. I should go."

"Shall I accompany you?

His words were chivalrous in an old-fashioned sort of way, yet I could tell that so much lurked underneath his politeness. I was confused, and the old, cautious me hesitated.

"No," I said, standing up too quickly. "I'll be okay."

Oba nodded, then gently brushed his lips against my cheek. "Dinner tomorrow, then?"

He'd given up too easily. I was disappointed. I smiled, then nodded. I left him on deck and made my way through the deserted hallways to my cabin.

■ ■ ■

I didn't see him at all while we were in port. I lingered on deck long after we had docked, hoping that I would catch Oba as he went ashore. My adventure would be that much more fun if I had someone to share it with. Once again, he was nowhere to be found.

Armed policemen patroled the dock in the back of an old blue pickup truck. I felt uneasy; I had expected crowds of people and vendors hawking their wares. Colorful buildings and houses were not far from the large pier where we docked. The clapboard homes were raised above the ground and the tide on unsteady-looking stilts, and instead of manicured lawns like those I might have found back in the United States, the front yards were strewn with debris or filled with vegetables still on the vine. Small children played in some of the yards; goats and chickens roamed through others.

I finally found the beach. Two small boats dotted the horizon. I lazed about, enjoying the crystal-clear waters. There was very little tourism, only poverty and pure white sand. Locals walked up and down the beach as I lay there. They stared at me, making me aware that I stood out from the group, probably looking more like them than the tourists I was with. I tried to relax and read but found myself staring into space. Thoughts of Oba's scent and his wise words kept coming back to me. I was looking forward to dinner.

■ ■ ■

Heads turned as I strode into the dining room. I was both glad and embarrassed that I had taken extra time dressing. The red, form-fitting wrap dress I chose was elegant and sexy. It made me feel empowered and daring.

Waiters rushed about the room, and the sound of silverware clanging filled the air. The room was full. Honduras seemed to have made everyone hungry. Oba was waiting for me at my table. His dress was simple but elegant; his clothing seemed to caress his body, accenting his sensuality. He stood as I approached.

"Did you enjoy Honduras?" He extended his hand as he spoke.

"It was beautiful," I said, leaning forward so he could kiss my cheek.

He pulled out my chair. I was surprised at the gesture. "Did you find it sad?"

"That too. But you know, everyone I saw seemed happy."

"Most probably were. Many people would look at the circum-stances there and immediately assume it had to be fixed. It is not uncommon to try to impose our terms of happiness on others. Not everything that is different is broken."

My tablemates joined us, and Oba was silent as we made polite conversation. He sat across from me, and I felt my face grow warm as he watched me. His eyes seemed depthless, hiding an unspoken invitation. Finally, dinner was over and I stood up to go, saying my good-nights to the other passengers at the table.

Oba stood, too. He placed his hand in the small of my back and guided me away from the table and out of the dining room. We stopped by the elevators. He wasn't going to ask twice, and I wasn't going to let him get away. My whole being seemed filled with anticipation.

"Do you think you could walk me to my room?" It was my turn

to do the asking. There was something in his manner that made me feel comfortable. I wanted him to be near me.

"Of course," he said. "Whatever the lady wants."

He seemed familiar with my room. "You have *this* room," he said. "This is the one where none of the electric appliances work."

"You would think they would fix that."

"They tried, but it is not possible. Nothing works here."

"Sounds to me like I should get a refund, then."

He chuckled, then encircled me with his arms. I inhaled deeply, drinking in his scent. "People come on this ship for the same reasons they want to come to these undeveloped ports. They are intrigued by its mysteries."

"I see nothing mysterious about not being able to dry my hair," I said, laughing.

"But that is part of it. This is the haunted ship." He opened his arms to indicate the ship.

"I know. I've been told. But I don't believe it. Don't tell me you do."

He kissed me then, fully and deeply. He pressed his body to mine and then parted my lips with his tongue, tasting me. The hardness of his body meshed with my curves.

The room spun.

"You Americans see only with your eyes," he said. "It's deeper than that. There are some things we are not meant to understand or control."

I didn't answer. He could believe what he wanted. I only believed what I knew for myself to be true. And right now, it was that it felt damn good to be in his arms.

Oba helped my clothes fall away and I didn't stop him. We lay on my bed, our bodies outlined by the moonlight streaming through my small window. He trailed kisses all over my body and then massaged me slowly. I felt sexual desire that I had not felt for months.

I shuddered at his touch. He was surprisingly gentle. He seemed to have a wealth of knowledge and he was using every bit of it to bring me pleasure. I spread my legs, welcoming the warmth of his tongue. He stroked me gently with his broad fingers, pushing me to climax. My breath came in rapid bursts.

I straddled him and searched for his pleasure zones, trailing my tongue along his chest. I teased his nipples slowly and he moaned, cupping my behind with his hands. I took his penis in my hand and felt him stop breathing for a moment. Oba slowly raised his hips, and I licked his penis, then sucked him like a lollipop. He gasped and I felt suddenly powerful.

In one movement, Oba flipped me over and guided his rock-hard dick home. It was my turn to gasp. He filled me up so completely, it was as if we were made for each other. I flexed my muscles, then spread my legs wider. I wanted him as deep as possible.

We moved together slowly at first, aided by the rocking of the ship, then faster. My heartbeat thundered in my ears. His face was strained and I could tell he was holding back. I wrapped my legs around him and pulled him closer to me with each thrust. Finally, we came together, then fell asleep in each other's arms.

■ ■ ■

In the morning he was gone, his scent still heavy in the air. I glanced at my watch: I'd slept much longer than normal. It was almost noon.

There was still no electricity in my room, but the shower was warm. I let the water cascade over me, thinking about my night with Oba. He was such an odd person, but so sensual. It then occurred to me that I did not know much about him at all. I didn't even know his last name.

■ ■ ■

Belize was more wonderful and wild than the travel agent said, yet very civilized. Dense mangroves grew not far from the muddy shores of the Caribbean waters. I spent my time exploring the ruins of the Mayan temples and enjoying the seclusion of our host for the day, the Jaguar Paw Resort. It was rustic and nestled deep in the jungle, by the banks of the Caves Branch River, said to be haunted by spirits of the early Mayan settlers. The quash and the nightwalkers roamed freely, but the wild beauty of the place was lost on me. Thoughts of my new friend on board the ship kept invading my mind.

■ ■ ■

"Abgele. Oba Abgele. No girlfriend, no wife."

We danced close together in the jazz lounge, his hand on my ass. I leaned my head on his chest, enjoying the feel of the muscles underneath his shirt.

"Where do you go from here? Back to Brazil?"

"I haven't decided yet."

I paused. My heart skipped a beat. "The cruise is over in the morning. What do you mean? Your airline ticket has to return somewhere."

"Right now I live on the ship."

"How does that work? I have never heard of anyone doing that before. Are you part of the crew and forgot to tell me?"

"No, I just have friends in high places. I go where I please right now."

The rational part of me wanted to shout out that that was the most ridiculous thing I ever heard. How did he live? But the romantic in me fell deeper in love at that moment. I imagined a life with no worries, sailing into the sunset daily.

"You could come home with me," I said.

He shook his head. "I couldn't. You and I both know it wouldn't be the same once we left here. There is something about the sea that is magical, and without it, it would all be different."

I was being unrealistic, but I still felt scolded. "I would like to see you again, though. Can we do that?"

We stopped dancing and he looked into my eyes. I knew the answer before he said it.

"What's done at sea—"

"—stays at sea," I finished.

■ ■ ■

On deck that morning, I expected to see him. At least to say good-bye. I stared at the door expectantly, wishing him to appear. My heart fell each time he didn't. As they called my group to disembark, I spotted Delroy.

"Have you seen Oba?" I asked. "I want to say good-bye."

He looked at me questioningly. "Who?"

"Oba Abgele. The man I was with? He lives on the ship?"

He shook his head. "I'm sorry. I don't know who that is. I don't recall seeing you with anyone." He paused, looking at me quizzically. "You have a safe trip home. Perhaps you will see him onshore."

I didn't. Disappointment flooded over me, but my memories were intact. Oba was as mysterious eight days later as he had been that first night on the ship, but he had given me so much.

I sighed and gathered my luggage. It was time to return to reality.

■ ■ ■

Two months passed. I stopped missing Ahmad, but I still couldn't sleep. Work was tough and I was having dreams about the moonlight and the ocean. It was always the same. I would be standing on a white, sandy beach, holding a lit candle. I would walk into the ocean and set the candle down. Then I would stand there and watch until it floated away. A dove would fly overhead, and then I was so overcome by a sense of loss, I would awaken.

Dark circles were appearing under my eyes. If I didn't know me better, I'd think I needed to see a psychologist. But I knew what the prescription should be without wasting my time. I missed Oba and his strange brand of wisdom.

Rather than stay in bed, I turned on my computer, opening the browser to my Yahoo! homepage. The news headlines sprang out at me. The *Sea Breeze II* had sunk. An overwhelming sense of loss overcame me. I had sailed on her only one time but had come to understand her magic. Tears came to my eyes as I read.

There were pictures. I held my breath. There she was, being claimed, sinking to her watery grave. I read further. There was no one on board. Mine had been the last journey. She was sailing to Europe, to be sold as scrap. Such a shame.

I enlarged the picture. They said that no one was on board, but it looked as if something or someone was on deck. It wasn't clear, but it looked remarkably like a bird. A dove. I read the message boards. There had been talk about it for weeks. The consensus was that it was an insurance sinking. The *Sea Breeze* was worth more underwater than the sum of its parts.

I thought of Oba. His broad shoulders. His smell. His mouth and the magic he had worked. *Where had he gone?* I hadn't heard from him even though I had given him my card, but I hadn't expected to. He'd been right: It *was* better this way. The moments we shared were frozen in time, still magical. Our week was wonderful, and it made the fact that I was coming home to an empty apartment not matter so much. But a big part of me wanted to at least know where he was.

I searched the Internet. Two hours later I found contacts at the cruise line that finally led me to the ex-captain of the *Sea Breeze II*.

At 10 A.M., I called him up. He didn't seem to mind my early call.

"I get lots of calls about that ship," he said. "She had many fans. People who sailed on her again and again."

I explained that I was looking for Oba, that we'd met and I wanted to contact him.

The captain paused. "You couldn't have met him."

"I assure you I did."

He paused again.

I went on quickly. "I just want to drop him a line. See where he ended up after the boat sank. He told me he was living on board."

The captain was quiet for so long, I thought he'd hung up.

"Oba Abgele died in an engine fire on the *Sea Breeze* over five years ago."

My throat tightened.

"Either you have a very vivid imagination, or you met his ghost. We knew the ship was haunted, but we never knew by whom."

In a few short days, Oba had helped me move on from my breakup. After being with him, I'd realized that I was more in love with being married than I had been with Ahmad, and that there were better things out there for me. I also learned that it was okay, sometimes, to just let things happen naturally and deviate from the plan.

Beyond that, he'd shown me that there are some things I am not yet able to comprehend and just have to believe in.

PINKTIARARAINBOWS

SékouWrites

The tiara didn't glitter as much after it was left on the counter of the bar—the black marble underneath it slick with the residue of spilled promises, splattered half-truths, and a misting of lust. Its absence of shimmer wasn't for lack of want—surprise maybe, fueled by the randomness of its new perch.

The tiara emerged only once or twice a year from the white box and padded sheets of cotton that buffered it. Always on the specialest of days, which made the tiara feel special, too. When it was taken from its box, the cotton peeled away slowly, Karra, its most recent owner, liked to gaze at it, tilting the tiara so that it caught the light and refracted pinkish rainbows up into her face. That happened more frequently when the tiara was still new, though. Before four moves had gradually relegated its yellowing box to the back of a tight closet, hidden by shoe boxes and buried under more current toys. For six months, the tiara had been forced to suffer the idignity of its box top being used as the resting place for an unwieldy purple sex toy called a Jelly Beaver—a salacious item that appeared soon after one of Karra's promising relationships ended abruptly. The things the Jelly Beaver muttered when returned to the tiara's box top after use were, by turns, appalling, torrid, and enticing.

Hours earlier, the Jelly Beaver had been knocked aside, and the tiara's box had been unearthed. Waiting by the bed, perched atop a crisp black shoe box, was a brand-new pair of stilettos. Below pink straps, their three-inch heels were sleek, smooth, and firm.

Clearly, it was another special day. The shoes. The clingy microribbing of the matching pink sweater. The dangerous slits in the skirt that was laid out on the bed. The extra time Karra was taking with her body, rubbing scented lotions into the most intimate creases of her skin. Definitely a special day. Getting into the mood, the tiara adjusted itself to radiate in more pronounced hues of pink. If it had known it would soon be forgotten on the bar of a trendy lounge, it might not have bothered. But probably, it would have.

The tiara's yen for travel and adventure was almost a birthright considering how it was created. Even though it was mostly constructed in Nashville, it never thought of itself as being born in any single place. Parts of it were birthed in different places, shipping codes and FedEx account numbers paving the roads, skyways, and byways to bring it together, bit by bit, over the course of two years. Looking at the tiara, no one would think that it took that long to make. Or maybe they would. Probably they'd have no thoughts about it one way or the other. The tiara possessed that taken-for-granted type of beauty: noticed, appreciated, forgotten.

The tiara enjoyed its Egyptian crystals most. Although the Swarovski at its apex was brilliant in the way that the sun might be considered to shine a little bit of light, Egyptian crystals usually came with vivid images of foreign accents and exotic fantasies. A pair arrived together, gleaming with a luminous amber color so dark it was close to chocolate. The crystals came with residual impressions of their time adorning the favorite choker of a woman known for her appetites.

Rich by inheritance, the woman had moved to New York for college, then flown back to Cairo immediately after graduation, finding the Hudson a poor excuse for the Nile. She was six feet tall, and her sienna skin and sharp features drew the eyes of both men and women when she walked through Khan el-Khalili, the crowded bazaar in the heart of downtown Cairo. The endless swirl of shouts and bargaining, colors and jostling, pale tourists and circles of old men sucking on three-foot-tall hashish pipes always gave way to let her pass. She would bargain for gems and jewelry because to pay the price first quoted was to be robbed. She'd then put them in a purple velvet sack and return home in the luxury of a Mercedes taxi.

She lived alone on one of the boats tethered along the large stone walls that bordered the Nile. When she decided to embrace her desires, she had a special raft made, just large enough to fit a king-sized mattress atop a waterproof box spring. Then she added a small motor and a thick canopy of silk that hung from a brass railing to hide her from sight. The top she left open so she could look up at the moon.

When night fell and the constant buzzing of cars died down to a nearly distant hum, she liked to drift down the Nile, the buttery skin of her naked body caressed by and tangled in burgundy satin sheets, her eyes idly watching the people on bridges above her as she drifted underneath. Eventually, her fingers would discover her nakedness. She liked to use both hands, letting each of her fingertips slide up and down, playing in her dampness, before she quickened their stroke into the featherlike touch that would make her shoulders tighten and teeth clench in a silent but powerful surge of ecstasy.

Often, she took younger men with her. She liked to ride them slowly, their arms pinned beneath her thighs, their eyes staring up at her bare breasts and the night sky above in awestruck rapture. She left just enough silk draped around the bed so that only those who found themselves directly above her raft could catch glimpses of her body rolling in slow waves, the dim sparkle of her amber-colored choker gliding up . . . and down . . . and up.

■ ■ ■

Looking at the tiara, its coruscating baubles and bejeweled wires, there was little that would remind you of the small woman most responsible for its creation. There wasn't much about her that seemed as exotic as the tiara, except maybe her shoes. Johnnie always could wear some shoes. With her heels on, she was just barely five feet, but there was not one day in the two years she'd toiled over the tiara that she hadn't had her heels on. They made her feel sexy, powerful, and, after all the years behind her, still able to command men's attention.

It wouldn't have taken her so long to complete the tiara except for the emotional distraction of divorce, and once, she'd taken the amber crystals out of the tiara to clean them and accidentally put one of them into a watch. The watch was a project for an old man in Chattanooga, a gift he wanted to give to his young nephew, Andre. His first *real* watch, the old man growled. Johnnie put an Egyptian crystal in the watch and charged the old man the price of a colored diamond. She didn't mean to, but she wouldn't have hesitated even if she realized her mistake, all his nasty phone calls well worth the markup. Later, she searched all over for the crystal and, perplexed by its disappearance, ordered another one from Egypt. Again consigning FedEx to connect her dots into art.

She liked to buy crystals from abroad. The fact that most of them came from overseas reminded her of her youth, when she wasn't frightened by the idea of grabbing a passport and jumping onto one of the modes of transportation that connect the United States to the rest of the world.

The idea of travel had never frightened her, but she'd never acted on it, either. She'd dreamed of flying away the summer after high school and arranging for a layover in Paris just long enough to race to the Eiffel Tower, her taxi weaving through traffic with breakneck precision. Once there, she'd take the elevator up to the second level of the tower, then run the rest of the way to the top, her coffee-brown legs devouring the steps two at a time.

At the summit she'd "accidentally" bump into the handsomest man who didn't already have a woman tucked under his arm. The view, she'd read, was too romantic to be enjoyed alone. She'd collide into him, using the ampleness of her rear end to enticingly cushion the impact. When he cursed her clumsiness, apologized, or began to ask for her number, she'd simply caress his face with her palms and kiss him until he began to kiss her back. She was a good kisser, she'd been told, especially when she shifted her weight so that her thigh pressed between a man's legs. It wouldn't take long for his body to respond, pushing into her with the firmness of longing. Teasing, she'd pull away and run back downstairs. The taxi would whisk her back to the airport, where she'd giggle when the other passengers asked if she'd bought anything in the duty-free shop during the layover, because their lives were so much more mundane than hers.

The fantasy, so many lifetimes old, felt gray and weather-beaten. But when she held a foreign crystal—the smooth, cool hardness of it feeling delicious in her palms, between her fingers, on her skin, and against her nipples—she could easily imagine the fantasy fulfilled rather than owning up to the life she had actually lived. She'd married her high school sweetheart, the gregarious math whiz who, the night he proposed, promised to take her around the world as many times as she wanted, but in twenty years had only succeeded in taking her from her apartment near Hadley Park out to the thirty-thousand-dollar condos on Harding Place.

The day her husband dropped the news he was leaving her, the whole venomous package cloaked in the enticing wrapper of an impromptu date night, she moved into her shop to cry, think, and order sex toys. Every day after that, when she heard him show up at work—his booming voice carrying through the front windows of her shop—she'd slip home and shower in their condo with only the ghosts of unkept promises and empty memories to keep her company.

Her husband owned the used-car lot at the corner of Charlotte and Fifty-first, and if she stood at the '92 Pathfinder that never sold, she could look down Fifty-first to the highway overpass and imagine she was speeding past, en route to someplace beyond Nashville's state lines.

To Johnnie's eye, Nashville was mostly green with lush leaves that swayed constantly, even without a breeze—seemingly fueled by the thick Southern accents that swirled around and through the city. All of which seemed pretty on some days and stifling on others, depending. When she drove up Charlotte, back toward town, she eventually crested a hill that would let her look straight ahead and see the ten skyscrapers of downtown Nashville reaching up like stubby fingers covered with glass. On the right, the BellSouth building rose like a two-pronged fork, its garish, neon blue bell looking down on the town like an evil eye conspiring to keep her trapped within city limits.

After the subject of divorce was broached, she couldn't sleep. Johnnie would lie awake in her shop, restless, then drive down to Charlotte early in the morning. Making U-turns in order to cruise the same four-mile strip in an endless loop until she saw the sun creeping over downtown in a sunrise that was always so shockingly beautiful, she could easily imagine herself transported to someplace tropical.

She'd dress for the occasion, a thick silver rope looped around her ankle above leopard-print slingbacks and below legs firmed from years of strutting about in four-inch heels. The shoes and anklet were constant, but her skirt varied, depending on the day, her mood, and what she'd already saturated the morning before. They were always short—tiny wisps of thin fabric that stretched taut across her full hips, the ripples of cloth straining to contain her. When she drew her thighs apart, the skirt's ripples rolled up into tidal waves. She liked the resistance against her skin, the private pleasure derived from knowing that just half an inch out of sight— right in front of her Brazilian-waxed lips—was a G-string equipped with a tiny vibrator. The remote control for its single setting of bliss was clutched in her right hand. She usually wore the unfinished tiara on her head, too, and a plain white collared shirt chosen specifically to belie the rest of her scandalous ensemble to anyone driving by.

Once she saw the first rays of the sun, she'd flick the remote control's switch at the next red light and try not to scream in pleasure. She'd squeeze her thighs together and imagine herself at the top of the Eiffel Tower kissing a beautiful stranger and then feel the moisture pooling between her legs, oozing down into her seat. She'd turn the vibrator off quickly, wanting to extend her pleasure and the amount of time she was distracted by it, but by the fourth traffic light it was all she could do not to break the steering wheel, her screams and pants barely muted by the full-tilt stereo and her foggy, rolled-up windows. Except for the early hour of her erotic escapades, she would surely have caused several accidents.

Even before he mentioned divorce, their marital strife had been the worst kind. He just stopped touching her. When she purposely rented movies chosen for the frequency and duration of sex scenes, then lounged beside him in silky robes arranged to fall open at the slightest touch, all he did after the movie was peck her on the cheek and jump on the Internet. Later, she'd find clumpy wads of Bounty in the bathroom trash can. That didn't make her feel pretty. But the tiara did. Days, when she was sitting at the back of her custom jewelry shop pretending to work, she would put the tiara on, strip naked—except for her shoes—and stare into the mirror until she felt beautiful.

The divorce happened on a day in September. A month of weekdays before she fully settled with the fact that she could not watch her husband, newly exed, sell cars in front of her shop's windows; no matter that the divorce papers decreed she was entitled to keep her shop and a percentage of his auto sales. She decided to wear the completed tiara to a Halloween party dressed as a princess. Then, over the next few weeks, she sold most of what she owned and decided to break the hold Nashville had on her by moving to Bridgeport, Connecticut.

She had a cousin in Bridgeport. An organic-living, wild-haired bundle of energy who, despite her years, always gave seasoned, well-rounded advice. Bridgeport, she'd e-mailed her, was at the beginning of an urban revitalization effort that was sure to shoot property values through the roof. It wasn't Paris, but it wasn't Nashville, so Johnnie packed what was left into the '92 Pathfinder, stole the keys, and made ready for her first real trip.

She bought a loft in the same industrial conversion complex as her cousin. Buying, to make the move feel more permanent and living in the same complex so that she wouldn't have to start her new social life from scratch.

"Do you still make tiaras?" her cousin asked while they were traveling I-95 south on their way to explore Manhattan. Johnnie didn't hear the question at first; the open road, the rapid flash of the highway's dotted white lines were reminding her of her early-morning drives. She had to cross her legs to contain the bubble of tingly swelling between them. Her thumb kept twitching, flicking the phantom switch of a remote control.

"What? Oh no, honey. I left the last one in Nashville. End of an era." She'd already decided not to make any more. They re-minded her of too many things. Held too much of her ex-husband within their multiple facets and ornate surfaces. They were a part of her past now. She'd find another hobby.

The memory of the little girl brought a bit of a smile to her lips. Not much, but enough. The girl had been crying in the car next to her when Johnnie pulled into a Mrs. Winner's franchise on her last day in Nashville. Frail, her shoulders bouncing in rhythm to noisy sobs, her thin arms folded across her chest, the girl was doing everything she could to keep her crying under control. Johnnie couldn't help but feel the need to ease the child's pain, so she did the first thing that occurred to her. She reached through the car's open window and handed the young girl her tiara.

"Baby," Johnnie cooed, "you're way too pretty to cry." The girl opened her eyes, her wariness of strangers co-opted by sadness, and sniffled once—a loud, clattering noise—as she looked up. Despite it all, she mustered the energy to be polite.

"Thank you, ma'am," she said, taking the tiara and placing it in her lap like it might break. Gradually, the sniffles and snuffles faded away as Johnnie walked toward the front door of Mrs. Winner's.

"Thank you so much," a woman said to her, thin fingers brush-ing Johnnie's elbow. "We just lost her father." The mother's eyes were red-rimmed, and her arms were laden with the sweet, sugary rolls that must have qualified as her brand of comfort food. By the time Johnnie got back to her Pathfinder with a bucket of food for

the road, a note scrawled in the penmanship of a child was waiting on her windshield.

"thanks again ~karra"

■ ■ ■

Andre would have noticed her even without the tiara. It twinkled atop the crown of her black hair, casting glints into far-off
corners of the dimly lit lounge whenever she tossed her head with
laughter. Her private collection of rainbows cruelly underscored
the fact that she was by far the prettiest woman in the room. He
watched her from the bar, tantalized, creating an imaginary world
around her so that she would be more than just another piece of
eye candy.

He'd been that way recently—admiring from a distance. Avoiding the dips and divides that were inevitable when the exotic high
drama of courting wore off. He was settling for eye candy these
days—no expectations, no rejections. But the woman had to seem
real to him, more than just a pleasant collection of inviting curves.

Looks only did so much for him now. He'd become immune
during his heyday. Been too often disappointed by beautiful
women who bounced into his bed, held his attention briefly, then
bored him into the abyss of disinterest with nonsensical patter
about boils and unsavory bodily functions. He knew what it was.
These women were so pretty no one had bothered to correct their
behavior, ignoring their personality flaws in consideration of their
genetic blessings. Typically, he needed more than that. So he created the details himself, avoiding almost certain disappointment:
the anguish of crossing the room to talk to a woman fine enough
to snag the lead in a hip-hop video, only to discover her English
was more broken than the motorcycle he'd almost wrapped around
a tree.

He took a swig of his drink and tried to determine what Tiara
Girl's poison would be. His uncle, a cantankerous old man, was a
lifetime bartender and he'd taught Andre to frame everything in
terms of liquor and its effects, reading people by what they chose
to imbibe. Andre looked over at her, eyes lingering longer than he

meant them to, and decided that if you asked her why she was wearing a tiara, you'd get different answers based on what she happened to be drinking.

If she was drinking champagne mixed with tequila (that suited her: nonconformist, gorgeous, with a hint of raunch), she'd tell you more than you expected to know: that it was symbolic of her search for the right man to make her a queen. Then she'd touch you and ask if you wanted to give it a shot. Gin? That would get her to tell you the truth. Something bland, like it being her birthday or a graduation celebration. If you asked her while she was drinking merlot, she'd wink and tell you that it made her feel pretty.

Not that she needed anything else to make her pretty. She was stealing the eyes of all the men in the lounge. Even the ones with dates were concocting lame excuses to stare and etch her into their memory for later use.

"Can you believe she's wearing a tiara?" Andre overheard one of them say, a contrived note of derision in the man's voice while his gaze hungered over parts of her body nowhere near the crown of her head. His date saw through the ruse, didn't like his diverted attention, but obliged him by leaning out to look anyway, her eyes helplessly falling toward the woman's hot-pink shoes.

Andre wasn't used to feeling like he was on the prowl. Years ago, someone at Arista had listened to his seventy-fifth demo tape and convinced someone down the hall to put Andre on the fast track to becoming the next crooning superstar. Many things had come easily after that, women among them. But that was then and this was now, four years later, when no one recognized him and the last remaining calling card from his fame was "Molasses," the hit single from his debut album. Eventually, he'd vacated L.A. and returned to his uncle's house in Chattanooga to lick his wounds and plan for the future.

Hours ago, he'd set out for Nashville. He didn't like to drive as much after the motorcycle incident, but he couldn't help himself. When Andre was a boy, his uncle had given him a watch with an amber-colored diamond and, ever since then, Andre had felt compelled to move, seek, and search. This was the third time he'd made the two-hour voyage to Nashville in the past week, searching for liquor and distraction. Tonight, he'd found both, an 8-Ball in one hand and a pen in the other, and he tried to figure out how he could manipulate the evening so that what he ended up writing down was Tiara Girl's phone number, instead of more lame song lyrics.

He glanced again. The tiara sparkled, throwing light airy rainbows across the room in abundance. She shook her head at something one of her girlfriends said, and he imagined her head rolling back and forth on a pillow beneath him, her bottom lip pinched into her teeth, her sculpted legs scissored around his waist as she rolled her hips up to greet his.

"Yeah," he imagined her moaning, digging her nails into his back and arms.

"Oh, yeah, Daddy," she'd whisper until she felt him widening inside her, thickening; then her arms would tighten around his neck and she'd beg him for it.

"Please," she'd groan, begging him to release himself inside her.

"Please . . . give it to me," she'd plead while she hooked her ankles together and bounced until her hips were slapping up against his so hard he'd barely have enough breath to call out her name—one hand groping for the headboard, trying to hold his body straight enough to catch every drop of the warm wetness she was throwing toward him.

He took a sudden gulp of his drink to shock himself out of the fantasy, then looked around the room, sizing up the other men who were hurling wolfish glances her way. Competition was steep. Pen still clasped in hand, he turned back to the bar, giving up for the moment, submerging himself in his Dead Sea of how-to-make-a-comeback worries and trying to settle his hormones.

"What's that for?" Up close, the beauty of her smile was blinding. Under the lights of the bar, her tiara glowed red, like a stop sign. He blinked, smiled, and shifted gears easily—like riding a bike.

"I'm going to write your phone number down."

Her eyebrows arched before she leaned over to ask the bartender for a glass of champagne. Then she turned back to him, the V-neck of her ribbed sweater hovering achingly close to his face, the swell of her chest pushing the fabric even nearer.

"From way over here?" she asked, amused. He swiveled his bar stool to face her, slowly took off his shades—Arista's stylist had told him that his dark eyes were intense and taught him how to use them. He'd retained most of her training long after the glitz had faded from his world. Even now, he was wearing what she'd taught him to: a multipatterned shirt that hugged his long torso and loose sandblasted jeans that kept him from looking too lanky. The shoes were the thing—she'd always emphasized the shoes. His were white leather with black piping, designed to stand out.

When you walk into a room, where do the eyes go? she'd asked him twice a day for the three weeks he'd been her charge. The face, the watch, the shoes, he'd learned to respond. He thought it overzealous at the time, but she'd dressed him up for a party and he'd noticed the women's eyes lingering longer over him. After that, he'd become a believer.

He was about to say something slick, something confident, like "I'll come get your number when I'm ready," but as he took off his shades, her eyes went large, the whites showing momentarily.

"Oh my God," she said. If he was smiling before, he was grinning after that. His fingers slid toward her forearm while he asked if she liked his eyes, not even considering the possibility of being recognized. He chuckled a bit, using the moment as an excuse to square up the room—sending a gloating glance to the fellahs and a "you wish you were her, don't you?" look to the ladies.

It was a familiar sequence of melody that pulled his attention back to her. She was singing. Standing there, inches away, radiating sex in her pink top, matching heels, and double-slit skirt, she was singing his song. And not "Molasses," the track everyone and their aunt Mabel knew. She was singing track eleven, the second verse, the one where his rich, Stevie Wonder–compared riffs had melted all over a Brooklyn break beat, imploring female listeners to leave the bedroom lights on so they could watch his tongue trek across the landscapes of their bodies.

He leaned forward and started to sing along with her—a quiet confirmation rather than a blatant call for attention. They stopped on the same note, in perfect sync, and smiled at each other. She was so busy staring that she didn't even notice the glass of champagne that had materialized at her elbow. He picked it up and held it between them.

"Maybe you need a drink." He expected his words to force her stare to shift itself into words—some spoken acknowledgment that she knew who he was—but she was beyond all that. She moved up onto the bar stool next to him and took a long sip of champagne. He had several inappropriate thoughts as he watched the thin cords of her neck as she swallowed. "And on my birthday, too," she said simply, the words falling out of pouty lips tinted with frosted promises.

During the height of his popularity, he'd shocked himself with how bold he could be—shocked even more to find that many women appreciated his frankness. He thought of this idly as he rubbed his index finger down the side of her champagne glass, soaking the moisture of condensation onto the tip of his finger, before running that coolness along the length of skin showing provocatively through the slit in her skirt. He relished how quickly her delicate features knit themselves into a frown, her back straightening as she shifted her weight. Trilling whispers and muted catcalls drifted over from the girls at her table. When he was done (it was a long slit), he parted his lips to suck what was left of the moisture off his finger. She flinched, unable to watch him complete the act, and he whispered, "Is there anything I can do for your birthday?"

"Two things," she said after a deep sigh, crossing her legs and smoothing her skirt. "One, don't do that again, and two, tell me if you're still married."

He laughed, not because it was funny but because he needed a second to catch his breath. His marriage wasn't public knowledge. At least, it wasn't supposed to be. A week before he got signed to Arista he'd met a woman at a house party. He remembered liking the way she wore a cut-up T-shirt without looking like she was underdressed.

When he signed the Arista contract, his boys took him on the requisite trips to several establishments where glimpses (and touches) of skin could be purchased for small bills, but that didn't satisfy him. He wanted to *share* his success with someone. On date number two he told her about his record deal. She was appropriately excited. Drove him to the mall to buy him a ten-dollar silver charm that she promised would keep his voice strong. He proposed on date number five, eager to have a private cheerleader, forgetting that he didn't really know her. It was only a matter of time. They'd separated too soon after the nuptials to have had any real life together, but, still, neither of them would file for divorce. It seemed so final. Plus, he still showed up at her house some nights—times when he mostly wanted to be held more than fondled. Mostly.

So, he decided to tell the truth, since she already knew it. "Yeah . . . but we're separated."

Well, some of the truth anyway.

"So you're still married." She cut to the core of it, clearly not intending to accept his offer of a comfortable half-truth that they could hide behind, take refuge in, until the deed—*deeds*—had been done.

"How did you know that, anyway?"

"I'm a fan. Big, BIG fan." She nodded to herself and ordered another drink. A vodka tonic this time, stronger medicine. Her girls had given up on her, and were eating and talking among themselves with the animated gestures and raised voices of tipsiness. Every so often, they'd steal a peek and smile, enjoying a vicarious thrill. He leaned into her to say something, but she stopped him with a hand on his chest, her fingernails poking into his pectorals. "I'm not going home with you, so don't even ask."

"Actually, I was just going to say that you're the most beautiful woman I've ever seen," he said, sitting back, "but since you brought it up, how about a compromise?"

She fidgeted for a moment before she answered. "Name it."

He liked her. She was passing his tests. His was an overly simplified SAT divided into two simple categories. Sexy? Check.

This wasn't applied to physical dimensions, had less to do with chest-waist-hip measurements and plenty to do with confidence and wardrobe. Game? Yeah. Most definitely. She exuded the aura of a down-for-whatever girl. She hadn't backed off of anything he'd thrown at her yet. At times like this he wished he had pushed for a divorce.

"Fantasy," he said, then stood to whisper what he meant directly into her ear. He made sure to throw his voice low and thick, keeping his lips so close that they brushed her earlobe and warmed it with his breath. When he finished, she blushed and kicked one of her legs unconsciously, but her eyes, on his, were steady.

"We need a theme. Travel." She spoke quietly but without a trace of shyness, then sat still to wait for him. He took his time, gracing her table of friends with a languid smile before he leaned into her ear again.

"I'd take you by the hand, right now, and lead you straight to your car. You'd barely have a chance to wave bye to your girls. I'd take the keys and make you ride in the backseat. I'd tell you to take your panties off and hand them to me when we got to your house. But if they weren't wet enough, I'd give them back to you, drive around some more, and make you try again."

■ ■ ■

Karra was twelve when she started wearing the tiara on her birthday—a year after the lady at Mrs. Winner's had given it to her.

Up until then, her tiara time had been more intimate—only wearing it when no one was around, no eyes to witness her secret father/daughter ritual. She would put the tiara on and play with miniature ponies until she got sleepy. She didn't particularly like ponies, but no matter the number of times she'd said this aloud, her father didn't hear her, chose not to believe her, or assumed she was being coy and continued to buy her toy ponies of all sizes at every one of her life milestones. False premise aside, the ponies became part of their history and, after he was gone, her playtime with them—the tiara perched upon her head—made her feel warm and fuzzy and snuggled. But only when no one was watching.

Not even Mom. It was after that first year that the tiara had become public—coming out annually to help her twinkle brighter than the people around her on her birthday.

So many years, so many memories later. She lived on her own now. An hour from where she'd been raised and twenty minutes from where she'd graduated from college. The tiara hadn't gotten much play during her college days. Mainly birthdays and a ten-minute stint during her graduation party. Oh, and that one time with Stan, the varsity football player.

The birthday ritual had slowly become sacred. Her self-homage. Something she secretly promised she'd stop once she got married. She was getting tired of waiting, though. Where the tiara used to make her feel pretty, now—pricked by her private promise—it reminded her of her desire for something that seemed so hard to come by in such a small, homogenous town.

Her friend Gisele had scratched that particular itch by importing someone, using the myth of the rich American (and her ample cleavage) to bring a husband back from their last vacation spot. They'd stayed two weeks in Negril, with the hot sand burning up through their feet and legs, then warming into other regions. It was only a few moments after their arrival that the idea of double beds in the same hotel room lost its appeal.

For her part, Karra tried not to think about the Pocket Rocket tucked inside her suitcase, its innocuous pink tube further obscured by the frosted Ziploc bag she'd wrapped it in. It wouldn't do to think about it. Once she thought about it, all she'd be able to do was lament the fact that the bathroom walls of their room didn't reach all the way up to the ceiling.

Gisele seemed to feel it, too—the aura of Eros that hung thick in the air of their hotel. It was even stronger on the beach behind their hotel, where a stroll in any direction—the sand pressing between her toes, the warm wind curling up against her back like an affectionate pet—made Karra feel like stripping for the next handsome stranger she saw. No, it wouldn't do to think about the Pocket Rocket in her luggage or the Jelly Beaver she'd left at home.

After the first hour on the beach, their excited chatter had died down. The effort of talking over the constant breaking and shushing of the waves seemed like too much effort, especially when there was so much idling to be done. She noticed Gisele make eye contact with a well-muscled Jamaican man—like anything Gisele ever did was subtle—and when he came over to flirt, his eyes resting more often below Gisele's chin than above it, Karra strolled into the ocean to give them a moment alone. When she came back—absent just long enough to drench her body from sandy French-manicured toes to just above nipples hardened by her own fantasy of quality time spent with a slow-accented stranger—they were gone. She hurried back to their room to unpack; couldn't get the Ziploc bag open fast enough.

Night in Negril was different. Soft. Undulating. Wet. Karra found herself thinking of it as a big, moist punany—her own—juicy and eager for the feel of hard muscle and large, slightly coarse hands. She wanted those hands to clutch, hold, and subdue her while long, slow pumps eased in and out of her until morning. The thought was enough to make her legs tremble.

The Pocket Rocket became her best friend, vibrating her into nirvana while she lay splayed on one of the recliners scattered across the long stretch of beach behind the hotel. Enjoying the thrill of pleasuring herself on the move, and fearful that Gisele and her new man would walk in on her if she did it in the room, she'd christened twenty different recliners by the time they checked out.

Gisele asked her to be the maid of honor at the wedding. Neither Karra nor Gisele expected it to last, but Gisele felt it was better to have been married once and divorced than not to have been married at all. Some days that made more sense than Karra liked to admit.

Back in Nashville, Karra was bothered by the flat land and the boxy grid of the street design. She wanted out. As a consolation prize, she became obsessed with the idea of sensuality in motion: the sense of something fleeting, almost ephemeral, but made poignant by the thrill of taking a risk. If she couldn't figure a way to get out of Nashville, if she couldn't find a man within

Nashville, she could at least have some fun. She had previously considered herself shy and was made into a liar by her actions, racking up stories the way one collects receipts—passing through men's lives like an errant bus, stopping just long enough to enjoy a moment before moving on.

There was the time she asked the corporate-suited brother for one of his chicken wings. All the more delicious (the moment and the food) because she'd walked into Hooters and sat next to him to do it. She'd seen him in the front window, hunkered over a large wooden tray of jumbo-sized chicken wings, orange and shiny with hot sauce. She had just picked up an application from B. B. King's. Not that she had the time, but what her day job lacked in the opportunity to vet possible soul mates she hoped she could rectify at B. B. King's. Who was she fooling, she thought, balling the application up into a tight wad just before she caught sight of him.

He was close to midnight in complexion and bald, with thin stylish glasses that made him look like he didn't belong in a town like Nashville. The spicy wings were making him hot, and silvery pinpricks of sweat shined out from the invisible stubble on his head. She wondered if she could make him sweat harder without even touching him. When he offered to buy her a plate of her own wings, she demurred provocatively: "I'd rather eat yours," she said, sucking on a piece of bone. Then she got up and walked out, satisfied with the sexual tension and the look of disbelief she was sure he'd be wearing for the rest of the week.

Then there was the painter. Later, he said he'd noticed her when she was still two blocks away, her peach shirt fluttering to reveal brief glimpses of her champagne-colored skin and gym-toned abs. He didn't know then that she was on her way to the same bar he was sitting in, a loose collection of married men using his visit to town for an art exhibit as an excuse to get out of the house. All that info came out of him in a gushing rush after she abruptly kissed him. At the bar. In the middle of one of his sentences. It was both impulsive and satisfying; the fact that she could make a grown man babble was its own reward.

She pumped a man's gas once. A dreadlocked brother in leather boots, creased linen pants, and a red-striped shirt with French cuffs. She was always attracted to the men who didn't look like they were local. He put the nozzle into his car—an expensive-looking collection of rounded curves—and was rooting in his pockets for money as he walked inside the gas station. When he came out, she was pumping his gas: black ankle-strap stilettos, miniskirt, black tank top, dark shades, and all smiles. He called her for a month, but the moment had traveled past her as soon as his tank was full.

Her "wild" phase had given her enough stories to feel less anxious. Slightly. By the time her birthday rolled around again, she was both jaded by risk and comfortable with it. She donned the tiara again, secretly hoping that by next year she'd be married off and could put the tiara to rest except for *inspired* special occasions.

When Karra saw him at the bar—his NBA-sized height taking up most of the space—she figured this would be her last bold, underscored, show-no-fear moment. When she recognized him, she had to fight every romantic impulse she'd ever had to avoid believing this was kismet, fate, her destiny. Unconsciously, she started playing with her naked ring finger, but the fact that he was still married threw a wrench into her plans to spend the rest of her life with him.

She needed a drink. She needed some backbone. She hoped he wouldn't challenge her after she said she wasn't coming home with him. She wouldn't be able to hold her ground twice. But she really, *really* wanted him to challenge her. Make a liar out of her. Prove that she was as hot in the pants for him as he thought she might be. But there was her dignity to think of. With the eyes of her girls darting over to watch her, she just couldn't knowingly sleep with a married man. Even if this married man was her favorite singer of all time. The one she had a screen saver of, the one she'd Googled once a month to see if he was up to anything new. Her very favorite. Of all time. And he wanted to take her home. She needed another drink.

The fantasy was fun. It helped. A happy medium, of a sort. She'd played with gusto. Telling him all the nasty things she would do to him if she had the chance. It made her self-conscious, the dirty talking and the fact that they were talking dirty in a room full of people, but the thrill of it outweighed the knot of embarrassment in her stomach. She told him she'd do things that she'd never dreamed of trying in real life. Her imagination fueled by his reactions (narrowing eyes, licking of lips, clenched fingers, the bulge in his pants). She whispered of taking him into an airplane bathroom, using two of her fingers to plunge herself—getting ready for him, making sure his large member would slide right in. Her other hand would stroke and squeeze to the rhythm of his own throbs—bringing him so close to the edge that, once she took him inside, she'd only have to pump once to feel him spasm into back-jerking spurts.

After that, he could barely contain himself. She quit the game then. Left him wanting more so he'd remember her, and maybe even track her down, if ever he got that divorce. Not that she was counting on it.

■ ■ ■

It wasn't until they were miles down the road, after her girls had finished teasing her about leaving her own birthday party for some stranger at the bar, that Karra told them who he was. When she did, the car fell silent. They pulled over and turned off the radio.

"Are you serious?" one of her girls asked. She nodded, her eyes locked into the distance of Nashville's flat, rolling darkness.

"And you didn't leave with him?" another asked.

"He's married," she replied simply.

"Girl, you're a better woman than I." This was from her best friend. They shared a love of most things, including tastes in men and music.

"Yeah . . . well, we *did* create a little fantasy." She smiled and they all squealed at once, lightness and laughter returning to the car as they begged her to tell them what happened.

They were all too tipsy and caught up to realize that the tiara had been forgotten on the bar. The bartender picked it up and put it in her bag out of spite for lack of a tip. I know just who to give this to, she thought.

■ ■ ■

The tiara twinkled shamelessly in the passenger seat. If it shined brightly enough, it might entice the bartender to put it on . . . and then it would be time to travel again. New journeys. New explorations. Hopefully beyond Nashville's borders this time.

THE FIXER

Sandra Kitt

The first time I saw him he arose from the sea in the night like Neptune, only naked. The water had been calm, flat, and impenetrable. His sudden appearance scared me, but when I saw how defenseless he was in the altogether, I realized I had the upper hand. I was protected in my swimsuit, aware that it was a public beach and even at midnight anybody could come along.

I didn't move. I just sat there watching the gently swinging pendulum of his penis—it was certainly long enough to qualify—wondering if I was hallucinating or just lucky.

The resort where I was staying in Sicily, below the fortress town of Taormina, was dead quiet this time of night. Spread out around colorful gardens and acres of pine trees were individual round visitor huts. I'm told the units are almost invisible during the day, from the sea and the opening of the bay. I glanced surreptitiously behind me to see if there was anyone else around, and, of course, there wasn't. All the action—the music and open-air restaurants crowded with late diners—was taking place in the town less than a mile away, and seven hundred feet above sea level. I had chosen to sit alone on the beach, facing out to the Ionian Sea, thinking what I was going to do with myself for the last few days of my trip to the Italian island. I was still pissed at being deserted by my two best friends, Janet and Sioux, who'd each abandoned our planned vacation.

I'd been left behind like excess baggage.

So here I was, sometime after midnight, searching the sky for constellations and watching the slow, silent glide of small boats across the opening of the inlet as they passed behind a large rock formation called the Isola Bella. I felt like the only person in the world, but his appearance proved me wrong. There were now two of us, like Adam and Eve. And you know what happened to them.

"Ciao," he greeted me, standing in the surf up to his knees, rivulets of water running off his body. Tall and olive-skinned, he had a narrow swatch of chest hair that ended just above his belly button and picked up again in a dark bush at his groin, seawater dripping from the end of his penis.

"Ciao," I answered calmly. It was one of the twenty-five words I knew in Italian. "Are you for real?" I asked in English.

"What do you think?"

He had an accent I couldn't identify, but his English was perfect. I could tell from the tone of his voice that he thought my question funny. He came out of the ocean, his hands sweeping water back from his short wavy hair, and stopped right in front of me.

I didn't move. My gaze was on his dick, which was practically at eye level. I don't know if it was deliberate or if he just didn't care. Suddenly, I didn't either. *Was* he for real? If he was a dream, he was the best one I'd ever had.

"Do I look real? Would you like to pinch me to find out?"

"Where?" I shot back, amazed that I had the audacity to tease him.

He laughed, checking me out.

"What are you doing on the beach at this hour? It is not safe."

"Are you saying I should be afraid of you?" Suddenly, a chill swept through me. Had I been foolish? But I didn't move.

He smiled. "Perhaps I am the one who should be afraid."

That I might pull you down onto the sand and have my way

with you, I thought. Then I shook my head. Where did that come from?

"As you can see, I am at your mercy," he said, sitting next to me.

He was completely at ease with himself, and I felt no threat. I might not have been so cavalier back home in Los Angeles, but Sicily, with its relaxed atmosphere and openhearted tolerance for joie de vivre, seemed a place to take risks. Life takes peculiar turns, and surprises come out of nowhere when you do things you wouldn't ordinarily do. Janet's encounter was a good example. Yesterday, she'd decided to have dinner with a shop owner, after spraining her ankle in his store. I'd told her she was out of her mind. Suddenly, it didn't seem so wild a chance to take.

The stranger seemed content to keep me company while he silently gazed out to sea. He'd found me doing the same, but there was no getting around the fact that he was still naked. I'd been feeling a sensual warmth and lethargy sitting in the water up to my hips. I'd even been thinking wickedly about taking off my suit and allowing myself a shameless lack of restraint. Like when I'm in the tub submerged in the water with just my knees and breasts bobbing above the surface. I close my eyes and feel the water gently buoying me, swaying me, lapping at my nipples and making them hard, stimulated by my own concentration and thoughts of erotic pleasure. I'd start to sweat in the scented heat. Perspiration would bead my cheeks and forehead. I'd spread my bent knees and feel myself opening, a delicious swirl of moist desire filling me.

His presence was starting to have an effect on me. Eighteen months had been too long a time since I'd last been with a man. I covertly watched him, my imagination creating possibilities. I wasn't desperate, but I was thirty-seven. Way too young to give up giving it up.

"Are you staying here at the resort?"

His voice jarred me back to the present. Flustered, I stammered. "Yes, I am. I came for the jazz festival."

The fantasy faded, but the pooling of warm desire increased between my legs.

"Alone?"

"No. I came with two friends," I answered with a half-truth. I thought admitting I was alone on this romantic Mediterranean island would sound so pathetic. And dangerous.

Sioux had returned to L.A. and her fiancé two days after our arrival, lured by two things: He'd sent her flowers by wire to make up for their pre-trip argument, and by her realizing that there was enough temptation in L.A. to possibly entice him to turn to someone else for solace. The expense of the trip wasn't even an issue since Sioux hadn't paid for most it anyway. Such are the privileges of being an account executive with a major airline. Janet had tripped and sprained her ankle outside a shoe store the day before and had accepted the attractive owner's invitation to let him take care of her.

I posed the same question to him.

"What about you? Are you on the island alone?"

His laugh was quiet but rich. "I am here with my quartet. We play in the festival every summer. I know Sicily very well. Your friends, where are they?"

"Out on dates," I lied. He didn't need to know that my friends were not returning for the duration of the trip.

I felt his gaze on me. I tried to pretend indifference to his presence, and confidence in my own.

"And you are here by the sea, daydreaming."

"I don't mind."

"I understand."

"You do?" I had a feeling that he did. "Can I ask you something?"

"Why am I swimming naked at night?" He laughed. "Why not? I could not do it in the day. But at night . . . the beach belongs to me. It is quite relaxing. Like when you take a bath, no?"

Yes, I thought, pleased that our thinking was the same.

"Aren't you afraid you'll be seen?"

"I have. By you," he murmured, low and caressing.

I felt my heartbeat skip. There was a slippery warmth between my legs, and he hadn't put a move on me.

"I didn't expect to have company, but you did not go to security."

"I'm thinking about it," I said, testing him.

"No, I think not."

He spoke with quiet assurance, in a way that made me feel like a coconspirator. I liked it. Suddenly, he reached out and touched my arm with a strong, cool hand. I jumped but didn't move away.

"Shhhhh," he whispered.

I sat still. His hand remained on my arm, and I sensed possessiveness to his touch that was exciting. His fingers became warm on my skin. At first I couldn't hear anything, except for the quiet roll of the water onto the shore and the swish of tree branches in a sultry breeze.

"Listen," he said, removing his hand.

I suddenly heard female laughter, then a man's voice. And then his laughter mixed with hers, light and playful. It sounded, at first, very far away. I looked around but only saw row upon row of carefully aligned beach loungers with blue canopies, waiting for the next day's arrival of hotel guests and day-trippers.

"There." He indicated with a nod.

I looked, and perhaps fifty feet away I saw movement. It took only a second to make out two bodies on a lounger where a man and a woman were making love, their bodies clasped together in need. The low murmuring of their endearments became moans that reached my ears. Listening, I was getting wetter, my heart pumping. I closed my eyes and looked away. I didn't need to see them. My body was in tune with theirs and, despite being in the open air, I felt like I was suffocating, my mouth dry.

From the distant lounger came the sounds of pleasure. There was something carefree and innocent about the couple's disregard of being in public, as if what they were doing was the most natural thing in the world. It was. Suddenly, all movement stopped and everything was quiet again. I didn't look to see what they were doing now.

"Are you ashamed that you listened?" he asked.

I shook my head, unable to answer. It wasn't shame; it was

envy. I looked at him, half reclined in the sand as he leaned back on his elbows. My attention was drawn to his penis, which had risen from his groin in full erection. I was glad to see he'd been equally affected.

"Have you been inside the Isola Bella?" he asked, pointing to the great rock outcropping that was like a sentinel at the end of the bay.

"I didn't know it's possible to get inside. What's it like?"

"A great cave dwelling. Dark and wet, but often warm. It's of historic value to this area, but it's also a place where lovers rendezvous. They are not supposed to, of course. Perhaps the couple couldn't get in tonight, and so they ended up here on the beach."

And we watched and listened, I thought, getting a vicarious thrill. Was he suggesting the Isola Bella to me? Did he think I would accept?

"What are you thinking?" he asked.

I was *trying* to think. "I don't know."

"I am sorry if they embarrassed you."

"No, no," I demurred. "That's not it. But making love is, well, so personal."

"No, not personal. Just life," he said philosophically, with a shrug.

Life. Yes, that's all it was. I hadn't been doing much living myself lately. I lifted my face toward the sky, felt my skin being kissed by the July breeze. I closed my eyes and inhaled the sweet scent of citrus, pine, the sea, him, as if all of it would renew me. I needed this trip to Italy for just a moment like this. I could reinvent myself from a successful TV producer with thirtysomething years, and one friendly divorce, behind me. Too much work and not enough play.

On my third day here, after Janet had limped away on the arm of her erstwhile rescuer, I went exploring the area around the hotel. I remember passing an old man walking his bicycle up a steep inclined street toward me. The basket over the front wheel was loaded with fresh fruit. He'd smiled and handed me an apple so fresh that it still had leaves attached to its stem. Just like that, instantaneous and unplanned.

"*Prego, mangia,*" he ordered me with a smile. *Please, you eat.*

A gift, I'd thought, readily accepting it. From a stranger. From the gods. Like the man next to me. I looked and found him watching me.

"Have you been to Sicily before?"

I shook my head. "This is my first time to Italy."

"How do you like it so far?"

"It's charming," I said, inhaling the sea air and immediately feeling giddy. Was it the air or him?

"What have you seen?"

I shrugged, embarrassed. "Not very much. I've walked the streets of Taormina and visited the daily market and the Piazza Duomo."

"Yes, the main church. Did you know that Taormina had once been a stronghold for slaves who had risen up against Rome?"

I didn't know, and I glanced at him suspiciously. "Why are you telling me this?"

"It's history," he said unapologetically. "This is an ancient city. Didn't you come to Sicily to experience and try new things? Have you forgotten so soon the couple down the beach? Don't be offended by the truth. Don't be afraid."

"I'm not," I said grudgingly, annoyed at having my dreamy illusions messed with.

He stood up gracefully.

"Would you like to join me?" he asked.

I forgave him instantly. How did he know?

He was too bold, too out there . . . too inviting. I hesitated, but I had a feeling of sudden urgency. This moment would pass. It was now or never. I knew that if I denied myself now, I'd have regrets later.

I stood up, too, and slowly peeled off my wet suit. The night air caressed my skin. I tossed the suit onto my beach towel and faced him. He smiled at me, dimples grooving his cheeks. I hoped it was appreciation for what he saw.

He held out his hand, and I realized he meant not to drag me to the ground and ravage my body like I wanted him to, but to lead me into the sea.

"I'm not a very good swimmer," I confessed.

"We will not be swimming," he answered, sounding a little amused.

I gave him my hand, and he held it with such strength and caring that I knew I was going to be completely safe. He walked into the sea, and I followed. The water reached his chest and then my neck until I was standing on my toes. I began to tremble.

"Relax," he whispered, drawing me close.

At last. I wanted to feel his hard body. I wanted to throw out inhibitions, home training, Sunday-school doctrine, and all those stories about serial killers. Suddenly, it seemed so easy to give in. I felt bold and fearless as desire won out against caution and good sense, neither of which had ever done me much good. Prudence faced off with a quickly rising heat of passion. I decided this was no time for logic. *Hell*, I was on vacation.

He held me against his body, and my feet lifted from the sand. His chest was hard and firm, and I was cushioned by the silky hairs. I put my arms around his back and held on. His dick was sandwiched between us, and I couldn't resist pressing my hips against him. He said nothing, but I heard the long, slow release of his breath as we entered the surf.

He turned me around so that now my back was against him. His arms around my rib cage and under my breasts supported me. My legs floated up toward the surface. I felt him push off and his legs also lifted as he began a strong scissors kick that took us a little farther from shore. The water was inky black, and I thought how easy it would be to push me under and hold me down. I rested my head against his neck, his chin against my temple, and silently dared him. Instead, he skillfully held us both aloft with a strength and power that amazed me. I suddenly glanced back to shore. The night lights positioned around the resort were like tiny pinpoints. The beach seemed a little too far away. Would we make it back?

"Are you okay?" he asked.

His breath fanned my cheek. I closed my eyes, exhilarated. "Yes."

"Good. Now I begin," he moaned softly.

A frisson of excitement tightened my stomach muscles. My hands were under the water, holding on to his arms. I felt the hard bouncing of his dick against me. He had me on the verge of total abandon.

One arm held me secure. The other hand found my breast, and sure fingers massaged my nipple. The sensation radiated out from the aureole, engorging my breasts and forcing a moan from my lips. His hand then glided down my stomach, causing a ripple of the nerves beneath, and his fingers threaded through the short, tightly curled hair.

He reached between my legs, and I went completely limp. The touch of his fingers made me catch my breath, the feeling was so exquisite. My inner juices made the motion slick and smooth, and I felt blood pulsing through my veins. I began to grind against his fingers, headed to a climax that would either kill me or make me reborn.

His finger slipped inside, and my toes curled. *Where has he been all my life?* I recalled every man I'd ever known who certainly knew how to do it but who didn't have even a fraction of the imagination and freedom of my sea god. Maybe that wasn't fair. He *was* a god after all.

I tipped over the edge. My mind went completely blank as I came, then lay limp in his arms, water splashing in my face. I didn't even have enough strength to cough when water went up my nose. My muscles still quivering, I released him. If he let me go now, the sea would have me. With my eyes closed I felt suspended, free of earth. The sensation lasted—along with the euphoria—until my feet touched bottom. They dragged through the silt and sand until we reached the shore. He carefully laid me on the sand and brushed my hair from my face. Oh no, *my hair!*

I opened my eyes and he was bending over me.

"How do you feel now?" he asked, smiling down at me.

"You've got to be kidding," I choked.

"You are like a baby," he chuckled.

"What do you mean?"

"You must learn how to *live* all over again."

He spread my legs. First he kissed me there, his tongue exploring me. I could count on one finger the number of lovers willing to do that. I lay there accepting his expert touch. I was still sensitive and the buildup to my peak was quick with a mix of pleasure and pain that left me panting.

I wanted to thank the forces in the universe that had brought us together and allowed me to take a leap of faith, unconcerned with where I would land, or if the fall would kill me.

I suddenly thought of Janet with her Italian stallion, and Sioux with her carefully selected fiancé. A silly grin spread over my mouth. I wanted to thank them, too, for leaving me alone.

I struggled to my elbows as he casually stretched out next to me, watching the sea. Was he already anxious to leave?

"Who are you?" I asked. Although a better question might be, *What have I done?*

"Does it matter who I am or who you are? Our names will mean nothing. Our background and history are pointless. Stay in the moment. It's all we have. Tomorrow is . . ." He shrugged.

"That's too mystical for me," I said, looking down at my body. It gleamed with moisture, and seemed lush and wanton as I lay there, naked. Two hours ago I was afraid someone would catch me on the beach in nothing but my swimsuit. Now I was naked with a stranger. I glanced at him again, still curious. "Do you do this every night?"

"Do what? Swim in the sea or seduce women?"

"Both."

He laughed quietly. "I do not plan these things," he said honestly. "There is enough planning in the other hours of my life. The music, and performing, and travel. The demands of agents, audience, and family."

Oh, oh. I *definitely* didn't want to go there.

"I can control at night what I can't always control in the day."

He dipped his hand into the water, scooping up a handful to watch it slip through his fingers. I was mesmerized as he let the last of it drop on my nipples.

"So, what did we just do?" I asked.

"I gave you pleasure," he said, his voice low and caressing.

So simple and pure.

I sat up and turned to him.

"But, why me?"

"Because you wanted me to."

"How do you know that?"

He smiled. "You didn't stop me."

True.

My gaze swept his body. His penis was limp again, lolling against the curve of his thigh. I boldly reached out and placed my fingertips on his chest. It was surprisingly warm. I let my fingers trail down to his navel. My eyes held his gaze. It was my turn to be provocative and eager.

He lay back but kept his eyes on me. I wasn't sure what I was going to do next. Foreplay was not my area of expertise, as one of my ex-beaux had told me. His loss, I thought as I dragged the tip of my nails across his abdomen. His skin quivered beneath my touch.

I knelt between his legs. As I began gently brushing the sand from his groin, his penis grew. My sea god continued to watch me through heavy-lidded eyes. I took hold of his dick, wrapping my hand around the cool, smooth length of it. I made the skin slide up toward the head and then smoothed it down again.

I got as comfortable as I could on my knees. Bending over his erection, I opened my mouth around the head and felt his penis grow even harder. He didn't make a sound, but his chest heaved as his breathing deepened, and his arousal tightened the sinews in his arms and legs.

I sucked him with reverence and slow, excruciating care. I was praising him. I was thanking him. I wanted it to be as good for him as it had been for me. His hips began to move, his breathing heavy and labored. I sucked harder, feeling his body stiffen. My own hunger grew in proportion to his, but it was my turn to give as good as I had gotten.

I stopped sucking and began licking him, just the crown of his penis. I teased the opening with the tip of my tongue, my breath fanning the flames of his desire.

I controlled his dick with my mouth, freeing my hands to stroke the sensitive skin on his inner thighs, his balls, around the base of his penis, and the penis itself until I knew he was ready to come. He held the back of my head, my mouth opened around him, my lips pressed into his salty hair as he came, his body trembling, knees bent to brace his feet in the sand. I released him from my mouth and sat back, my head spinning with the exhilaration that enveloped us both.

I thought about the couple we'd witnessed earlier, making love. I wondered if we were being watched.

Water rushed over us. The tide was coming in. It was no longer late at night but very early morning. The sky had lost its stars and now glowed in a cobalt blue dawn. I became aware of my surroundings, aware of myself. Naked, on the beach with a stranger whose dick I had just sucked.

He sat up and looked at me. I could now make out his face, the set of his eyes, the shape of his mouth. But I didn't want to know anything more.

"You see, the night holds mystery and surprises," he said

"Only here in Italy," I sighed, feeling satisfied and renewed.

"It can happen anywhere. It's always up to you."

I nodded, knowing he was probably right. "I've got to go," I said.

We stood up together. I grabbed my towel and wrapped it around my chilled body. He watched me, then bent to pick up my swimsuit and handed it to me.

"So. Now day comes," he said, reaching out to stroke my cheek.

His caress was unexpected, and a lovely thought, after everything. I think I understood what he meant. "Yes," I answered. I didn't know what else to say, as the dawning light drew us apart and reality intruded.

We stared silently at each other. Then, without another word, he turned and waded back into the sea to disappear smoothly and without a ripple beneath the water. His head surfaced some distance out, getting smaller and smaller as he swam away. I wondered if I would see him again.

■ ■ ■

I woke with a start, as if realizing I was late for something. I looked at my watch and was not surprised that it was a little past noon. I stretched like a satisfied cat as I tried to recapture what had happened the night before. But had it really happened? I sat up and looked at myself in the bureau mirror opposite the bed. My hair didn't look any worse for wear, especially after having gotten wet the night before. I yawned and realized my jaw was sore. I felt different all over.

Oh yes. Something *definitely* had happened the night before.

The day was already half over and the night only six hours away. I was wondering if he would be on the beach again. This was my last day on Sicily. The trip had been broken almost from the start. Last night it had been fixed. I had yet to pay the fixer for his services.

I opened the window of my hotel room and leaned out to embrace a day glorious with sunshine. The beach area was already packed with visitors who'd claimed lounge chairs early. Even if I'd wanted to sit on the beach for an hour or so, it was impossibly crowded. My customary lounger was occupied. The space in the sand where I'd spread my towel the night before, and where my sea god had come ashore to delight me, was covered with bikini-clad sunbathers and naked babies playing in the sand.

Heads moved and bobbed about in the dark blue waters of the sea as people swam and cavorted. There were at least four small motor launches close to shore, soliciting passengers for a sail along the coast to one of the other bays or grotto caves. The narrow strip of land connecting the end of the beach to the Isola Bella was crawling with people. I smiled complacently. I'd already seen some of the sites, thank you. I knew that when I left Sicily the next day, it would be with a unique souvenir and irreplaceable memories.

I took the three-minute cable-car ride from the lower town up to Porta Ferdinanda, the arched entrance of Taormina. The main street, Corso Umberto, was packed with tourists and music lovers who had arrived for the jazz festival. It was fun to see so many visitors with brown skin who looked like me, although I knew that most of them were not American. I felt somewhat fraudulent being there since I had yet to attend a single concert or performance. But Sioux, Janet, and I had gone to one of the popular nightclubs when we first arrived.

Melodic arrangements wafted out from every street and alley of the small city, blended with the laughter and conversation of hundreds of people speaking a polyglot of languages. I enjoyed the sounds knowing that somewhere within the fortress walls was a performer with whom I'd made beautiful music. I slowly walked the cobblestone streets with no particular destination in mind, wondering if I'd see or hear him.

I stopped at a café and requested *mangiare una piccolezza*, a snack, for my first meal of the day. In just five days I'd grown fond of eating gelato, the creamy Italian ice cream, or sipping cappuccino in the open-air cafés, protected from the sun by a colorful awning or umbrella. Today I had an ulterior motive: people-watching and wondering if I'd see him. And if he should happen by, what then?

The anticipation kept me excited and hypersensitive. My skin tingled with the tactile memories of his touch. My breasts seemed to yearn to be enveloped and massaged, my breathing never quite settling down to normal. I was waiting. I thought I spotted him at least half a dozen times as I wandered from one performance to the next. Was it the bass player behind the dark glasses in the Brazilian band? Or the drummer in another from Tunisia?

The sun was starting to set, casting long, flat shadows on the buildings and streets in front of the town's major cathedral, as I sat through my final concert. There was a trio of black Frenchwomen in the audience as well. We chatted and shared stories about our travels. They wondered at my traveling alone, but I didn't explain how that came to be. After the performance they invited me to join them for dinner. I accepted.

We found an interesting restaurant situated in an alleyway with wide and deep ascending steps. The tables were set in a manner so that there were diners above and below us. The restaurant was semienclosed by the walls of the buildings on either side of the dining area. The lighting was low and romantic, with fat candles in the middle of every table. My acquaintances and I enjoyed a leisurely meal getting to know one another better, punctuated with boisterous laughter over our cultural observations from both sides of the Atlantic. We were aware that we drew the attention of a table of men seated nearby, and at least one of the women accepted a discreetly passed note from a man at the next table.

I was aware that before last night I might have missed today's opportunity. Before Janet and Sioux left me, we would have been three average African American tourists huddled together because there was safety in numbers. I wished them both well, but I knew I was the one who'd hit the jackpot.

Finally, around midnight, after exchanging e-mail addresses and wishing one another a safe trip home, I had no choice but to head back to my hotel to pack and arrange for transportation to the airport the next morning. All the while my mind was on the beach, the quiet sea, a stranger from the water. I was anxious about what could happen, what I would find, if I went down there. So I didn't go.

It was as if I wanted to solidify the previous night. Hermetically seal the adventure in my heart and mind. Not mess with a good thing. I woke panicked around two in the morning. Was I out of my mind? Why deny I wanted to go back to that place he had taken me to before? I didn't bother with a swimsuit. I hastily wrapped myself in a towel and went down to the beach.

He wasn't there.

Disappointed, I sat on the edge of the sea with my knees drawn up for warmth. Close enough to the water that it just reached my toes. I closed my eyes . . . and waited. I had to reconcile myself to the truth. Last night had been an apparition. One of those timeless moments slipped into the ordinariness of our lives. The water crept beneath me. I gasped at the cold. How long was I willing to wait?

Where was he?

I opened the towel and lay down on the sand. I had abandoned all reason and propriety because once in a lifetime means just that. I had no regrets, but I was still consumed with wishful thinking. The water rolled over me, almost touching my breasts. The next wave could cover me, pulling me out to sea.

My hands covered my breasts, wishing they were his.

"May I?"

I sighed and opened my eyes. He was standing over me, wet and naked.

"Please." Did I sound relieved?

He took my hands and pulled me to my feet. I couldn't see his features in the dark, but his presence was oddly reassuring and familiar. His hands holding mine made me feel safe.

"I almost did not come," he said with a sigh.

"Why?"

"Last night was perfect."

"But you changed your mind," I noted, feeling triumphant.

"Yes. Because . . . last night was so perfect."

We smiled at each other in agreement.

"You are leaving," he said.

"In the morning."

"Did you enjoy your vacation in Italy? Will you return someday?"

"Yes, and I don't know," I answered. "I'd hoped to hear you play. I couldn't find you in town."

"I'm glad you didn't."

He was right. It would have changed something.

"But, we have this time to say good-bye, yes?"

"We never officially said hello," I reminded him.

"We didn't need to."

He turned me around and put his hands on my shoulders, pulling me back against his body. His penis, erect and hard, nestled at the small of my back. I tried to slow my rapid breathing, not wanting to rush it because I knew this would never happen again.

"There is a legend about Neptune," he whispered softly against my ear, his hands gentle and soothing as he stroked me. "In ancient times, a Greek with his crew sailed his vessel into this place. An offering was prepared for Neptune. But the sea god was very angry because the liver of the sacrifice had not been cooked well. Neptune caused the water to swell and smash the ship. All the crew perished except for the leader. He survived by holding on to a piece of his wrecked vessel as it was carried by waves into the bay to shore. Neptune saw the shipwrecked sailor but decided to let him live.

"The Greek found the island beautiful and eventually returned to his homeland and persuaded his people to return with him. It is said this is how Taormina came to be. Because Neptune saved the life of one Greek sailor."

Was he my very own sea god? I hadn't realized that I might have needed to be saved. What was the moral of the story?

I felt his hands on my breasts, at first merely stroking and cupping them with his palms, playing with my nipples, squeezing them until they were hard. I'd felt like I was on a precipice of anticipation, building all day. Now it seemed possible to come with just his hands massaging my breasts, but that's not what I wanted. My knees were quivering so I sank down to the sand. My towel was soaked but I lay back on it, positioning my body like an offering. He stretched out beside me. His hand glided over my stomach, then moved between my legs. The touch of his fingers was a balm, a blessing as they found my lips and worked themselves in and out. I lay open and willing and completely unafraid.

"Come with me, please," I said. I wanted him to join his body with mine.

"Another time," he whispered in my ear.

So I consented to a promise I knew neither of us would keep.

I felt the spiral of sensual tension start under his fingers. I tightened my thighs, focusing on that one spot, that one feeling. He continued massaging between my legs, creating another eddy of pleasure, another rippling climax.

A moment later he took his hand away and kissed me lightly, sweetly. I lay there as the sea flowed over me. It cleansed my body, cooling me, slowing my heartbeat. When I could finally open my eyes, he was gone.

I didn't feel him move away, didn't actually see him leave. There was no splashing of water as he reentered the sea, and no swimming figure disappearing toward the horizon. One minute he was there, his hands performing magic on my body; in the next he was not.

I didn't feel bereft or surprised. I felt serene and liberated.

I lay listening to the unique sounds of the night, the gentle rippling of the water, imprinting the moment on my brain. After a while I got up, rinsed my towel in the surf, and dragged it around my body. I thought I heard something but could see nothing. I heard it again, someone calling from the sea. It sounded like "*ciao, bella.*" I smiled to myself and headed back to my room.

■ ■ ■

Janet told me all about her adventures the next day at the airport in Catania. She never once asked if I'd had a good time. To be honest, I hadn't given much thought to her or Sioux the last two nights. And I had no intention of ever telling either of them about him. The way I see it, they'd forfeited the right to know when they went off to do their own thing. I was sure neither had experienced Sicily the way I had. Neither would later be able to describe a single thing they'd done on the island, or repeat any significant history . . . or legend.

Janet decided on the flight back that she didn't think she'd ever want to visit Sicily again but had heard that Paris was a happening place. I didn't tell her about the new friends I'd made in Taormina who lived in the City of Lights and invited me to visit. Paris was definitely on my A-list. I had learned in Sicily that I could have a most excellent time without a plan, and without friends, anywhere.

Later I would pull the memory of what happened on the beach from the back of my mind, dig it out of my files of fantasies, and relive those moments in moonlit water whenever I wanted. I came back home with a better appreciation of time and opportunity. And with the knowledge that some things are better left unsaid.

SOUTHERNMOST TRIANGLE

Preston L. Allen

I do not drink margaritas, I do not fish, I do not like gays or Hemingway, and yet I find myself leaving my honey and my honeysuckle Atlanta for the coral paradise of Key West.

Because Mavis is horny.

I drive through Miami, then South Miami, then Kendall, then Homestead, then Key Largo. U.S. Highway 1 thins to one lane. There is water on both sides: the Atlantic and the Gulf of Mexico. Big deal. They look the same to me. Now there is the seven-mile bridge. Didn't Schwarzenegger blow that up in that movie with Jamie Lee Curtis? Now there is land again. Key West. The smell of hibiscus and salt water. The squawking of sea birds. Shell shop after shell shop after shell shop.

And the people. It is a theater of the absurd. The attire is shorts and sports caps, straw hats, fishing hats, and sandals, and goofy touristy T-shirts, and bikinis, even on bodies—both male and female—unfit to wear them. I feel out of place in my coat and tie.

The white people here are dusky from the sun, the black people here even blacker. The look in everybody's eyes is the look of the lazing house cat. The look says, I have eaten, I have scratched, now let's get down to the serious business of stretching out and sleeping all day. An apathetic joy rules the southernmost city in the continental United States. It reminds me of my honeymoon in the islands: Jamaica, the Bahamas, Roatan, Trinidad, Barbados, Grand Cayman, Grand Turk. Becca made me do it. What a Grand bore. Sand. Water. Funny accents. A bunch of sunburned tourists milling about in a small space.

And don't let me start on the gays. I could go on all day. Or perhaps I should say all night. If you pass through Key West at night, you will see the army of dark-haired, bare-chested boys on their scooters. You will see the army of men come out to greet them with kisses and dollar bills. You will witness the brazen back-alley transactions taking place anywhere and everywhere except for maybe the privacy of the back alleys. My bad. Well, of course, the *back alley*.

I pull my Range Rover into their drive, and Chaddy meets me there. He's outside watering his ragged lawn. He is waiting for me.

Chaddy is a brown-haired, brown-eyed, block-headed man with a high forehead still clinging to the memory of curly locks from its youth. He's wearing a khaki T-shirt, baggy shorts, and flip-flops. He drops his hose, which continues to spray, *fshzzz*, and he runs across the yard with his hand extended.

I shake his thick, wet hand. Everything about Chaddy is thick—his cheeks, his shoulders, his fingers. He's a middle-aged man coated in baby fat. He's pumping my hand in his soft, wet grip as the hose goes *fshzzz*.

He's saying, "Good to see you, Cedrick. Good to see you again."

He's pumping my hand like he won't ever let go, as if what happened the last time I was down here three years ago never happened. The hypocrite. He makes me want to puke. Can't he see that I am cringing?

I am going back and forth about punching him right in his thick, sunburned face when Mavis appears on the porch. Mavis in a lavender short set. Mavis with her dreads tied into a single, thick, nappy ponytail. Mavis with her bright eyes. Mavis with a mouth like smiling hearts. Mavis whose skin reminds me of caramel cream. Mavis with legs that go on forever. She smiles at me with eyes half closed. It is a message that takes my breath away, and I am lost.

Chaddy catches me looking and chuckles. He knows the deal. He says brightly, "I've got the whole day planned. Oh, the things we're going to do, Ceddy."

I hate when he calls me that.

Nobody calls me that. It sounds too much like his name. His hand is on my shoulder now. I am walking toward their house, a small colorful box with a high wooden fence and a very large yard full of weeds. I am on the porch. I am hugging Mavis.

Breast against chest, groin against groin, the slightest of grinds, and I remember the way it used to be. How good it is to hold her again. Her softness. Her curves in my hands. I want to lick the smell of spring flowers from the folds of her skin. I want to put my hand on her ass. But after what happened last time, I'm not sure just where we stand.

She bends slightly so that her face is near mine. She is half a head taller than both Chaddy and me. I look into her sparkling brown eyes. She kisses me on the lips. Tongues slide between lips. We're so desperate we clack teeth. I taste her. I am lost again.

I hear Chaddy behind me: "Mmmm. *Niiiice.* Well, let's get started. There's so much catching up to do."

Mavis pulls her lips from mine and scolds him sternly, "Turn off the hose, Chaddy."

He runs to his errand. *Fshzzz.*

Mavis and I kiss again.

I am so hard.

■ ■ ■

Chaddy has the day planned. As always, we make our way on foot. Now we are inspecting shells at Art by the Sea. Now we are perusing novelty condoms at Condom Conundrum. Now we are standing at the landmark that reads, SOUTHERNMOST POINT CONTINENTAL U.S.A. It overlooks the sea, this rusting, gaily colored signpost. On a clear day, I am told, you can see Cuba, which is only ninety miles away.

Chaddy is so clever. He spits on the ground and says, "That spit, my friend, is officially the southernmost spittle in the continental United States." Then he farts. "That fart is officially . . ."

He laughs at his own joke. I don't. Mavis chides him: "Behave!" But she titters, amused.

Now his arm is around her. They have their backs to me. They are looking out toward the sea, toward where they say Cuba can be seen on a clear day. Today is a clear day. I don't see Cuba. I look at them like that. They are exactly what they appear to be. A contented middle-class couple with grown kids they see only on holidays. They are schoolteachers, both of them, Spanish and music. They met in the Peace Corps. Chadwick and Mavis Flaherty. Democrats. Liberal. The southernmost interracial couple in the continental United States.

What do I look like standing there in my tie and coat on this clear, hot day looking at them? I look like just what I am. Upper middle class. Okay, wealthy. Yes, I've got a couple mil salted away for a rainy day. I'm nearing forty, a partner at Baker and Steele in Atlanta. I've got kids living at home, twelve and nine, a boy and a girl, Cedrick Robeson Alderman III and Abigail Rebecca. I'm a Republican. My wife, Rebecca, Becca, is white. I don't apologize. I don't explain. I am in love with Mavis Flaherty, and it is ruining my life.

Now we are eating salads at Eden by the Sea. They are both vegetarians. I want a steak, but I'm trying to be nice. When in Rome . . .

I drown my leaves in oil and vinegar and dig in halfheartedly. It is crunchy and cold. I watch their love play, the way he places the celery against her lips, the way she places the lettuce against his. Mavis says he got her into leaf loving. But every once in a while she sneaks out behind his back to Burger King or KFC. She is a Southern gal, after all. Has to have her fried chicken. Her grease. In fact, sometimes, when he's out of town, she cooks steak or pork. Other than that, she claims, she is one hundred percent faithful to him. And this I know because I've tried unsuccessfully to see her behind his back.

There are no secrets between them. None at all. Which perhaps explains why it ended between us the way it did three years ago.

He's stalling. We need to get down to business, but Chaddy is stalling. I can feel it.

The sun is dying beautifully in the west. Darkness is encroaching. I hear the buzz of gay motor-scooter boys as they begin to appear like pretty-faced ghouls. Chaddy and Mavis Flaherty are necking on the picturesque corner of Duval and Eaton like horny teenagers. He is wearing white-on-white kente cloth. She is wearing a white sundress quite filled out with her hips. His hand is on her ass.

He's stalling. He fears what I am going to say.

I'm standing at their side, in my tie and jacket, smoking a cigarette. Wondering if I will go through with it. I have fears, too.

You see, I love Mavis. And she loves me. But not in the way she loves Chaddy.

And I hate him. And he loves her . . . and me. And maybe he loves me in the same way he loves her.

This is our pitiful triangle.

I have no problem having sex with another man's wife, especially a white man's beautiful black wife, especially a woman who can make me rock hard with a touch, but I draw the line at having the husband whisper, "I love you, Ceddy. Oh my God, I do!"

I am a 100 percent heterosexual male.

■ ■ ■

When I met Mavis some four years ago, my beloved Becca and I were having extended-family problems, which had my head in a real bad place. I had come to Key West to work on the ARCO case, which by the way I engineered and won. I am a tenacious litigator and negotiator. I am good at getting what I set out to achieve.

It was a hot, rainy night. Mavis was singing at a lounge called the Bogey Bacall. She was singing "Misty" and doing a damned good job of it. She is a contralto, which is the right voice for that

song. As a matter of fact, "Misty" had brought Becca and me together, so there was that.

Mavis sang as I downed my whiskey sour and ordered another.
When she finished, she sang it again, as though she'd read my
mind. And the rain kept coming down.

I found her to be a strikingly beautiful woman, and I became
consumed with her presence. My eyes followed her deliciously
swaying movements. Her chocolate skin. Her lustrous salt-and-
pepper locks. Her full backside. Her legs that went on for days
and days. She was nothing like Becca, a thin, small, blonde
thing. A waif. This was a *woman* before me, full, graceful, and
strong. I began to imagine what it must be like to hold her and
to be held by her. I would like to make love to a woman like
that.

Indeed, my childhood at our Cambridge estate and my school-
ing at Exeter, Yale, and Harvard Law had afforded me few en-
counters with qualified *sistahs,* as they say. I had always subscribed
to the philosophy that blondes have more fun. Becca is a judge's
daughter. I don't apologize.

I was much surprised and pleased when after her last song
Mavis, billed as Mave, came over to my table, as they were bring-
ing me a third whiskey sour. I think I said something corny like,
"Sit, you're the woman of my dreams."

She sat, and we struck up a conversation. Her voice was as sultry and sexy as a love song. Her accent was Southern without
sounding backward or ignorant. She was the most beautiful
woman I had ever met. I was entirely under her spell.

I learned that she was an educator. The singing was something
she did on the side for extra money, she explained. She came from
a family of musicians spread out over Memphis, Mobile, and New
Orleans. You should meet my brother, she said. He did session
work with the Temptations. And my uncle played bass for the
Nevilles. And my sister—you would have liked my sister, she
said—but she's not with us anymore.

I nodded sadly, and she smiled a weak smile that reminded me
of someone I used to know, and then continued to chatter on,

mentioning names and more names of singers and musicians, some of which my clouded mind told me that as a black man I should have heard of. I kept nodding. I kept smiling. I kept thinking how lucky I was that she was still smiling at me. Then she said that she was married.

"Uh, but," I slurred.

"Oh no," she said, putting her hand on mine. Her touch sent electricity through me. "You should meet my husband. He would approve of you."

We stood up and stepped out into the rain.

■ ■ ■

It rained, man, it rained.

The sweet smell of rain. Rain is a portent, no doubt. We had no umbrella. She had walked to the club, and my car was back at my four-star. Key West is a walker's paradise. She took off her shoes and held them in her hands as she tipped through the settling water in her bare feet. Wound around each of her curvaceous ankles was a ring of tiny, bright shells strung together by a kind of knotted twine. I followed her through the rain, newspapers held over our heads. Watching her pretty feet. Watching her shapely bottom.

On the porch of their house, she winked at me and said, "I can't wait. I need to try some of this now. I am so wet."

She went down to her knees.

The gate of their high, unpainted fence was still ajar, and I worried that passersby could see us from the street. Then the door of her house swung open. There stood her husband, a blocky white man. She was on her knees with my dick in her mouth in the rain, as he stood mute in the open doorway checking me out.

He extended a hand and said, "I see you met the wife. Come in. Come in, you'll catch your death of cold. I'm Chaddy."

But I couldn't move. I couldn't budge. Mavis wouldn't release me until I had come on her tongue.

■ ■ ■

There was no time for the bedroom. My ravishment took place on the couch. Her mouth on my mouth. Her mouth on my nipples. Biting hard, harder, until I cried out. Her mouth on my dick.

Mavis had small breasts but big nipples. I sucked on them. Her pussy hair was unshaven and wild-smelling as she pushed it into my face. She tasted like sweet, earthen rain. My dick replaced my mouth in her bush. Her pink, naked husband, with his hand on my back, assured me, urged me on. Mavis's husband held my hand as I fucked her. It was . . . weird.

I fucked harder. I was trying to prove something. I was trying to show him up. Then Mavis climbed on top and fucked me. She showed me up. Then she fucked him. And he her. But she wanted my dick in her mouth, too. In her ass.

We tried a couple ways, but I was either too big or his kept slipping out. It worked better when she got on top of him facing him (though I missed seeing her face—she has beautiful dimples) and I positioned myself carefully behind her. She had a big ass, so it was nice. Her back door was as accommodating as her front, a bit tighter perhaps, a bit dryer. We found our rhythm after a few tries. It was real nice. We all came at the same time and collapsed in a heap. Then she climbed over him and kissed me on the mouth. Just the tip of her tongue touching my lips delicately and those doe eyes fixed on me with something like love. In no time, I was hard again. I am Superman tonight, I thought. Superman!

I entered her. She sighed against my ear. The fabric of the couch moistened with our juices was cool and wet against our joined skins as we began to rock again. There was a smell all around, of perfume, baby lotion, salt water, and hibiscus. I did not come this time, though she did, but we made sweet friction like that, and held each other until the sun came up.

Her husband, worn out from the earlier configurations, slept contentedly beside us.

■ ■ ■

In the morning, there were quieter though unabashed introductions all around, a shower (the three of us), breakfast, and a tour of the house. Back in the living room, I spotted the framed portrait of the young woman on the mantel—I picked it up.

Chaddy and Mavis were behind me. Chaddy was chattering on about something mindlessly. Mavis put her hand in mine. She explained about the picture: "That's not me. I never looked that pretty even when I was that young."

"My God. She's . . . beautiful," I said. "I mean, you're beautiful, too."

"Thanks. It's my sister. The one I told you about. The one who died in the accident. We kinda look alike. Everyone gets confused."

I nodded.

"Wasn't she pretty?"

I nodded sadly at the photo of her dead sister. Then I looked up from it. "You're pretty."

I was going to say something further, but Chaddy had put his mouth on her nipple, and her hand had fallen from my hand to my crotch. I had to meet the ARCO people at noon. We still had a good hour left. We went into the bedroom.

It was a good hour.

I still could have gone either way, I guess. But I went back to Atlanta and my family with my head full of ideas. Becca was so beautiful. My children. Key West had all been a dream. I tried to behave as though none of it had happened. This was the end of it, I decided. It was a onetime thing. Leave it at that. But I found myself like some teenager sneaking off to masturbate in the restroom at work every day. I went online and viewed the bodies of nude black women. I was hungry for it. I rented porn and got Becca to watch it with me. She liked it okay. She thought she understood. She blew me without my asking. She was very wet when I fucked her, but said no to the anal. "For your birthday," she promised with a reassuring kiss. This was our deal. Anal once a year, if I was a good boy. "You know I have to build up to it."

It took four weeks of that before I called them. Chaddy answered the phone.

"Hey man."

"Hey man."

"This is—"

"I know who it is." He chuckled. Not maliciously. "We couldn't get you off our minds, either."

"Yeah." I was relieved.

"Mavis is something else, huh?"

"She sure is."

"I'll tell you something. There's been no one since you. We haven't even thought about it. Anybody after you would be a letdown."

"I got some time next week."

"We'll be here."

"Okay."

"She is beautiful, isn't she?"

"Yes," I said. "You're a lucky man."

"The way she sucks your dick—beautiful. You are beautiful," Chaddy said.

■ ■ ■

Over the next few months, I had nothing on the brain but Mavis. She was a most frustrating contradiction.

She would lie with me in bed and sing to me until I was asleep. She would awaken me with a breakfast of fruit juices she had hand-squeezed especially for me. Mango, lemon/lime, papaya, pineapple, sea grape. She would paint my fingers and toes to match hers. She would put rings on my toes and kiss them. With scented oils, she would grease the hairs of my pubis and brush them flat with a soft-bristled hairbrush. She would go to sleep with my penis in her mouth. All this she would do with her husband there. She would never see me alone.

Over the months of our loving, I tried to tell her. I tried to explain, but he was always there so I had to say it in code:

"One black woman, just one my whole, entire life, before I met you. Back in prep school. I was fifteen. I could have loved her, and perhaps I did, though my father says no. She was a teacher. She was older than me, of course, but young, in her twenties, and very beautiful. She had a rich honey-brown complexion. She had a pretty face, like yours, with such big, sensuous brown eyes. Her breasts were small, like yours, and with the same big, dark nipples. Her hips were wide, and her backside was broad and as perfectly rounded as a basketball. And she was a tall woman with long legs."

"Like mine?"

"Just like yours. But yours are better."

"She was either a giraffe . . . or a man in drag," Mavis joked.

"Don't be silly. She was beautiful—like you. And she was my piano tutor." Hint. Hint. I looked longingly into her eyes.

"Oh," she said, the light beginning to dawn, "you like long-legged musicians."

Before I could answer, Chaddy interrupted, spoiling the mood.

"Ah, the music thing," he said, and he was off on one of his tangents. The great musicians he had known in his life. The musical talent he had introduced to the world. The children at the school with promise he had his eye on. On and on he yapped. But Mavis sat enraptured, listening to him.

I got so miffed whenever it ended like this, with him taking her attention away from me. I would sulk. They pretended not to notice.

It mystified me. How could she not want to be with me?

Over time, my jealousy turned to fatalism. I had to have her for myself or I would put an end to it. I would go home and never come back. I tried several times to end it, but they would call, "We're sorry. We didn't mean to hurt you. We love you. Let's give it another try," and I would board a plane or jump in the car and come down.

They owned me. The way they were playing me, I was losing my mind. This woman, Mavis, so beautiful, so warm and willing, she had me quite under her spell.

The way she could get me hard again by rubbing the head of my dick against her untrimmed bush. The way she would drain every drop out of me. The way she would lie asleep on her stomach with her ass exposed. The way her pussy would open like a flower inviting a kiss. A lick. It really is the most beautiful pussy. Its lips are red and wet and always swollen within its unruly tangle of black curls. Always ready. Mavis used to complain, "It's always wet, Cedrick. Wet for you." I believed her.

Chaddy agreed. "You see," he would say. "This is why we need you. Her pussy is never wet like that for me. Since you have come into our life, Ceddy, we have wanted no one else."

Then he would pat me on the back, congratulations for a job well done. Or he would peck me on the cheek.

Which I did not like.

■ ■ ■

Now I have driven down to tell them how it's going to be from now on. But Chaddy is stalling on the picturesque corner of Duval and Eaton in his white-on-white kente cloth, necking with Mavis as the sun sets.

I begin to make indignant noises in my throat. I toss my cigarette, still burning, near his feet. Chaddy gets the message and we begin to make our stumbling way back to the colorful little house that the Flahertys call home. Yes, we stumble. I forgot to mention that we had stopped off at several bars where I drank more than I should have. Key West is a drinker's paradise. I drank because I am steeling my resolve.

I follow them into the house and close the door. We are stumbling against each other. Tottering. They reek of the sweetness of liquor. They are holding each other and trying to hold me. I am struggling not to be touched, especially by his big, thick white fingers. I am at the end of my manners. The thing has to be said. I have driven almost half a day to say it, so I must say it. I have given up so much. I push away from their grabbing, their tickling, even from her lips on my neck. I escape to the other side of the room, where I am free of them, where I can say what I've come to say.

I am at the fake fireplace, its mantel lined with photographs of Mavis and Chaddy in happy embrace, and of Mavis's talented big sister who had died so tragically, and of their two children, Gregor, a musician, and Devonia, a dancer, both of them happily unsuccessful in their arts and working as educators until they "make it." They are tan in color. Their faces are beautiful like their mother's. They are thick and block shaped like their father. They remind me of my own sad children in that way.

I turn back to my giddy, groping hosts. I stand in silence at the mantel until they feel the weight of my intent. Their playfulness comes to an end. Chaddy falls heavily onto the couch and lowers his head. He does not want to hear what I have to say. Mavis remains standing, her hands on her hips.

I begin, "You know why I'm here. You know why I've come."

Chaddy puts his head in his hands. He shakes it from side to side. "No. No. Don't do this, Ceddy. Don't. You'll ruin everything."

I am looking at Mavis, and she is looking at me. There is a warning in her eyes.

But I have no choice.

■ ■ ■

On the last day of our loving three years ago, I followed the Flahertys to school.

It was one of those mornings after a rigorous night of fucking. I had grown reckless. I had Mavis on the brain. I planted myself outside the window of her classroom. They were playing the bells and drums that day. I thought I recognized the song. It was a German thing from my piano lesson days. I peeped through the window to see her teaching. I had seen Mavis sexually in every way. I wanted to see another side of her. I wanted to see her with her class. She spotted me and warned me away with a stern look. After the bell rang and the students began shuffling off to another class, she came outside to where I was sitting under a palm tree. We were alone at last. She had only a few minutes before the next bell. I told her in a breathless rush.

"I love you, Mavis."

"I love you, too," she said.

"Then leave with me. I will divorce my wife tomorrow. I will divorce her yesterday. I want to be with you."

"But I love Chaddy."

"Always Chaddy," I seethed. I sucked my teeth in disgust. Her classroom was filling up with students. There was the beating of drums and the tolling of bells. A few faces peeped through the window. I reached for her. "But you said you love me, Mavis."

"I have enough love for both of you."

"Who do you love better?"

"You are my lover. But he is my husband."

"Oh!" I released my anger then. "But what kind of husband is he to let his wife sleep with other men? He's kind of a punk, don't you think? My dick is bigger than his."

"Cedrick," she said, "you are fortunate that we both love you. Otherwise Chaddy and I would be very upset by your words."

"You're going to tell him?"

"There are no secrets between us."

"Jesus Christ. Jesus Christ," I said. "I can't believe you're going to tell him what I said. This is private between us."

"There is no *us* without Chaddy."

"What! Are you crazy? Don't tell him."

"In fact," she said, pulling out her cell phone.

I fled from the southernmost schoolyard in the continental United States. I ran back to their colorful house, where I was staying. I opened the door of my Range Rover and got inside. This was the last day of our triangle, I feared. It was my seventeenth trip down "on business" to be with them. People were getting suspicious. Becca certainly was. It had become so much a part of my routine that I had a number of personal things—underwear, toiletries, a spare shirt and pants—in their closets and cabinets. Would they return home and catch me in the act of packing my things? Shouldn't I just leave everything here and go now? Chaddy, though a pacifist, owned a handgun. I sat in my car and did nothing.

She came back to me on waves of tears.

■ ■ ■

Year one at Exeter, I was fifteen.

Naomi was a teacher. She was tall with long legs. She was my piano tutor.

She taught me to play "Misty," through which I met Becca, who was also her student at the girls' campus. But that is another story.

She wore her hair in big, natural dreads. She had dimples. She was the only black person at Exeter who paid any attention to me. True, the others were mostly cooks and cleaners and security personnel, but they had skin that was the same color as mine and they ignored me. I know that I was a student and that my station in life perhaps was off-putting to them, but I was completely alone. I was away from my family for the first time, and the white people (I don't want to call them deliberately racist because I am not so harsh in my judgment of other people's insensitivity)—the white people were not always kind to me, the little black boy who was as smart and as wealthy as they were.

Naomi would dry my tears at night and give me her shoulder to lean on. Her breasts to sleep on. And in the general frustration with which love confuses itself with lust and anger and sympathy, Naomi took to jacking me off with her talented hand when the unfairness of my situation seemed too much to bear. She offered up her delicious puss for the suck when I believed, yes, truly believed that I could not make it to the next day, that I simply could not go on. She taught me to fuck like a strong, strong man who could make her come over and over again, in the puss, in the mouth, in the ass, and I loved her and she loved me.

Though my father still says no.

She was a woman of low morals, he explained. A tramp. A cheap slut. A whore. You'll meet many more of those before it's all over, let me tell you.

I disagree. And it was a mean thing for my father to say.

When Naomi's indiscretion was discovered, her employment at Exeter was abruptly terminated.

I never saw her or heard from her again.
She never even tried to call.
That was the greatest blow to my heart.

■ ■ ■

It wasn't until years later, through a subtle conversation with her baby sister, that I learned what had happened to Naomi.

"Car accident . . . maybe suicide."

"Suicide?"

"Maybe. Some boy or something at one of those ritzy schools she used to teach at. She started to tell me about it when it went down. Said it was embarrassing. She was crying a lot over the phone. Promised she would give me the scoop when she got back home. She never made it back home. It was a mess," Mavis said.

"A mess? The car accident?"

Chaddy put his hand on my back, dropping in his two cents again. "She was pregnant," Chaddy informed me. "The kid had knocked her up."

■ ■ ■

When Mr. and Mrs. Chadwick Flaherty got home from school that day, Chaddy was more jovial than usual. I was sitting on the couch, fully expecting them to curse me out, or worse. But they were playing with my head again. He told me a joke that he got from one of the kids that day in school, and then he laughed at it. Mavis kissed me on the lips and asked if I wanted to take a shower with her. I shook my head no. Chaddy said, "Well I sure could use a shower," and off they went laughing into the bathroom. Of course, they left the door open. I listened to them frolicking in the shower. Then they turned off the water and I heard them in the bedroom. Chaddy called out, "Ceddy, come in here. It's lonely without you."

"Come on, Cedrick. Come to bed, baby." It was Mavis's sultry voice. My siren song.

I got up and went into the bedroom and sat down on the edge of the big bed where we all three had slept the past two nights.

They were already naked. They undressed me until I was naked, too.

I would like to say Mavis alone undressed me, but that would not be entirely true, no more true than when at night as we all lay in bed after our fucking and I felt a hand on my dick as I was trying to get some sleep that it would always be Mavis's hand. Nor if I felt a mouth on my neck would it always be hers. Nor did I like his strange little comments as he watched me and Mavis fucking: "What a magnificent dick. It looks so tasty." Or Mavis blowing me: "I could help with that, really, if you like." Or me coming on Mavis's stomach or in her mouth: "Yummy, yummy, yummy, that looks *gooood*." And then he would proceed to lick my come from whatever part of her body I had come on.

What is true is that I would always push him away. I am not like that. I am not a pervert.

I was naked in bed with them on that last night of our affair, three years ago. I was holding Mavis close. Holding her, kissing her, running my hands over her tiny breasts and her big ass, but holding her like a shield. Chaddy was rambling, "I love you, Ceddy. Oh my God, I do. I love you. I forgive you for trying to take Mavis away from me, and she forgives you, too. Don't you see we love you? Love means never having to say you're sorry."

But it was too late. I was loving Mavis hard. My fingers were in her pussy. My tongue was in her ass. I was not asking her to forgive. I was asking her to choose. She who had always lived in a liberal world of musicians and artists. Choose the one who loves you most jealously. Choose the one who loves you best. I would never let another man love you. My love would be big enough for you.

I rolled her onto her back, hooked her long legs over my shoulders, and I took my dick, which was bigger than his, and I pushed it into her pussy, which was always wet for me, and I began to fuck her. I fucked her harder than I ever had before. She noted the difference. Her pussy was sopping. She was screaming. She never screamed unless it was anal, and then not like this. I put my back into it and gave it to her hard. I felt her working her hips back at me. I felt her scratching my shoulders with her painted nails. I fucked her and fucked her.

Chaddy was breathing hard, but he had stopped his gabbing. Usually, when I was rocking Mavis, he would be playing with his dick or he would place it in her mouth. This time he just sat naked against the pillow, his dick limp. I fucked her. She pulled me down. She held on to me and fucked me back. She held me tight. She put her lips against my ear and whispered so that only I would hear. "I love you more. I love you more. I don't want to be with two men. I never wanted to be with two men. Keep fucking me. Keep fucking me. Fuck me harder. I love you."

She put her face against my ear, and I felt the warm tears. I knew I was right. I knew I was right all along. She was mine. Mine.

But Chaddy was not beaten yet. He crawled over to us like he sometimes did when he wanted to get a better look. He lowered his head until his eyes were on a level with our thrusting pelvises. Let him look, I said to myself. Let him see how it should be done. Fuck him. He lost. She's mine. Once you go black . . .

Chaddy watched as I put on a show of pure brute sexuality such as he had never seen before. Mavis was sopping her juices all over their bed and whispering love in my ear. Her orgasms had her twisting beneath me. Her ponytail had come undone. Her dreads were splayed out on the pillow like tentacles. Then Chaddy reached between us and pulled my dick out and put it in his mouth.

"What the fuck?" I shouted.

He managed two quick sucks before the spasms hit me. I gushed into his mouth. My head was spinning. I grabbed hold of his balding head to steady myself.

"Mmmm," he said, smiling up at me. Licking his lips.

"The fuck!" I roared, and then I was on him with my fists.

Mavis was hitting my chest, slapping my face, and screaming at the top of her lungs: "Leave him alone! Leave him alone! You bully! You asshole! I hate you! I hate you! I hate you, Cedrick. I hate you!"

■ ■ ■

Oh Mavis. Oh Mavis.

Did you tell Chaddy about the secret things you whispered in my ear that night? Did you tell him about the letters?

But that was then, and this is now, and Chaddy's sunburned head is in his hands. Chaddy is saying, "We love you. We love you, Ceddy. There's been no one since you've been gone."

Mavis's hands are on her hips. There is a look of warning on her face. I don't care about Mavis's hands on her hips or her hard face. I don't care about Chaddy's sobbing, his pleading. I am going to say what I came here to say.

"It took me three years and a lot of soul-searching—"

Chaddy wails, "Mavis loves you. I love you. We were faithful to you."

"—but I can no longer live a lie."

"No, no," wails Chaddy. "Don't break us apart."

"So I'm here to ask Mavis to come away with me. To marry me."

Mavis scowls at me and says, "You ass," but it is just a mask.

She had written that she loved me. She had written about the confusion that was her feelings. She wanted me as much as I wanted her. She cared about Chaddy, but sometimes she just got so tired of the lifestyle. Sometimes she wanted just one man in her life. One man who could please her. One man who could rock her world and make it stick. A *real* man. She had written that she was horny for me and that there was only one way for the horniness to go away that she knew of, and that way was swinging between my legs.

And I was horny for three years reading her letters. Her pleas. But I finally found the strength. Yesterday I told Becca that it was over. That I love someone else.

I tell Mavis, "No woman should have to go through what you go through with him."

Mavis snaps. "What do I go through with him? What? You tell

me. You ran out on us. You didn't stay to work it out. One little argument and you were gone," she says. "After all he did for you—you hurt my baby. I'll never forgive you."

I protest, "But you love me."

Chaddy sobs and sniffs loudly on the couch.

I go over to Mavis and touch her cheek. She slaps me hard on the face.

"You said you loved me, Mavis."

"Love you?" Mavis says. "I was nice to you today because that's the way Chaddy wanted it. He was so excited to have you back, I said okay, what the hell. Let's try to make this thing work. But it's not working. He's so kind, he's so open, he's so generous, he can't see you for what you are: a selfish, insensitive, mean, hateful, jealous man. Don't you see he loves you? He shares with those he loves. He loves me, so he lets me have you. He loves you, so he lets you have me. Love is about giving, but you—you want everything for yourself. Love can't exist where there is greed." She shakes her head. "Look at you. What about your poor wife, the mother of your children? Did you already leave her? Shame on you. I don't see what Chaddy sees in you."

"What!"

Mavis goes over and sits on the couch beside Chaddy, who rests his head on her shoulder.

I am not going crazy. I take out one of her letters. I say to her, "But what about this? The letters."

"Letters?" Mavis says.

"This! You said you love me." I hold it up. Yes. She sent me many letters, at least two a month. Becca finally got hold of one of them about a month ago. I had to make a choice. I chose Mavis.

But Mavis looks genuinely perplexed.

"I didn't write you any letters."

We look at each other trying to figure out what's going on, until from Chaddy there comes a sickly sound, a sort of a rumble that swells from a place deep down. He raises a hand and says, "I wrote them, Ceddy. I'm sorry." Then he turns to Mavis. "I'm sorry, honey. I loved him."

Mavis is cradling him in her arms and cooing, "It's okay, baby. We don't need him. We'll get along fine without him. We'll find someone else. Someone who will love us both."

I am standing there, stunned.

Then Mavis looks up at me and says, "Get out of our house, Cedrick. You're no longer welcome here."

"But—"

"Just get out. Get out," Naomi's baby sister says.

ANGELA

Carol Amorosa

His potent sexuality notwithstanding, Angela made up her mind not to let Blacks weasel his way into her pants. Sinewy, magnetic, and intense, he seemed the right salve for the horny bug bite she'd gotten, predictably, upon landing on the island. He was friendly enough and had already insinuated himself into her yard, but she'd had an affair end badly last trip down. So she vowed next time around that her sexual attentions would be lavished on a lover and not just a fuck. In addition, the intelligence she'd gathered on Blacks suggested thievery, a fierce temper, and a strong suspicion of crack smoking.

She accepted his offer to go to the disco that night with her resolve firm. It would be something to do in a one-horse town, and at twenty-nine he'd be good company, mediating between her old bones and the pubescent rude boys who dominated the dancehall. Angela was in her midforties, didn't look it, but was ever fearful of being outed. She was even more sensitive about her age because she usually ended up with younger men.

She dressed purposefully—clothes she could move in that would show off her molded slimness and hide her potbelly when she danced: capri pants she'd made from brown damask brought back from Gambia, a slinky gold spaghetti-strap camisole that hung below the belly yet above the butt, and her trademark red Converse All Stars.

Angela brushed her teeth, fastened some tiny pink flower clips onto her black curls, now irretrievably nappy from the humidity, dotted rose oil on her wrists, then slicked her lips in coral. It was his lips that she found most perilous. They made her more aware of her own and a little envious. The color of raw liver, well shaped and inviting, they seemed to draw her to him.

■ ■ ■

She stepped into the tiny kitchen of the rented three-room cottage, settled on for its proximity to the sea, though it had "no aesthetic." To simplify her too-complicated world, Angela judged her man-made surroundings as being with or without aesthetic, and placed the living and breathing into those two classes as well. She couldn't help it; her women friends were all foxy, she loved horses and leopards, and she was only attracted to top-of-the-line men.

The kitchen was the least inviting of the rooms, with peeling faux marble Con-Tact paper over rotted wood serving as a counter, a rusted two-burner stovetop, and a cruddy "stainless"-steel sink with a leaking faucet. She washed out her rum glass, its cheesiness providing better service now than when it was host to supermarket-brand jelly. A shot or two of white overproof rum with a drizzle of lime was her afternoon's sidekick while she worked. She placed the glass in a rusted iron drainboard beside a couple of chipped Chinese plates and tinny forks with bent tines.

The kitchen was filled with aromas: a Julie mango ripening in sweet orange acidity, a succulent cashew fruit from the backyard tree fermenting too quickly into brown, and the cloying, scented cloud of a browning banana. Below, the trash, a black scandal bag tied on a hook, exhaled the stink of a rotting snapper carcass, the remains of a late lunch. Life hurries back to its maker rapidly in the tropics and faster still by the sea.

Angela first came to Jamaica on the urging of a friend, also a

painter, who'd been bedazzled by the light at the sea and the sultry, smoky blue of the hills. On that trip she'd experienced her first
hurricane in the tropics. True, as a child the family would make
annual pilgrimages to Puerto Rico to visit the dwindling relatives
there, but those trips were relegated to Christmastime when all
was calm.

She admitted to no one that she felt blessed by that experience.
Only the most intolerably God-fearing who lived in the wake of a
storm's destruction could see it as an act of Providence, and she
chose to have as little to say to those folks as she could. But the
hurricane's fury and ever-changing light touched her irrevocably.
She saw the sky during breaks between ferocious outbursts of wind
and torrent become a screen of cool silver that cast a blue glaze
over the sea and turned luminescent the pale papaya trees outside
the guesthouse where she was staying. Those moments of calm
were infinite and portentous. She was captivated and knew then
that Jamaica would demand some of her best work.

■ ■ ■

Then there were the men. Mikey, a "red," of mixed African and
Scottish blood, small and tight with a black man's nose and a
white man's butt. Uncharacteristically, he was nearly her age, but
he had a fetching boyishness about him. They used to duel with
hoses behind her rented house, then, laughing, their clothes soaking wet, make sloshing love on the hammock.

Mikey was a small-town man, kindly but of limited intelligence
and, more dismally, even less curiosity. But he worshipped and
doted on her, and they'd had some grand times together. Their
lovemaking on occasion was spectacular, as he showered the same
indulgences on her pleasure that he did on her comfort, fucking
her deeply with finesse and real emotion. At night, they'd put a
mattress on the floor of the enclosed veranda and fuck for hours,
the heat of their passion gently cooled by the night air.

Angela had grown to love him and longed for him when they
were apart—but, after two years, she'd gotten weary of his dull-
ness. She'd betrayed her feelings, and they began to bicker. They

called it quits. A foreign woman ending a serious affair in a small town in Jamaica runs down the town as well, she'd learned, when she lost her status as "Jamaican by experience." Soon after she was treated like a stranger by merchants she'd shopped at for years, and ignored by everyone in Great Bay who knew Mikey. And that was almost everyone in town. Even some of the many expats who'd been in her position one time or another seemed to take sides against her.

■ ■ ■

Angela walked into the nondescript parlor and then the bedroom, which was not much more than a painted wooden armoire squared into a corner—a safe haven for mosquitoes—and two creaky single beds on either side of the room. She opened the door to the veranda—breezy, isolated, and with a luscious view of the sea over sentinel boulders and the fisherman's cove that lay one inlet over. She stepped outside to retrieve some paint pots, her watercolor pad, and a jar of water with two sable brushes lounging against the neck. Angela wiped the brushes clean with a paint rag and looked at the painting she'd begun that afternoon; her critical eye rested on the page. She'd spotted a pelican sprat fishing just off the rocks, his bloated beak breaking the water. He'd been kind enough to linger, allowing her to possess his image before he dove into the inky blue current. She'd finished off the aquarelle and gave thanks. She closed the book and brought it inside, knowing it needed work.

Angela turned on the outside lights, secured the windows and doors, then headed up the road to meet Blacks.

■ ■ ■

Angela began staying in Belmont after being edged out of Great Bay the year before. She'd come for two months in the winter and a week here and there other times during the year when she could get away. Belmont was another fishing village, characteristically so, smaller than Great Bay, with fewer Americans but more Germans. She found out right away that it was a major transshipment point for Colombian cocaine. She'd have to keep her New York guard up; the bad business vibe was palpable. But Belmont was picturesque, lined with coves, secret parking lots for paint-peeling wooden boats laden with seaweed-soaked nets and fish pots—formidable traps of honeycomb wire and wattle. The inlets were attended all day and much of the night by generations of fishermen, their spindly dog-bone knees peeping out from under ripped shorts and worn rubber Wellingtons. She loved to get up at dawn and walk the road, looking down into their world, gathering images and the warmth of the waking sun.

After finding Belmont, Angela met Sweats. And, immediately, she put him in the "booty call" bin, knowing she was his booty call as well. He was educated but had a slumbering chi, no worldview, and was always "begging" her for something because he expected everyone else to save him from his material and moral misery. There was little fetching about him. Not even his big dick, which he used perfunctorily and with little engagement. Like Mikey, he'd cook for her. It was one of the few things that gave him pleasure. He was a decent cook, but, like his fucking, his fare didn't much rouse her.

She began to drift back to Mikey but didn't want to give up the convenience that Sweats offered. Plus, having two men was a great rejuvenator, better than a tit-lift. Having to hustle at work wore her down, and she'd begun to feel old, not getting as much attention on the street back in New York. Both men accepted her split time: Mikey because he still loved her, and Sweats because he had nothing invested. Then, satisfying a lifelong dream, Angela went to Cuba. There, Enrique the *brujo* divined that her "younger lover" was no good and that all there was between her and her "light-skinned man" was sex. *"Mentira?"* his rum-soaked mouth purred voyeuristically into her ear: "Is that a lie?" Forced to reckon with the truths she had been resisting, she felt cheap. She returned to Jamaica and ended it for good with Mikey, found Sweats smoking crack, and gave him his walking papers as well.

■ ■ ■

Angela found Blacks, a cigarette dangling from his lips, sitting on the wooden railing outside Timer's shop, where he'd first chatted her up. Timer was a soft-spoken Rasta man, philosophical in that fuzzy Rasta way but not tiresomely doctrinaire. He was astute enough to keep references to the divinity of Haile Selassie at a minimum when she was around. His great failing was his womanizing. He used his shop as a recruitment agency, and he seemed to exact few requirements from witting and unwitting applicants: Anyone with an X chromosome was welcome. Never mind that Timer had a German wife of twenty years and eight mixed children in the house in the back. Almost fifty and Rastafied, with mixed blonde and gray dreads reaching past her knees, Timer's wife, who'd come to Jamaica as Barbara, was now Ethiopi-I and so out of her head that she believed she was breeding soldiers for Jah's army.

The shop sold everything from flip-flops to fishhooks and overproof rum. Its centerpiece was a rickety table out front, the seat of some fierce domino matches. Timer was also known to retail an occasional spliff to a small clientele. His was one of the few commercial establishments that stayed open nights, attracting a collection of regulars and itinerants ranging from the completely mad to girlie-girlies, obnoxious braggarts, and just plain folk.

Angela found herself here most evenings, oftentimes with her friend Indiaman, who had a whip-sharp intelligence and quirky sense of humor, but who skated precariously around the edge of madness. Nights in Belmont without a lover were tough, tougher when spent in a makeshift home with "no aesthetic." The distractions of the shop helped pass the time. It was here from her regular perch she'd seen K.K.'s sister, a bruiser of more than two hundred pounds, deck her lover for not handing over enough cash, and Mrs. Walker chase her philandering husband down the road with a machete after finding him with his dick in the mouth of sixteen-year-old orphaned Cassandra, a sad, lost little thing who was looking for love in all the wrong places.

Blacks and Timer were brethren, as close as one could get to true friends. His homemade shack was in the lane about a hundred feet behind the shop, and he'd often roast a snapper or jackfish from his catch on a wood-burning grill Timer had set up out back. Soon after they'd met, Blacks had invited Angela over for some foil-roasted silver snapper. She'd watched as, intently, he palpated the fish, rubbing its belly with salt and pepper, then slitting its side and inserting scallion links and threads of Scotch bonnet pepper. Finally, he blanketed it lightly with thin tomato rounds. Blacks then wrapped the fish in aluminum foil before setting it over the fire. She had a hint that his handling of the snapper was a metaphor for the way he'd make love: a skillful and patient buildup to a deliciously satisfying climax.

Angela discovered one day during a visit to Timer's that Blacks was nearly illiterate. Noticing him staring at a page in the *Daily Gleaner*, she asked him what the story was about. "Me no know," was all he said, his eyes not meeting hers. Angela redoubled her resolve to stay away from him, irritated with herself for being drawn, again, to an uneducated man—true, she was in rural Jamaica where the literacy rate was under 40 percent. But she constantly saw herself falling short of standards she set for herself and imagined her family and friends in perpetual judgment of her decisions. Then she'd felt embarrassed for Blacks, imagining how painful and demoralizing it must be for him.

Despite this, and to her surprise, they'd found much to talk about, and she was grateful that it was almost never about getting into her pants. Blacks was a virtual encyclopedia of the bush and sea. Fed up with the beatings and belittling, he'd left home and school in the hills at fifteen; he was drawn to the sea. His vast knowledge of curative herbs was the legacy of a resourceful mother and Obeah uncle, known throughout the parish for his ability to commune with the spirits to effect cures. The sea ran atavistically through Blacks's veins. He'd told her about cutting grammar school, lured to the ad hoc ponds sprung up after the summer rains, where he'd splash about trying to capture fish with his hands. Vivid, too, were the recollections of the beatings awaiting him on his return home, a neighbor's report of his exploits having reached the yard before him.

It was, by now, a game for Angela to try to prize the "real" name out of the many Jamaicans she'd gotten to know only by their nicknames. She wondered whether Blacks would reveal his. She ran into him one day standing on the road in a ripped mesh marina having just returned from sea. As she approached, she was accosted by his gleaming blackness. Shaded even darker by constant exposure to the sun, he was almost ebony in the light. The nickname was inescapable, but she was now more curious about his given name.

"So, what's your real name?" she asked him.

"Me no tell nobody, but meh tell you," he said, smiling broadly, his teeth white against his skin. "Meh born Derrick Trevor Wedderburn."

"And when did they start calling you Blacks?"

"Dem call me Blacks when me a pickney, but me no like dat and me always fight dem. But den me learn to love meh color ca' it de one the Father born me wid. Since den me love when dem call me Blacks."

■ ■ ■

Angela found Blacks one morning tinkering with the motor of a friend's perpetually moribund Ford Cortina. He looked up, grabbed a Red Stripe from the cooler, and, leaning against the rusted fender, launched into a ferocious riff on how he was going to build his mother the most elaborate cottonwood coffin, then shoot her in the middle of the night with his speargun.

The vituperative was inspired by his last night's dream of a time he cut school to go fishing, got busted, and was then beaten mercilessly. His mother took salt to the wounds by taking the fish to market to sell and pocketing the cash. His protests merely elicited from her, "I need the money more 'an you." But the next day, Angela saw him jumping onto a minibus heading for his mother's yard to care for her after she'd stumbled and sprained her ankle.

She found that they were becoming friends, but Angela was dutiful in reminding herself that these seat-of-their-pants guys were masters at the cultivation game; she could imagine any number of reasons, besides friendship, for which she was being primed. Was this why he seemed to enjoy her company, seemed to be opening up to her? Vulnerability is rare in all men, she knew, but especially in a hard-skinned, knocked-about Jamaican man.

■ ■ ■

As they walked up the road to the Pebble Beach Disco, Blacks stopped along the way to greet brethren and variously encourage or discourage the kids fishing with long lengths of string off the seawall. As they walked, she gently reproached him for his sugges-tion that he drink a combination of a bush he called *medina*, and ganja leaves. She'd brewed it the morning of her last departure and within half an hour had fallen back into a deep sleep. She had to scramble herself and her bags out of the house not to miss her plane, causing her to wonder if he'd purposely prescribed a sopo-rific. Blacks simply laughed, protesting that for him it worked wonders, better than the coffee he'd given up when he went Ital.

It was about eleven, somewhat early, when they arrived. The flat, sandy ground that served as a parking lot and entrance to the outdoor club was sparsely set with young men in B-boy garb smok-ing ganja. Blacks surveyed the dancehall beyond, his head turning slowly to take attendance. She wondered if he was looking for any-one in particular. She had heard rumor of an incident at Pebble Beach in which Blacks, brandishing his speargun, threatened to skewer a youth who'd tauntingly accused him of being a batty boy. In Jamaica, the last thing you want to be called is a faggot. A quiver of alarm went through her.

The most blissed-out ragamuffins were skanking, glued to posts they'd staked out on the cement flooring not far from the selector's booth, at the ready nonetheless to do battle if his lineup didn't hit the spot or if he overextended or offended in his rap. There were few tables—most folks didn't sit down in the dancehall. Glaringly obvious, but customary, was the paucity of women. Angela had heard several sobering stories of gang bangs in the old fishing boat on the sand, and knew that a number of the girls who were here courted trouble. Most of them were under twenty and were squeezed into spandex pants and tube tops, their taut Brancusian curves spilling out of their clothes.

"Me wan' a Red Stripe. Ya buy me one, mon?'"

"Sure, Blacks, but didn't you catch thirty pounds of snapper last night? You should be buying me the drinks."

She was pushing it. She knew how hard it was for a fisherman to make a living: The waters here were drastically overfished, and rainstorms, breeze, and passive resistance on the part of the fish made it fools' work. At the same time, she was preemptive with everyone in town about not footing Belmont's alcohol consumption bill.

"No problem. Me pay nex time," he replied.

He then headed toward a darkened corner of the dance floor while she turned to the bar. It was a long wooden counter covered in yellowing white Formica, the same scratched and warped surface that covered the rickety domino table outside Timer's shop. Rings of condensation lay on the counter where icy Red Stripes and Heinekens paused making their way from cooler to customer.

"One cold Red Stripe and a white rum with one chunk of ice, please," she made a general announcement. Two women in stained white short-sleeved shirts and short black polyester skirts, their bellies spreading over their waistbands, sat on low stools behind the bar ignoring her. Angela waited. As she was about to repeat her order, the younger looking of the two—Angela judged her to be about twenty-two—stirred and sullenly served her the drinks.

"How much?"

"Hundred an' ten."

"Thanks." Angela handed her a bill for five hundred Jamaican dollars. She debated, then decided against tipping—most Jamaicans didn't and there were times she ruefully stuck to a "when in Rome" policy—and stuffed the change into her pocket. Beer in one hand, rum in the other, she made her way over to where Blacks stood against the bamboo screen that separated the bar from the dance floor. Angela allowed herself a good look as she neared him. He'd started moving easily to the raga dancehall. His movements were loose but understated, sensual. And though he was moving for himself, it was still inviting.

She was sure his ancestry was Senegalese. Wolof: His ears were tiny and round like a jelly roll, his eyes almond-slit—tonight, as most times, the whites deeply veined with red. His skin was near ebony. His shoulder-length dreads were perpetually chaotic, sweater yarn fine. In remembrance of his diving and shoot-fishing days, long gone now, they were tipped in gold. Tonight he'd strewn most of them under a straw jockey's cap he'd plaited. She admired him for his lack of vanity, for not constantly grooming his locks like the rent-a-dreads, arranging them just so, then tossing them with self-satisfied theatrics. On the other hand, she thought he could be so much more fetching if he took better care of himself. But, then again, she reminded herself, that wasn't any of her business.

He wore a crisp white marina mesh shirt incandescent against his skin. His dungaree overalls crackled in their newness; one strap of the bib he'd left undone to flap easily as he moved. He seemed taller than what she'd guessed was his six-foot-two frame, and his muscles gleamed under the bare bulbs. She saw him in shoes for the first time. They were huge, cheap, hard brown, parochial-school brogues, which he left untied; they threatened to fall off should he lift his feet from the floor as he danced. Not to be out-done by the eighteen-year-olds, Blacks was sporting a pair of blackout sunglasses, titanium rimmed and lozenge shaped. A spliff stuck to his lower lip looking small and white like a fleck of saltfish.

"Here's your Red Stripe."

"Give tanks."

"No problem."

"How much ya pay?"

"Hundred ten for the two."

"Ya tip the gals?"

"No, they were feisty and I just figured they wouldn't feel no way 'cause Jamaicans don't tip."

"Yah, mon, dem gals feisty, me know 'em, but dem need the

money more 'an you," he countered as he took a sip and looked around. "You arright here or you wanna move to the nex part?"

"Let's stay here for a little while." Angela stopped and smiled to herself, thinking back to what Blacks's mother had said when she'd pocketed his fishing take: "I need it more 'an you."

He was reeling from the ganja. She'd gotten used to his daytime herb haze but had never seen him in this outer realm. Angela figured in the rough daily life he led, he probably needed to check out. "Yeah, Jamaica is beautiful, but rough," was how she'd counter the all-inclusive bunch she'd meet just back from a week cloistered at Hedonism, believing they'd found their island paradise. "Just go see the movie *Life and Debt* before you book your next trip. Or take a walk through the backstreets of MoBay when you get off the airplane," she'd tell them, offering a reality check.

Angela was cushioning herself with overproof rum. She needed the overproof to feel comfortable. His age. The fact that she was being seen with him and not Sweats. That she was one of the only women there—and a foreign one at that—and skanked just like a Jamaican meant she was being checked out big-time. Tanned, her Latina self passed as a "brownin'," or a "coolie," folks with East Indian blood. But now, still with her New York pallor, she had to gird herself against the "white woman" leers. So Angela welcomed the searing sweetness of the rum as it eased down her throat numbing her lips and tongue.

They danced mostly side by side, raga dancehall-style. From time to time, hand held high in the air, a cigarette threaded through his fingers, he'd move out to face her, but neither fell into step with the other. It would have been a green light for her to do so. Thus she kept to her own rhythm so as not to invite trouble, and he to his.

"Me wan nex Red Stripe," he said some moments later. " 'Ere buy me a nex beer and yerself a nex rum." He handed her a note for a hundred Jamaican dollars. Okay. She'd sport the ten dollars and a likkle something for a tip this time.

"Okay. Soon come."

The alcohol hit her as she turned back to the bar. She needed to steady her inner, more than outer, equilibrium. Angela ordered the drinks and, as she paid, felt a closeness behind her more personal than the crush of people pushing into the bar. She turned to see Jah Guide, a local Rasta, in his forties, on her ass. A once fine man, he'd been finished off by a broken love affair with an Australian woman ten years his senior. She was an actuary with a prominent insurance firm; he was just a bumpkin with no education but a lot of drive, at least back then. His drinking ruined them; then it put the finishing touches on him. About all he could muster now was an unlicensed taxi service and a dabble in the crack cocaine trade.

"So, a wha' a gwaan, Angela? Me beg ya a dance?"

"I'm serving drinks right now, Jah Guide. Maybe a little later?"

"Who you serving drinks to? You know should be me." She could sense that alcoholic's aggression beginning to well and wanted to get away.

"Just a friend who likes his Red Stripe real, real cold. Likkle more, eh?"

But he'd already given up and was looming over the girl behind the bar, gruffly demanding both a rum and a fuck, his words slurred and his head drooping.

When she found Blacks again, it was as if nothing had changed in her absence: the hypnotic music, the dancers, the expression on their faces erotic and beatific, but curiously not sensuous. Angela figured they must crave this suspended animation that annulled the grim reality of the day-to-day. She wondered whether she used Jamaica to suspend the realities of her own life, the constant struggle for cash and recognition, her own unyielding self-criticism, the loves that sometimes come but always go. At the same time, she knew the luxury of her own troubles compared to theirs and the chimera of deliverance that drugs give. She thought of the words of Elean Thomas, a Jamaican elder, speaking just before her death, of her battle with alcoholism: "When you're drunk, you're never out of it. Even if you're lying down on the road, you're still clear, clear."

She eased the frosty bottle into Blacks's hand, wondering

whether he could feel its cold wetness through his fisherman's calluses; then she slipped back beside him. He turned to face her moments later, a faint inscrutable smile on his face. She stole a glance upward from time to time at his mahogany-stained lips, as closed and still as a Mende mask.

Angela was feeling no pain now, anesthetized enough to not care about the offensive lyrics—those she could make out—which beat up on batty boys and laundry-listed Beenie Man's conquests and Shaggy's infidelities. Whatever happened to "Get Up, Stand Up" and "Time Tough"? she thought, shaking her head.

A soca interlude provided relief, then back to the dancehall. When Elephant Man's "Log Out" was up, she finally began to squirm. "Ya don like Elephant Man?"

"Especially not this tune. It's homophobic."

"Is wha?"

"No matter . . ."

"Yah ready?"

"Yeah, let's go." Once before he'd offered to walk her home from the disco, but she politely, and firmly, refused.

She noticed that more than several youths turned to watch them leave. It gave her a twisted feeling of pride and irritation. In her tipsy state, she fantasized that there was desire behind their glances. She thought of an old Spanish expression: *Vacas viejas dan buena leche*—"Old cows give good milk." But these young testosterone-laden men of limited sexual wisdom left her cold. And she resented them for taking the liberty to clock her so openly.

They fell into step with each other once they turned onto the road. They walked, first in silence, but the sexual charge was too strong. She tried to defuse it.

"Was that fun?" she asked him.

"Yeah, mon. But if me no go, if me stay a yard or a meh bed 'an smoke a spliff, me crisp."

"I hear you, but I love to boogie, and here, if you miss one Sunday night, you have to wait a whole week for another chance."

They passed the lane leading to his yard. He took her hand.

She eased out of his leathery grasp. He said nothing. They walked in silence for some minutes.

"Uh . . . do you think you could find me some more of that corkscrew bush? I wanna start drinking the tea here and maybe take some back home with me."

"Yah, mon. It grow in me friend yard in Whitehouse."

"I thought you told me you had no friends."

"Ah true. Me say friend, but me no mean it. Me jus know 'im."

"Like Timer?"

He considered. "Yah, mon. Like Timer."

■ ■ ■

They were at the gate to her yard now, still and silent for some seconds.

"Make we sit on the veranda, meh tell ya how fi roast bonito on a wood fire."

"Yeah, but just a few minutes, cause I'm getting tired." How pathetic, she thought.

They sat, about a foot apart, on the concrete veranda railing. He reached for her hand again, this time more assertively. Cursing herself, Jamaica, and all the men she'd ever known, she didn't pull away.

They sat, silently, motionlessly, as her heart began to pound. Then he drew her slowly toward him. He held her for a moment against his chest and put his lips to her forehead. They were fleshy and firm like a baby's leg. She lifted her arms and took hold of his shoulders as she tried to quiet her heavy breathing.

"Come 'ere."

He lifted her up onto his leg and encircled her in his arms. With his strong fingers he pushed her curls onto her scalp and began to suck on her cheekbones, the bridge of her nose, her eyelids, arousing her more with his gentle tobacco breath. She massaged the muscles around his shoulder, turning them liquid beneath her hands. Then she lifted up his shirt and began to kiss his chest, leathery and taut as a Masai shield, stroking his flesh with her tongue. She felt his sweat on her lips and on her breath.

When her teeth found his nipples, he groaned softly from deep within his belly.

He cupped her chin in his hand and raised her mouth to his. He brought his lips to hers and engulfed her. His tongue, raspy, flat, and wide, blanketed hers as he probed deeply, teasing, bringing her to that threshold of pain that heightened her pleasure.

She pulled back to suck hard on his lower lip, tempting its resilience with her teeth. Then she slid her tongue under his upper lip, running over his gums like fingers over piano keys. His hands were on her ears now with feathery caresses against her lobes.

"You win," she murmured. "Let's go inside."

He gathered her up and carried her to the door. She tottered in his arms while she unlocked it. She left the door open to let in the moonlight and the blessing of the surf.

He brought her slowly to the bed—time in Jamaica moves languidly, even when making love—and lowered her onto it. He slipped her out of her shirt, her pants, her bra, like he was skinning an eel underwater. She groaned, her arms over her head, reaching. More rapidly, but with the same purposeful languor, his overalls, T-shirt, and outer of two pair of briefs were delivered to the bed on the other side of the room. His erection was mighty under the baggy briefs, his thighs solid and slick as an octopus, his muscles entwined flat against the leanness of his legs. He was like a colossus come up from the sea. She feared looking upon his face.

He slipped onto the bed, scrunching down his briefs and mounting her light as a secret. Condom unfoiled in a seamless choreography, his member, long and already gleaming with precome, found its way into her embracing pussy. He stroked, rode, wined, and loved her, it seemed, with everything that was in him, all the hidden pain. She struggled to hold on to her mettle, determined not to surrender all of herself to him, and, if not to best him at his own game, to give him a good run for his money.

They swelled and ebbed, swelled and ebbed. He eased her onto his belly, then, gently pushing back her shoulders, brought her face to within arm's length as she straddled him. He wanted her to see him smile, and she could almost see, through her own wetness, tears in his eyes. Then they tangoed, their sweaty bodies making the move easier, as he slid her around and under his waist until he was over her, without ever missing a beat. His body swimming, his face opening into a sigh, he came. It was his first gasp when the midwife slapped life into him and his last breath all at once.

It was always a while for her first time, but he had that gift of being able to stay hard after he'd come. He nurtured her until she ripened, then tore open, her flesh breaking through her skin, her clit engorged within the fortress of her legs. He held her firmly against him to still her thrashing. Once quieted, she slowly opened her eyes.

"Ya arright?"

"I'm okay."

He sat up, pulled a spliff out from behind his ear, lit it, and lay back down beside her, one hand absentmindedly stroking her sweat-soaked curls. He lifted her head to his chest. She lay still for a few minutes, inhaling his scent and the ganja.

As he opened the door to pee, she got up from the bed, felt a slight chill, and grabbed a length of African fabric from the closet shelf, then went into the bathroom, peed, and washed her face and her pussy, leaving them both wet. When she came back, he was standing in the doorway, dressed, the sea sky a waterman's blue behind him, the sun threatening to be born again. He drew her to him. Kissing her on the head, he said, "Likkle more," turned, and was off.

She dropped onto the bed, flung open the wrap, and allowed herself to ooze off to sleep. She awoke an hour later, just before six, knotted the wrapper around her waist and stepped outside, smiled at the burgeoning sun, and turned on the tap in the outdoor shower. Back in the bedroom, she began to straighten up. She retrieved her flung underwear and hung her pants up in the closet. Reaching into the pocket for the change from buying the drinks, she noticed it was gone.

THE GRIM GUMBO OF LOVE

Jervey Tervalon

Banking over the Mississippi, high above the gigantic blue-green S of the river, the sky was unusually clear, even restful. Then the plane descended, and the thick tropical humidity appeared, a gray opaqueness ready to envelop him as soon as he stepped outside of the air-conditioning. Besides the flying cockroaches, the stickiness was the thing August disliked most about returning to New Orleans, his hometown.

He found his father, Winston Landreau, former World War II staff sergeant, retired ten years from the post office, waiting for him at the luggage carousel, hunting cap on, dressed in well-worn jeans and work shirt, permanent scowl securely fastened on his brown, weathered face. August couldn't believe that he was in New Orleans spending time away from work and his new wife, time he couldn't afford. Guilt that he wasn't a better, more attentive son set the trap, and that early-morning phone call from Daddy, wanting company for a drive back to L.A., had sprung it. What had he said? "You don't have to, but I could use your help with that drive. I ain't as young as I used to be."

So there he was, looking at the man who was his daddy, this man who could curdle milk with his sour smile.

"How was the flight; ya get sick?"

"Naw, Daddy, I'm fine."

"Fine? What's fine, fine like a woman? Like wine?"

August shook his head. "It's just an expression, you know. I'm okay."

"Say that then! Say what you mean!"

"I've got to pick up my bags," August said, hoping to put some distance between them, but no such luck: His father followed at his heels.

What had it been, almost a year since Daddy drove down alone to New Orleans, taking little-traveled highways, to tend to his infirm mother? She recovered before he arrived and had dinner miraculously ready for him when he arrived there three days later than expected. Daddy didn't fly; he professed to hating the act of getting somewhere too fast and missing the great deserts, the vast, monotonous vistas of twisted cacti and abandoned motels from Los Angeles to New Orleans. August suspected he was just too cheap to pay for a ticket.

"You gonna give your Grumma a heart attack trying to make you happy."

August took a second to let his father's statement sink in. It was best not to overreact and get lassoed into an argument.

"How's that? What did I do?"

"You got her cooking like she's never seen a stove and bugging me about what to fix you since you're not supposed to be eating no meat, so she went down to the fish market for oysters, but she's sure you gonna want something else."

"I eat oysters; you know that. I'll eat anything she wants to cook."

"Oh, that's mighty big of you, boy."

August sighed deeply.

They finally arrived at the baggage claim. Nobody seemed to be in a rush, particularly not the skycaps: two fat, dark-skinned men in green uniforms, larding it up at a counter, conversating. When August's luggage tumbled down from the chute, he had no problem walking past them, even though he'd misplaced his baggage ticket.

"They didn't stop me for my claim ticket," August said, turning back to look at the two skycaps still chewing over their conversation.

"Maybe you look honest, or they don't know any better."

They exited the airport into air so humid it felt like a wet rag against the face.

"Hot as the dickens!" Daddy said to nobody in particular, as he strolled ahead of his son. August was a little irritated that his father let him carry both suitcases. Sweat almost blinded him when they stopped at a well-preserved bloater from the early seventies. Daddy opened the trunk in a flourish.

"Throw them in," he said.

"Could hide a couple of bodies back there," August mumbled, peering into the depths of the Dodge Swinger's trunk.

After an annoyingly long drive, they reached the twisted knot of the downtown junction, and the car eased off the Chef Highway and descended below the levees and the grayish water that surrounded them on all sides into a slow moving drag that dead-ended into a weatherworn shotgun shack with its front door open to the elements. Inside, a naked lightbulb illuminated what had to be an unimaginably filthy mattress.

"Hey, some poor people, downtown, yeah," his daddy said.

They drove by the whitewashed tombs of Lafayette Cemetery, then through narrow streets with shotgun houses fallen into disrepair, but still handsome. Daddy parked the car in front of Grumma's tidy duplex with a plaster statue of the Virgin Mary on the kerosene-scented soil of her front yard. There she was, out on the porch waiting for them, hands on her hips, looking strong and youthful. Her hair was cut blunt and short. He missed the long, thick braid that used to run down her back. He hurried from the car to the porch and paused for a moment, embarrassed about having to kiss her wrinkled, olive-colored skin.

"Auggie, my Auggie's back," she said, with that Brooklyn accent by way of New Orleans's Ninth Ward. She fought through the cocoon of his shyness and kissed him, and clutching his hands, she led him through the cluttered front room to a nearly century-old photo of his grandfather who looked more postmortem than in the vigor of life. There were more portraits of relatives in dusty oval frames, but he never cared to look at those ancient, dead Creole faces, staring at him with Latin/Irish/African eyes. No, those people might have been his blood, but he didn't care about that. They just made him feel that he would die sooner rather than later.

Grumma sat him down in the bright, snug kitchen, next to the window fan in front of the screened back door. She hurried over to the icebox, got a can of Dixie beer, and popped it open for him.

"My boy got to eat!" she said, smiling broadly, and then began to bread oysters. The smell of them frying in hot oil made him deliriously hungry. He settled back in the chair and sipped the cold beer, content with the sound of whirring fans.

"Don't you worry, don't worry at all. These oysters are ready, yeah," she said, bustling around the table and quickly filling it with an elaborate spread: spinach in a piecrust topped with bacon and cornmeal, fresh succotash, red beans and rice along with the fried oysters.

"Go ahead and eat, my boy, your daddy's always slow."

After Daddy came into the kitchen, she dished them up plates and they ate quietly and intently, except for Grumma, who sipped a beer and watched them enjoy the food.

"It's great, Grumma," August said, still chewing.

"You need some more, yeah," she said in response, and turned to the stove to bread more oysters.

August sighed, happy to not be moving, not headed to a destination with more ambivalence than desire.

Then there was an explosion behind him like a gigantic sledge-hammer striking sheet metal. He pitched forward, splashing beer onto his teetotaling father.

"What's wrong with you, you gump! You never heard thunder before?"

"I guess I forgot how loud it is."

"Welcome back to New Orleans."

August smiled awkwardly as more thunder reverberated through the kitchen. Home would take some getting used to. How could he forget thunder loud enough to make him wish he wore Depends?

After dinner, Grumma occupied herself with straightening up the cluttered bedroom of the small shotgun house where Daddy slept. She was boldly attempting to get all of Daddy's clothes, fishing and hunting gear, and his ever-growing stack of newspapers organized so that August would be able to sit in the big chair to watch television.

"Grumma's not working too hard, is she?" August asked his father.

"Yes, indeed. She's always cleaning and scrubbing. By the way, did you tell her you ain't gonna be staying here?"

"No, I haven't told her. I thought you were going to tell her."

"Me?" Daddy laughed. "You better tell her before she gets that bed made up for you."

August got up from the table feeling bloated and overfed. He trudged into the living room, where Grumma was carefully tucking a corner of fresh sheet beneath the mattress.

"What do you need, baby?" she asked, wiping her damp forehead with her sleeve. "You want the fan on?"

"Sure, Grumma, but I'm going to be staying at a hotel in the French Quarter. I don't want you going to extra trouble just for me."

Grumma paused, one hand on her hip, the other smoothing back her hair as she thought.

"I'll go with you . . . got to get ready," she said with a determined smile, and it was back to action as she hurried to the bathroom in the rear of the shotgun house. Relieved that she wasn't too disappointed about his plans, August returned to the kitchen for another beer. Daddy was in the middle of a game of solitaire at the small table.

"So, what your grumma say? Did you make her cry?"

"No, she's okay. She's coming for the ride."

"Hot dawg, you done it. She don't leave unless it's for Mass. She's coming to see what kind of dump you left her for."

"There's no space here, Daddy. I'm twenty-nine; I can't be sharing that little bed with you."

"Oh, be quiet, you big hippo, and get your bags so I can drive you there."

Soon they were back in Daddy's land boat, cruising slowly down by the weatherworn storefronts and homes of Conti Street. Stretched out on the backseat, August surveyed the crowds walking along Canal. He saw a few long-legged women in hot pants and miniskirts, and a few wild-looking bikers hanging out in front of a bar with an ominous black leather door.

"Hey, Gump, keep your eyes open for the motel because I'm making only one stop."

August refused to become annoyed. Street addresses were impossible to find, but maybe it was because it was dusk and the orange light of sunset washing the narrow streets obscured the numbers. Finally, he made one out, a faded address above a drain grate. The hotel had to come up in the next two blocks.

"Daddy, it's coming up."

Grumma pointed to a wooden house, which looked to him to be something like a horse stable.

"When I used to be a little girl, I lived in something just like that house. And you know, it was right around here if my memory is holding up."

"Yeah, did the place look spooky like it does now?" August asked.

Grumma smiled. "Spooky? I suppose."

He fished around for another word while ignoring his father mumbling about the silliness his son talked.

"I read a novel about vampires that took place here. It made the French Quarter seem like a place filled with ghosts."

She laughed and took the time to twist about in the car seat to look him in the eye.

"What's so spooky about the French Quarter? Just a lot of people wanting to get drunk. Yeah, some of them tourists do want to talk about Marie Laveau. But you know she wasn't nothing. People back then talked about Zabo Countess. She was the *real* voodoo queen."

"Zabo Countess? Was she African or something?"

"Oh, I don't know. Zabo Countess was a tall, dark-skinned woman who scared the hell out of people. But nobody talked about that Marie Laveau. Zabo Countess had everybody worried that they were gonna find something bad hanging from their back door, like a salted chicken heart or something. Or that crows were going to fly in your house, and that would be it.

" 'Course I never was afraid of her. Grumma Mayda took me to the French Quarter when I was a little girl. Used to have them boards back then, to walk over the mud on. Zabo Countess had everybody, colored or white, worried that she'd put some kind of spell on them that they'd step off into knee-deep mud if they saw her coming. But my Grumma Mayda wasn't afraid. Zabo Countess thought she could do that, make Grumma Mayda step in the mud to get out of her way. But she wasn't having it. Grumma Mayda stood there like she planned to knock the stuffing out of that woman if she came an inch closer. Zabo Countess cursed us, put her fingers to her lips, and flung them down, and she spat on the board. But that didn't make Grumma Mayda move. Zabo Countess frowned and stepped into the mud to let us pass."

"That happened?"

"Yes, and that's how we got cursed." Grumma laughed after she said that.

August had never heard his grandmother talk about her child-hood, and it made him feel good, but Daddy continued to frown and shake his head.

Finally, the traffic began to move and they inched closer to the Hotel Toulouse. Daddy managed to slip into the loading zone ahead of a particularly aggressive taxi, whose driver was trying to kamikaze into position for the hotel.

Daddy waved him off and refused to let him in. The taxi driver hit the horn, blaring at them. Red in the face, Daddy leaned across his mother and shouted out the window, "Jackass!"

After cursing him and shaking fists, August and Daddy noticed Grumma sitting with legs crossed, looking not so much angry but more bothered and bored by the commotion. With her glasses perched forward on her nose, she ignored them and fiercely read a prayer missive. Finally, she looked up, shaking her head.

"Mama, are you okay?"

"Everything's fine."

"Fine? What do you mean by that?"

"Fine. That's what I mean, fine. Now, are you ready to go?"

"Yes, Mama," Daddy said, and pulled his hat lower on his head.

August kissed his grandmother good-bye. Daddy gunned the engine, and with tires squealing, forced his way into French Quarter traffic.

August sighed, wiped the sweat from his brow, and lugged his bags into the hotel.

■ ■ ■

After surveying the pleasant and clean hotel room, and discovering that the door leading out to the rickety veranda actually opened and he could look down onto the street, August stretched out on the big bed and thought about being alone for the first night since he was married. On a hot night in the French Quarter, he was ready for anything that his temporary freedom would bring him. For weeks before the trip, he'd fantasized about the possibility of genuine temptation—of resisting the charms of a beautiful woman, to flirt and to be flirted with, to actually have something to feel guilty about.

But first, he would have to call Sophia. He had a generous and trusting wife whom he doubted he deserved. She wasn't jealous, didn't browbeat him, didn't demand that he account for his time, didn't know about his overly active fantasy life. He didn't want to cheat on Sophia but couldn't figure out how he wouldn't. It made him feel a little queasy, this being dishonest. He wanted her to love him and be married to him, so what option did he have? Telling the truth about desires that he didn't understand seemed stupid. His buddy Tim told him about this strip joint in the Quarter that supposedly would rock his world. He wanted his world rocked, he certainly did, but before that, he needed to make the call, check in, and make sure he had a real world to return to.

"Hi, hon!" he said, genuinely excited to hear her voice over the phone.

"How was the flight?" she asked, her voice as excited as his.

"I sat next to this really sweet housewife from Florida. She confided in me about her alcoholic father and all kinds of stuff, but her husband seemed a little nervous about this big black guy talking the whole flight to his wife and daughter."

Sophia laughed, then asked, "How's your grandmother?"

"She looks great. She made a great meal for me, but when Daddy was dropping me off he almost got into a fight with this little Spanish-speaking guy."

"Your daddy? He's seventy, fighting out in the street?"

"He's like that, hot tempered and irritable, but loving and gentle in his own way. He only whipped me three times. All justified, I think I set the house on fire for all three of those whippings."

"August, the call is costing us, so no more reminiscing. I'll call you tomorrow at the same time. I'll be counting hours until you return to me."

"Hey, that's a line from a Sarah Vaughan song. Which one?"

"August, don't be so goofy. I miss you."

"And I miss you, too."

"You see, we miss each other."

"And that's why we're married."

"You looked so sad boarding the plane."

"I hate flying."

"How about me, weren't you sad to leave me?"

"Sure. I had a fantasy that the plane was going to blow up and I'd never get to see you again."

"That's romantic."

"Getting blown up?"

"No, you are in your own bizarre way, but you should go to bed, it's eleven thirty there."

"Good night, my love," he said in his best Barry White baritone.

"And good night to you, my silly lover."

Click. He listened to the dial tone for a moment and realized that he was lonely. Just six hours ago he kissed her good-bye. The exhilaration he had felt earlier was gone. He was alone and suddenly exhausted, but restless in the way that the thought of getting undressed and going to bed had no appeal. He lay in bed thinking about Zabo Countess lurking on the veranda peering at him with dead eyes and waiting for the moment that he would fall asleep. No, sleep would not work. Up, off the bed into the reassuringly bright bathroom to wash his face and comb his hair. Then he returned to the bed and searched through his tightly packed luggage for his pocketknife. Sure, it wasn't much protection, but it was something. He put the knife in his pocket and headed out into the hallway, down the stairs and through the lobby.

"Which way to the Café Du Monde?" August asked the nattily dressed doorman.

The clerk said, without looking up from a computer terminal, "Right out the door. You'll run right into it."

The doors slid open and he stepped out into the humid night, which was just as fucking sticky as the day. From a distance he could see the thick crowd streaming along Bourbon Street. When he reached the intersection, he looked around him and marveled at the sheer number of people meandering about. Preppies, rednecks, B-boys, Japanese tourists, mimes and human robots on crates, gorgeous girls of every color, and quite a few gorgeous gays of every color.

August stood behind a fire hydrant hoping to watch the scene, but a horse and buggy slid in front of his vantage point. His boy Tim said, "Nu Awlins. The city care forgot. So wild you could rub pussy on your head all night long," but August didn't like that particular image, a little too raw for his tastes. People were spilling out, almost dancing into the street, in every direction. Crisscrossing along Bourbon Street, he dodged a couple of drunken cowboys clutching hurricane glasses. He navigated through the crowds to the other side of the street where a small knot of men were clustered in front of a club. Must be lewd, August thought, looking up at the sign featuring a huge pair of hot pink neon tits, and snugly tucked between those big breasts was the word *drink*, also in neon, a Mardi Gras green that flickered off and on.

Working his way forward, until he stood in front of the broad window that offered a view of what the nightclub had to offer, he caught a glimpse of what captivated so many men: On the stage was a dancer, a black woman with a wonderful ass, wearing tassels over her breasts and a G-string. A stupid song blared from somewhere on the stage, distracting him. She began grinding her hips toward him, and almost instantly he knew where he'd be the rest of the night, if not the rest of his life. He glanced disapprovingly at the horny tourists surrounding him; she was too good for those losers. She slid her arms behind her head and swayed sensuously. Her long legs and beautiful ass entranced him, but then a hawker appeared—a short, fat white guy with a derby on—and broke the spell. The hawker looked over the crowd of lusting men while he sipped a beer, then as if he had a schedule to keep, parted them with the ferocity of spiel so loud and obnoxious, August almost ran for cover.

"Y'all come in. Come on in! Come on now! See what the girls got to shake in your face. Why the hell not come in and enjoy an ICE-COLD BEER?"

August marveled at how the hawker said "ice-cold beer," like ice had just been invented.

"And see our fabulous assortment of erotic dancers, performing for your viewing pleasure."

But the crowd began to disperse. "NO COVER! ABSOLUTELY NO COVER! FOR THE PRICE OF AN ICE-COLD BEER YOU CAN SEE MANDY DO THE WILD THING ONSTAGE."

But it was no good; the crowd moved on to other venues, leaving August alone at the big window. Then Mandy turned to him and began to bump and grind, faster and nastier, lower and lower, until she was almost squatting. Her hands ran along her stomach and breasts, and then she arched her back and those breasts were within reach; only a quarter inch of glass separated them from his greedy hands. Then she turned her back to him and began to rotate her ass to a new, more seductive beat. Mesmerized by that tiny G-string, those gorgeous hips, and all that flesh, he couldn't move. She was the mongoose and he the snake—stupid, unable to even go inside and find a table. Somebody tapped his shoulder, an overweight black man wearing a Harley-Davidson T-shirt.

"Have a seat, enjoy the show," he said in a friendly enough voice. The bouncer revived him, but the reality of the dankness of the run-down club disoriented and disgusted him, so he returned to Bourbon Street.

Damn, August thought as he wandered along, oblivious to the raunchy partying going on around him. He wanted to go back and wait for her to finish for the night; maybe he could buy her a drink or something. Yeah, right. Her boyfriend probably sits in the front row and is strapped like everybody else in New Orleans.

Naw, he thought, it's not worth it. And so, momentarily composed, he continued along the street, with his eyes open for a sight that could dull the image of Mandy dancing lustily onstage. A man with a placard sat slumped on the steps near the entrance. August read the sign as he passed: REPENT SINNER OR BURN IN HELL. What an endorsement, he thought, as he searched for the quickest path to the front of the line, but there was no slipping ahead of this crowd; he received a few unpleasant stares from a couple of guys as he lingered at the edge of the crowd hoping to cut in. The bouncer waved a few customers through, and the big window was momentarily clear.

A big-breasted blonde girl, who couldn't have been older than twenty, danced on the stage of the packed club. She stopped dancing and held her oblong breasts above a water basin shaped like a tulip, and a man in a cowboy hat rushed forward to wash them. At first he seemed reluctant, delicately dabbing at each one, lingering touches and caresses, but then he began to eagerly soap them up. All the while, the blonde girl seemed pleasant and unperturbed. She didn't seem to mind the shouts and laughter from the audience or the red-faced cowboy who at that moment lost self-control and plunged his face between those two big soapy breasts. A couple of bouncers forcibly escorted the happy cowboy outside, and things calmed down and the blonde returned to dancing. Somehow, though the blonde was awfully cute, she didn't do it for August.

He worked his way out of the strip joint. At another club down the street, he looked through the big window and saw a half-dozen white girls in tiny bikinis, and all the girls looked amazingly alike: pert breasts, firm little behinds, long legs, and all of them seemed to have unusually broad shoulders. August stepped back to read the neon sign above the store window: BOYS! BOYS! BOYS! THAT LOOK LIKE GIRLS GIRLS GIRLS! They did look like girls. Yeah, they looked better than a lot of the girls he had seen tonight, he thought as he hurried back to the club where Mandy worked.

She wasn't onstage, and the club was dead. Pissed that he missed her, he sat in an empty booth in the back, thinking it was time to call it a night. Then he saw her burst out of the kitchen, almost clocking a waitress with a swinging door. She wore low-riding jeans with the thong underwear showing and a sliver of a bikini top barely able to restrain her peach-sized breasts. She looked better in clothes than naked. She sat down at an empty table and began to smoke a cigarette. He watched her awhile, wondering when she'd start the rounds for lap dances. After the third cigarette, she looked around and then stood as though she were ready to leave. He had to make a move. He gathered up his nerve and walked over to her table. He stood behind the chair farthest from her and waited and waited for her to notice him. She didn't.

"May I sit down?" he finally asked.

At first she looked bored; he figured he ought to just slip away and deal with rejection, but then she smiled.

"Sit if you want. I'm off work."

"Thanks," August said.

She lit a fresh cigarette and turned her attention to a big-breasted girl onstage.

"Bitch can't dance," she muttered to herself.

"What?" August asked.

She shook her head.

"I wasn't saying nothing. So what's with you? You want a date with a dancer?"

He didn't know how to respond. Was she hooking?

"You don't know how it works? I'll be up front with you because I can tell you've never done this. If you want me to come with you, you got to pay, but you probably don't have the cash to afford me. What are you anyway, a college student?"

"No, I graduated a couple of years ago. I teach high school."

"You're still a college boy, stuck on yourself."

She sneered at him, but the sneer turned into the sexiest of smiles.

"So you have money. You got a hotel around here?"

"Yeah."

"You want to spend some money?"

"Sure, I think," he said, feeling very uncomfortable.

She sneered again. This time, though, the sneer lingered.

"Do you want a date or what?" she asked almost angrily.

"Yeah, I guess."

She laughed, making her look even more beautiful. His judgment was completely gone, disappeared like the sweat from his brow when he first saw her dance. He couldn't rely on usual reluctance to commit to anything. It was a struggle to keep from signing over his traveler's checks to her.

"So, what you gonna do?" she asked, sounding less than patient.

"I don't have all this very clear . . . about the date . . . where do we go . . . I mean I don't know if I want to . . . you know, fool around, but you're so beautiful it's hard not to want to."

She laughed and turned to him. "I'm tired of this fucking place. Let's go."

She was up and walking to the door while August was still wondering if he could go through with this shit. He followed her outside and then his eyes took over. In the streetlight, she seemed more spectacular. He expected her to be wearing heels because her legs were so long and her ass so high, but she sported flat sandals that tied around her ankles. He imagined himself worshipping her feet, coming down with a sudden foot fetish.

"Where you from?"

"L.A., but I was born here."

"What you doing, visiting relatives?"

"How'd you know?"

"It's obvious. Anybody can see you're from down here. You Creoles look alike, always marrying your cousins."

He didn't know what to say to that, so he just shut his mouth and stayed on her heels, mesmerized by her swaying ass. Away from Bourbon Street the crowd thinned. Late as it was, walking toward Jackson Square was a little unnerving. They approached the rear of the unlit Cabildo, and the night seemed even darker; the imposing structure blotted out the light from the shops and cafés. Grim wrought-iron railings that stretched the length of the uneven brick walkway made August flash on a scene from Jack the Ripper and how he left a prostitute's intestines dangling from the sharp spires of wrought-iron railings for the bobbies to find. And here he was, following a prostitute, lusting wildly for her, and at the same time, in the back of his mind, he could picture himself floating down the Mississippi with a bullet in his brain.

"Schoolboy, hurry it up. You don't want to slow down in the dark. Get your ass mugged."

That was reassuring, that she worried for his safety. She slowed to his pace.

"You know, if I didn't have a gun in my purse, I'd leave you here."

They turned a corner and there was his hotel. He stood looking at it like he had never seen it before.

"Did I tell you I was staying here?"

Mandy shook her head. "No, but I'm good at guessing. This hotel got mentioned in the *New York Times* because it's cute enough for snobs but it's reasonably priced. You got a little snob about you, so I figured you might be staying here."

He shrugged, feeling more than a little exposed. Then she reached around and squeezed his ass.

"I work on the clock, so if you don't want to spend a gang of money, you should invite me up to your room."

August took her by the hand and rushed into the lobby, ignored the nod of the night clerk, and rushed to the elevator. There, he waited impatiently for the elevator doors to open, to let him get out of the sight of all these reasonable folks who weren't bringing a prostitute to their rooms.

Finally, the door opened and he rushed in so quickly that he almost bumped into a well-dressed man.

"Don't rush around so much. Nobody knows you with a working girl, and I don't think they'd care. This is New Orleans. You supposed to get some."

August reached his room and as he unlocked the door, Mandy slipped around him and glanced about with a look of some disgust.

"Damn, they certainly gave you a shitty room. You got a view of trash cans?"

"From the other veranda you can see the street, and I got a good price."

"Hope you did because that's where those frat boys piss."

She sat down on the edge of the bed, made a circle with her finger. "Like I said before, time is my money. What do you want? Full service, two hundred for an hour and that includes a blow job and massage. If you just want a massage and blow job, that's one hundred fifty for an hour. See, normally, I charge that for a half hour, but since you seem like a gentleman and ain't just about getting some pussy, I cut you a deal and you don't got to tip me."

"Thanks," he said, unsure of what to do next.

Her eyes flashed. "You need to make up your mind, what's it gonna be?"

"Full service is what exactly?"

"I do everything, suck you and fuck you. Does that sound good?"

"Yeah," he mumbled.

"Then you need to put two hundred dollars on that table so I can get to work."

August turned around and reached the the secret stash of money he kept in a belt pocket. The zipper stuck and he had to go into the bathroom and unfasten the whole belt and pull at the zipper before he could get the pocket to open. He had four hundred-dollar bills, took two out, and put the belt back on. He returned to Mandy, and instead of putting the money on the table, he held it out for her.

She shook her head.

"See, you put the money on the table and I leave it there until the deed is done. That shows good faith on both our parts."

August nodded.

"Now watch this," she said. She stood up and slid off her jeans. Actually, she more or less peeled them off. All she had on was that thong that fit her high, round ass perfectly.

"You want me to keep my shoes on?"

He nodded and watched as she stood like a crane and worked the sandals back on.

"Now, you need to get naked; otherwise you won't get your money's worth."

August took his clothes off with more ease than he thought he would. He maneuvered around and tried to slip into the bed, but she grabbed him by the hand and pulled him over. He tried to conceal himself, but she pushed his hand aside and looked at his penis for a moment. It seemed clinical to him until she touched it, just a fingernail on the shaft, and he shuddered.

"Wow, you must not get much," she said with a smile.

She ran her red lacquered fingernails along his penis down to his balls until he was rigid. Then she took his penis into her hand and licked below the head, and he shuddered again.

"You know you're gonna come before the main course. That wouldn't be good, would it?"

"I don't know," he mumbled.

"You married, right?" she asked as she slipped his penis into her mouth.

His knees buckled as she sucked him.

"What? You can't answer that question?"

He looked down to see she had somehow slipped a cherry red rubber onto his dick.

"Yeah, I am."

"Your wife don't do this to you?"

He hesitated, but she looked up at him, waiting for an answer. If he wanted his dick sucked, he needed to answer.

"No, she doesn't do that."

She sucked him until he moaned.

"Why won't she suck your dick? Does she think she's too good to have your dick in her mouth?"

Suddenly, he was soft.

"I don't know. I guess she doesn't feel comfortable doing it. I never asked her."

"Maybe you should."

She put her lips around it again, and magically he was hard again. She did something with her hands and tongue, and he was rapturous.

Then she stopped.

"You're about to come."

She turned away and slid onto the bed. "I should give you a massage to slow you down. I don't want you coming so fast."

He nodded, content to go in any direction she led him.

"Roll over," she said.

She straddled him and began massaging his back. For a moment, he was relaxed, like there was nothing to feel tense about, nothing wrong about having a beautiful naked woman, built like he had never seen a woman built, rubbing his back. How could there be anything wrong with that?

"You like a massage?"

"Yeah, I think I do."

Then she grabbed his balls and roughly squeezed them.

"Hey!" he yelled, and jerked away.

She laughed.

"You didn't like that?"

"No! It hurt."

"Sometimes hurt is good. Roll back on your stomach and I'll try something else."

He rolled over and she spread oil on his back. It felt good as she worked it into his skin.

"You like this?" she asked as she straddled his ass. After a few minutes she leaned over and whispered into this ear, "You trust me?"

"Huh?"

"You trust me to try something else, seeing that you don't really know much about sex?"

"I know about sex," he said, turning onto his side, almost knocking her off.

"You know about what most young men know, how to stick it in and how to come."

He shrugged.

"You want me to show you something?"

"Okay," he said.

She gestured for him to roll onto his back.

She massaged his feet; then her strong hands worked their way up his thighs and on up to his ass. She worked his cheeks hard, then suddenly she shoved two fingers into his butt. He tried to pull away, but her weight was on him. Once he got over being startled, he relaxed, and she worked her fingers in and out of him until he bit the pillow. He didn't know if he liked the sensation, but he couldn't help being on the edge of orgasm.

"Oh, now you're gonna come again. We can't have that."

She disappeared into the bathroom and he heard water running. She came back drying her hands on a towel.

"Roll on your back," she directed.

August rolled over and was amazed at how big his condom-wrapped penis looked.

She squatted above him, almost lowering herself onto his dick but stopping.

"What? Why'd you stop?" he asked with urgency.

"Do you really want to do that to your wife?"

"Do what to my wife?"

She brushed the tip of his penis with her vulva. His mouth fell open, anticipating her finally fucking him.

"Why'd you bring up my wife? It's pretty late in the game to try to make me feel guilty."

"What do you have to feel guilty about? You ain't done noth-ing but get a massage, a kinky massage, but it's still a massage. You haven't done the deed."

"You gave me head."

"Head ain't adultery. Bill Clinton proved that."

"I don't know."

"And you didn't come. If you don't come, it ain't shit."

"But I want to come now. I want to fuck you."

She laughed and lifted herself higher every time he strived to shove it into her.

"See, I'm saving you. You don't want to ruin your marriage. Save it for your wife. Rock her world. Otherwise, I can tell you things are going to go badly for you. You'll never find happiness and your wife will hate you."

"Are you a fortune-teller?"

"Yeah, I do that in the mornings and some afternoons."

The way she smiled, he didn't know if she was joking.

"If you quit now, this won't matter. It'll be a dream and you'll think about it and you'll get hard and excited and you can do it with your wife. But if we do it, then, like I said, you gonna pay for it. When you're driving back to L.A. with your daddy, you'll hate yourself, and then you'll tell yourself you won't confess. But it'll eat at you, and you will confess, then she'll cry and you'll feel like shit. I wouldn't say this, but you do love her. It shouldn't matter to me, it's your business, but you do love this woman. I know this like I know you paid me two hundred dollars."

He sighed with frustration and covered his face with a pillow. "How is this good faith? You tease me and instruct me about being good, and you're a prostitute."

"Sure, I am. That's why I'm trying to help you, plus my hour is up."

"Okay, you're right." He sat up and looked at his ridiculous erection and the happy red condom covering it.

"I love her. I do. I just want more. I don't want to be trapped."

"It's all in your head," she said, and pointed at his head and then the tip of his penis.

"What?"

"You're not trapped. Don't worry about that. You're free to be good to your wife, and if you're good to her, she'll be your freak. Trust me."

Mandy started to dress, turning around to slip the thong on, then her jeans.

"But I'm so hard, you can't leave me like this."

"I won't," she said. And slipped between his legs, put her hands on his thighs, took his penis into her hand, and touched her tongue to the underside of it. He came and came and came. Gasping and clawing, trying to reach the surface, get a breath of air, fill his lungs so he could go back down. She pushed him back, held on to him until he spasmed into exhaustion.

After a moment of silence, she pointed to his penis and the sagging condom. "That's amazing. I've never seen a condom that full."

She slipped it off him and flushed it down the toilet.

"I don't think I could've made you come any more if I would have fucked you for the next hour."

"Yeah," he said, still trying to catch his breath.

Dressed, she glanced at her watch. "I got to go."

"How'd you know about me driving back with my father?"

"How do you think I know? It's voodoo."

"Voodoo?"

"Your grumma knows about it."

She leaned over, gave him a kiss on the cheek, and waved at him as she closed the door.

He shook his head, collapsed on the bed, and fell asleep.

He dreamed about his wife, saw her walking along the beach with someone other than him, saw her in the arms of another man, and he woke crying.

■ ■ ■

He did most of the driving back to Los Angeles because Daddy wouldn't go faster than fifty-five. They didn't argue, because August had too much on his mind. He'd bought Sophia a Coach purse from Dillard's (the price astonished him, but he knew she liked them) and an ankle bracelet.

"Can't wait to get home," he said, but his father was asleep against the door, hat pulled low on his head.

He remembered kissing Grumma good-bye, and she said, "Hope you had a good time."

"I did," he replied.

"That's why you need to go home now," Grumma said, and her eyes were on him for a long moment.

"You're right. I do need to go right now."

And now, thinking about it as he drove through the hot West Texas desert, it seemed that all love was voodoo, at least some of the time.

BLACKBERRIES

Nalo Hopkinson

"You want some blackberries?" I asked Tad. "They grow wild all along here."

In fact, blackberry bushes lined the narrow winding road as far as the eye could see. I walked over to the nearest one, where there was a clump of fat, ripe fruit hanging just about level with my mouth.

"You crazy, Shuck?" asked Jamal. "Those things are growing by the roadside with all this pollution! You gonna make him eat those?"

As if to prove Jamal's point, a semi came hurtling down the road, careening around the curves, belching blue smoke. It was huge and it stank, but there were still three cyclists riding in its wake. They had serious gear on and straddled serious racing bikes. One of them looked sure to overtake the truck at the next bend. I shook my head. Vancouver. Gotta love this city. I'd only been living in her three years, but already she had my heart, with her tree-hugging, latte-sipping, bike-riding ways. Some girls are just like that. I waved a wasp away from the bunch of blackberries I was eyeing and pulled the ripest ones off. They just fell into my hand, staining it a little with juice.

"Here," said Tad. "Lemme try 'em."

Jamal sighed and rolled his eyes at his boyfriend. "Your funeral, sweetie."

Tad smiled and made a kissy face at him. "And I know you'll look hot at the wake, so cute in your tux."

I put one of the blackberries into Tad's mouth, enjoying the warmth and slight dampness of his tongue against my fingers. Tad had the kind of plump, ripe brown lips I liked. I imagined crushing the berries against them and licking the juice off. Shit, the things I was thinking about my oldest friend.

Tad bit into the berry. He raised his eyebrows in surprise. I grinned. "The blacker the berry," I told him. He responded with that flirty grin I remembered so well. Oh, gay boys could make me so randy. Gay boys and mouthy femmes.

"Come on, Jamal," Tad said. "You really need to taste one of these. Here." He took a berry from me and waved it in front of Jamal's face. Jamal looked skeptical.

"Just smell it." Tad put the berry under Jamal's nose and winked at me. "You know how they say the way to a man's heart is through his belly?"

"That's no belly," I pointed out.

"You know it," Jamal said. "I don't spend all that time in the gym for nothing." Jamal was wearing denim shorts that looked like they'd been sewn right on him, and a sinfully tight white tank top. Like many black men, he didn't have much body hair to obscure the view. The white cotton made his skin gleam. His chest was a map of every workout he'd ever done. He was long and lean to Tad's short, rotund muscularity. Ah, so what? I bet my arms were bigger than his. I bet I could take him. I felt the warm pulse come and go in my clit and smiled. That was the thing with me and some guys: this balled-up heat, this combination of competitiveness and good, hard wanting. A lot would satisfy it. Wrestling, maybe. Or . . . no. Shut it, girl. I didn't know if I could flip these boys. Even if I could make them, just for a little while, hard for someone with girl bits, would it be someone like me? Every fag I knew was fascinated with breasts, and I was a little deficient in that department.

Jamal got a good whiff of the blackberry, and his face changed. He practically sucked it out of Tad's fingers. Tad laughed.

Two lanky white guys in surfer shorts and skateboarding T-shirts scrambled around us on the narrow verge, trying not to stare at the tableau of three black folks together in the same space. Not a sight you saw a lot in Vancouver. They headed toward the entrance to Wreck Beach, the smell of weed tailing them.

I slurped down the rest of the berries. "C'mon," I said. "Let's go." We continued along the roadside.

Jamal and Tad were up visiting me from Seattle. Tad and I had been buddies when I still lived there. We'd known each other since school days. Sometime near the end of high school, Tad had come out to me; like I hadn't guessed! With his example to follow, I'd come out to myself—a good obedient black girl from a fine Christian family, engaged to a minister in training—and fled into the arms of outcast women like myself with no plan of ever looking back. Tad and I had stayed fast friends, but we'd stopped the outrageous flirting with each other that we used to do. No need, right? Now that we'd each shown our true colors and didn't need the other as a shield anymore. Except when Tad contacted me a few weeks ago, we'd fallen right back into the sexual innuendo, the teasing. It felt familiar. Tad was my home. I'd invited him and Jamal to visit me and Sula, and I was thrilled when they accepted. The guys had landed at Vancouver airport a scant two hours ago. I'd whisked them off immediately to show them Wreck Beach.

We were at Trail Number Six, the path that led to the beach. "Nearly there," I told them. I took the first few steps down. Tad and Jamal followed me, then stopped to look around. We were in a forest—dark, damp, and cool. Lean old maples stretched forever to reach the sky. The footpath angled sharply down in steps hewn out of the earth and shored up with planks. A deep ravine dipped down beside the footpath. It was overgrown with saplings, tangled black-berries, and undergrowth. Here and there, a few giant rotted tree trunks jutted up out of it, looking like a giant's caber toss. "*This* leads to a beach?" said Jamal.

"Yup," I replied. "It's about twenty minutes straight down, ten if you're fit."

"Lawd a mercy," muttered Tad. "The child still has a taste for hard labor."

I smirked at him. "Ready to hike?" I asked.

Shot through with bars of precious sunlight from above, a yellowed maple leaf drifted slowly down into the ravine. The leaf was the size of a turkey platter.

Jamal looked at me, a gleam in his eye. "Ten minutes?"

"For me, anyway," I said. The gauntlet had been laid down. Would he pick it up?

"Betcha I can do it in seven."

"You're on!" I burst past him. He yelled and ran to catch up. I knew this path well, could do it in the dark. I had, one night, with my girlfriend, Sula. And when we'd made it to the beach—well, mosquitoes bit me that night in places no mosquito had any right being.

I grabbed a sapling for purchase, slid around that little dogleg you get to about a third of the way down. I shouted for the joy of it.

"Please be careful, both of you!" yelled Tad.

I stopped, looked up at Tad a few yards above me. He was skating and slipping on the pebbles. He skidded to one knee, grimaced as he skinned it. He'd stopped about an inch from the edge. Jamal looked down. It was a steep drop over the side.

"He's right," I said. "I'll race you, but let's not do anything stupid, okay?"

Jamal measured me with his eyes. I let him look. My sawn-off jeans showed the bulges in my thighs, and my arms strained at the sleeves of my T-shirt. I was a fair match for him, and we both knew it.

"All right," he replied. "Nothing stupid. We take it easy. But I bet you I'll be the one to make it down there without breaking a sweat."

"In your dreams." I turned and kept climbing down, Jamal neck and neck beside me.

"Tad, you okay up there?" called Jamal.

"You bitches better slow down!" he shouted back.

"Yeah?" I said to him. "You gonna come down here and make us?"

Tad chuckled. "I bet you'd like that."

I could hear him puffing, his feet landing heavily on the steep stairs, but Tad didn't ruffle easily. Like when he'd come and pulled me out of my parents' house, where my dad had me under house arrest for the crime of being a bulldagger. Dad had reached for the baseball bat he kept behind the couch, but Tad just grabbed it away from him and calmly told me to pack a bag, he'd wait for me. Been too long since Tad and I hung out.

"I can smell the sea," Jamal said.

"Yeah," I told him. "I love this part. The forest belongs to the land, but as you come farther and farther down, the sea starts to peek through. You smell it first, then you begin to see it. A few more steps, and . . . ah. There she is."

We were at the landing, just a few yards above the beach. The sand stretched out on either side with the water just beyond it, its gentle waves licking at the beach. The sea smelled like sex. Off in the distance, the Coast Mountains marched away from us, range upon range, disappearing into the mist.

Jamal stood tall, but he was breathing hard, and I could see the beads of sweat on his face. I bet they tasted like the sea. "Little winded, there, Jamal?" I teased him.

He sucked his teeth. "Don't give me that, girl child. Look at you."

He was right. I was puffing a bit myself, and my T-shirt was soaked. I pulled it over my head. I never wore a bra. Jamal literally jumped. I calmly tucked the end of the T-shirt into my belt. "What?" I asked him. "I told you it was a nude beach." You weren't supposed to get naked until you were actually on the beach, but I was feeling the devil rising in me. Wanted to see how Jamal and Tad would deal.

Tad had caught up with us. He burst out laughing when he saw me. "Susanna Paulette Avery, you're still flat as an ironing board!"

"Don't talk shit, Tad. This a thirty-eight-inch chest. I work out hard to get this chest."

"Chest, yes. But where are the titties, girl?"

"On your momma."

Now Jamal was laughing, too. He looked relieved. Probably cause he didn't have to look at bouncing boobies on me. Even with my shirt off, lots of people still mistake me for a man. Nipples a little thicker than on most guys is all.

I pointed to the Johnny-on-the-spot off to one side on the landing. "You guys want to use the facilities before we go down?"

"Nah," said Jamal. "We can piss in the bushes if we have to . . . oh. Excuse me, Susanna. Unless you want to." He gestured toward the toilet. Damn. Show a little bit of girl parts, and he goes all gentleman on me.

"No." I moved past him and headed for the stairs. "And shut it with the Susanna crap. Everybody calls me Shuck."

"Except your daddy!" Tad sung out. Giggling, he brushed past me on the stairs and raced down to the beach. "He calls you . . ."

"Don't start, Tad!" I ran, caught up with him, tackled him to the sand.

"Ow! Big meanie." Laughing, Tad got me in a choke hold, pinned my back to the sand, one arm behind me. The buttons of his shirt were plucking at my nipples. They swelled. I got my legs around Tad's body. Men have the upper body advantage; women have the lower. I twisted, flipping Tad like a turtle. I sat astride him. Jamal ran up and stood there, watching us both with a shit-eating grin on his face.

"Now," I said to Tad, "*what* does my dad call me? Tell me." And I started tickling him.

Tad wriggled helplessly under me. "Bitch! Stop it! No!" He giggled, tried to slap my hands away, but I kept moving them, kept digging my fingers into his tummy, his sides, the bit along the bottom of his belly.

"Here, let me help," said Jamal. He knelt at Tad's head, grabbed his arms. Laughing, Tad struggled, but Jamal held him fast. I kept tickling. Tad started to squeal.

"I think you men need to go to the other part of the beach," said a firm woman's voice.

I looked up. She was pointing to where the gay men usually hung out. She looked part Asian, part something I couldn't identify. She was completely naked, all soft curves, about fifteen years older than me, with a relaxed, amused grin. Just the way I like 'em. I stood up off Tad.

"Yes, ma'am!"

"Oh," she said, hearing my voice. "Maybe not." She'd pegged me for a woman.

"Where is it?" Jamal asked her.

She pointed, but I said, "I can show you." I took Tad's hand, pulled him up off the sand. The woman raised an eyebrow at me, but only said, "I'm sure you can," and sauntered off.

I watched her departing behind: chubby and round, like two oranges. I bet that ass felt good in the hands. It was bouncy, too. "Gotta be jelly," I muttered.

"Cause jam don't shake like that!" Jamal finished. We laughed, punched each other's shoulders.

I led the boys farther out onto the beach, to a nice patch of sunlight. Sunlight, like black people, was a rare and precious occurrence in Vancouver. Tad and Jamal stared around them. Even in early fall, some people still came down to the water. There was a mound of sand, human height, with a sand sculpture of a naked woman carved into its side. Over to our right, someone had stuck bleached fallen logs into the sand, angling them together into the shape of a teepee. Over to our left an elderly Asian woman and man, nude, sat on towels with their chess game on the sand between them. Three ruddy children and their dog played with a bright green ball. The children's laughter and shouting and the barking of the dog ascended into the cool autumn air and were thrown back from the forest behind us.

"Water? Pop? Smokes?" The vendor strolling the beach was male, stocky, white. He swung a bright red cooler from either hand. He wore sturdy rubber sandals, a money pouch around his waist, a sun visor on his head and a bow tie around his neck, all in the same red as the coolers. Nothing else. Tad's face as he spied him was a picture.

"We don't have anything like this in Seattle," he murmured.

"Hey, Philip," I called out.

The vendor smiled when he saw me, and came over. "Hey, Shuck," he said. "Nice day, eh?"

"Beauty," I agreed.

Tad quirked an eyebrow at me. "Beauty?"

I shrugged. "Been here three years. Starting to talk like the locals. Philip snickered.

"You guys thirsty?" I asked them. They nodded. So I bought some pop off Philip.

"Smokes?" Philip asked again. "I got tobacco and, um, herbal."

"Reefer?" asked Tad. "You selling reefer out in the open like this?"

Philip just grinned.

"Shuck," said Tad, "we're the only black people as far as the eye can see. You know that if some shit goes down with the cops, we'll be the ones doing jail time, not him."

"Just chill, man," Philip told him. The borrowed black phrase sounded odd in a white Vancouverite's mouth. But hell, probably no odder than me saying *beauty*.

"This is Vancouver," I told Tad. "*And* it's Wreck Beach. If the cops start picking people up here for smoking weed, the jail'll be overflowing in an hour."

Tad shook his head. " 'S'alright anyway, man," he told Philip. "Thank you."

"You guys have a good day, then," Philip replied. He nodded at me and continued down the beach.

I turned to hand a can of pop to Jamal, and my mouth went dry. He'd kicked off his sandals. As I watched, he stripped off his tank top and shorts and slipped out of the skimpy black jock he was wearing underneath. When he bent down, the hollow that muscle made at the side of his butt cheek was deep enough that I could have laid my fist inside it. Graceful as a dancer, he flicked the jock off, tossed it on the pile of his clothing, rolled it all up into a cylinder, and stood. Tad gave his lover's body an admiring gaze. Jamal took the can of pop I held out to him, somehow managing to do so without looking directly at me.

For a while we all just stood, uncomfortably silent. Sucking on the drinks gave us something to do with our hands. I led them to a pile of flat rocks, comfortable as armchairs. We sat and looked at the people around us, looked out to sea—anywhere but at each other.

Not too many people out today; it was early fall and a little bit chilly for the beach. Two more nudists were playing Frisbee not too far from us; both appeared to be in their sixties. He was tanned with a fall of long white hair tied into a ponytail, and elaborate mustachios. Both forearms a rainbow of tattoos. He carried his firm potbelly on his sturdy thighs like a treasure chest. She had long blonde hair, a beautiful and weathered face, a toughness and pride to her movements. She had knotted a burgundy lace shawl around her hips, not that it hid anything. It seemed to be just for pretty. And she was pretty. Her breasts bounced and jiggled as she leaped, laughing, for the Frisbee. She caught it, went and took the man by the hand. Together they walked over to a group of three children frolicking by the rocks. They had a family picnic over there, spread out on towels.

"There's kids here," said Tad.

"Yeah. Everybody comes."

"Doesn't it get a little racy for them to be out here?"

"No. Anybody starts to make out in public, people will stop them."

"Oh." He looked a little disappointed.

"Of course, what happens in the bushes isn't exactly public. . . ."

Jamal snickered.

". . . I'm sure there's a lot that goes on that we don't see." Hell, I'd played my own reindeer games here. That night with Sula and the mosquitoes, for example. No one was allowed down here at night, but we'd managed.

Over to our right, a young woman sat fully clothed on the sand, her knapsack beside her. She had a sketchbook. She seemed to be drawing the mountains in the distance. The two surfer dudes we'd seen earlier were skimming wakeboards in the shallowest part of the water, hopping onto them and riding parallel with the shore.

"There's nobody in the water," Jamal said.

"Nah, not much. It's cold and there aren't any waves. That's not the attraction of this beach."

"No?" Jamal replied, a teasing tone to his voice. "Then what is?"

Tad gasped and grabbed my arm. "What's that?" he hissed. He pointed toward the water.

Jamal looked where Tad had pointed. "Shit. Is it a dog?"

I smiled. "Seal. Harbor seal."

"For real? A live seal?"

"For real."

The seal had surfaced not twenty feet offshore, only its head visible. Its fur was black and shiny, its eyes large and curious in its big round head. It was staring at the surfer dudes.

"It's just curious," I said. "Don't make eye contact with it. . . ."

Too late. The seal had turned to look at us and had seen us staring. Shy and cautious, it disappeared back into the water.

"Fuck, that's wonderful," whispered Tad.

"Yeah," Jamal replied. He leaned back against Tad's chest with a happy sigh. He leaned over and patted my hand. "Shuck, thank you for letting us visit. Really."

"No problem." They were gorgeous, sitting in a love knot like that. I think that was the moment I decided to see if I could turn them both on to me, just for the afternoon.

"Hold this for me, will you, baby?" Tad handed Jamal his empty pop can and whipped his shirt off. He'd gotten a belly since I saw him last, and his arms and thighs were heavier.

"Being in love suits you, sweetie," I told him. "You look good."

He looked embarrassed. "Fat, you mean."

"No, I mean good. Like you'd be good to hold."

Tad raised an eyebrow at me. Jamal chuckled. "Oh, yeah. I just wrap my arms and legs around him and ride all night."

I gave them both a measuring stare. "Yeah, I can imagine." Jamal stared me back down. Tad just looked uncomfortable. Shit. Had I pushed too far? Maybe this was a bad idea. Tad was my friend, had stood by me all these years. I didn't want to ruin that over a fuck. Better ease up a little, figure myself out. I stood up and said, "Okay. Let me take you to where the boys are."

■ ■ ■

Never mind the cooler weather; gay Wreck Beach was hopping. A large man in a small, frilly apron circulated through the crowd, selling martinis right off the tray he balanced on one hand. There was a volleyball game going on farther down the beach, a serious game. I recognized those four guys; they came down here a lot, but I never saw them cruising. They really just enjoyed being naked in the sun. One of them jumped and spiked the ball hard, sending his opponent sprawling when he tried to stop it. A few people watching them applauded.

Down by the water, some diehards were trying to swim. Better them than me. They had little triangular purple flags stuck in the sand near their towels. A nudists' club, then. Three women and a dog lolled on the sand. They nodded and smiled at me. I nodded back. A man lay on a towel on his stomach, his perfect bottom upturned invitingly to the sun, and to the eye. A few guys just strolled the beach, alone, their eyes alert for opportunity. And there was plenty. The twinks were twinkling, the bears were bare, and the bushes were shaking. Before winter, certain of the man-handling men of Vancouver seemed determined to get in every last bit of naked cruising on the beach.

It was rockier here. Back at my and Sula's apartment, my shrine had a collection of rocks I'd collected from Wreck Beach, all colors. All worn smooth by the water. We picked our way across the rocks and sand.

The three of us had drawn instant attention the second we

crossed the invisible dividing line between the straight part of the beach and this one. No surprise; we had us some permanent tans. Up in the city, being black could get you followed by security guards when you went into stores. But down here, it was a different matter. Most of the guys who scoped me for a girl immediately switched their attention to Tad and Jamal; those greedy two were loving every instant of it. A hairy man with a tall, thin body gave Tad a melting smile. "Hello," he said as he walked by.

Tad dipped his chin in response. " 'Ssup," he growled, all serious and street, but when the man had passed, Tad grinned and gave himself a thumbs-up.

Jamal was likely to get whiplash, he was working so hard at seeing everything there was to see. "It's hog heaven up in here!" he hissed at us. He was getting his fair share of appreciation, too.

My shoulders were getting warm from the sun. It wasn't too bright, but it could still burn. I fished the flat plastic bottle of sunscreen out of the back pocket of my shorts and smeared some all over my upper body. Better protect the nips. Then I flipped the bottle at Jamal. "Here," I said. "Put some sunscreen on that pretty behind."

He caught the bottle, looked at the label, sneered at me. "Girl, what you think I need this for? Got me more melanin than alla these motherfuckers out here!"

"All right, but don't come crying to me when your hide gets hard and leathery like somebody's old wallet." I held out my hand for the bottle. Jamal cut his eyes at me, but he put the sunscreen on.

An older man came walking past us. He looked white, but he was tanned a deep brick red. His skin had settled into soft folds on his body, and he clanked when he moved. I spotted a pinkie-thick rod through each nipple, plugs and multiple rings through his ears, and a bunch more rings and rods through his dick. There were probably more I wasn't seeing. Tad shuddered, but I thought he looked really interesting. Had to admire his dedication.

Then I got a better look at one of the men coming out of the water. Could it be? I wasn't sure. He saw us, altered his trajectory so that his path would cross ours. Dragonfly tattooed on his left thigh. Yes, it was him!

As he passed by, he looked Jamal up and down, slowly. "Mmm," he said, "chocolate." He walked on, gazing back at Jamal now and again. He flagged down the martini seller.

"What the fuck was that?" said Jamal.

I chuckled. "He didn't recognize me."

"Where you know him from?" Tad asked.

"Shuck," said Jamal, "can we find somewhere to sit that's a little bit private? All of a sudden, I'm not digging these guys so much anymore."

Perfect. Just my chance. "They're not all like that, you know," I said. But I led them to the place I had in mind, a private little patch of sand surrounded by scrubby trees. Good, no one was using it just now.

"Where do you know him from?" asked Tad again.

I pointed to a large flat-topped rock. "You can sit there," I told them. "It's almost like an armchair."

"Susanna . . . I know you when you get like this," Tad said. "What's the story with that guy?"

I grinned. "You gonna take those clothes off? It's warm down here."

Jamal put his clothing down on the rock and went to undo the fly on Tad's jeans. Tad made a show of slapping his hands away, then submitted. I sat on the boulder that was conveniently near the flat rock and watched. Triumphantly, Jamal yanked the zipper down.

"Wait, sweetie, wait," Tad said. "Gotta take the shoes off first." With a shy glance at me, he sat on the rock, put his balled-up shirt next to Jamal's clothing, and started taking off his runners. To keep him company, I took off my sandals, put them on the boulder beside me. Tad got his shoes and socks off, snuck me a glance again, rocked his jeans off his hips, and pulled his legs out of them. He was wearing black cotton shorts underneath. So modest. He rolled the jeans up beside the other clothing.

"Stand up," I said. "Let me see you."

Slowly, he did. His thighs were thick, his calves full and muscled. "Well, look at you," I told him. Jamal was smiling at me thoughtfully. Was he egging me on?

"Lover," he said to Tad, "turn all the way around for your friend. Let her look at you."

He *was* egging me on.

"The two of you are shameless," muttered Tad, but to my surprise, he did what Jamal asked. I took my time admiring his butt, the fullness of his belly. He turned to face me, but I'd barely glanced at his package in his shorts when he sat down. "So," he said, faking nonchalance, "you gonna tell me about that guy?"

"You wanna know what happened, you have to take the shorts off."

He cocked his hand on his hip. "Is the story worth it?"

"Worth seeing you in the full, glorious flesh? It's a high price, baby, but I think I can meet it."

He made a face at me. But he looked pleased, too. This felt good. This felt like the way we used to tease each other. I just wanted to push it up a notch, that's all.

Maybe Tad was thinking the same thing because all of a sudden he pulled his shorts down, stepped out of them, grabbed them up off the sand, and sat down. He tossed the shorts onto the pile of clothing and turned back to me. "There," he said. He crossed his hands in his lap, conveniently hiding his crotch. "So, tell me the story." Jamal sat on the warm sand beside Tad's knee.

"All right," I said. "You asked for it."

I settled comfortably on my boulder, leaned forward. "Well, Sula and I have this game, right? Every so often, one of us dares the other one to do something outrageous. If you chicken out from doing whatever it is, you lose, and you have to be the other person's sex toy for a night; do everything they say."

"Ooh," said Jamal. "Kinky." He stroked Tad's calf.

I snickered. "You don't know the half of it. One time I lost on purpose. Could barely stand the next day, after Sula got done with me." The memory of that night was making my nipples crinkle up. All those girly pantyhose that Sula owned had made the most fiendish restraints. I didn't know I could bend in some of those positions.

"You're stalling, Shuck," said Tad.

"No, just setting the story up. 'Cause this one time, I took her up on her dare. There's this gay bar called Pump Jack's, a men's bar. I'll take you there on Friday. Sula said she wanted me to go in there and get one of the guys to let me jerk him off."

"No!" said Tad.

"Yes. And I did it."

"With that guy we just saw?"

"With that guy."

"How?"

"I went to the bar in drag. . . ."

"In a dress?" asked Tad.

Jamal chuckled. "No, silly. She went in guy drag."

Though, come to think of it, I pretty much look like I'm in drag when I wear a dress, too. "Yeah," I said. "Little goatee, little bit of extra swagger in the walk. Wore my regular clothes. Walked right in. I mean, I go in there as a chick, so I thought the bouncer would recognize me. He got this look like he almost did, but then you could see he didn't make the connection. I didn't speak the whole time. Ordered a beer at the bar by pointing at the draft spigot. When I started drinking it, I knew I'd have to do something soon, before I needed to go and piss."

Tad was shaking his head. "Susanna, you are something else."

"Susanna left home. I'm Shuck."

"What happened then?"

"I saw this guy looking at me. That guy. The one on the beach. I started staring him down, looking him up and down. If I did that to a woman, she'd probably run a mile. But this guy, he came and sat next to me. Said hi. I didn't answer; just pointed with my chin over to the bathroom. Shit, I didn't think it would work! Figured he'd see I was a woman, and I'd have to pass it all off as a joke.

"But that didn't happen. He just gave me this rude, slow smile. Leaned over and whispered that he'd see me in there. And off he headed, to the john.

"My heart was fucking hammering in my chest, I tell you. But I put down my beer, followed him. He slipped into a stall, and I slipped in behind him. He reached for me, but I didn't want him touching me too much. Women's skin has this soft feeling, you know? Even mine. Didn't want that to give me away. So I pushed his back against the stall door. I sat on the toilet, unzipped him . . ."

"Shit, that's hot," said Jamal. He was leaning forward, his mouth a little open. His cock was firming up. I was getting a tingle in my shorts, too, telling this story.

"He was hard the second I got his dick out of his pants. I slid my hands up under his shirt, grazed his nipples, pulled on them a little."

Tad swallowed.

"I ran my tongue around the head of his dick. He moaned, kinda low. I held on to his dick, gave it a good squeeze. It jumped in my hand."

Tad got this odd look. He squeezed his knees together and said, "You know, you better stop talking like that; else you might see something you don't wanna see."

Oh yes. Now we were getting somewhere. Jamal looked up at his lover, gave him an evil grin.

I stared right into Tad's eyes. "What you covering up there, Tad?" I said. Jamal snickered, but I held Tad's gaze like the headlights hold the deer's. "Something I'm saying getting you horny? Something about the way I pinched that man's nipples and took his dick in my fist and slid up and down, squeezing whenever my fingers went past the head?"

Tad gulped. He cupped his hands tighter around himself, but he wasn't fooling me; those hands were rubbing up and down, ever so slightly.

"You didn't know I did guys, did you? Only sometimes, Thaddeus. Only when the man is as gay as I am, and there's no hope in hell of pretending that the sex we're having is straight sex."

Jamal shot me a look. Was that admiration? I set my focus back on Tad. Jamal could match anything I could dish out, throw the challenge back in my face. We understood each other. Tad was the one I'd have to convince, if this was going to happen.

"Tad," I said.

"Yeah." His voice was raspy.

"You know what I did next?"

"No."

"I had my fist around that dick, feeling the little surging swells as he got more turned on. I took the other hand away from his nipples. . . ."

"Aww!" protested Jamal.

"Hush, you," I told him. "I took my hand and slid it flat down his belly, toward his cock. Held the head in one hand, just pumping a little, back and forth . . ."

"Oh god," whispered Tad. He was openly stroking himself now, hiding the view from me with one hand, sliding the other up and down over his cock and balls.

". . . held that head and drew my nails, very lightly, up the underside of his cock."

Tad's mouth opened.

"He moaned again, louder this time. He leaned back against the door. He had his hands at the top of the cubicle, hanging on to either side. I could see the muscles straining in his arms."

Tad made a little breathy noise.

"He got a drop of pre-come at the tip of his dick, just twinkling in the eye. I rubbed my thumb in it and used it to moisten the head of his dick."

Jamal moved in closer to Tad, laid his head on Tad's knee. Tad jumped and Jamal stroked Tad's inner thigh. "Shh, baby, it's okay," he said. Tad's eyes flicked from Jamal to me—a desperate, needy glance.

Jamal chuckled. He ran his tongue along the outside of Tad's thigh, licked his lips, and said to me, "So, did you suck him off?"

"Jamal!" Tad sat up straight. His hands slipped a little, and I could see his cock—compact, dark like the rest of him, with a pretty pink tip. Nice. "Jesus Christ, Shuck. You're my friend. We shouldn't . . ."

Jamal pressed Tad back against the rock, stroked his tummy. "Don't fret, Daddy. This is fun." Bless the boy, I thought. He looked back at me. "So, did you?"

I shook my head. "Suck him off? Not my thing. You know what I did instead?"

"What?" whispered Tad. Jamal gave him an encouraging smile.

"I spat on the place where my hand and his dick met, got it nice and wet. I started pumping him really slow."

Jamal ducked under Tad's leg, moved Tad's hands away from his cock and balls, held them out, away from his body. "Like this?" he said. He spat on Tad's erect cock. Tad gasped. His hands made clutching motions. Jamal let them go. Tad held on to Jamal's shoulders, threw his head back. "Like this?" Jamal asked again, and started sliding Tad's cock in his fist. Fuck, they were lovely together.

"Kinda like that," I told Jamal. "Keep going." I opened my own knees, thumbed my shorts open, and yanked the zipper down. I could smell my own musk. I slid my hand between my belly and the spread-open zipper. No underwear; I mostly don't bother with it. The crisp curls of my pubic hair were damp. Jamal dipped his mouth down to Tad's cock, ran his tongue slowly around the head of it. Now both Tad and I were moaning. I splayed my legs wider. My fingers found the folds of my pussy. They were hot and slick. My clit was puffy between them. It jumped at my touch, at the sight of Tad, eyes closed, mouth open, his hand around the back of Jamal's neck. Tad was bucking his hips now, slowly, popping his cock in and out of Jamal's mouth. Jamal, greedy Jamal, kept reaching for more.

"Jamal," I said hoarsely. "Can you get to your knees?"

Jamal made a garbled sound of assent around Tad's cock in his mouth. Tad reacted to the vibration with a slight shudder. Somehow Jamal managed to get into position. He spread his knees for traction, released Tad's cock from his mouth, and started tonguing Tad's balls. His perfect ass was displayed to my view, firm and dark as a cherry; two halves with the split between. With my three middle fingers I started rubbing my pussy, fast and flat against my clit, fingertips dipping into my cunt with each push. I was creaming inside my shorts.

There was sweat running down Tad's chest and heavy belly.

More of it beaded in his tight, short hair and the beautifully groomed goatee. "God, you two are hot," I muttered. Tad opened his eyes, saw me looking, squeezed them shut again. He slowed his incursions into Jamal's mouth. I got a flash image of a black-furred head disappearing shyly beneath the water. Oh no you don't, Tad. I wasn't going to let this scene end here.

"So that guy in the bathroom?" I said to them.

"Mm?" mumbled Jamal, around a mouthful of Tad's cock and balls.

"I'm working him up with one hand. I hold the other hand up to his mouth. I'm still not talking, but he gets the idea. He starts licking my hand. Gets it good and wet."

"Shit," whispered Tad. But the rhythm of his hips had sped up again.

"I took that hand, cupped his balls with it. But just for a second." Remembering that forbidden night got me even wetter. I kept working my clit, slipped a couple of fingers on the other hand into my cunt, just at the entrance, beckoning against the front wall. Shit, shit, yeah. "Then," I said, "I slipped my hand past his balls, back, until I touched his asshole. He jumped a little."

So had Jamal. The motion pushed his ass out even further into relief. His little pink rosebud of an asshole winked at me. I could see the curling black hairs that ran from the small of his back down toward it, like an arrow. *Here's the honey. Here.* Jamal had one hand on his own dick, stroking hard.

"I slipped one fingertip in. . . . " I said.

Tad started to pant. His eyes were wide open now, fixed on Jamal's busy mouth.

"His asshole squeezed tight around my finger, like a little kiss. Then it opened up for me."

Jamal was making little groaning noises around Tad's cock. I pushed off from my rock, dropped to my knees beside them. Knees would pay for that later. My clit under my strumming fingers felt like a marble in syrup. The fingers of my other hand stroked hard against the spongy ridge just inside my cunt. It pushed back. Soon. "I . . . " My body was shaking, my crotch jutting toward Jamal and

Tad. My thigh muscles knotted. It felt good. "I pushed one finger inside him. Then two. He took them both."

"Shuck," muttered Tad, "it's . . . I'm . . ." Jamal had his fist clamped tight around the base of Tad's cock, his mouth working the head. His hand between his own legs was almost a blur. He was screwing his ass around in the air. He looked so nasty.

"I plunged those fingers in and out of him, feeling him clasp them with each push. His dick was hard as iron in my hands."

The letting-down feeling started inside me, muscles starting to push down and forward. It was like I needed to piss.

"He slammed his shoulders back against the door. His crotch was arched way out. He was calling out for Jesus. He started to come. It spurted . . ."

Tad made this low, deep growl. His body began to spasm. Jamal pulled his mouth away so we could watch the gouts of juice rhythmically pumping out of Tad's cock. He stared, intent, at his lover's crotch, then came himself, hard and roaring.

That put me over the edge. My hand was flying at my clit, my forearms like cables. My own body pushed my fingers out of me, and I let go, and I was flying. I howl and laugh when I come, and I squirt. Lots. When I was done, the front of my shorts was sopping, and Tad's foot and Jamal's knee were in a puddle of girl-juice-soaked sand. I collapsed onto my side, breathing hard. It was going to be hell getting the sand out of my dreads.

I heard a noise behind us. I pulled my hands out of my pants and rolled over. Two eager heads had just pushed through the bushes to see what all the commotion was about. "Oh, excuse us," said the two men. They tromped away, giggling. I heard one of them say, "Was that a *woman* with them?"

Jamal started laughing, a low, slow roll. He put his head on Tad's knee and said to me, "Girl, you are some dirty bitch." He reached out and high-fived me. Our hands made a wet noise as they slapped together.

Tad still looked a little sheepish, but his whole body was more relaxed now. He leaned back against the rock, stroked Jamal's head. "Is this Canadian hospitality, Shuck?" he teased me.

I put my head against the warm sand, reached out a foot, and slid it along first Tad's leg, then Jamal's. I was going to have quite the story to tell Sula tonight. I admired our skins, the three shades of brown against the pale sand. "Look at us," I said.

"Three black sheep," Jamal joked.

"Three blackberries," I replied.

Tad gave a happy sigh. "And such sweet juice."

LA SEGUA

Brandon Massey

When Daniel saw the woman at the bar in San José, he thought he must have been dreaming.

The bar was La Terraza. It was in El Pueblo, north of the center of San José, a bustling district of shops, restaurants, art galleries, and nightclubs that resembled an old Spanish village. On that balmy March evening, the cobblestone streets and rain-forest flowers were still wet, evidence of a thunderstorm that had struck only an hour ago. The storm clouds had departed as suddenly as they had come, the velvet sky so clear that volcanic mountains were visible on the horizon of the Central Valley. All sorts of people, tourists and locals alike, meandered along the narrow sidewalks, weaving in and out of bars and clubs on a current of laughter, chatter, and salsa and merengue music.

Daniel had visited La Terraza during the first week of his vacation to Costa Rica, on a tip from a native who'd praised the bar's drinks. He'd spent a lot of time there over the past three weeks, drinking Cuba libres and ruminating on his depressing life.

The bar staff spoke fluent English, the food was delicious, and the drinks were potent enough to knock you into dreamland. Which is precisely where Daniel reasoned he must be when he'd sat at the counter contemplating the depths of his third Cuba libre and turned to see a woman who bore a flawless likeness to Jasmine Hart.

At eight o'clock on a Friday evening, the bar was only a quarter full, mostly with regulars. A bald, fortyish American man in a dark suit and a loosened tie sat at one end of the bar, sipping an Imperial cerveza and reading the *Tico Times*, the country's English-language newspaper. A young Latin couple who loved to drink shots of *guaro* as much as they loved to publicly grope each other occupied a table facing the idyllic courtyard. The bartender stood at a sink, his back to Daniel as he washed glasses.

The woman sat three stools down on Daniel's left. As improbable as it seemed, she *had* to be Jasmine Hart. The similarity was uncanny.

Although Daniel had last seen her in high school in Illinois, almost fifteen years ago, he would never forget her face.

How could he ever forget The Most Beautiful Girl in the World?

She wore a red sundress that hinted at the exciting contours of her body—a figure that looked as ripe as it had when she'd been the captain of the cheerleading squad. Thick auburn hair cascaded to her shoulders in gentle waves. Her cinnamon skin glowed golden in the bar's light.

She was turned slightly away from him, her gaze resting on the TV at the opposite end of the bar, picking at a plate of plantains. Her profile—chocolate brown doe eyes, pouty lips, button nose—was enough to convince him that she was Jasmine Hart.

Strangely, he hadn't seen her enter the bar. It was as though he had turned and she appeared, like a fantasy materializing in the flesh.

He must be deeper in his cups than he'd realized. Was he on drink number three, or four? Daniel couldn't remember. Dwelling on his pathetic life tended to make him lose track of how much he drank.

Feeling his gaze on her, she shifted to face him, tucking a strand of hair away from her eyes.

Jasmine used to brush away her hair just like that. Daniel had
sat across from her in chemistry class, sophomore year. He'd memorized her movements better than the periodic table of the
elements.

It *was* Jasmine.

But why would she be here, thousands of miles away from
Illinois?

A smile flickered across her face. Was that a spark of recognition in her eyes? It couldn't be. She wouldn't remember him.
They'd hardly ever talked.

Before he could stop himself, he'd opened his mouth.

"Forgive me if I'm wrong," he said. "But have I seen you somewhere before?"

It was the worst opening line from the Book of Bad Opening
Lines. But the liquor had loosened his tongue, and it was the first
thing that popped into his mind.

Her smile broadened.

"You know, I was thinking the same thing," she said, her voice
as sexily husky as he remembered. "Did you go to high school in
Illinois?"

"Zion-Benton," Daniel said. "Go Zee-Bees . . ."

"Oh my God!" She burst into a high-pitched laugh and covered her mouth. "Is your name David . . . no, Daniel?"

"Daniel Price. And I know who you are, you're Jasmine Hart."

She nodded. "Wow, this is so funny! What're you doing here?
Costa Rica—a long way from home, isn't it? Are you on
vacation?"

"Something like that," he said, and realized how mysterious he
sounded. But he liked how the words came out and didn't elaborate. "You?"

"Same thing, I guess," she said. A shadow flitted over her face.
"I flew in a couple of days ago."

Daniel discreetly noted her ring finger. It was bare, but a ribbon
of skin was lighter than the rest of the finger.

Three weeks in the Central American sun had tanned the ring

mark on his own naked finger. One of the first things he'd done after arriving in the country was leave his ring in his hotel room.

Imagine this. Me and Jasmine Hart, playing hooky from our spouses, meeting in a bar in San José . . .

He quickly nixed the fantasy. He wasn't in Jasmine's league. Back in school, she'd dated Reggie Taylor, an All-State running back. Daniel remembered the guy as clearly as if school had ended yesterday. Jasmine and Reggie had dated throughout school and been high-school royalty. They'd been prom king and queen at least twice, voted Most Likely to Succeed, *and* Most Likely to Get Rich and Famous. When their names were announced at graduation, the student body had roared with applause, as if they were superstars.

Daniel had been an average student: not athletic enough to be a jock, not smart enough to be a nerd, not handsome enough to be a ladies' man, not edgy enough to be a bad boy. He was merely in attendance, sliding by with unremarkable grades and lackluster achievements. When he crossed the stage at graduation, he'd been greeted with perfunctory handclaps.

Although some underachieving kids graduated from high school and blossomed into successful adults, the line charting his life had continued along the same dull, average course. He got a business degree from an average school. He married an average-looking girl he'd met in college. He landed an average job at an insurance company. He lived in a Chicago suburb, in a subdivision full of average homes.

And now, at thirty-one, his marriage teetered on the brink of divorce and he'd been pink-slipped from his job—calamities that commonly befell average guys like him.

This trip to Costa Rica, funded with his severance package money, was his last-ditch attempt to figure out how his life had gone so wrong and what he was going to do about it.

Meeting Jasmine here, and discovering that she remembered him, seemed like divine intervention. A sign that he was meant for bigger and better things.

Above average things.

Jasmine watched him with an expectant smile.

He wished he had a glass of water because his mouth was dry.

"How long are you staying here?" he asked.

She shrugged. "Until I've found what I'm looking for."

"What are you looking for?"

"What are we all looking for, Danny?"

His wife, Stacy, was the only one who called him Danny, and she'd reserved that name for intimate moments in the bedroom. Hearing his name roll so easily off Jasmine's tongue sent a pleasant shiver down his spine.

"Happiness, the meaning of life?" he said.

"I was thinking—a good time. Scratch that, a *great* time."

Her eyes sparkled.

A great time.

Was she flirting with him?

Under normal circumstances, the thought would have been ridiculous. This was *the* Jasmine Hart, the queen of Zion-Benton High School, and she looked more gorgeous now than she ever had during her school days. But since graduation, he'd started to go bald and had gained so much flab that his wife once complained that he looked like a black Pillsbury Dough Boy.

As he looked at the gleam in her eyes, however, the idea didn't seem far-fetched at all.

"A great time," he repeated.

"You know what that is, Danny? Or have all those years with wifey numbed your senses?"

"How'd you know I was married? I'm not wearing a ring."

"Don't have to. It's practically stamped on your forehead, baby."

He touched his forehead, as if he would discover a giant M painted there in red.

She reached across the counter and held his hand. Heat flared in his loins, and he began to feel a little dizzy.

This was unbelievable. She *was* flirting with him.

Daniel felt such a surge of lust that he was unable to speak.

"It's all good," she said. "I'm married, too. I don't know how much longer I'll be married, though." A shadow passed over her features.

He cleared his throat. "Did you marry Reggie Taylor?"

"Now that's a name I haven't heard in ages. God no. We broke up two months after graduation. He was the biggest ho in the world."

"No kidding? I always thought you guys would be together forever."

She laughed. "We've got a lot of catching up to do, don't we, Danny? Why don't you come a little closer and buy me a drink? I won't bite." She smiled mischievously.

Feeling more intoxicated than ever—and this time, no credit to the rum—he moved awkwardly to the stool beside her.

That was how it started.

■ ■ ■

Two hours and several drinks later, Daniel and Jasmine left the bar and took a taxi to his hotel in Barrio Amon, the city's historical district.

He was staying at Hotel Santo Tomas, a French Victorian mansion formerly owned by a coffee baron. He'd learned about the hotel on the Internet, while furtively planning his hiatus from his life. When his severance package came through, he'd booked a room for a month.

Daniel hadn't told Stacy about his trip until a week before he was scheduled to leave. Predictably, that night they'd had their worst fight ever.

As they crossed the quiet lobby to the main staircase, Jasmine grasped his hand.

He blushed. No one here knew his real situation. To the hotel staff, he was a bachelor who'd fallen into a little money and had come to Costa Rica for a respite from the States. Guilt covered him like a heavy coat.

"Nervous?" she asked.

"Nah," he lied. "Feeling good."

"Really? So you've done something like this before?"

"Something like what before?"

"You know. Fool around."

"Well . . . not really."

"Good, I want to be your first." Jasmine smiled.

They climbed the steps.

Daniel suddenly had the feeling he was being watched. He looked over his shoulder.

One of the housekeepers stared at him from a doorway across the lobby. It was the man who cleaned his room each morning. A short, dark-haired native, he trudged about the hotel with downcast eyes and a grim expression, never speaking. Daniel had said *hola* once, but he'd ignored him.

The housekeeper had never looked at Daniel directly—until now. Daniel couldn't read the man's expression. His face was a blank stone tablet.

"Come on, Danny." Jasmine's grip tightened.

Daniel turned away, still feeling the man's gaze on him, and followed her upstairs.

■ ■ ■

On the staircase landing between floors, Daniel said, "Did you see how that guy was staring at me?"

"What guy?"

"One of the housekeepers. Short, dark-haired guy across the lobby."

"Maybe he was staring at *me*." Nudging him to the wall, Jasmine stood in front of him and draped her arms around his neck. "I have that effect on men sometimes, you know."

Her perfume, a spicy fragrance, filled his head like a fog. She kissed him—a soft, teasing touch on the lips.

All thoughts of the housekeeper left his mind. He wound his hands around her narrow waist.

I can't believe I'm with Jasmine Hart, I just can't believe it.

Smiling at his shyness, she put her hands on his and urged his fingers down to the firm swell of her butt.

She felt so good that Daniel wanted to cry.

He tightened his hold on her hips, as if holding fast to a dream he didn't dare let slip away.

Jasmine kissed him again, her tongue lingering on his lips.

He felt as though he would explode, and they hadn't even done anything yet. It was as if he were an overexcited teenager kissing a girl for the first time.

"Come," she whispered.

He followed her up the last, short flight of steps, and along the dimly lit hallway, to his room near the end.

His hand trembled so badly he could barely dig the key out of the pocket of his khakis. He fumbled to unlock the door.

"Here." She placed her hand on his, helped him insert the key in the lock, and turned the knob.

"Sorry," he said. "It's just that I've always dreamed of you—"

"I know," she said, then guided him inside and shut the door behind them.

■ ■ ■

He had a spacious, tastefully decorated room. King Louis XV furniture. Hardwood floors adorned with Persian rugs. Bright paintings of tropical lands. A bay window offered a view of the glittering neighborhood.

A collection of scented candles stood on the dresser, courtesy of the hotel. Jasmine asked him to light them while she went to the bathroom.

As he lit the candles, he noticed his wedding ring lying on the bureau. It shone like a watchful eye.

None of the downtown hotels had air-conditioning, and he could've used it. The ceiling fan suddenly couldn't keep him cool enough.

The ring stared at him accusingly.

You promised to be faithful to your wife.

His conscience was reprimanding him. It sounded a lot like Stacy.

He'd never cheated on Stacy, not once in eight mostly miserable years of marriage. He'd been a nice guy, had tried to be a good husband, and though he'd been tempted many times, reverence for his vows had kept him faithful.

But every man has a moment of weakness.

And his had finally arrived, packaged as Jasmine Hart.

The ring seemed to glow.

You promised to be faithful.

Jasmine knew he was married and could care less whether the ring lay in view. But he couldn't stand to look at it.

You promised.

He swept the ring into a drawer, out of sight.

■ ■ ■

Jasmine emerged from the bathroom wearing a lacy red bra and a thong.

Daniel sat on the bed, gaping at her.

"God, you're beautiful," he said, his voice hoarse.

She sauntered toward him, knelt in front of him, and spread his legs.

He sat there as if he were a puppet, willing to let her pull his strings however she desired.

She put her hand on the bulge in his slacks and kneaded it. He groaned.

"I've been wanting this since high school," she said.

"You . . . you *have?*"

Massaging him, Jasmine nodded.

"Sophomore year, chemistry class," she said. "Remember?"

"How could I forget? You sat next to me."

"I wanted to sit *on* you, Danny. Sit on you and grind. But all that dumb high-school popularity shit . . . I could never be who I wanted to be, be with the guy I really wanted."

"Me?"

"Of course. I used to hope you'd talk to me." She sighed with regret. "But you never really did."

He didn't know what to say. Jasmine had wanted him? He hadn't thought that she had been more than peripherally aware of his existence.

I wanted to sit on you, Danny. Sit on you and grind.

To think that he'd spent the last ten years of his life—two in courtship, eight in marriage—with Stacy, who, even on her most glamorous day, could never compare to Jasmine.

He might have even married Jasmine.

It was an awe-inspiring thought.

As his mind reeled, Jasmine rose. He looked up at her, over the mounds of her luscious breasts.

"Would you leave your wife for me?" she asked.

He hesitated only a moment. "Yes. Yes, I would."

"Don't you love her?"

"Not as much as I've always loved you."

"Oh, Danny, that's so sweet. And it's what I'd hoped to hear."

"It's the truth. I've fantasized about you forever."

"Undress me?"

With clammy fingers, he unhooked her bra, let it fall.

Good Lord.

She smiled. "The thong, too."

He slid the garment down her legs, and she was revealed in all her glory.

Someone needed to pinch him. This absolutely could not be happening to him.

Perhaps he had passed out at La Terraza after too many Cuba libres, and even now was asleep, drooling on the counter.

"Not a dream," she said, with a gentle smile. "You'll see . . . later."

He was going to ask her what she meant, but then she climbed on the bed, showing her butt to him, her beautiful bare ass, and when she invited him to join her, he couldn't strip out of his clothes fast enough.

■ ■ ■

Afterward, they lay together in the sweat-dampened sheets, the flickering candle flames the only lights in the room.

"That was good," she said. "Did you like it?"

"This is the best night of my life." Daniel sighed.

"Then you had a *great* time."

"*Great* doesn't describe it. It was *unbelievable*."

"Good." She snuggled against his chest, her breaths deepening as she drifted into sleep.

Daniel saw the message indicator blinking on the telephone on the nightstand. The phone hadn't rung since Jasmine had been there, so someone must have left the message while he'd been at La Terraza.

Only one person could have called: Stacy.

Perhaps she sensed, by some woman's intuition, that he was cheating on her.

Daniel was surprised to realize how little he cared.

He pulled Jasmine closer.

He had told Jasmine he would leave his wife for her, and he meant it. He'd come to Costa Rica because he was contemplating a divorce and wanted time alone, to sort out his thoughts before making a decision and going home.

But since he'd met Jasmine, did he really have to go back home at all?

He could stay here with Jasmine, and they could build their lives anew, together. Hell, Costa Rica teemed with U.S. expatriates.

It was a deliciously appealing idea—the sweetest idea he'd had in years.

Perhaps a life of being average finally was behind him.

Smiling, he went to sleep.

And awoke in a nightmare.

■ ■ ■

He lay in bed, and Jasmine lay beside him, eyes closed. She idly massaged his chest; her nails were painful. He looked down and saw that, instead of fingers, she had a set of sharp claws. Shredded skin, like wood shavings, covered his chest.

As he drew back in shock, Jasmine sprang up and opened her mouth, revealing long fangs dressed in saliva. A serpent's tongue slithered around her black maw. She had bulging red eyes, like blood blisters.

A rumbling voice sounded in his head.

You've renounced your wife, Daniel. Now you belong to me.

Her eyes burned like the flames of hell.

You'll always belong to me. . . .

The monster came forward, as if to give him a deadly kiss.

Daniel screamed.

■ ■ ■

And woke up, the scream trapped in his throat.

Morning sunlight sifted through the curtains. The candles had burned down to nubs. Heart banging, he turned to look beside him.

Jasmine was gone.

But there was a note on the pillow, written on the hotel's letterhead, in elegant handwriting he recognized as Jasmine's. It was the same as when he had graded her chemistry papers years ago.

Sweetest Danny,

Thank you for an unforgettable night. Let's do it again. Can you meet me at La Terraza tonight? Ten o'clock?

Jasmine

He thought about the bizarre dream. Jasmine with claws, fangs, and demonic eyes? It was nuts.

You'll always belong to me. . . .

It was guilt speaking to him, that's all. The monster symbolized his shame or something like that.

As unsettling as it had been, the dream merely proved that he had a conscience. It wasn't as though he were happy that he had cheated on his wife. It was nothing to boast about. But he'd done it.

And he'd do it again.

He was a new man now, with a brighter future.

Whistling, he hopped out of bed to shower.

When Daniel stepped out of the shower, the phone was ringing.

He answered it. "Hello?"

"Hi, Daniel."

It was Stacy. Her voice, usually high-pitched and demanding, was oddly flat.

He scratched the back of his neck. Something was wrong.

"How are you?" he asked.

"Did you get my message? I called you last night."

He saw the blinking message light on the phone. Damn, he had forgotten about that.

"I didn't get in till late," he said, casting about for a plausible lie. "I'd had a few drinks and—"

"Were you out with another woman?"

"No," he said, a bit too quickly.

He expected Stacy to press the issue, but she only sighed. She sounded tired.

"Is everything okay?" he asked.

It was a dumb question to ask. He had left her at home while he spent a month in Costa Rica to decide whether he wanted to be married anymore. How could anything be okay?

"I'm pregnant, Daniel," she said.

"What?" He nearly dropped the phone.

"The doctor confirmed it yesterday. I'm pregnant, Daniel, with our baby."

She started to cry. He realized why she'd sounded exhausted— she'd probably been up all night crying.

He didn't know what to say to her. He was afraid to say anything because he might confess what he'd done.

He plopped on the bed. As his wife wept, his hands found Jasmine's note.

Let's do it again.

"I want you to come home," Stacy sobbed.

She'd never asked him to come home. Not once. When he had announced he was leaving for Costa Rica, "to clear his head," she threw a vase at him and chased him out, screaming, "Fine, take your black ass down there, I hope you catch malaria!" And whenever she'd called, it had only been to cuss him out.

But she had humbled herself to ask him to come back. Only real pain would drop her to her knees like this.

But he didn't *want* to go home.

Maybe if she had called him yesterday morning, he would have acquiesced. But this morning, he had a new lease on life.

"I'm sorry, but we'll have to talk about this later," he said.

Her answering wail pierced his eardrum.

He removed the phone from his ear and hung up.

■ ■ ■

Daniel wanted to see Jasmine sooner. The phone call with Stacy had put him in a sour mood. Jasmine would lift his spirits.

But he didn't have her number. He didn't even know where she was staying. In the heat of last night's passion, he'd forgotten to ask those basic questions.

No matter. He would see her tonight.

He went downstairs for breakfast. After he got some coffee and food in him, he hoped he could figure out what to do about Stacy.

He chose his customary spot in the open-air dining room: a corner table that offered a view of the immense swimming pool. A "tropical" continental breakfast buffet—papaya, mangoes, bananas, pineapples, pastries, juices, and the country's renowned coffee—covered the polished bar.

Daniel heaped his plate with fruit and avoided the sweets. He wanted to trim his pudgy forty-inch waist, to look good for Jasmine.

An older gentleman named Cortez, who usually worked during breakfast hours, was there. Like most Costa Rican men, Cortez was short and compact. He had a full head of gray hair, a broad face, and large, muscular hands due to the years he'd spent laboring on coffee plantations.

Cortez greeted Daniel with a formal bow as he returned to the table.

Daniel liked the guy. Fluent in English, Cortez had fed him a lot of valuable information about things to do in the country. He'd told Daniel about La Terraza, in fact, so he was indirectly responsible for Daniel hooking up with Jasmine.

Although diners typically got coffee for themselves, Cortez flipped over a cup, and then started pouring coffee and cream into the mug simultaneously from separate decanters, the customary manner in which coffee was served there.

Daniel hadn't been a big coffee drinker before visiting the country, but he'd quickly become addicted to Costa Rica's national drink. The golden bean was such an integral part of life there that he'd heard of mothers feeding a weak mix of coffee and milk to their nursing babies.

"*Buenos días,*" Cortez said. "You look like you've had a long night. Meet a nice Tica?"

"Matter of fact, I did meet a very nice lady last night. An old friend from high school. I met her at La Terraza, the bar you told me about."

"Ah, an old flame." Cortez grinned.

Sipping coffee, Daniel blushed. "We weren't exactly flames when we were in school. But things change when you grow up." He thought about the things Jasmine had said and done. In spite of his mood, he had to smile. "Man, do they ever change."

"Are you going to see this lovely Tica again?" Cortez asked.

"Going to see her tonight. But I've run into a problem."

"Problem?" Cortez's eyebrows arched.

Daniel gazed into his coffee. He wanted to share his predicament with someone. Cortez was in his sixties and married for a long time. Daniel thought he might be able to drop some wisdom on him.

"I've never told you this, but I'm married," Daniel said. "I left my wife in the States, told her I needed some time away. We've talked about getting a divorce but haven't made any steps to do it yet." Daniel sighed. "She called me this morning. She's pregnant with our baby."

"*Muy malo.*" Cortez's eyes widened. "You say you met this Tica last night, she was someone you knew from school?"

"Yeah, but she's not the problem. The problem is, I don't know what I'm going to do about my wife. How can I divorce her if she's pregnant? That's cold-blooded, man."

"*Sí,*" Cortez said. His eyes were intense. "Tell me more about this Tica."

Why did he want to keep talking about Jasmine? Hadn't he heard what he'd said about Stacy?

Daniel shrugged. "Her name's Jasmine. She's beautiful, she was a cheerleader in school, everyone loved her, but I never had a chance with her. Or so I'd thought."

"Please explain, Daniel." Cortez's face tightened.

"Turns out she was crazy about me in school. I'd had no idea. Anyway, like I said, we met at the bar, by coincidence really, and hit it off. I can hardly believe that it happened. The chances of me running into her here must've been like ten million to one."

Cortez didn't smile at Daniel's luck. He frowned.

"I must ask this." Cortez reddened. "Did you have . . . relations with her?"

Daniel grinned. "Oh, yeah, I sure did. And it was incredible, man."

Cortez's frown deepened.

"Be careful with this Tica," he said. "Very careful."

"What're you talking about? You know her?"

"You should go home to your wife, my friend. Today. You would be safer at home with your wife."

"Go home? You've gotta be kidding me. What—is Jasmine some drug lord's mistress or something?"

Cortez leaned over the table. His eyes fixed on Daniel. His face had paled.

"Do *not* meet this Tica again. It may already be too late. Go home, please."

"I don't want to go home!" Daniel said, smacking his fist against the table and involuntarily knocking over the coffee.

Muttering in Spanish, Cortez touched the gold crucifix that he wore around his neck and then hurried away, disappearing into the kitchen.

Mopping up the spilled coffee, Daniel shook his head.

Stay away from Jasmine? Go home?

What in the world had the old man been talking about?

He hoped to pry more information out of Cortez, but another server took over his duties.

Daniel stopped the waiter. "Where's Cortez? I need to talk to him."

"Mr. Cortez is working elsewhere on the property," the waiter answered, as if he'd memorized the response.

Puzzled, Daniel began to eat. He kept a lookout for Cortez, but he didn't reappear.

Cortez was avoiding him. But why?

■ ■ ■

When Daniel headed down the hallway to his room, he found the housekeeper, who'd stared at him so strangely last night, hurrying out of his room, pushing a cart laden with cleaning supplies.

Daniel started running toward him. "Wait, I want to talk to you."

The man glanced over his shoulder at Daniel.

Last night, perhaps because of all the rum he'd drunk, Daniel had been unable to discern the look in the man's eyes. But he saw it now.

Fear.

"Come back!" Daniel yelled. "I only want to talk!"

The man deserted his cart in the middle of the corridor and fled to the end of the hall. He disappeared through a door that led to the stairwell.

Daniel gave up chasing him. He wasn't going to pin the guy down and make him talk. It wasn't that important to him.

He went to his room. The housekeeper had finished his cleaning duties: The bed was made, outfitted with crisp sheets.

A slip of paper lay on the center of the mattress. It was the note Jasmine had left for him.

Three words had been scrawled hastily, in red ink, at the bottom of the paper: BEWARE LA SEGUA.

Frowning, Daniel studied the note.

What the hell was La Segua?

He had a decent grasp of Spanish, thanks to four years in high school and two more in college, but he'd never heard of the word.

And why was the housekeeper warning him about it, then taking off like a thief in the night?

"Superstitious nonsense," Daniel said to himself. Although Costa Rica was an advanced nation with a high literacy rate, some of the natives still harbored all manner of backward ideas. The housekeeper must be one of them.

Cortez had seemed like a cool dude, but maybe he was loony, too.

Daniel was a rational guy. He didn't believe in UFOs and ghosts and bullshit like that. Some of his older relatives did—his grandma had a treasure trove of ghost stories—but he was a die-hard skeptic. Everything had a logical explanation.

He hated to throw away the note, since Jasmine's handwriting filled the upper half of the page and reading her words sent a charge of anticipation through him, but the housekeeper's stupid message had ruined it, like a splash of mud on a rose.

Cursing, he crumpled the paper and flushed it down the toilet.

■ ■ ■

Daniel spent much of the day downtown, at the Mercado Central. It was one of those clear, balmy days for which Costa Rica was famous. The outdoor market was crowded with a mix of tourists, brown-skinned natives, and beggars. Vendors and buyers haggled, dark-haired children scampered about, and spicy aromas, wafting from lean-to concession stands, scented the warm breeze.

Browsing the long rows of goods, Daniel refused to think about the housekeeper's nonsensical message and Stacy's announcement. He was determined to enjoy himself. He was in a tropical paradise and was going to see a gorgeous woman tonight.

Life wasn't perfect, but it was damned good.

He bought a silver necklace at a great price. A gift for Jasmine.

Later that night, leaving the hotel en route to his date with Jasmine at La Terraza, Daniel felt someone watching him.

He felt a gaze on him as he caught a taxi. Glancing over his shoulder revealed only the doorman, who was turned away from him.

Riding in the taxi through the traffic-packed streets, Daniel kept looking out the rear window. No one appeared to be following him, but a nagging feeling told him that he was being watched.

He had to be overreacting to Cortez and the housekeeper's weird behavior. Who would want to follow him? He was no one special.

At ten o'clock sharp, he pushed through the doors of La Terraza.

Jasmine waited for him at the bar.

"Thank you, Lord," Daniel said under his breath. To be honest, he'd been worried that she would stand him up, that she had come to her senses and realized that he was far too average to be with her.

But she was here, wearing a green dress that displayed her figure to startling effect.

When he reached her, Jasmine embraced him, pressing her breasts against his chest.

"I missed you, Danny," she said, her breath warm and sweet.

"Missed you, too," he said.

She clasped his hands in hers. "I want to go for a walk through El Pueblo."

"Sure." He was so happy just to be with her, he would've walked around the rim of a volcano with her.

Hand in hand, they left the bar and strolled on the narrow sidewalk, threading their way through the noisy, Saturday-night crowds.

Across the street, Daniel noticed a car—a blue Nissan Sentra—and wondered if that was the same car he'd seen earlier, driving several lengths behind his taxi.

Paranoid delusions, man. Let them go.

"Talk to your wife today?" Jasmine asked.

"Yeah, I don't want to go into that, though," he said. "It'll spoil the mood."

"Are you leaving her for me?"

"Jasmine, it's kinda complicated."

"I'm never going back to the States, Danny. I'm making this my home. I want you here with me."

"I want to be with you, too, but it's just not that simple."

She pulled him off the sidewalk, into an alley. Low stucco buildings surrounded them. Coppery light barely illuminated the length of the passageway. A sickly-sweet odor—the stench of garbage—reached him.

Jasmine pushed him roughly against the wall and unbuckled his belt.

"What . . . what're you doing?" he asked.

She sank to her knees in front of him.

Although he was nervous, he was excited, too. He knew what she was doing, all right, and he didn't want to stop her.

He loved spontaneous sex, especially in public, fantasized about it all the time. But Stacy was too much of a prude to ever do anything like that.

But Jasmine didn't care.

She unzipped his pants and dug his erection out of his boxers. Taking it in her fingers, she looked up at him, her eyes shining.

"You're something else," he said, almost panting.

She kissed the tip, her tongue fluttering across it. He moaned.

"Do you want to be with me, Danny?"

He didn't have to think about it.

"Yes . . . yes . . ."

She ran her tongue along the shaft. A spasm of pleasure almost buckled his knees. Jasmine smiled.

"Your wife's never done this to you, has she? Do you love me more than her?"

"Oh God, yes . . ."

She drew him possessively in her mouth.

He bit his tongue to stifle a shout. Tilted back his head and closed his eyes. Gave in to ecstasy.

She worked him in and out, in and out.

Shuddering, he lowered his head and looked at her.

And saw the monster from his nightmare, gazing up at him with bloodred eyes full of devilish pleasure.

You belong to me, Daniel.

He screamed.

He pushed the creature away and frantically pulled up his pants.

When he looked again, the monster was gone. Jasmine sat on her butt in the alley, looking up at him with confusion.

"Danny, what's wrong?"

He started to reply, but then looked into her eyes. They had glints of red, like flecks of blood.

A sly smile slid across her face.

"Oh shit," he said, hardly able to breathe.

"Renounced your wife, Danny," she whispered, in a voice that was like Jasmine's, but was cold and evil. "Now you're mine."

She opened her mouth wide. She had a long, black, forked tongue, like a serpent. Her mouth, full of fangs, dripped with saliva.

She hissed.

Daniel screamed and broke into a run.

Running down the alley toward the street, he saw the blue Nissan he'd seen earlier. It was parked at the curb.

Cortez hopped out of the passenger side and opened the rear door.

"Get inside, quick!"

Daniel didn't ask any questions. He dove into the backseat.

The car squealed away from the curb.

Daniel turned and saw Jasmine at the mouth of the alley, watching him, a faint smile on her face.

Now you're mine.

■ ■ ■

220   Brandon Massey

The housekeeper from the hotel was driving, his gaze focused on the road.

Cortez leaned over the passenger seat and examined Daniel. His face was grave.

"Are you okay?" Cortez asked.

"What the hell is going on?" Daniel said.

Cortez looked anxiously at the rear window. "She is La Segua."

"Who the fuck is La Segua?"

"Not who, *what*," Cortez said, crossing himself. "I know you are a man of reason, but you must listen and believe."

"After what I saw back there, I can believe anything."

Cortez nodded. "It is an old legend. Many years ago, La Segua was a beautiful Tica in Cartago, our old capital. She was in love with a Spaniard who broke her heart. His betrayal cursed her. She became a monster. But she looks at first like a beautiful woman."

Daniel shivered, glued to his seat, waiting for Cortez to finish.

"La Segua tempts men who are away from their wives. If the husband falls to temptation, La Segua will possess his soul."

"But she looked just like Jasmine, knew stuff about me from years ago—"

"La Segua is very powerful and very evil. She uses your dreams to tempt you."

Daniel sat shaking his head. He wanted to cry. Or drown himself in endless Cuba libres, to wipe away the memory of what had happened.

"Juan," Cortez said, nodding to the housekeeper, "he recognized La Segua when you brought her to the hotel last night. He had fallen to La Segua before. We broke its hold on him, but he lost his tongue forever."

The housekeeper glanced in the rearview mirror at Daniel and smiled sadly.

"You guys have been following me, haven't you?" Daniel said.

"*Sí,*" Cortez said. "Juan saw the letter La Segua had left in your room. We wanted to help you get home, where you might be safe. You must confess your sin to your wife and ask her to forgive you, Daniel. That may break La Segua's spell."

Daniel knotted his hands. Although every reasonable brain cell in his mind protested, he had no choice but to believe the legend. He had seen the creature with his own eyes.

It had all been too good to be true. The real Jasmine would never want him. How could he have been so stupid?

And he'd had sex with that . . . that *thing*.

He wanted to jump in a bathtub and scrub his skin raw.

They braked at a red light. Daniel glanced out the window.

A woman baring a mouthful of fangs pressed her face against the glass, red eyes fixed on him.

You belong to me.

Daniel screamed. "She's out there, let's go!"

"Please." Cortez grabbed his shoulder. "It is only an old woman. Look again."

Slowly, Daniel turned his head and looked.

It was indeed an elderly lady. She was getting inside a car parked along the side of the road.

"Jesus," Daniel said.

"La Segua's grip is strong on you," Cortez said. "We must hurry."

"Where are we going?" Daniel asked.

"To the airport," Cortez said.

■ ■ ■

They parked at the departures terminal at Juan Santamaría International Airport.

Cortez had packed Daniel's luggage. He helped him remove it from the trunk.

"I guess I should thank you," Daniel said. "But my head is spinning."

"There is one more thing," Cortez said. He withdrew a tiny box from his pocket and gave it to Daniel.

"This a good-luck charm or something?" Daniel asked.

Cortez nodded. "The best you could have, my friend."

Daniel opened the box.

Inside was his wedding ring.

Cortez clapped him on the shoulder. "Good luck. I will say prayers for you."

Daniel stood at the curb, watching the car vanish into the fog.

Someone brushed past him, jostling his luggage: a woman, with burning red eyes. She leered at him.

Renounced your wife . . .

He choked back a scream, not wanting to make a spectacle of himself, and lowered his gaze. He rolled his luggage toward the terminal entrance.

When he looked behind him, he saw that it was only an ordinary, blonde-haired woman.

I can't go on like this. I'll go crazy.

He slipped his wedding ring on his finger, as if it were in fact a talisman that could ward away evil.

Suddenly, he couldn't wait to get home.

■ ■ ■

The earliest return flight to Chicago was scheduled for the next morning. Daniel purchased a ticket and slept in the waiting area.

He slept fitfully, and it had nothing to do with the lumpy chair on which he rested. La Segua plagued his dreams, taunting him.

You cannot escape, Daniel. You belong to me.

When morning came, he called Stacy to tell her he was on his way home. When she didn't answer the phone, he left a message on the voice mail.

"Stacy, this is Daniel. I'm coming home."

He had planned only to give his flight arrival time and then hang up, but he found himself continuing to talk.

"I've been thinking about us, and our baby, and to be honest . . . I've been an asshole. I've been selfish. I've taken you for granted, for a long time, and I'm sorry. I'm really sorry. This whole trip of mine was a mistake, but it's made me realize some things about myself, about us. I want us to work on our marriage. I want us to work on it and set things right for our baby. I hope you can forgive me, honey. I'll see you this afternoon."

Daniel hung up. Tears streamed down his cheeks.

He'd been so caught up with emotion that he'd forgotten to give her his flight information. He called back and left another message giving his flight arrival time and asking her to pick him up.

When he finally took his seat on the airplane an hour later, he stared straight ahead. He was afraid to look around him and see a red-eyed woman leering at him.

Thankfully, La Segua did not appear during the flight.

Daniel dared to believe that his heartfelt message to his wife had snapped the curse. He hadn't said anything about committing adultery, but maybe he didn't need to. He'd admitted his other mistakes. Wasn't that enough?

After his flight arrived at Chicago O'Hare International Airport, he rushed to the baggage carousel, claimed his luggage, and went outside to wait for Stacy to pick him up.

He hoped that she'd gotten his message, hoped that she even wanted to see his face again.

He didn't see La Segua outside the terminal, either.

The whole experience was starting to feel like a bad dream, a nightmare from which he had finally awakened.

Daniel had been waiting outside for about twenty minutes when their SUV appeared, inching along the road toward him.

From the distance, Stacy was a shadowy figure behind the wheel.

He became absurdly certain that, instead of his wife, La Segua was driving their car. Stacy was going to get out and have fangs, claws, a snake's tongue, and crimson eyes, and she was going to leer at him and laugh at how she had fooled him into thinking he'd broken the curse; but in truth, he was doomed, fated to forever be bound to the infernal creature.

The SUV parked ahead of him. The tinted windows prevented him from seeing clearly inside.

On shaky legs, he went to the driver's side of the vehicle. The door opened.

Stacy climbed out, looking her ordinary, plain self.

Thank God, he thought. The curse really was broken.

He rushed forward and grabbed her in a crushing embrace.

"Stacy, I'm so glad to see you. I'm sorry for everything I put you through. I love you. I love you so much."

She hugged him tightly. "Welcome home, Danny."

He held her closer, full of gratitude.

Squeezing him tighter, she put her lips near his ear and spoke, her voice like stones scraping across a floor.

"You belong to me. . . ."

HAWAII FIVE-OH!

Tracy Price-Thompson

As I waited in line at the security checkpoint dressed in a tight designer T-shirt and a pair of comfortable cotton shorts, I was so hyped I could barely contain myself. Graduation was over and my hard-earned vacation in paradise was about to begin. Just watching my carry-on bag and Fendi purse slide through the X-ray scanner sent a shiver of pure excitement through me.

For a country girl from Tennessee, I hadn't done half bad. My newly earned law degree was soon to be my ticket out of the backwoods and onto the payroll of one of the most prestigious black law firms in the city of Memphis. I'd worked damn hard to graduate in the top 10 percent of my class, and I'd worked even harder to land a dream job that came complete with a great salary and top-notch benefits.

I'd recently moved out of my college dorm and into a small apartment on the outskirts of town, and was looking forward to beginning my new job in two weeks' time. But that was after my graduation present, courtesy of Uncle Junior and Aunt Gracie. They'd flown in from New York City to proudly watch me walk across the stage, then greeted me on the other side with an all-expenses-paid, one-week trip to Hawaii!

The airport was jam-packed with business travelers and struggling college students heading home for the summer. I wasn't the least bit fazed by the security checkpoints or the delays. This would be the first time I'd ever flown over an ocean, and even though it would have been cool to have a road dawg to travel with, I was thrilled beyond words at the thought of spending a week on an island rumored to be the closest thing to paradise.

An hour or so later, I had boarded the airplane and was buckled into a coach seat. I was sandwiched between a middle-aged Asian man on my left and a cutie-pie–looking brother on my right, who was slouched in his seat with his long legs splayed out in the aisle.

"What's up?" the brother asked, nodding in greeting as I smiled in return. He looked mixed, but with what, it was hard to tell. His skin was nutmeg brown and his teeth were dazzling white, but that head full of jet-black curly hair was truly an amazing sight to behold. It was neatly trimmed and tapered on the sides, and accentuated his dark eyes and flawless skin to a tee.

I turned away from him and glanced at the man on my left, who was resting his head against the window and reading a newspaper written in what looked, to my untrained eye, like Japanese.

The overhead bins were completely full in my immediate area, so I used my toe to nudge my carry-on bag farther under the seat in front of me. I then sat back and tried to relax as the flight attendants made sure everyone had on a seatbelt and the storage bins were secure.

This was only my second time on an airplane. The first time, I'd taken a brief trip in the sixth grade after I'd won the state spelling bee and was invited to Washington, D.C., to compete in the nationals. That trip had been so long ago that I'd just about forgotten what being up in the air was like. As the plane taxied down the runway and elevated itself into the wind, I clenched my armrests and gritted my teeth as I tried to stop my ears from popping and my poor stomach from hurling.

"Are you okay?" the brother asked. I managed to open one eye and nod weakly. "Take a few deep breaths," he urged. "Liftoffs can be rough, but we're reaching cruising elevation and things'll settle down in a few moments."

I took his advice and gulped deeply, trying my best to hold down that mocha caffe latte that I'd sipped before boarding. Each time I opened my eyes I found him staring at me, a look of deep concern creasing his handsome brown face.

"Better," I said after a few minutes, slowly releasing the armrests and settling back into my seat. "I'm feeling much better. Thanks."

He smiled and nodded. "Good. Wouldn't want you to be sick all the way to California. My name is Kemo. Is this your first time flying?"

I shook my head quickly, not wanting to come off like I was straight from the country woods, even though I was. "I'm Ronica. Ronica Montgomery. I've flown before. Just makes me sick sometimes, that's all. What about you?" Like the attorney I'd be as soon as I passed the state bar, I shifted the conversation in the direction I preferred it take. "Do you fly very often?"

"Two, three times a year."

I shifted in my seat, giving him my full attention. "Oh really? Are you from Tennessee or California?"

He shook his head. "Neither. Actually, I live in Hawaii. On the island of Oahu. My parents are divorced, so I fly back and forth a couple of times a year to keep both of them happy."

My eyes widened. No wonder he had such beautiful sun-baked skin that seemed to contrast with his silky hair. I'd seen photos of Hawaiians in the brochures inside my travel package, and many of them were truly brown and beautiful, but this guy was deeper than that. He had some black in him, some straight-up African, and it took me all of two seconds to figure him out: Black man goes to an island and hooks up with a local girl. Presto, abracadabra, allakhazam! You get a cutie like Kemo out of the mix.

"So you're Hawaiian, huh? Wow. I've never met anyone from the Hawaiian Islands before."

He shrugged. "Actually, I'm black. I was born in Hawaii and I still live there, but I consider myself black."

Coming from a school the size of mine, the shortage of eligible black men had become painfully apparent painfully quickly. Those who weren't gay were either playas, committed, or, heaven forbid, into white girls; and the few biracial men on campus were the products of what some sisters thought of as these unholy black man/white girl unions.

I crossed my leg and smirked. "Well, you might consider yourself to be black, but what does your mother think you are?"

He stared at me for a moment, then asked, "What are you trying to say, Ronica?"

I held up my hands in mock surprise. It was always my mouth that got me into trouble, and I'd been told more times than I could count that I needed to save my quick tongue for the courtroom.

"Sorry," I said. "I wasn't trying to imply anything. Nothing at all."

He nodded and then grinned. "Well, since you asked, I'll tell you. As a proud black woman, my mother thinks I'm the best black man that has ever walked the face of the earth. She stayed in Hawaii after divorcing my Hawaiian father because she liked the culture and wanted to raise me in a stable environment. She retired from the police force last year and moved back home to Tennessee, but she loves the fact that I'm walking in her footsteps. In fact, I work out of the same precinct that she once worked from, and it cracks her up to think of me sitting at her old desk."

"You're a cop?" I asked, amazed. With his baggy pants, oversize T-shirt, and Air Force Ones, who would have thought it?

"No," he corrected me. "I'm a police officer. An officer of the peace."

Something about his smile made me want to flirt, and I smirked at him sexily. "Yeah right, a peace officer. You look more like a D.T. No, you're a five-oh. Hawaii Five-Oh."

He put his head back and laughed, flashing dimples and showing his perfect pearly white teeth. Chocolate had never looked so fine.

"You've got jokes, huh? Actually, parts of that old TV show were shot right in downtown Honolulu. In an area called Waikiki."

I stared. "That's where I'm staying. I'm heading to Hawaii on vacation, and I'm staying at the Hilton Hawaiian Village in Waikiki."

He nodded again. "You'll love that area. Plenty of tourists and shops and nice places to eat. But be careful, okay? Honolulu has a pretty high crime rate in the tourist district, and a lot of vacations get ruined when people are careless about their wallets."

It was my turn to nod. I took his words as good advice and filed them away for future reference.

Kemo and I chatted all the way to Los Angeles, pausing in our animated conversation only twice when we excused ourselves for bathroom breaks. Due to my hectic class schedule, my college dating experiences had been highly sporadic. I sat mesmerized by the sound of this man's voice, and the bright flash of his smile had me feeling warm and gushy inside.

I told him about my small, churchgoing family in Tennessee, and he was amazed to learn that besides my aunt and uncle in New York and a cousin back home who was a year older than me, my parents and I were pretty much alone.

"I can't even relate to that," he said. "No one is ever alone in Hawaii. Hawaiian families are very large, and our families are called our *ohanas*. Everyone is either your auntie or your uncle, and all your friends are really like cousins."

Now that was something I couldn't relate to, so I nodded politely and listened while he talked about his home as the plane began its descent in Los Angeles.

As we disembarked from the airplane, Kemo helped me with my carry-on bag without my having to ask, and it felt good to be seen chatting with such a fine brother as we strode through the terminal and toward our connecting gate.

"What seat did they assign you for the next flight?" he asked as we arrived at a crowded gate. A short line of people waited at the check-in counter. As I headed toward a row of empty seats, I noticed we were surrounded by an abundance of Asians sprinkled with a few white folks and a couple of women who I thought were probably Hawaiian.

I glanced at the boarding pass I clutched in my hand. "I'm in 21B," I said. "How about you?"

He looked disappointed. "I'm in 13A. But that's okay, we'll still be able to wave at each other."

I nodded, although I was disappointed as well. My final semester of school had been rough. It had been a long time since I'd had such a stimulating conversation with a man, and I didn't want it to end.

"Watch my bag?" I asked, nodding at my carry-on bag, which he still held in his hand. There were a few minutes left before boarding time, and I wanted to duck into the restroom to wash my face and freshen up.

Kemo grinned sexily. "You trust me like that?"

Damn he was fine!

I shrugged and slung my purse over my shoulder, then busted him checking out my hips on the sly. "There's nothing much in there to steal," I said with a sexy grin of my own. "Unless you like silk thongs."

He laughed out loud, then waved me away as I shook my stuff toward the ladies' room. Once inside, I glanced at my reflection in the mirror above the sinks. Still feeling the heat of Kemo's glow, my grin was bright and wide.

■ ■ ■

He was such a gentleman.

"Thanks," I said, holding out my hand to take my bag. We had boarded the aircraft and he had bypassed his seat in row 13 and carried my bag back to row 21, where I waited for an elderly woman to get settled into her window seat so I could sit beside her.

"I got it," he said, lifting the bag easily and allowing me to catch a glimpse of his muscular arms. He had a great body, thick and hard, just the way I enjoyed my men. I couldn't do a damn thing with a chicken bone. I liked me a brother who had some muscle on him.

I smiled my thanks and sat down in the middle seat with my purse on my thighs. I was reaching for my seatbelt when Kemo sat down beside me, with an electric grin lighting up his face.

"Is this seat taken, ma'am?" he joked.

I gave a short laugh. "The flight is full, so I'm sure it is. You'd better move before somebody comes over here and embarrasses you."

"Don't worry about it, sweetie," he said. "I got this."

I just shrugged and looked at him like he was crazy. I hated to have to watch the brother get told off, but he didn't seem the least bit stressed. Although my eyes lit expectantly on each passenger who approached our row, none of them stood over him and demanded their seat.

"You looking for somebody?"

I nodded and laughed. "Hell yeah. The person who paid for that seat you're sitting in."

"You want me to move?"

I shook my head and tucked a stray braid behind my ear. "No, I don't. I'd love to chill with you all the way to Hawaii, if I could."

He reached over and put on his seatbelt. "Well, you can, so relax. I changed my seat, so you're stuck with me for the next five hours."

It was going to be five hours of bliss because I was already taken with Kemo and I barely knew him. That didn't stop my heart from fluttering wildly or cause that hot feeling that had been building between my legs to subside.

Kemo had a great sense of humor and told me all kinds of stories about growing up in Hawaii. He lowered the armrest between our seats, and we turned toward each other as best we could, huddled together in our private world. Kemo made surfing and swimming in the Pacific Ocean and baking under the island sun seem like magical adventures, but he also talked about his job as a police officer and how some of the people he had to lock up were the same people he'd hung out with as a teen.

"There are no strangers among Hawaiians, Ronica," he said wistfully. "Every event is like a family reunion. When you live on an island, especially one the size of Oahu, everyone practically knows or is related to everyone else."

I nodded, awed. I came from a small farming community, so I could relate to knowing all your neighbors, but I envied those who had large families to share their lives with. Just seeing the pride and love in his eyes when Kemo spoke of his family and friends was wonderful.

"So, what else are you into besides water sports?" I asked, snuggling toward him in my seat. It was frigid in the cabin, and the stewardess had distributed travel pillows and light blankets.

"I'm into football," he said. His broad shoulders and muscular frame made me believe him. "I played at Moanalua High School, and now I volunteer to help coach there during the season. What about you? Do you play any sports?"

I shook my head. "Nah, not really. I cheered for a minute during junior high, but once I hit high school I dedicated myself to academics because I needed to get a full scholarship to college."

"Oh yeah?" He looked impressed. "You went to college?"

I nodded proudly. "Sure did. In fact, I just graduated from law school two weeks ago. I have a job lined up at one of the hottest law firms in the city, and this trip is a graduation gift from my aunt and uncle before I settle down to working full-time."

"Wow," he said, nodding. "You're a big-shot lawyer, huh? That's great."

I shrugged like it was no big thing, when in actuality getting my law degree had been the most difficult thing I'd ever done. "Well, I still have to pass the bar, but the firm I'll be working for helps with that. They give us study materials and a mentor to make sure we pass it the first time around."

Kemo took my hand, and sexual heat surged to my clit as he raked his finger lazily across the center of my palm. His lips were only inches from mine. "You seem like a smart girl, Ronica," he said, his voice low as he enveloped my fingers in his large, manly hands and pressed his lips to my thumb. "I'll admit that I'm attracted to sexy sisters, but it's the attractive and intelligent sister like you who turns me out every time."

I had no idea what to say. Men didn't compliment me on my intelligence every day, especially not men who looked like Kemo and made my body melt with just a glance. Without thinking, I leaned forward and kissed him, my lips parting under his, our tongues dancing as though we were all alone.

"Damn," he said as we broke contact, smoothing my bottom lip with his thumb. It was only the confines of our seats that stopped me from pressing myself against his chest.

"Let's switch seats," he whispered, and although I was puzzled, I didn't protest. Gathering our blankets, he stood up and allowed me to slip into his seat, then he sat down in mine. Moments later I understood why.

We sat in such a way that we were almost facing each other, but now Kemo's broad shoulders blocked the elderly woman from my view, and me from hers. He tucked one end of my blanket behind my shoulder and used the rest of it, and his own, to form a tent draped over our bodies.

Then his lips were on mine, nibbling and sucking, his tongue probing and teasing, and with his hand concealed beneath the blanket, he palmed my hip and then let his fingers travel up my waist before cupping my breast and slipping under my shirt to thumb my nipples.

I moaned into his mouth, knowing that the passenger sitting across the aisle behind me couldn't see a thing, and neither could the old lady snoozing in the window seat.

It was all I could do not to scream as my breasts swelled under Kemo's touch, my nipples erect between his thumb and forefinger as his tongue played wicked games in my mouth.

I squeezed my thighs together and rolled my hips in a slow fucking rhythm as my clit throbbed, and before I could stop myself I came, right there in my chair, releasing a long shudder into Kemo's open mouth.

"You like that, baby?" he whispered, his fingers still fingering my nipples.

I nodded, trying to catch my breath. "Oh yes," I said, but I wanted more.

Kemo understood, and moments later I sucked in my breath and snagged my bottom lip between my teeth as I felt his fingers crawling up the leg of my shorts searching for that hot wet spot between my thighs.

I shuddered softly as he massaged my wetness and then slid one finger inside me. He fucked me with his finger as his thumb pressed down on my clit, and as the second orgasm tore through me, much more powerful than the first, I grabbed his wrist with both hands and pushed his fingers inside me as deep as possible, my back arched completely out of the seat, my pussy clenching tightly.

It took me a few minutes to recover, and I sighed as Kemo withdrew his fingers and then licked them one by one.

"Yumm . . ." he murmured. "Cinnamon."

"Let me do something for you," I begged, squeezing his dick through his pants and reaching for his belt buckle. "Your turn now," I whispered as I stroked him under the blanket. I knew I couldn't satisfy him right there in his seat, but I was so hot and hyped that I was willing to do something freaky and outrageous like sneak into the tiny bathroom and suck him off until he exploded.

But Kemo shook his head. "That was for you, Ronica, but don't worry." He pressed my face gently toward his shoulder. "Don't worry," he said again, "I'll get mine later."

■ ■ ■

Nestled in the clouds and soaring high above the ocean, Kemo and I held each other and chatted for the next few hours, and by the time we landed at the airport in Honolulu, I was experiencing a mixture of emotions. Of course I was excited to be embarking on the vacation of a lifetime, but even though Kemo had promised to get his later, he still hadn't offered me his telephone number or told me how to contact him, so I was also a bit sad that I'd be parting company with a sexy man who was beginning to feel like an old friend.

We walked into the terminal holding hands. As we waited for our luggage to appear on the carousel, Kemo gathered me into his arms and I pressed myself against the rock-hardness of his body. I stared into his beautiful dark eyes and couldn't help reaching up to run my fingers through his jet-black hair.

"That was the best flight I've ever taken," he whispered in my ear, nuzzling my lobe with his tongue. "Have a great vacation, Ronica. Maybe I'll see you around."

Another wave of disappointment surged through me, but I put on a bright sexy smile. After all, I was nobody's innocent virgin, and getting a little bit on an airplane did not a relationship make. I comforted myself with the fact that I'd had two orgasms in one day, and courtesy of a real, live man at that, even though I would have been happy to get busy with him in every imaginable position. Kemo's deliciously thick fingers beat my overworked vibrator any day.

"Sure," I answered as I grabbed my oversize suitcase from the conveyor. Kemo lifted it easily for me, then extended the handle and pivoted it toward me on its wheels.

"Can you manage this?" he asked.

I nodded, waving him off. I was feeling rejected, and deep down I wanted him so badly, I could hardly stand myself. "I'm good," I said, balancing my smaller bag atop the larger one, purposely avoiding his gaze.

"There's a counter across the way where your hotel representative will pick you up, okay? I have a car coming for me, so I gotta run." He touched my shoulder. "Mahalo for the cinnamon, Ronica. I'm gonna taste you all night long."

"Peace," I said softly, then turned and wheeled my suitcase over to the information counter.

■ ■ ■

The Hilton Hawaiian Village was some kind of beautiful. After checking in and having a valet take my bags, I made my way to the twelfth floor. The room was da bomb, and the view from my balcony was exquisite. The stars were bright and low-hanging, and the lapping of the ocean was hypnotic as I watched the waves crash against the beach in a pristine white foam.

Even though it was just after 8 P.M. local time, I didn't feel tired at all. It was the middle of the night back home, but I was too hyped up to have jet lag. I leaned against the balcony railing and watched the throngs of people on the beach below. I was amazed that people were still swimming in the near darkness, and the sight of laughing children and affectionate lovers made me wish I had someone to share the magic with.

An hour later I had taken a quick shower and changed my clothes. I freed my mass of braids from their clip, allowing them to swing freely down my back. I'd glanced at the room service menu, but then reminded myself that I hadn't come all the way to Hawaii to sit up in my room eating alone. There was so much action going in the hotel complex and out on the streets that I decided to get out and get right in the middle of it.

Heeding Kemo's warning, I checked to make sure my bank card was in my wallet. I had about eight hundred dollars in spending money, with two hundred of that in cash and the rest in my checking account. I counted out five twenties and folded them tightly, then rolled them inside a pair of tube socks, which I then crammed into the front pocket of a pair of blue jeans that were folded up and sandwiched in the middle of my suitcase. I took the remainder of my cash and rubber-banded it tightly. I then stuck it inside my bra, securing it to the inside of my generous cup with a small safety pin.

I was set. I put my wallet and my room key in my purse, and headed out the door.

The night air was warm and pleasing, and my eyes were wide as I tried to take in and comprehend all of what they saw. I'd picked up a small tourist map from the front desk when I checked in, and I found myself walking in the midst of a heavy crowd in the heart of Waikiki.

I was amazed at the multitude of people, and of the different races and ethnicities as well. It freaked me out a little when I stopped at a restaurant called Cheeseburger in Paradise, and even though the staff looked almost entirely Asian, their speech patterns and accents sounded just like mine. I had to remind myself that no matter how remote it was from the mainland, Hawaii was simply another state in the union. The island people were as Americanized as I was.

With the crowds at their peak because of tourist season, it was impractical to expect to get a table all to myself, so I agreed to join a group of travelers who had recently been seated. They were a mixed group of students from California, a bit younger than I was, but energetic and friendly. It wasn't long before I was deep in conversation with them, and when it was time to leave, a blond-haired guy named Mack asked me to join them at a nearby club.

"C'mon," he said with a big crooked grin. "This is Hawaii." He held up a closed fist with his thumb and pinky fingers extended. "Hang loose already!"

What the hell, I thought. I didn't have a whole lot of experience partying with white people, but there was a black guy and two other black girls in the group, so I jumped into a taxi with them and laughed and talked shit like the college student I once was.

Traffic was monstrous! We seemed to inch along at a snail's pace as we drove the length of Waikiki. Thirty minutes later we climbed out at the Ala Moana Center.

"Upstairs," Mack hollered, grabbing my hand and pulling me along with him. "The party is upstairs!"

I wasn't really a dancer, but in this little bistrolike club, you didn't have to be. It was so jam-packed with people that I naturally swayed with the crowd. Although I had a brief moment of discomfort when I noticed the only blacks in the house were the ones I'd come with, I relaxed when I realized that I was among people of color, even if they weren't quite as brown as I.

I grooved on the dance floor with Mack, who was quite attractive and more than a bit drunk. After downing about four beers I was feeling pretty good myself, but I wasn't crazy. Mack had nice features, for a white man, but I'd never been attracted to whites in that way. I pushed him off when he grabbed my ass and growled, "Can I spend the night with you?" I was too nice to tell him that laying up with him wasn't even a remote possibility. After being with Kemo, Mack paled in comparison.

It was close to 5 A.M. when I finally made it back to the Hilton, and jet lag combined with all the beer I'd drank had taken its toll. The crew from California waved good-bye from the taxi as I made my way shakily toward the bank of elevators. Minutes later I'd staggered to my door, swiped my key card, kicked off my sandals, and passed out on the bed.

■ ■ ■

I awakened the next morning to a stream of sunlight and the sound of a vacuum cleaner being run in the hallway outside my room. Damn! I sat up, then grabbed my head and winced. Alcohol always gave me a headache. It didn't matter if I drank beer, wine, or liquor; it all had the same effect.

I staggered from the bed and over to the sliding glass doors, which I pushed open to let in some fresh air. Making my way to the desk, I found the room service booklet and ordered up the biggest breakfast on the menu. I figured I'd take a shower while I waited for my food, and then eat my headache into oblivion.

I'd just pinned up my damp braids and applied coconut-scented lotion to my body when there was a knock at the door.

"Just a second," I called out as I buttoned my silk lounging robe and opened the door. I let the waiter in, then picked up my purse from the floor where I must have dropped it the night before.

Moments later, my head wasn't the only thing pounding. My heart was hammering, too. My wallet was gone. My mind went on rewind as I tried to remember when I'd last seen it. At the restaurant. I was saving my cash for gifts and incidentals, and I'd paid for my dinner with my bank card, just as I'd planned to pay for all my meals. I hadn't taken it out in the taxi, so somebody must have picked my pocket while I partied in the crowded club.

"Um," I mumbled to the waiter as I looked for the bra I'd worn the night before. "Gimme a quick second, okay?"

I found my bra on the floor on other side of the bed, and after unpinning and unwrapping my cash, I paid for my meal and gave the waiter a nice tip.

"What do people do," I asked as he uncovered my plates and prepared to leave, "when they've been the victim of a pickpocket here in Honolulu?" I knew I had to cancel my bank card, but I was sure there was more to it.

He looked at me. "Has that happened to you?"

I nodded.

He shook his head sadly. "Honolulu can be a thief's paradise. It's a shame when visitors to our island are subjected to these kinds of crimes. You must contact the HPD and file a complaint."

"HPD?"

"Yes, the Honolulu Police Department. Their number is in the visitor's packet that you should have received when you checked in."

I thanked him again, and sat down to eat my breakfast. Aside from my bank card, there hadn't been much of anything in my wallet. I'd taken my driver's license and cash out earlier in the evening, but the theft of my bank card meant I wouldn't have access to the money that was in my account.

My headache was raging by the time I finished eating. I couldn't believe I'd become a victim on my very first night on the town, and I chided myself for drinking too much and for not being more cautious. I dressed quickly in a white tank top and a pink miniskirt that complimented my brown complexion, then rifled through my visitor's packet and found the telephone number of the police department.

The desk sergeant promised to send someone over to take my report. While I waited I called information and got the number to my bank, then called the lost and stolen card department and had my account suspended.

I still had a little cash, and since the bank promised to issue me another card within twenty-four hours, my vacation wasn't going to be ruined. I was looking forward to visiting an area called Diamond Head, where the rich and famous lived in beautiful mansions. As soon as the police took my report, I planned to catch a trolley in that direction, headache or not.

I sat outside on the balcony thumbing through a stack of brochures while the maid changed the sheets and freshened up the bathroom. She'd just finished up and was preparing to leave when a knock at the door startled both of us.

The word "Police" was barked on the other side of the door, and the housekeeper gave me a questioning look.

"Go ahead," I told her, since she was much closer to the door than I was. "I'm expecting them."

But I wasn't expecting what greeted me as the door swung open. He stood there wearing the uniform of Honolulu's finest, and damn did he look good.

"Kemo," I breathed, rushing over to do the door, almost knocking the poor maid down in my attempt to reach him. She gave me a dirty look as she left the room. "What are you doing here?"

He flashed me a broad dimpled smile, and I became instantly wet. "You called, didn't you?"

I laughed as he entered my room, closing the door behind him and unbuckling his holster.

"I smell cinnamon," he said, coming toward me with a sexy, deliberate look in his eyes.

I laughed again. "I called to report a theft," I said, backing toward the bed. "Not to order room service."

Kemo took off his cap and draped his holster across the desk. And then he was all over me, squeezing me to his chest, his hands roaming every inch of my body.

"Ronica," he moaned into my neck as his kisses left hot streaks on my bare shoulders and collarbone. "This time I'm going to do you right."

Kemo took me outside on the balcony, and I didn't resist. He kissed the back of my neck as I leaned against the stucco wall, and with his fingers roaming my breasts and teasing my nipples, I pressed back into his hardness, my moans spilling into the salty air.

"That's it, Ronica," he whispered, fumbling with his zipper and belt. "Enjoy yourself." The next thing I knew, my skirt was up and his fingers were pulling my thong aside, delving into the sweetness he was becoming to know so well.

"Don't worry," he whispered in my ear. "I've got a glove."

Anticipating what he had to offer, I sighed and allowed my eyes to take in the beauty of the horizon and the whiteness of the sand, the teal-colored water rushing toward us in high waves. Kemo withdrew his fingers, and I felt something thick and hard.

"Hurry," I whispered, spreading my legs slightly and tilting my pelvis back to meet him.

Kemo held me by my hips as he entered me, and it seemed like miles of dick slid into me before he filled me completely. He fucked me with long, slow strokes, sliding what felt like ten inches so deep inside me that my eyes closed with each thrust.

All kinds of feelings were swirling through me. The hard hotness of his rod banging against my cervix, his fingers massaging my clit, the ocean breeze cooling my skin, and the vision of paradise filling my eyes. Moments later an explosive orgasm ripped through me, and I felt so limp I could have collapsed and fallen over the balcony.

Kemo was close to coming, too. He deepened his thrusts, gripping my hips and banging me so hard that shock waves streaked through my pussy like fireworks.

He kissed my neck when it was over, and all I could do was grin stupidly over my shoulder. "Hey," he said softly, turning me around to face him and holding me gently in his arms. "How about I wash your back and you wash mine?"

I was surprised. "Don't you have to get back to work?"

Kemo shook his head. "Actually, I worked last night. I was just getting off shift when your call came in. I volunteered to swing by here and take your report on my way home."

Moments later we stood naked in the shower under a stream of steaming water, and for the first time in my life I experienced the thrill of having a man wash my body. Kemo squeezed soapy water over my shoulders and licked my nipples as bubbles cascaded over my breasts.

His body was more than magnificent. It was powerful and chiseled, and his dark skin was mesmerizing. When Kemo slipped down to his knees and lifted one of my legs over his shoulder to bury his face in my crotch, licking and teasing, it was all I could do not to rip down the shower curtains as another orgasm tore through my weakened body.

"I'm off for the next few days," he told me, his fingers trailing through my braids. "How about I demonstrate my aloha spirit by showing you around the island?"

And show me he did. With Kemo as my guide, I visited Diamond Head beach, where we climbed a beautiful but daunting peak, and then we visited Kaneohe, where he showed me a ladder called the Stairway to Heaven that ascended the entire length of one of the furry green mountains and disappeared into the clouds.

Kemo spent four glorious days making sure my island vacation was a true slice of paradise. We visited a small tourist town on Oahu's North Shore called Haleiwa, where he fed me the most delicious shrimp scampi from a roadside truck, then took me to a luau at an ocean resort called Germaine's.

I spent the next two days sunning on the beach alone, but on the last day of my vacation, Kemo and I said our good-byes over a cup of Jamba Juice at a local stand. "I'll be back in Tennessee for Thanksgiving," he told me. "Maybe we can get together, yes?"

I nodded. We'd become so close in such a short time. But I had a new job to look forward to, and Kemo had his own responsibilities to attend to. November was such a long time away. "Yeah," I said, swallowing hard. "I'd really like that."

■ ■ ■

My flight was a red-eye and scheduled to leave at midnight, so I caught the hotel's airport shuttle at 10 P.M. To my surprise, the terminal was almost empty, and the whole experience of checking my bags in and getting my boarding pass was uneventful. I was riding an up escalator to the gate level of the terminal, and feeling sad about the paradise I had to leave behind, when I heard a sexy voice behind me.

"I smell cinnamon."

I whirled around and ran to Kemo, breathing in his aroma, amazed to be in his arms once again.

"What are you doing here?" I asked happily. "I thought we agreed that this afternoon was good-bye?"

We stepped off the escalator and Kemo put his hand in the

small of my back, gently guiding me toward the down escalator and the terminal's exit.

"One more time, Ronica," he said, leading me outside toward a police cruiser that waited at the curb. He held open the front passenger door and waited for me to climb inside.

I paused at the open door, staring at him like he was crazy, and scared that we'd get caught if I got inside.

He laughed. "Don't worry, baby. You're in good hands. I'm a 'cop,' remember?"

I got in.

I sat there shivering with anticipation as Kemo drove to the outdoor parking area and pulled the cruiser into a near-empty area, then chose a spot close to a grove of palm trees.

"Hawaiians bend over backward to show their guest the aloha spirit," he said. "So before you leave, I'm gonna bend you over and show you some of the best aloha you've ever had."

He took me right there. Under the darkness of the sky and facing a grove of luscious palms, Kemo bent me over the hood of his police cruiser and made love to me, first from behind and then stretched out on the hood of the car with the stars kissing and illuminating our half-naked bodies.

An hour later I boarded my flight, enjoying an ache between my legs that I knew would last for weeks to come. And as the airplane rose into the sky above what had become my paradise of love, I said good-bye to the island of Oahu and to a wonderful lover who had made this my vacation of a lifetime.

I snuggled into my seat and closed my eyes, completely satisfied because I knew no matter where life took me, the memory of Kemo's touch would always be a delightful reminder of my Hawaiian vacation. As I headed for home, I fell into a deep sleep with a smile on my face and the sweet taste of aloha on my lips.

FORT JESUS

Sandra Jackson-Opoku

What! You're writing a book about Hector Guzman? Man, don't mention that wigger's name. Don't care if he *is* dead. I don't respect nobody who ain't respected me.

It's like this, Kwesi. Jamaicans got this expression, What nuh good in the marning, 'ard to be good in the aftanoon.

Heck's name brings up things I'd rather not remember: A woman who should have been mine. Islands I once loved. Montego Bay, Mombasa. Especially Mombasa. I'll probably never see that place again.

I realize it now, years later. No chance that shit would have ever fit together right. We were like Columbus when he crossed his fingers and set off for the Indies. Hector Guzman sent us to the wrong Africa, and we were fool enough to go.

Anyone who asks me, I'll tell them straight. Tiger Lemieux ain't no artist, he's an artisan. I'm an old-fashioned craftsman, except I build films, not furniture.

Was I just another nigga bamboozled by The Man? There were more headaches on that shoot than you could shake a dick at, and Heck had his stubby little Johnson in all that shit. After all, Mombasa was his baby. Going all the way to Africa to shoot a dramatic sequence for a music video, a ten-minute minimovie about a girl ghost who haunts Mombasa Harbor. It seemed foolishly expensive to me. We could have put that shit together in the studio.

But Heck insisted that "Brown Girl, Blue Island" had to be shot on location, and that location had to be Mombasa. Who was I to argue? His record company was footing the bill. If they had that kind of cash to burn, I was there with a match.

You remember the script? An African warrior tries to rescue the maiden he loves, who's been captured and imprisoned at Fort Jesus. She drowns; he's enslaved and stolen away across the ocean. Her ghost haunts Mombasa Harbor from that day on, waiting for his return.

I have this thing about African islands. I fell in love with my first one right out of film school. I went to Robben Island as production assistant on a Nelson Mandela documentary for Italian TV. Your girl Grace was in it, too, back when she was trying to go Afro-pop. Remember, Kwesi?

Any sister from the townships could have sung circles around her. Instead we get Grace Witherspoon hamming her way through a music number that had as much to do with Nelson Mandela as Huckleberry Hound. Warbling "Nkosi Sikelel' iAfrika," the South African national anthem, like it was *Madame Butterfly* or something. Floating through prison cells in a ball gown. You would think she was the one who'd spent twenty-two years on Robben Island. She was trying to get some kind of crossover action going, but it didn't work. Grace Witherspoon wasn't nobody's Miriam Makeba. Sorry, Kwesi, but it's the truth.

When she found out I was going back to Africa, Grace begged to tag along. She thought an appearance in one of Heck's music videos would give her sagging career a shot in the arm. If she didn't mind paying her own way, I'd find something for her to do.

I remember it like yesterday. That's when I first met you, man. Your gigolo days. Grace came in from Europe dragging you with her like a puppy on a leash. BYOB: Bring Your Own Boy-toy. Don't play shamed now, Kwesi. It ain't every young man who can pull a sugar momma.

Grace thought she'd get to play prima donna like on that Mandela project. When it didn't go down like that, she flounced off the set. You'd left by then, but you must have heard about how the shit hit the fan like a load of elephant crap.

Hector billed himself as some kind of coproducer. We'd already taped his sequence in London. He had no scenes with the African cast, but he knew people in Kenya and wanted a free trip.

It always struck me as a big contradiction, those medieval stone fortresses along the African coastline—the swaying palms, the white sands, then bam! Buckingham Palace.

You remember where most of the shooting took place, right? Fort Jesus, way up on that ridge overlooking the entrance to the old port. How come those pillaging Europeans loved to give their outposts such pious names? Like the Lord himself had blessed them. I guess the Almighty couldn't make up his mind. That fort changed hands no less than nine times between the Portuguese and Omani Arabs. When Kenya became a British colony, they used it as a prison for guess who? Africans, whose land it was in the first place.

Heck was just the latest in a long line of white boys to come pushing up into somebody else's place: eating their food, breaking and taking their shit, sleeping in their beds—with their women, no less. If I had been a Mau Mau warrior, I'd have dynamited that thing into rubble come independence.

A Portuguese fort on the Indian Ocean—absolutely the wrong place to set a story about the transatlantic slave trade. The arrogance of my own ignorance, helped along by Heck. I cringe when I think of it now. The biggest holocaust in human history, and there I was, trying to stage it thousands of miles from its origin.

Maybe that's why it never really got off the ground. Maybe I was being punished by my ancestors for misrepresenting Mother Africa. It seemed from the get-go that the whole production was cursed. Ghosts of the Portuguese and British, the Africans and Arabs, breaking lenses and overturning props, kicking sand in the cameramen's eyes and trying to drown my cast.

You ever visit a place and get these vibrations, man? History rushing out from the bricks and stone. You can just see the troops charging, hear cannons firing. You smell the blood of history's unhealed wounds. Oh, you like that line, huh? Maybe I'll be a writer like you when I grow up, Kwesi.

It's where I first saw two girls looking out onto the Indian Ocean. Standing there at Fort Jesus, each of them striking in their own different ways.

One was petite and dark, juicy as a mango. The other was long and brown like a cinnamon stick. Two African girls on vacation from college, one a West African and the other a mixed-race Kenyan. They were staying at one of those inns along Tagli Beach.

They wore one-piece bathing suits. The *kangas* wrapped around their waists stirring in the wind. Shreds of fog drifting around them. They stood with hands shading their eyes, looking out across the water at something it seemed that no one else could see.

I found out later that they were at the wrong place, waiting for one of the tour boats to dock. But at that moment I could imagine them as two sexy ghosts, looking for their African prince to come back across the water.

"You've found what you're searching for, sisters. Tiger Lemieux is on the scene."

I know it was lame, but did Cara have to look at me with such dismay?

"What's the matter? Cat got your tongues? *Sprechen Sie Deutsch? Habla español? Parlez-vous français?*"

One girl giggled; the other one frowned. One turned toward me; the other leaned away. I did what any filmmaker does who wants to capture a thing of beauty before it slips away. I promised to make both of them stars. Now, if somebody wanted the lead in one of Tiger Lemieux's *private* productions, I wouldn't have kicked either of them out of bed.

You remember that pretty little chocolate thing? Dimples so deep you could get lost in them. Ass like a pair of perfect Georgia peaches. Labadi was her name; The Body was more like it. Talk about a fine brown frame. That sister had curves on her that just wouldn't quit.

Cara, now that one was more than a little standoffish. How could any woman in her right mind resist me? Still, Labadi managed to talk her into coming along to cattle call the next morning. To seal the deal I took them out dancing that night. I waited up the road while they crept away from their guesthouse, sneaking away from Cara's old watchdog of a granny.

You remember the smell of that Mombasa nightclub, Kwesi? The place was little more than a beachside shack, smelling of fried fish, fresh beer, and the ocean. The crash of incoming waves was backbeat for the music on the box—a mishmash of Swahili taarab, Afro-pop, hip-hop, reggae, and country. I've never figured out why Africans love country music so damn much.

A full moon shone down on the dance floor, nothing more than a wooden deck built out over the ocean. If you got too drunk or danced too wild, you were in real danger of toppling into the drink. I'd actually seen it happen. It was a German tourist, couldn't hold his liquor. Doing his jerky little white-boy dance too close to the edge and tumbling over backward. The local barflies got a good laugh out of that one.

We took our drinks to a table outside where the air was fresher and the light was brighter. I wanted to be able to feast my eyes on the two beauties at my side.

Cara seemed just on the verge of blurting out some deep, dark secret. She would stop speaking midsentence and just stare off in space. Labadi flirted up a storm. And boy, could the two of them dance. You talk about sexy, that was foreplay on the floor. Kept me with a hard-on all night long.

Neither would dance alone with me. Whenever I pulled one out on the floor, I'd look up and find myself dancing with the two of them. A couple of times they ignored me completely and danced with each other.

You ever been double-teamed by two beautiful females? That shit will make you dizzy. They were like the waves underneath the dance floor: one tugging me onto shore, the other pushing me out to sea. I don't know if I drank too much or got dizzy from the motion of the ocean. I do remember that at the end of the evening I was too messed up to drive.

It's a lucky thing I hadn't hooked up with two female thugs. That shit has been known to happen out there in Kenya. I could have been robbed blind, stripped naked, carjacked, cut up, and dumped in the Indian Ocean. I vaguely recall Labadi driving, Cara riding shotgun, and me curled semiconscious in the backseat.

I had a blinding hangover the next morning when they picked me up, barely in time for cattle call. Labadi had found a script in the glove compartment and read it from cover to cover. I'd promised her a role as an extra, but did I really want to lose her fine self in crowds of funky locals? What about the role of Sherifah, the tragic heroine?

I hadn't yet cast the female lead, the role I'd all but promised to Grace, although she was twenty years too old for the part. Still, good black don't crack. Your boo wasn't half bad to be in her forties. Plus, we had lucked out with an excellent local makeup artist.

Maybe we'd have been able to pass Grace off for a nineteen-year-old virgin if it hadn't been for Labadi, begging and pleading for a video test. She even hinted that my cooperation might soon be rewarded. I wasn't thinking about sex right then. The Mombasa sun was screaming in my eyes, the ocean waves beating in my head, the sand shaky under my feet. I didn't put up much resistance, but I did have the presence of mind to insist on one point: that Cara also read for the role.

My instincts were right, tore up as I was that day. For all her sparkling personality, Labadi couldn't act her way out of a paper bag. She froze like a statue in front of the camera. No matter how many takes, she'd find a way to flub her lines.

Quiet Cara was another story. In front of the camera, she came to life. That blinking red light seemed to jolt her out of whatever trance she was in. She had that thing you couldn't put your finger on. It glowed in her face, her body, her voice. Cara had the brooding, mysterious air that was perfect for the role of Sherifah, the ghost girl.

I began to understand how directors fall in love with their leading ladies.

If Labadi was pissed that her friend beat her out for the part, she didn't show it. She acted like it wasn't no thang, and I put her on the payroll as my personal assistant.

I was digging on Labadi, who acted like she was interested. I was still intrigued by Cara, who didn't seem to want any part of me. For all her openness before the camera, she avoided me when we weren't working. It wasn't my style to be pushing up on no woman who didn't want me. She was fine, all right. But then her girlfriend was, too, and a hell of a lot friendlier.

Maybe they had it all decided between them. Who would get the role, who would go for the man. I had no choice but to go along with the program. I gave Labadi the attention she wanted and Cara the space she needed. I tried my best to avoid any mess.

I had enough trouble with Hector on my hands. He was changing sets, rewriting scripts, bossing people around. He seemed to think that "Brown Girl, Blue Island" was his show. It may have been his song, but it was my production.

His mother should have named him Jody, the man who sneaks in the back door after other people's women. What, you don't know that military marching song? Well, you must have heard Johnnie Taylor's tune: "Ain't no use in going home, Jody's got your gal and gone." It wasn't long before he was sniffing Labadi. Flirting, buying gifts, meeting her for drinks. She said she didn't encourage him, but I never heard her say no.

I don't know just how close she let Heck get. She was cockteasing me for damn sure. She'd let me do a little kissing, a little feeling through her clothes. But when it started getting heavy, she'd pull away.

"Oh, Tiger. You are a very naughty boy," she'd laugh

I don't know if she was using Heck to make me jealous or the other way around, but she had much game. Sistergirl knew how to sidestep. For someone who was such a master player, Lady Labadi wound up playing herself in the end.

Hector Guzman was the single most useless person on the entire set. Some white folk like to deputize themselves niggerologists, guardians of a culture we're too stupid to look after ourselves. Heck thought he was the only one who knew the African way of doing things. I knew he was showing off for Labadi's benefit. He figured he'd win the woman by outblacking the black man.

"As an ethnomusicologist, I can say without hesitation that . . . yada, yada, coconut wata. I've always understood the Bantu way of being as . . . blah, blah, blah, and blasé wee."

For the sake of peace, I played along. If I wanted to avoid trouble, there were four people I'd have to feed with a long-handled spoon: your girl Grace, who loved to stir up shit; Lady Labadi; Hector Guzman; and Cara's grandmother, the one who owned that ho house where you and Grace were holed up. Ain't no wonder there were so many endangered species in East Africa. Big Granny was frying them up in her game kitchen. You remember that notorious old girl known all over Mombasa for her elephant trunk and Nile crocodile. "Any meat you want to eat." That was her.

Big Granny made it clear she didn't want me around those girls, especially Cara. But I don't think she would've minded having a piece of me herself.

The day we shot the Fort Jesus exteriors, I sent Labadi, Grace, Guzman, and Granny on a long boat ride. I think you went, too, didn't you, Kwesi?

I didn't want anyone hovering around. It was just me, the actors, and two cameramen on the set. One camera was high on a turret above Fort Jesus, shooting down at the parapet below. The other was out in the water, sitting on a motorboat with me.

There's this sequence where the warrior rounds up reinforcements and storms the fort with spears and cutlasses. He finds his way to his ladylove's cell and sets her free. The Europeans are following in hot pursuit. Having no other way out, he grabs her hand and together they leap from a parapet into the sea.

We were shooting just the two leads that day. We didn't have enough bank to bring in stunt doubles. I never planned for anyone to actually jump in the drink. I did a long shot with the two of them perched on the edge of the parapet. We'd already had some greenboard with them leaping from a low wall, holding hands. I would lay down some special effects in the studio later, then cut away to them in the water.

The scenes at the fort went off without a hitch. The harbor shots were a different matter. I don't know how many takes we did with Cara and the male lead. We just couldn't seem to get it right. The man is treading water, desperately searching for Sherifah. He finally sees something in the distance and paddles over to it. But what he finds is her lifeless body floating facedown in the water.

I finally got it wrapped and told the actors to climb aboard.

I looked over and noticed Cara still floating there. I saw a wave wash over her and her body being pulled under. I'm not the strongest swimmer in the world, but I jumped in and grabbed her, trying to hold her head above water. The useless cameraman didn't even help. Just stood there like a fool, filming the whole damn thing. I still got that tape, Kwesi. Sometimes I get in a deep funk thinking about Cara and find myself playing it over and over.

I dragged her deadweight over the side and got her on board. Nobody else knew what to do, so I did my best to revive her.

Kwesi, that's some eerie shit, soul kissing an unconscious woman. I parted her cold lips, pressed mine against them, and started breathing air into her lungs. The salt water on her tongue tasted like tears.

The driver gunned the engine and raced for shore. I tried desperately to keep a rhythm going, pumping her chest and blowing into her mouth. We bobbed up and down, her body slipping and sliding on the wet deck.

■ ■ ■

By the time we were tied up on dock, her chest had begun to move. She started coughing, then her eyes flew open. I'll never forget the look in her eyes when she came to. Her hands reached up, I thought to hug me. But no, she was pushing me away. She turned her head to the side, retched, and started crying.

At first I thought she was weeping with relief. But when the tears kept coming, I started wondering if Cara had been deliberately trying to drown herself and was mad at me for saving her life.

"Are you all right? Should we take you to the hospital?"

The girl seemed like she was swollen with tears. Like all the salt water she swallowed was finding its way out through her eyes.

I carried her to a shelter on the beach we'd been using as a greenroom, and spent hours trying to calm her down. It was like trying to settle a fretful child. I'd sit there patting her back and watching her weep. When she'd drift off, I'd ease up and try to slip away. She'd wake up and start crying all over again. Finally, I just gave up and lay down with her.

Man, you're a pessimistic piece of shit. You know that, Kwesi? I know exactly what you're thinking. What, you some kind of fucking saint? When I met you, you were freaking with Grace Witherspoon, and I know it had to be some kinda kinky shit. Don't be looking down your nose at me.

I had no intention of taking advantage of a vulnerable woman, all right? I wasn't even turned on. I just couldn't think of anything else to do.

So I took her in my arms and kissed her. Surprisingly, she didn't pull away. The woman who wanted no part of me was now unbuttoning my shirt and unbuckling my belt.

When men get caught doing something they shouldn't be doing, been somewhere they shouldn't have gone, they always say the same shit.

"I was caught up in the heat of the moment."

That's bullshit, boy. Your body ain't no toy that takes off when you wind it up. See, when the dick gets hard, the head gets soft. The blood rushes from the brain into other parts and you can't think straight.

Lying next to her on dry land, I could still feel the motion of the ocean. I was back in that motorboat locking lips with a drowning woman. Every so often I'd go limp. I would stop and try to reason with myself.

"Tiger Lemieux, you old heinous bastard. Get your dick back in your pants."

But she wouldn't turn me loose. The woman was ravenous, hungry as the ocean. I was just a sailor in a whirlwind. But getting inside Cara was like trying to squeeze a size 10 sausage into a size 2 casing. I was ready to give up, but she kept pulling me back down. I positioned myself between her legs one last time. Her hand guided me in, while her body seemed to be pushing me out. I only got it in as far as the tip.

She was so tight, so wet. I put my finger down there to test it and was shocked as hell when it came back bloody. I think I came more from amazement than excitement. I don't think she did. In fact, I'm almost sure she didn't.

I was watching her face the whole time. Her eyes were squeezed shut and she was biting her lip, like a kid waiting for the doctor to stick the needle in. Suffice it to say that Tiger Lemieux wasn't rocking her world at that particular point in time.

Hey, it wasn't the biggest nut I ever busted, either. But something about that moment was incredibly sweet. Cara gave me a part of herself that had never been touched. I found myself wanting to give her something back. This earring here—the tiger's-eye I'd worn in my left ear since I was nineteen years old. I took it off, placed it in her palm, closed her hand, and kissed it.

Both of us were so sore afterward, we had to go sit in the ocean. The next day we shot at Makupa Market. You remember all the colors, the *kangas* and cheap fabrics. The smells of fresh produce and rotten meat. It's the scene where Sherifah's prince sees her buying fruit, falls in love, and follows her home. Cara carried a basket of plastic mangoes on her head. I couldn't understand why we had her toting artificial fruit when there were real mangoes everywhere. Then I realized she wasn't one of those African women who grew up balancing things on her head. Every few steps she took, the basket would fall, the plastic mangoes rolling on the ground. Finally, the stylist got some pins and fastened the whole contraption to her headdress.

I noticed in a close-up shot that she wore my tiger's-eye—not in her ear, but pinned to her costume. Not since that Cracker Jack ring I gave a girl in grade school had I been more proud to see a woman wearing something of mine.

Hector stuck his big shaggy head all up in the shot, frowning and poking away.

"I don't know about this, Tiger. Would a traditional Swahili woman have worn this kind of jewelry at that point in history?"

Hector couldn't get to me, not even when he pulled it off and left a rip in her costume for the stylist to sew up. Cara and I, we were mooning like schoolkids. I was worshipping like you did at the throne of your diva. You sure did love that opera singer's funky drawers. Well, that same simpleminded, blushing grin that came over your face when Grace Witherspoon would swish her narrow ass across the room—I had it.

Cara and I spent the next few days making out like high-school kids. Kissing, touching, feeling—all above the waist. I had blue balls for days, but you know what? Making out with Cara was nothing like Labadi's cock-teasing. Cara wasn't playing games; she just needed a man to take his time. It was all warm-up, just gunning the engine before driving the car. Meanwhile, I was busy getting to know that long, tall body.

Naw, she wasn't built like no brick house. She didn't have an ass and a half like Labadi, no basketball breasts like Big Granny. But you know what they say, man: More than a mouthful is wasted. Besides, she coulda been chairman of the Itty-Bitty Titty Committee, but the girl had some thick, juicy nips. Poked out like Hershey's Kisses jumbo size, just begging to be tasted. We had to mash those suckers down with tape every time we shot, just so her nipples wouldn't upstage the scene.

What did I do about Labadi? Nothing, man. I just tried to avoid her. I didn't want to rub her nose in it, but I was no longer feeling her. She'd had her chance.

One day I took Cara behind a boathouse to work on the next scene, and spent time working on her.

"Tonight?" I asked, when I came up for air.

When she blushed and nodded yes, I was the happiest man on Mombasa. Even when I looked up and saw a figure standing down the beach, binoculars trained on us. Hell yes, it was Heck. Who else? I didn't give a shit. Let him watch all he wanted. He sure wasn't getting none of that brown sugar.

We had shot a full day, finishing up around sunset. I sent the gang of four on another errand so that Cara and I could have some time to ourselves. I later found out that you commandeered the car and had Heck drive you to the airport. If only you had waited, Kwesi, my life might be different today.

No knocks, just a key turning in the lock. I could see Grace standing in the hallway light. Behind her were Labadi and Big Granny.

"Are you in there, Cara?" Grace called out. "Hector said you were so ill you had taken to your bed."

It was a lie, of course.

Grace stepped in, then stopped when she saw us. Everyone else piled up behind her. I could see Labadi in the background, rising up on tiptoe to peek around her shoulder.

"What's the matter? Is she all right?"

Grace leaned against the doorjamb, smirking like a little carnivore. "I don't think she's up for any visitors right now."

"No visitors?" Big Granny pushed Grace aside, barging in like a Mack truck. The woman's eyesight must have been pretty bad. She made it all the way over to the bed before she realized that Cara wasn't alone in it.

"Who is in there with you, Cara? Not that Negro boy from America."

You believe that shit, Kwesi? "That Negro boy from America."

We were trying to pull on our clothes, while Big Granny was yanking the covers off and yelling.

"This boy is seducing my granddaughter. I will kill him. Where is my knife?"

She ran out to go look for it. I didn't need much imagination to figure out what she planned to do with it. To make matters worse, Labadi had plopped down on the bed.

"What has he done? Did he take advantage? The man is no good, do you hear me? Rubbish, filth!"

"Nothing happened, but even if it had, it wouldn't be rape." I was pulling my pants on. "We were making love."

Kwesi, can't nobody say "fool" like an African woman.

"Fool! Her fiancé was killed less than one year ago and Cara almost lost her mind. She came here to get herself sorted out, and look what you have done to her! If she succeeds in drowning herself next time, it will be on your head."

Big Granny was back in the room by then, brandishing a carving knife, elephant-trunk-slicing size. It took both of them to hold her back. The knife dropped to the floor and skittered under the bed.

"My grandchild was a virgin," she screamed. "You have spoiled her innocence."

Grace shook her head and blinked her eyes. I could see her mouthing the word.

"Virgin?"

Lost hers so long ago, she probably couldn't remember what being a virgin felt like.

Labadi tossed me a poisonous look.

"Of course, you realize that we are finished."

I guess I'm just a dog at heart, but something about that filled me with regret. I know you can't have your cake and your pudding both. But look at how unfair this all was. Damn near lynched, just for trying to love a woman. I reached out and grabbed Cara's hand. After all, we were free, black, and over twenty-one.

"I don't know why everybody's got their asses out of joint. I'm leaving now, but I'll see you later, Cara."

She looked just like a little girl, frightened and confused. I think she even got up and reached out her hand to stop me from leaving. She whispered the strangest thing. I didn't know what to make of it then, but now I know just what she meant.

"It's really you. You came back to me again."

Big Granny jumped between us. That old girl could move pretty fast for someone her size. She didn't have the knife on her, but she still could have done me some serious damage.

But it wasn't Granny who wound up stabbing me in the back. Labadi went around telling everybody I had taken advantage of a local girl, a virgin with good marriage prospects.

I had seen only one side of Mombasa until then—the party side. I soon got to meet two other sides—Islamic law and the lynch mob. I was no longer welcome at the bar I frequented; there was an article in the newspaper about a foreign film production corrupting the morals of local youth. A rumor was circulating that our film permit might soon be revoked.

I was pulling away from the hotel one morning in my rental car when an older woman walked up to me. She gestured for me to roll down the window, which I did.

"What is it, ma'am?" You know me. Good old Southern boy; Mama taught me to mind my manners. I figured the old lady needed directions or maybe wanted a lift.

She hissed at me in her language. It might have been Swahili for "fool!" She then raised a hand and slapped me. Can you imagine? This proper Swahili matron, wrapped in robes and veils from head to toe, went after me like Muhammad Ali.

I gunned the engine and screeched off before she could get in another hit. I looked back in the rearview mirror and saw that a small crowd had gathered around her. Her finger was raised, pointing accusingly in my direction.

I knew my days on Mombasa were numbered. I had to double up efforts to get things done before my time ran out. Cara was always on my mind, but I made no effort to see her. I figured that after the project was in the can, we'd get another chance to be together.

I had a mess on my hands. How to get the African crew and cast, who had been moving on tropical time all along, to suddenly get cracking. My bedroom business was the talk of the town, and I had lost their respect. People didn't show up on time, if they did at all. Two women quit without notice, and we had to scramble to find another stylist and makeup artist.

Big Granny came to me on the set one day, all sweet and appeasing. I should have been suspicious at the sudden switch from Lorena Bobbitt to Mother Love. She was willing to have Labadi call off her dogs, but there was a stipulation. I was to meet her at the inn later that night. She made it clear what was expected of me.

Man, what could I do? I was trying to save my show. I went down there with my condoms in my pocket. To my surprise, Labadi was the one waiting for me in bed, fully clothed.

Lady Labadi was a freak from first peek, just like I figured. She pulled this strip of cloth from under the pillow and blindfolded me. Started planting wet kisses all over me, from the top of my head to down where the sun don't shine. I let her get it out of my pants, play with it a little. But man, my heart just wasn't in it. Why'd I keep at it? Hell, you're a man, Kwesi. Would you say no to some free pussy?

There was a knock at the door. Labadi answered.

"Come in, please."

A silence in the room so thick you could hear people breathing. I tore off the blindfold. Cara stood in the doorway, looking at me with my dick hanging out.

"You see what kind of person this is?" Labadi lectured. "He lured me here to Granny's room, then tried to take advantage behind your back."

When Cara backed away, I started after her, until Labadi whispered words that would stop any red-blooded black man cold in his tracks.

"If you go after her, I'll call the police. I will tell them I was raped here tonight."

It didn't matter anyway. She still called the cops on me. I had never been in trouble with the law, and now I was brought in for questioning on rape charges. Rape!

I didn't want to spend the rest of my life rotting in no African jail. What else could I do? I closed up shop and crept out of Kenya, one step ahead of the law.

So how did Cara wind up with Hector?

I wish I knew, Kwesi. I wish I knew. Whatever the reason she married Heck, it wasn't for his money. Cara Bondi wasn't no ho. If anybody was the ho, I guess it would be me.

The budget was toast. I had already taken the white folk's money and spent most of it. Besides, there was my professional reputation. I had to put up or shut up. I had a bunch of B-roll I couldn't do a thing with, and no way could I go back to Mombasa. I decided to take the show to Jamaica, do a down and dirty shoot, get into the studio, and slap something together.

I knew Cara had quit college by then and was modeling in Milan. She never answered any of my phone calls, so I FedExed her a message. Would she consider coming to Jamaica and reprising her role? I didn't get an answer, so I was shocked as shit when she actually showed up—on guess whose arm?

I wasn't about to let some lame white dude play me like a grand piano. Take my woman without a fight, like Ole Massa on the plantation. I got Cara alone and pleaded with her to give me one last chance. Even after she'd been in his bed, I was willing to take her back.

I asked her to meet me at the hotel bar one night. Cara didn't come, but Heck did. Do you know the fool had the nerve to lecture me?

"If you ain't learned a lesson in life, learn this, youngblood. There is just so much shit a woman will take. Creeping with her best friend, that's where most of them will draw the line."

You talk about seeing red? This wigger leaning on the bar sipping his rum punch, done already ripped off my people's music and copped my woman. Here he is trying to school me in my very own language. Hell, no. I had no other choice but to go upside his head. Lucky for him, the bartender pulled me off before I did much damage.

Now, Kwesi, you know I'm a lover, not a fighter. This wasn't like me at all. All Hector got was a little lightweight ass-whipping. Me, I was the loser in the end. After that stupid fistfight, Cara wouldn't even acknowledge me, and I almost screwed up my career. Not only did Heck threaten to kick me off the project, he promised that I'd never direct another music video.

Well, as you know, nothing ever came of that threat. Heck soon had another set of problems to worry about. Cedella and the twins. His first wife shows up unannounced, dragging those brats along with her. You ever met Heck's kids, man? Ain't they 'bout the strangest set of twins you've ever seen? The little girl near 'bout as black as my boot, the boy so white he's almost albino. Here come all three of them, hanging their asses out on my video shoot.

Heck and Cedella had been separated for years but never actually divorced. She must have thought she still had a claim staked. There was this ugly public scene between them, where she accused him of fucking the local color. I guess she had it in her mind that Cara was a Jamaican girl.

Heck came running to me with his tail between his legs. Cedella would cut him some slack if he let her star in his music video.

"I'll forget about that business at the bar, if you'll do me a favor and get her off my back."

Cedella was already haunting my set like a fucking ghost, she might as well get to play the part. I don't have a problem admitting it. "Brown Girl, Blue Island" is not my finest moment. Cedella turned out to be an even lousier actress than Labadi. Whenever it comes on MTV, I have to change the channel. I can't stand seeing Cedella playing the role that was supposed to be Cara's.

So now you know, Kwesi. Whenever I hear Hector Guzman's name, the frustration comes rushing back. Do you know what it's like to have something you want taken away from you? Of course you do. Grace Witherspoon. So you know how I feel.

Look at us. Both of us tight with the old ladies we got, getting soft and stupid over lost loves. It's always about the one that got away. Out of all the women I've had in my life, I'm still carrying around the ghost of this one.

They say there is one kindred spirit made just for you. The way Cara acted, it was like she knew me from somewhere else.

Cara was the ghost girl waiting by Mombasa Harbor, and I was the African prince from across the waters. You can grin all you want, my man. I truly believe we might have had our chance at eternity, if only it had been right from the start. But what nuh good in the marning, 'ard to be good in the aftanoon.

Good luck with the book, man. Hope Heck ain't been playing Jody to your old lady.

LA LINEA NEGRA

Melvin E. Lewis

On the first day of his trip, Michael saw Omara. They looked at each other. A dark-skinned Latina with wild curly hair and thick lips, she spoke English fast, with a New York accent. Her chocolate skin shined in the sun. Her hands were cocoa squeezed from the nut. Her legs were firm like mangoes and teeth white like coconut milk. Omara's eyes traveled slowly over Michael as she held his image in her view. To Michael, it seemed her Spanish was even faster, as she flipped between languages as often as she smoked cigarettes. Omara was the tour guide. Smooth and sophisticated, she handled the group of tourists well, answering questions easily and noting points of interest with a sure hand.

Omara was born near Manatí, in a sugarcane county in Puerto Rico, a hundred miles west of San Juan. When her family migrated to New York City, her father became a custodian in Harlem. A dark-skinned man who spoke Spanish at home, he raised three daughters in the projects of East Harlem and fought back when he heard people call him a coon, or a nigger. When he was cleaning, people thought that because he spoke Spanish, he didn't understand what was said around him.

Michael was born at home in a farming community. His family

had migrated from Meridian, Mississippi, the same time as Omara's moved to New York. He was the first person in his family to travel outside of the United States. Omara was the only one of three daughters to graduate from college and return to live in Puerto Rico.

■ ■ ■

The Center for Caribbean Studies had placed ads in *Encore*, the *Black Scholar*, the *Guardian*, and the *Daily Worker* about a twenty-three-day political study tour of Puerto Rico. Michael was one of ten participants. Back in D.C., he'd taken two Spanish classes from a Cuban exile journalist. Now, words were flying around his neck and face like bullets. They chased him and creased his brow. They parted his hair as he walked *en las calles de Puerto Rico*, "the streets of Puerto Rico."

In San Juan, Michael lost his fear of foreign words. He went running every morning looking at the countryside. He started collecting pebbles and rocks after he ran. When he cooled down he'd put broken granite, red, copper, and sandstone pebbles in his back pocket from each part of the island that his feet had touched.

He noticed new places each morning as he went farther into the city. He started running six miles on his first day, and by the third day he saw the bakery open, where the big commercial laundry moved its trucks in the morning, and where the men gathered to throw horseshoes.

At home, in Washington, Michael had watched Spanish-language movies and Mexican soap operas to prepare for his trip. He'd listened to Argentinean musicals and would understand some of it, but he was lost in San Juan. He had to repeat himself. He didn't roll his Rs. He couldn't remember where to put the accent in words. Sometimes *puertorriqueños* spoke Spanish and left off the endings, or dropped a syllable. Some days Michael couldn't speak Spanish at all.

Puerto Rico was not like the southern United States or Africa. It was another part of a triangle, a mixture of African, Taino, and Spanish blood, their common bond, their nationality. Salsa was

Puerto Rico, the beat and culture. Afro-Atlantic bands played instruments that Michael had never seen; they used horns and drums to push the music. His brain was being pushed upside down by his third week in San Juan. Salsa brought him back to life. He didn't need to understand the words. The music invited him into the song. He watched the bodies, footsteps, and toes of dancers and felt he could *baliar,* "dance." If he could dance to the rhythm, hold the music in his hips, Michael thought that he would be able to grasp the words in his mind.

In San Juan he'd start his day by running. He'd open his door and walk to Ashland Avenue. The busy street was a crossroads between *tres cosas,* "three things," and *tres mundos,* "three worlds." The first was the tourist section with old walk-up hotels, then the small retail businesses where only Spanish was spoken, and then the entrances to neighborhoods. English was the language of the Yankees, or the foreign tourists. By the third day he had extended his run to ten miles each morning. He saw schools open and where the buses took poor women to clean the houses. At 7 A.M. neighborhood *borinquén,* Puerto Rican women, stood on street corners in their head wraps and uniforms, ready to travel to the exclusive gated communities outside San Juan, near the beach.

Eventually, Michael learned when to speak which language. At business programs and receptions, Spanish was required like panty hose and a business suit. When he went into the city he studied words and phrases to function in Spanish. Away from the tourist areas no one spoke English to him. If he wanted faster service in the tourist section, he sat with the other members of the group and spoke English. When he wanted to observe life, he sat apart, while the tour guides asked for directions and information in Spanish.

At first, Omara shook her head at his Spanish, her earrings swinging about her face.

"Please do not speak Spanglish." She laughed. "Speak to me in either Spanish or English. I don't like it when you mix up the languages."

Michael could not think in Spanish; it took him too much time to organize the words for complete thoughts. He couldn't make quick comebacks in Spanish. After a week he listened to the music in small cafés each night and enjoyed the tenors hitting high notes as they sang. It didn't matter if Smokey Robinson was singing in English one night or Roy Brown in Spanish the next; they both reached his soul with the music, mood, and melody. He started to understand and dream in Spanish. He started to dream about Omara. He wrote her a poem and kept it in his pocket.

Omara spoke Spanish when she made love. She sang in Spanish when she cooked and was critical of Latinos who moved to the United States and lost their language or who never returned home. She told Michael that they lost part of their soul.

When the group was picked up each morning, Michael would read the headlines in the English and Spanish newspapers while the tour bus headed into traffic. They would cover two different worlds. He would highlight terms and words he didn't know. He tried to do crossword puzzles in Spanish and wore out an eraser. In the evening he walked to the public library or took a bus to the University of Puerto Rico (UPR) to use the reference material. Michael watched the news and learned expressions. He practiced the pronunciations and accents of the broadcasters.

Across the street from UPR was a McDonald's. When he was overwhelmed and his brain hurt, he went there to relax. He ordered his food in Spanish, and the french fries brought back a piece of home.

He was not a total stranger there, and people no longer asked him where he was from. They knew that he was an *extranjero*, "a foreigner," and that was enough. During the first two weeks, people asked him where he was from so often that he started making places up. One day he was from central Ghana; another, northern Nigeria; and the next, eastern Ethiopia. Saying he was from rural Africa stopped people from asking him any more questions. On his last day an attendant asked him in Spanish to say something in an African language. He smiled and replied, "*Amai vaswera sei?* I asked about your family in Shona."

Being from Washington via Mississippi caused a lot of small talk that Michael could not understand; some days he wanted to be invisible, to walk among the people without speculation of race and nationality. When one of Omara's old boyfriends saw them eating dinner in a quiet corner of a candlelit restaurant in the mountains, he called her and asked about the "Black Yankee." When Omara was with Michael, his obsidian color defined her.

Puerto Rico had its own flavors and pace. It was not like traveling farther south in the Caribbean, where he could imitate the English and Creole accents and say he was from Brooklyn. Riding public transportation in Trinidad and Grenada was easy. When he ate in local markets, people left him alone, assuming he was a returning child of the Caribbean. There, Michael lived as a native, going to ska or calypso concerts, eating in the towns and visiting local beaches where you could sit all day by the ocean and watch the sun sink into the water.

In Puerto Rico, language was power and authority. Outside San Juan he never heard Puerto Ricans speak to each other in English. Maybe it was the national question. Federal court hearings and the post office test were in English only. English was imposed on Puerto Rico like bombing the hell out of the islands of Vieques and Culebra, and button-down long-sleeved shirts and ties. Most of the time the temperature was eighty-two during the day and seventy at night. Wool-blend suits, ties, and panty hose made as much sense as space heaters and the signs that read, WE SUPPORT THE NAVY TARGET PRACTICE IN VIEQUES AND CULEBRA ISLANDS.

■ ■ ■

The first week, Omara led the group around the archipelago. They traveled to the mountain chalets, and learned about the history and resistance in Puerto Rico to Spanish colonialism and then *el imperialismo* of the United States. They heard the fire in the people's national anthem of Puerto Rico. It was what the Puerto Ricans sang when they wanted to celebrate *their* country. The official national anthem of Puerto Rico was "The Star-Spangled Banner."

In La Parguera, Michael and Omara walked away from the group at the bay where the petrochemical plants were. They went to the waterfront and read plaques for the sailors lost at sea. They looked silently out at the horizon as the waves rocked the sea-walls. Off in the distance they saw wild horses running along the shore.

Omara watched Michael beneath her lashes. He was tall and dark, his hair cut close to his head. He was friendly but reserved with a quiet energy. He always had questions about her country, and she liked talking to him about Puerto Rico and his childhood in the South. She wanted to get to know him better. She didn't know what drew her to him—an American—when there were so many of her countrymen around. Michael seemed to exist in his own world. When she'd see him running in the early morning, it was as if no one else existed. Or maybe it was his love of Puerto Rico, evident every time she showed him a new part of the island. Omara started making tea for Michael from the Campeche tree roots to protect him while he ran in the mountains. She'd bring it over after he returned from his run, and they would take turns sipping from the cup.

One morning Omara sat unnoticed smoking on her porch as Michael returned from his run. She watched him walking up the hill to his cottage. His long legs were strong and muscular. He'd taken off his T-shirt to dry himself. He had curly hair on his chest. Her eyes stroked his nipples, shoulders, and arms. Omara put out her cigarette and stopped smoking around Michael. He was raising the tide in her sea. That night she dreamed about him and woke up sweating.

In the dream Omara and Michael lay under a cecropia tree beneath its silver-bottomed leaves. She reached out for his hands, pulled him close, and kissed his temple and cheeks. Omara pulled up his T-shirt and kissed his neck and combed the hair on his chest with her fingers. She tasted the salt on his skin as the morning sun dried the grass next to them.

That night Omara dreamed she was back in Harlem jumping rope. As she jumped, her friends sang: "Who'll take the girl with the African booty? Michael will take the girl with the African booty."

■ ■ ■

During their second week, they went to Vieques. The road to Vieques was a slow twist that went through the eastern part of Puerto Rico. They detoured through El Yunque to see the rain forest. Dense with foliage, and warm and humid, it was a perfect home for the native frogs, iguana, and caiman unique to the rain forest. *El coquí* was a small frog that sang only in Puerto Rico. Michael thought Omara was a *coquí* because her song was more beautiful in Puerto Rico.

The waterfront of Playa de Fajardo was a busy fishing port. From there it was a two-hour boat trip to Vieques. The group left on a ferry into a choppy sea.

The people of La Isla Nena, Vieques's more common name, were mostly brown and black workers. Scattered throughout were schoolgirls with yellow and pink ribbons holding their pigtails, some with little puffy naturals. The ferry arrived first at Isabel Segunda, on the west coast of Vieques. The seafront felt like the area beneath Cape Coast Castle in Ghana. The turquoise water and colorful boats disguised years of bloodshed and brutality. There was an underlying sense of pain and an echo of voices. In the slavery museum in Charleston, South Carolina, Michael had felt spirits touch him.

Death and deceit were in the roads of Vieques, the same as Mississippi. The people and the land felt the same. Michael watched the people in the streets. The frame houses carried him back to his grandparents' farm and aunts' porches. He saw children playing on the side of the road shooting basketballs from dirt courts, and he was home.

Vieques was a zoned island. The natives could live on only 30 percent of their land. They could not walk or travel on most of it. The majority of the blue water and sand were for the United States. The rich soil was fenced and reserved for military use.

Santa Maria, Vieques's main city, was a dying town. Many of the young people had moved away. The schools of once-healthy fish, near the Canal de Vieques, had died or were diseased. Locals fished near Saint Croix. You could even hear Spanish at the piers of Frederiksted, a city in Saint Croix close to Puerto Rico.

Most of the natives followed the fish and lived in the water-fronts on Saint John, Saint Thomas, and Saint Croix in the Virgin Islands. They went to pick crops in Hawaii. They migrated to Miami, and some went to work in the oil factories in Christiansted and Trinidad.

The waters around Vieques were filled with the metals of wasted bombs. People looked tired and sickly. There were more children with cancer in Vieques and its sister islands of Culebra and Culebrita than in Three Mile Island.

Michael thought of the translation of a folk song, "*Cuba, Qué Linda Es Cuba.*" "How beautiful my country is, now that the Yankees have left."

Omara had told him that she wanted her country to have independence, to determine *themselves* what happened on their land.

"Vieques was a symbol of how the United States treated Puerto Rico," she'd told him, waving a hand to encompass the island, her many gold bracelets jingling. "The American navy moved people off the land at the start of World War II, and they never returned home."

■ ■ ■

Michael ran an easy seven-, eight-minute mile most days. The morning after going to Vieques, he ran for two hours straight, to the city walls. He needed to run out the air he felt backing up in his lungs, choking him.

Vieques reminded him of rural parts of Mississippi, but the flowers were different. Gorgeous and abundant, they grew in colors and combinations he'd never seen. Flowering plants in coffee cans sat on every front step. His grandmother's front porch was filled with cuttings and pinches from public park plants. He would have had to carry a shopping bag of cuttings home for her.

Omara's parents had left the sugarcane fields for New York and she'd returned home. Could he return to the Deep South? Could he live in the Caribbean or Africa?

Vieques had given him a bit of the Delta's depression. It took him home. He thought he'd left Mississippi in his past. The land, the pace, and the people were the same here. The soil was rich, like the black mud of the Delta, and the pace was slow. He could smell death and the blood in the earth. He bent down and picked up a handful of dirt and let the wind blow it out of his hands. His father and grandfather could've harvested crops on this land.

Michael's mother, Selma, had kept him close in Mississippi, not wanting her son to be another Emmett Till. Michael loved Mississippi, but he couldn't blossom there. Selma and Brooker loved the Mississippi soil and their family farm, but they loved their children more. So they left the South and all they knew. Their children would not live in danger or go to second-class schools, while they paid first-class taxes.

■ ■ ■

At the city walls Michael pushed against the forty-two-foot-high sandstone bricks, their thickness almost twenty feet. He looked at the entrance to Puerta de San Juan. The walls were built to protect the city and port from cannon fire. When the United States landed in Puerto Rico, they didn't bother with the walls; they simply stayed and never left.

In El Condado, an enclave along the beach in San Juan, Michael noticed the colorful stores and artists' shops. He stopped near Calle Fortaleza to get the address of the kite store that sold the bright kites flown in the park in front of El Morro, the fort. He'd thought about asking Omara to join him one day in the park. He would show her how to fly a kite and watch as the wind pressed her dress against her body.

Michael asked Omara to meet him at the kite store the next day. They met at a café for a *café con leche*, then walked down the cobblestone streets of San Juan to the kite shop. Omara picked bright ribbons for the streamers of Michael's kite. They took the kite to the park and watched it play in the wind, rolling and dipping over the grass. Michael showed Omara how to fly the kite, and he watched as the breeze pressed her dress against her legs.

Later, Omara suggested a restaurant with a view of the city

lights. They ate rice and black beans, shrimp, plantains, and a green salad. Then she fed him *hojaldre* cakes, made with ginger-bread, for dessert. That evening Michael spoke only Spanish. Watching Omara's lips helped him find the right words. Omara was pleased.

On his way home the next day, he passed a music store. He went in and saw a musical instrument that was played by scratching a silver comb on one side and rubbing a stick on the metal ribs on the other.

Michael asked the sales clerk when they were added to a song. He laughed and said, "When you feel the beat. Like when the soup is good, you add a few more spices to the pot to make it better. You will know when."

Michael followed the cashier to the register and, after buying the instrument, asked if he could return in a few days to practice.

The clerk shrugged and smiled. "*Cómo no*. Of course."

■ ■ ■

Omara and Michael strolled along the beach in Vieques ahead of the group. She asked him how he started running. He told her that running came easily to him. It was peaceful and allowed him to see the early morning and the fish and vegetable markets open. He especially liked to run in the rain. Back in D.C., he ran around the Potomac River Basin every morning.

Omara looked out to the ocean. The rest of the group was catching up to them. She was silent for a moment; then she asked Michael if he would go out with her later that night to hear salsa music. Michael couldn't think of anything he wanted to do more.

He had only seen Omara in casual clothes. That night she wore a fitted white dress, unbuttoned at the neck, and open-toed heels. Her hair had been curly and full. She'd cut it short that day. It was even curlier now and complemented her bone structure. She wore long silver earrings that caressed her shoulders every time she turned her head. Omara's arms and legs were bare. She had red lips, toenails, and fingernails. A red heart on a silver chain hung down the opening of her dress and stopped above her breast.

Michael wore a Caribbean shirt and bracelet he'd bought that afternoon. He liked the soft cotton guayabera and the Taino-designed jewelry. His penny loafers were polished and his linen pants freshly pressed. Michael put his hand in Omara's hair and touched a curl. He told her he liked her haircut, that it showed more of her face.

In the bar, Omara and Michael drank beers and *chichaitos*, a Puerto Rican drink of rum and anise. Omara loved to salsa. Her bare legs were strong and shapely and shone in the lights. Michael watched her as she danced, liking the way she moved her hips and how she turned on her toes. Omara danced and danced, smiling and laughing. As she took his handkerchief and wiped the sweat from her face and chest, Michael thought he wanted to spend the rest of his trip with her.

The next song was "Chan Chan," an Afro-Cuban song. Michael caught Omara's hand and pulled her toward him, and they slow danced. Omara relaxed into Michael's arms and smiled at him. They looked deep into each other's eyes. Then she smiled and told him that they could go back to her place.

There was a half-moon over San Juan Bay. Omara lived on the second floor of a two-flat apartment building facing the Atlantic. Her windows overlooked Ocean Park. They could hear the waves from her balcony. They kissed on the balcony and felt the ocean on their faces. They held each other and looked out at the sea. Omara turned and faced the water.

"In my parents' house, I was called *la negra de la casa*. I was the darkest of the girls, and I always felt the need to achieve. We don't celebrate the African part of us. We were supposed to improve the race. That meant dating and marrying people lighter than you. I never date white men or men lighter than me. I don't want to be a fantasy or exotic." She sighed. "Being around you makes me think about New York. I love New York, but here in Puerto Rico, I'm a person. In New York, I was *Puerto Rican*." She laughed. "Americans would murder my name. They called me O'Mary, O'Martha, or they'd give me a nickname. Can you imagine some-one named Todd coming here and we call him Pedro instead?"

Michael took off his shoes and then Omara's sandals. He knelt on the ground and massaged her feet. *"Dime"* came on the radio and they slow danced barefoot. Omara whispered close to his ear, "Your color reminds me of the Nina Simone song: 'Black is the color of my true love's hair.'"

Michael sat on the wicker couch and pulled Omara onto his lap. He opened the buttons of her dress. He licked from her neck to her navel. Her breasts filled his hands. He kissed them. The ocean spray wet his fingers and her chest and bare legs. He licked the mist from her body.

Omara spread her legs around him, drawing him close. He slipped a finger inside her. She squeezed her muscles and held him tight. She felt the salt from the sea touch the tips of her nipples. Omara opened her legs wider and Michael entered her. She twisted her knees around his back and locked her ankles. They danced and danced. She bit his neck, moaning, *"Dime. Dime.* Tell me." Her dark brown nipples turned purple. She would not let Michael's body go soft. She came and came. She moaned words in Spanish that he did not know, but he understood their meaning. He watched her as she came, her head thrown back, her eyes closed, lips open. Then he came with her.

■ ■ ■

"Abrázame. Besáme. Hold me. Kiss me," Omara whispered. They were like a needle and thread sewing a patch together. Michael listened to her heartbeat as she lay against his chest and the wind moved the leaves of pink lilies. Omara turned to Michael.

"I want to show you *mi santuario*, where I go when I need to reflect, to hear the birds sing and to pray."

They left the apartment and walked to an alcove just under her balcony cut into the rocky face of the mountains near the beach. In the alcove were vast pools of water left when the tide had gone out. Michael could see small turtles swimming. They held each other as the moon shone down in shimmers of light illuminating the water. They turned to the beach and walked toward the ocean.

It was so clear he could see the sandy bottom near the shore. He turned to Omara. "Let's go swimming."

"Not at night." She shook her head. "It's not allowed. And I don't have my suit."

"There isn't anyone around," Michael said, spreading his arms to encompass the beach. "You don't need a suit. Let's go swimming."

Omara shook her head. "What if someone comes?"

"Then they'll see us naked."

Michael took off his clothes and jumped in the water. The summer heat felt good when he surfaced. There were turtles and schools of iridescent fish in the surf.

Omara looked at him. "*Tu eres loco*. You are crazy. If you get arrested, I'm not going to call your embassy. I won't translate for you in court." She laughed, but she thought that his body looked beautiful in the moonlight, and she liked that he was impulsive.

"*Esta bien, señorita. Basta ya.* Okay, okay, lady. Enough already. When did the United States open a consulate in a colony?"

"You'd better come out. You didn't come all this way to get into trouble." Omara laughed.

"I was in trouble when we started looking into each other's eyes." Michael laughed, running out of the water and grabbing her in a wet embrace.

They closed their eyes and kissed. They were one body with four arms, one body with four legs. Michael and Omara were a week of rainbows kissing the sky. They were flying too close to the sun with wings made of beeswax and honey.

Michael felt he'd come so far to find home.

Omara felt she could finally be at peace here.

"I love you," Michael said.

"*Tu te amo*, Michael. I love you, too," Omara said. Then she asked him to stay with her in Puerto Rico.

CONTRIBUTORS

Preston L. Allen is a recipient of a State of Florida Individual Artist Fellowship in Literature. His short works have been published in numerous literary journals, including the *Seattle Review*, *Crab Orchard Review*, *Gulf Stream*, *Asili*, and *Drum Voices Review*. His collection, *Churchboys and Other Sinners* (Carolina Wren Press, 2003), is the winner of the Sonja H. Stone Prize in Literature. His novels *Come with Me, Sheba* (Writer's Club Press, 2004), *Bounce* (Writer's Club Press, 2003), and *Hoochie Mama* (Writer's Club Press, 2001) are available on Amazon.com. His erotic fiction has appeared in the *Brown Sugar* series, the combined stories making up the novella *Nadine's Husband*, which he is currently completing. He lives and teaches creative writing in Miami. He can be reached at pallenagogy@aol.com.

Carol Amorosa has been a published journalist for fifteen years, covering music and events in Africa, the Caribbean, and the Latin world. She has been a closeted writer of fiction for nearly as long. She travels widely but has roots in Jamaica and Mexico. This is her first published work of fiction.

Deep Bronze is the pseudonym of a writer who enjoys traveling abroad and looks forward to her next trip to West Africa. The mother of two, she is engaged to a Senegalese musician and storyteller. A native of the Midwest, Deep Bronze lives on Chicago's Southeast Side with her family. She hopes to publish her own collection of erotic stories. Her story "Rendezvous" appears in Zane's *Chocolate Flava* (Atria Books, 2004).

Nina Foxx is the author of *Dippin' My Spoon* (Manisy Willows Books, 2000), *Get Some Love* (Avon Books, 2003), *Going Buck Wild* (Avon Books, 2004), and *Marrying Up* (Avon Books, 2005). She is also the coauthor of *Do the Write Thing: Seven Steps to Publishing Success* (Manisy Willows Books, 2002). Her travel essays have appeared on BlackWordsOnline.com. She is working on her sixth novel, *One Step from Crazy*, which will be published in summer 2006. Originally from Jamaica, New York, she now lives in Austin, Texas, with her family.

Nalo Hopkinson was born in Jamaica and spent her early years in Jamaica, Trinidad, Guyana, and the United States. She now lives in Toronto, Canada. She is the author of three novels, *Brown Girl in the Ring* (Warner Aspect Books, 1998), *Midnight Robber* (Warner Aspect Books, 2000), and *The Salt Roads* (Warner Books, 2003), and a short story collection, *Skin Folk* (Warner Aspect Books, 2001). She has edited the anthologies *Whispers from the Cotton Tree Root: Caribbean Fabulist Fiction* (Invisible Cities Press, 2001) and *Mojo: Conjure Stories* (Warner Aspect Books, 2002), and coedited *So Long Been Dreaming: Postcolonial Science Fiction and Fantasy* with Uppinder Mehan (Arsenal Pulp Press, 2004) and *Tesseracts 9* with Geoff Ryman (Edge Press, 2005). She is the recipient of the World Fantasy Award, the Sunburst Award for Canadian Literature of the Fantastic, the Gaylactic Spectrum Award, and science fiction's John W. Campbell Award for Best New Writer. She's working on a new novel in which menopause is magic.

Sandra Jackson-Opoku is the author of two novels: *The River Where Blood Is Born* (Ballantine/One World, 1997), winner of the Black Caucus of the American Library Association Literary Award for Best Fiction of 1998, and *Hot Johnny and the Women Who Loved Him* (Ballantine/One World, 2000), which ranked on several local and national bestseller lists. "Fort Jesus" is excerpted from her novel in progress, *God's Gift to the Natives*. Another chapter, titled "Iguana Stew," appeared in the 2005 edition of *Brown Sugar 4: Secret Desires*. She has earned such awards as a National Endowment for the Arts Fiction Fellowship and Illinois Art Council grants. She is assistant professor and fiction coordinator in the Master of Fine Arts in Creative Writing Program at Chicago State University.

Sandra Kitt's first mainstream novel, *The Color of Love* (Signet, 1995), received critical acclaim and was optioned by HBO and Lifetime. Her novella in *Girlfriends*, an anthology from Harper-Collins in 1999, was nominated for the NAACP Image Award for Fiction that same year. Sandra is considered the foremost African American writer of romance fiction and was the first black writer ever to publish with Harlequin. In 1994, she launched the successful Arabesque line with her novel *Serenade*. In 1995, she received a Waldenbooks Award for her second Arabesque novel, *Sincerely*. A frequent guest speaker, Sandra has appeared on *Today* on NBC, Black Entertainment Television, and *Good Morning America* on ABC. Her latest novel is *The Next Best Thing* (BET/Arabesque, 2005). A native of New York, Sandra holds bachelor's and master's degrees in fine arts. She can be e-mailed at author@sandrakitt.com.

Melvin E. Lewis's writings about the Caribbean have appeared in *Afro-Hispanic Review*, *OBA Songs*, *Presence Africaine*, *Wasafiri*, and *NOMMO: A Literary Legacy of Black Chicago (1967–1987)*, edited by Carole A. Parks (OBAhouse, 1987). He will have poetry in the forthcoming issues *Obsidian III* and *Gargoyle*. His work has appeared in the anthologies *Beyond the Frontier: African-American*

Poetry for the 21st Century, edited by E. Ethelbert Miller (Black Classic Press, 2002), *The Black Panther Party Reconsidered*, edited by Charles A. Jones (Black Classic Press, 1998), and *Fast Talk, Full Volume: An Anthology of Contemporary African-American Poets*, edited by Alan Spears (Gut Punch Press, 1993), among others. He can be reached at mlewiswriter@aol.com.

Miles Marshall Lewis is editor of the literary journal *Bronx Biannual* and author of the hip-hop memoir *Scars of the Soul Are Why Kids Wear Bandages When They Don't Have Bruises* (Akashic, 2004) as well as a book on Sly and the Family Stone, *There's a Riot Goin' On* (Continuum, 2006). Born and raised in the Bronx, he currently lives in Paris, France, with his partner and child. Lewis has written for *The Believer, The Nation, Essence, Rolling Stone, Blender*, and many other periodicals, and his erotica has been published previously in *Brown Sugar 3: When Opposites Attract* (Washington Square Press, 2004). He is completing his first novel, *The Magic Kingdom of Christmas Muse*. For more information, visit www.MilesMarshallLewis.com.

Glenville Lovell was born in Barbados and now lives in Brooklyn. He is the author of four novels, *Fire in the Canes* (Soho Press, 1995), *Song of Night* (Soho Press, 1998), *Too Beautiful to Die* (Putnam, 2003), and *Love and Death in Brooklyn* (Putnam, 2004); several short stories; and a number of prizewinning plays.

Brandon Massey is the award-winning author of the supernatural thrillers *Thunderland* (Kensington, 2002), *Dark Corner* (Kensington, 2004), and *Within the Shadows* (Kensington, 2005). He also edits the black horror and suspense anthology series *Dark Dreams I, III*, and *III* (Kensington, 2004). He lives near Atlanta, where he is at work on his next thriller. For more information, please visit www.brandonmassey.com.

Sékou Writes is the editor of *When Butterflies Kiss* (Silver Lion Press, 2001), a serial novel in which ten writers each wrote one chapter of the same story. During the 2003 New York International Fringe Festival, SékouWrites coauthored and costarred in a spoken word theatrical piece designed to explore the modern black male experience. SékouWrites is also the creator of the Black Men on Black Love seminar series, which has evolved into an online column at www.sekouwrites.com. Most recently, Sékou's fiction has been published in *Intimacy: Erotic Stories of Love, Lust, and Marriage by Black Men* (Plume, 2004) and the premiere issue of *UPTOWN* magazine. He holds an MFA in fiction.

Jervey Tervalon's latest novel, *Lita* (Atria Books, 2003), is the sequel to *Dead Above Ground* (Pocket Books, 2000). He teaches at the Ralph J. Bunche Center for African American Studies at UCLA and lives in Altadena with his wife and two daughters.

Tracy Price-Thompson is the *Essence* bestselling author of *Black Coffee* (Random House, 2002), *Chocolate Sangria* (Random House, 2003), *A Woman's Worth* (Random House, 2004), and *Knockin' Boots* (Random House, 2005). She is the coeditor of the major anthology *Proverbs for the People* (Kensington, 2003). Visit her Web site at www.tracypricethompson.com for further information. She can be reached at tracythomp@aol.com.

ABOUT THE EDITOR

Peter McClusky

Carol Taylor, a former Random House book editor, has been in book publishing for more than ten years and has worked with many of today's top black writers. She is a contributing writer to *Sacred Fire: The QBR 100 Essential Black Books.* She is also the editor of the *Brown Sugar* erotic series: *Brown Sugar, Brown Sugar 2: Great One Night Stands, Brown Sugar 3: When Opposites Attract,* and *Brown Sugar 4: Secret Desires.* She has been featured in numerous magazines and newspapers, interviewed on TV and radio, and her fiction and nonfiction have appeared in many publications. Her online relationship column, "Off the Hook: Advice on Love and Lust," is featured on Flirt.com. She lives in New York and is at work on a collection of her own stories. She can be reached at Carol@BrownSugarBooks.com. For information on *Brown Sugar* or *Wanderlust,* visit www.BrownSugarBooks.com.